ANDREW G.
NELSON

QUEEN'S GAMBIT

ANDREW G. NELSON

Published by

Second Edition: February 2019

ISBN-10: 0991129725
ISBN-13: 978-0-9911297-2-0

Printed in the United States of America
1 3 5 7 9 10 8 6 4 2

<u>DEDICATION</u>

To my wife Nancy; without your love, support and constant
encouragement this book would never have been possible.
Thank you for always believing in me.

And to God, through whom all things are possible.

Romans 8:28

Other Titles by Andrew G. Nelson

JAMES MAGUIRE SERIES

PERFECT PAWN

QUEEN'S GAMBIT

BISHOP'S GATE

KNIGHT FALL

ALEX TAYLOR SERIES

SMALL TOWN SECRETS

LITTLE BOY LOST

BROOKLYN BOUNCE

NYPD COLD CASE SERIES

THE KATHERINE WHITE MURDER

THE ROASRY BEAD MURDERS

NON FICTION

WHERE WAS GOD? An NYPD 1st Responders Search for Answers
Following the Terror Attack of September 11th, 2001

UNCOMMON VALOR – Insignia of the NYPD ESU

UNCOMMON VALOR II – Challenge Coins of the NYPD ESU

ACKNOWLEDGMENTS

The book you hold in your hand would not have been possible without the influence of some very special people. Each left a marked impression on me and I am forever grateful.

To: Dennis, Richie, Teddy, & Tony –
Thank you for your influence, support and friendship.

To the Sheepdogs –
The men and women who don their uniforms, each and every day, to protect the flock from the wolves of the world.

Fidelis Ad Mortem.

Love is like a game of Chess.
A boy plays and he is always afraid of losing his Queen.
A girl plays and she is willing to risk everything just to protect her King.

- Author: Unknown

CHAPTER ONE

Northeast New Hampshire
Tuesday, October 16th, 2012 – 12:14 p.m.

Hunting Keith Banning was like trying to catch a ghost.

It had been nearly six months since the two men had battled it out with each other. The fight had effectively ended in a draw, with Banning fleeing, a knife wound to his leg, and Maguire racing to defuse the explosive vest Banning had strapped to Melody Anderson's chest. Since then, Maguire had dedicated every resource at his disposal to pursuing the man.

He crouched down on the rocky outcropping and peered out into the valley below him. Anticipation and frustration seemed to be Maguire's constant traveling companions lately.

In the beginning, the New York State Police investigators assigned to the *Banning Task Force* had been reluctant to share the information they had compiled. Maguire understood their apprehension, even if he didn't agree with it. They had lost two of their own and didn't want to risk anything jeopardizing their investigation. However, as the leads began to dry up they reluctantly came to accept that their case had gone cold. At that point, it didn't seem as if they had anything to lose.

Maguire brought a wealth of investigative experience to the mix, along with certain financial assets, which gave him a lot more resources at his disposal. He also wasn't encumbered by the same jurisdictional restrictions that they were.

A gentleman's agreement was reached that dictated if Maguire uncovered anything he would not take any action without notifying the state police, unless there was an imminent threat to Maguire, Tricia Browning or an innocent bystander.

While Maguire had agreed to the conditions, he certainly had no intention of complying with them.

In the end, Keith Banning was a killer, living in a twisted fantasy world where he viewed the conflict between himself and Maguire as part of some deranged chess game. It was a game that Banning would never quit playing until one of them was dead and Maguire fully intended to provide that closure to him via a well-placed shot to Banning's head.

It might have sounded cold and ruthless to some, but the reality was that Banning had long ago crossed a line from which there was no coming back. Maguire had seen it before; some people just developed a blood lust. During the fight at Melody's house he had seen that same look in Banning's eyes; the absence of any compassion or empathy. People had ceased to exist to him. They had devolved into nothing more than game pieces to be used, moved, and sacrificed for nothing more than his enjoyment.

There would be no rehabilitation for him. A prison cell simply held no meaning. For Keith Banning it would be a place to plan his next move, waiting for the opportunity to strike. Maguire could not accept that risk. As long as Banning breathed air he was a threat to the people Maguire loved.

Banning had already been linked to the deaths of five people, including Maguire's parents, and he was considered the prime suspect in the deaths of at least a dozen others. Tricia Browning, Maguire's old high school girlfriend, still had not been found and it was unclear whether she was alive or dead.

The investigation had proven to be both physically and mentally exhausting.

While they all still referred to him as Keith Banning, for the sake of investigative consistency, it seemed that no one knew who Banning really was. In all, they had uncovered at least seventeen different identities, but the vast majority proved to be nothing more than wild goose chases. As if the personas he had created were designed, not for his benefit, but to sidetrack anyone looking for him.

The state police had gone to great lengths to plaster Banning's photograph all throughout the North Country. In the beginning the leads came in droves. He had been seen from Canada to D.C. and as far west as Indiana. In each case investigators were sent, but it was either a case of mistaken identity or they arrived too late. It had become readily apparent to those on the task force that Banning was toying with them.

The latest sighting had brought Maguire up to this remote hunting cabin in northeast New Hampshire.

He had slipped in under a waning crescent moon, taking advantage of the minimal ambient light, and set up an observation post about three-quarters of a mile from the cabin. The cool weather helped to create a nice contrast for the thermal imaging goggles. He had kept it under observation for two days, but there had been no movement in or around the place. When he was absolutely sure that there was no one watching him, he made his way slowly down the mountainside.

An examination of the cabin's interior, along with the surrounding area, revealed indications that *someone* had been there recently, but nothing that would specifically link it to Banning. It was either a case of mistaken identity or just another game of cat and mouse that he was playing.

Maguire reached into his jacket pocket, retrieving his cell phone and called the now all too familiar number.

"Please tell me you found something, anything," said the voice that answered.

"It's empty."

"Fuck."

Lieutenant Dennis Monahan sat behind his desk, at the New York State Police, Troop B Substation in Keenseville, New York and clasped his forehead with his hand.

"There are signs that someone has been here, but nothing that indicates it was Banning," Maguire replied. "I'm guessing it was just someone who may have taken a wrong turn."

The lead had sounded promising when it had first come in. A local resident had been out raking his leaves and had observed an old pickup truck, with New York plates, heading up the mountain. He thought it was suspicious because there were only two other houses further up the road, one of which he knew was supposed to be vacant.

Maguire had been in Nashua, New Hampshire conducting some re-interviews when the call had come in. Being so close he had offered to do a quick sneak and peek. Given his background as a former U.S. Navy SEAL, he certainly had the capability to do it covertly. No one had wanted to generate any more attention than absolutely necessary; in order to avoid the risk of possibly spooking Banning.

Monahan rubbed his weary eyes.

How much longer will this go on? he wondered. *Something had to give eventually, didn't it*?

"What's happening on your end?" asked Maguire.

"Nothing," Monahan replied. "Everything has pretty much dried up. In fact I'm beginning to get pressure from Albany to start releasing personnel back to their units. The feds pretty much pulled out after the TV cameras left. In fact, all I've got left now is a Border Patrol agent acting as an intermediary with DHS."

"Not to sound too pessimistic, but he'll probably be gone after the first week in November."

Monahan grimaced on the other end, because he knew Maguire was right. Everyone did the right thing when their political reputation was on the line, but once the votes were cast next month things would go back to normal soon enough.

"What are you going to do now?" Monahan asked.

"I'll take a second look around the perimeter and see if I can pick up anything," Maguire said. "Then I'll do a follow-up interview with the witness. Maybe he can remember a bit more of what he saw."

"Ok, well call me if you find out anything else."

"I will," Maguire replied and ended the call.

He sat looking out over the picturesque valley in front of him. Directly below, a crystal clear blue lake sat nestled in among the trees, reflecting back the image of the white clouds that hung in the sky, above the water. The fall colors were beginning to take hold with splotches of red, orange and yellow mixed-in with the green leaves. It was like an autumn painter's pallet. In just a few short weeks it would all be gone, replaced with a blanket of snow that would last well into spring.

Maguire felt a sense of weariness now, as he looked out at the foliage. The beauty he saw belied the truth, which was that death was coming soon. Like winter, Keith Banning was waiting for the right moment to strike.

Would he be ready for the coming battle?

"Not like this," he said out loud.

The hunt had been taking its toll on him lately. He couldn't remember the last time he had been back home or the last time he had felt the warmth of her skin on his.

He looked down at the phone, selected a number and waited for it to connect.

"Hey, cowboy," Melody said when she answered. "When are you coming home?"

"I was just thinking about that."

"Don't think about it too long, I need you back here in my arms."

"Where are you?" he asked.

"I'm in Maryland, right now," she replied. "I couldn't take being cooped up in that fortress you created for me any longer; not knowing when my brave knight was going to come rescue me."

Maguire had not wasted any time after the attack at Melody's house. He had overseen the complete overhaul of the security arrangements. In addition to the physical security changes at the home, there was now a twenty-four / seven protection detail that accompanied Melody and her executive assistant, Genevieve Gordon, wherever they went.

At first Melody pushed back on the increased security, but Maguire held his ground and she ultimately relented. Well that wasn't exactly accurate. After the incident she had purchased the land across from her home on Meadow Lane and had a pier constructed. She conceded the new security arrangements on the condition that Maguire relocate his houseboat from the other side of the Shinnecock Bay to the new dock.

Maguire protested, but they both knew it was only a token attempt. It still afforded him a certain level of autonomy, at least for now. Plus he also enjoyed being closer to her.

"It's not that bad," he replied. "Is it?"

"We've reached a modified agreement," Melody said.

"Like how modified?"

"The bedrooms and offices are off limits, along with the gym."

Maguire thought about that for a moment. He knew just how intrusive a protection detail could be, but at the same time there was a very good reason for having them there. Melody and Genevieve were two very strong-willed personalities, so he knew that it was best to pick and choose which battles he fought with them.

"That's fine," Maguire said. "What's left for you to do down in Maryland?"

"Nothing, it's just a pit stop actually. Gen and I went to the R&D facility in Montana for a visit. I left her out there for a few extra days while I came back to do some paperwork and a bit of lobbying in D.C.," she replied. "I'm just waiting for her to get here and then we will fly back to Long Island together. We should be home tomorrow afternoon. What about you?"

"I'm finishing up here and coming home."

"Seriously?"

"Yep, as much as you have missed me being in your arms, I've missed holding you in mine as well, angel."

Melody leaned back in the burgundy leather wingback chair, swiveling around in it, until she was staring out the panoramic office window toward the rolling hills in the distance. She found herself biting her lip at the image that was playing in her mind.

"For how long?" she asked.

"Well if you're kicking the security people out of certain parts of the house, I guess you're going to need someone to keep a closer eye on you for a while."

"Then again, you're the kind of bodyguard a girl could get used to."

"My place or yours?" he asked.

"You sound tired, James," she said. "Come over to the house when you get back. Let me watch after you for a while."

"Okay, I'll call you when I get into the city."

"Be careful, cowboy."

"Always, angel," he replied.

Maguire stood up and walked back toward the cabin. He would take one last look around and call it a day.

Fifty feet away, mounted about half way up the trunk of one of the innumerable red spruce trees, a camouflaged wireless security camera sat nestled among the branches. Like a silent sentinel, it sent its signal to a transmitter which then broadcast the feed through the airwaves.

A little over one hundred miles away, the man known simply as Keith Banning, sat in front of laptop computer watching the image in real time. It was the first time since that fateful evening in May that he had laid eyes on his adversary. In a way he felt a sense of relief. He had begun to worry that the state cops had shut him out.

He reached down and grabbed the pack of cigarettes off the desk. Banning withdrew one, lighting it up and inhaled deeply.

He had toyed with the cops for months hoping to instigate a response. Finally, he saw a glimmer of hope that their game could begin anew.

It's good to see you again old friend, he thought.

Banning leaned back in his chair, propping his feet up on top of the desk, and looked out the window of the cabin. He took a long drag on the cigarette and tapped the ash out in the ashtray.

Maguire had finally initiated the first move in their latest game. Now it was his turn to repay the favor.

CHAPTER TWO

Manhattan, New York City
Tuesday, November 6th, 2012 – 9:45 p.m.

New York State Senator Alan McMasters sat on the couch, his elbows resting on his knees and his chin pressed against his clasped hands, as he watched the television set in front of him. Sitting beside him was his wife Jill, a former sports reporter for ESPN, whom he had first met at a charity golf outing fifteen years earlier.

Tonight the two of them watched as the local election races began to get called. Directly behind them was his inner circle, the key members of his campaign team, which had worked tirelessly to get him to this point. In addition, there were also those individuals who would make up his transition team, should the need arise.

Twenty floors below them, in the ballroom of the Waldorf-Astoria, over a thousand friends, campaign staffers, and supporters had gathered to watch the returns coming in on the large projection screen above the stage.

McMasters and his wife watched as a perky, twenty-something reporter began reading off the latest numbers along with the projections. "...and in the New York City mayoral race, with sixty-three percent of the vote in, we are projecting that State Senator Alan McMasters will win."

Around him the room erupted in cheers.

Jill McMasters leaned over and wrapped her arms around her husband, who continued to stare at the screen in disbelief.

"Congratulations, Mr. Mayor-*elect*," she whispered in his ear and gave him a kiss.

For the last few weeks the pundits had all been reporting on the growing surge of popularity for him. Despite the platitudes from the press he had forced himself to remain grounded. Politics was not for the faint of heart and he knew that bigger careers than his had been crushed on the jagged rocks of reality by simply choosing the wrong word at the wrong time.

As he continued to stare at the television screen, he felt like a weary marathon runner who had just crossed the finish line in first place.

He dropped his head into his hands and said a silent prayer.

After a minute, Mayor-*elect* Alan McMasters got up from the couch, a huge smile appearing on his face, and began shaking the hands of the well-wishers who closed in around him. Jill McMasters took the opportunity to walk across the room and peer into the adjoining suite where their two children, thirteen-year-old Robert and eleven-year-old Lauren, were holed up playing video games.

Lauren was the first to look up, hearing all the commotion in the background.

"What's going on?"

"We're going to have to start packing."

"Why?"

"Because your daddy won the election and we are going to be moving to Gracie Mansion."

Robert looked up from his game. "Why do we have to move?"

Jill smiled. "Because that's where the mayor and his family live."

"The mayor now doesn't live there."

"Well, we are a family that believes in up-holding traditions and I think it is rude to turn down living in the house the people of New York City provide to their mayor."

Gracie Mansion had been built in 1799 by Archibald Gracie and was a private residence until 1896 when the municipal government took control of it. In 1942 Fiorello LaGuardia became the first New York City Mayor to use it as his residence, a tradition that lasted until 2001 when then Mayor Rudolph Giuliani moved out because he was getting divorced. New York City law prevents the use of Gracie Mansion by anyone other than the Mayor, his family and visiting public officials, even if just for an overnight stay. Since then, the residence had remained empty and was used only for official events.

Robert groaned audibly. "Do we have to change schools?"

"No, you and your sister will still go to the same school."

"Fine," Robert said.

"Will I still have my own room?" Lauren asked.

"Yes."

"Ok."

And with that the trauma of the move came to a speedy resolution, as the kids redirected their attention back to their respective video games.

Kids are so resilient, Jill thought, as she walked out of the room and rejoined the party.

When the handshakes and congratulations were done, Alan McMasters walked over to where Richard Stargold stood talking to Tom Murphy, McMasters' chief of staff.

"Just the two men to whom I need to speak," McMasters said. "Let's go somewhere quiet."

The three men stepped into the adjoining room, which had been set up as a pseudo-office, and closed the door.

McMasters was the first to break the silence. "What the hell did we just do?"

Murphy and Stargold both laughed.

Over the summer, McMasters' opponent, Jesse Walters, had unleashed a vicious partisan advertising campaign that attacked

McMasters' career in the state senate. It was particularly effective and it appeared that Walters would ride a wave to an easy victory, but then, for some inexplicable reason, the campaign turned their focus on McMasters' military career.

The backlash was immediate and swift.

While McMasters refused to comment on the smear campaign, a new advertisement, paid for by a military veteran's political action committee, began to run. It showed a grainy black and white video of a young Marine Lieutenant coming out of doorway, supporting a wounded soldier, and taking him to safety. The screen faded to black with a caption that simply read: 'McMasters opponent says service doesn't matter, tell that to this Marine. Better yet, tell it to Jesse Walters on November 6th.'

Overnight, the course of the election had changed.

Jesse Walters tried desperately to get ahead of the controversy, but it was all for naught. His campaign now found itself making excuses and trying to clarify things, while McMasters took the moral high ground. In the end, Walters' campaign managed to snatch defeat from the jaws of victory.

"Well Rich, we've spoken about this before, but now it's real. You know how I feel. I can deal with the politics, but policing is not my forte. I need someone I can trust, someone who I know has got my back. What do you say? Will you be my police commissioner?"

Stargold stood there for a moment, letting the significance of the moment sink in. He had spoken with his wife Mary and James at length about the offer. Both had encouraged him to accept it, pointing out the obvious career implications. Rich had risen in the ranks of the United States Secret Service, achieving the coveted slot of Special Agent in Charge of the New York City Field Office. It was something he knew; something with which he was comfortable, but this was an entirely different animal.

Even though running the New York Field Office was a highly sought after position, it was still just one of the Secret Service's

136 field offices worldwide. Accepting the position of New York City police commissioner would put him in charge of a department more than seven times larger than the Secret Service and with an operating budget of nearly four billion dollars.

The reality was staggering.

The New York City Police Department was officially established as a municipal police agency in 1845, but its roots date back much farther, to 1625, when an eight man Dutch *night-watch* patrolled the streets of New Amsterdam, now the southern tip of Manhattan. From those humble beginnings, the department grew to its current strength of over 35,000 sworn officers plus another several thousand support staff. Not only was it the largest police department in the United States, it was actually larger than some countries standing armies.

The NYPD was unique in that it was completely self-contained. In addition to its impressive manpower levels, it boasted a wide array of specialized units, including the Emergency Service Unit, the NYPD's version of SWAT, Aviation Unit, Harbor Patrol, Mounted, Canine, Intelligence Bureau, Narcotics, and Organized Crime, to name just a few. In addition, after the terror attacks of September 11th, 2001, the Department formed the Counter Terrorism Bureau to address the threat posed to the city. Ultimately the reach of the CTB expanded beyond the streets of the Big Apple and into numerous foreign cities including London, Paris, Madrid, Tel Aviv, Hamburg, and Toronto.

Stargold took a deep breath as he formulated his response.

"I get to choose my people?"

McMasters looked over at Tom Murphy and smiled.

"Rich, you work for me," said McMasters, "but who you choose to work for you is entirely *your* decision."

"Ok," replied Stargold. "In that case it would be my honor and privilege to serve as your police commissioner."

McMasters and Stargold shook hands, consummating the deal.

"Gentlemen, I do believe this calls for a cigar," said Murphy, who walked over to the desk and opened a wooden humidor. He removed three cigars, clipping the ends and handing one to each man. After lighting them, the men enjoyed a moment of light banter and laughs, as the stress of the decision making dissipated with each puff.

"Tomorrow we'll have to sit down with the transition team, along with the mayor's representatives, and begin to get things rolling."

"I'll notify Washington that I'll be retiring in January," Stargold said.

"Tippi Fisher is going to be Deputy Mayor for Operations. Officially, her office will be the *go to* for the day-to-day operational stuff, but I expect direct communications on anything that you consider important. I am a firm believer in the open door policy."

"I understand completely."

"Have you given any thought to what changes you might be making?" McMasters asked.

"Honestly, I haven't really allowed myself to think about it. I don't think I wanted to jinx anything."

"Well I certainly appreciate that, Rich."

"Try to remember that when the press is beating you up, Alan," Murphy interjected.

"Point taken, Tom," McMasters said. "That being said, is there anyone on your short list, Rich?"

"Yeah, actually there is," Stargold replied, "but getting him to sign on might take more than a little bit of work."

"You can always invite him out and I'll put on an all-out charm offensive."

"Oh I think he'll do it," Rich said. "What I'm going to owe him is an entirely different story."

"Is he worth it?"

"He's worth more."

"Then let me give you a word of advice. If you hold him in that high a regard, then don't accept no for answer. It's how I felt about you from the beginning. I never had any question that on January 1st I'd be swearing you in as my police commissioner."

"Thanks for the vote of confidence."

"Well, now that we have that resolved gentlemen, I guess it's time to go out and celebrate."

"After you, sir," said Rich.

The three men exited the room and rejoined the party. Stargold made his way over to where Mary stood talking to Jill. The two women looked over at him as he approached.

"Well, did Alan get his way?" Jill asked.

"I don't think there was ever much doubt," Rich said with a smile.

"Congratulations, Rich," Jill said. "You'll make a great police commissioner."

"I hope so. I can't imagine anything more daunting from a law enforcement perspective."

"Do what Alan does, surround yourself with the best people you can find and you'll breeze through it."

"You sound like Alan now."

"I taught him everything he knows," Jill said with a laugh.

"Behind every great man is an even greater woman," replied Rich.

Jill looked over at Mary. "Oh I see you've taught him well."

"It hasn't always been easy," Mary said.

15

"It never is, Mary," Jill replied. "Well, I guess I better rejoin Alan. We're going to have to go down to the ballroom and thank the troops."

"Have fun," Mary said.

"I will, dear. I'll call you later in the week. We can go and get lunch."

"Sounds like a plan."

"You take care of her, Rich. She's a real gem."

"Oh, that I know."

Jill turned and walked over to where her husband stood. A moment later Tom Murphy ushered them toward the door and they made their way to the ballroom where the supporters were now celebrating the election win.

"You ok?" Mary asked.

"Yeah, I'm fine," Rich responded. "I just never really thought this day would come, to be honest."

"You know you can do this, Rich. You're smart; your people have always respected you, and you know how to get things done."

"That's not the hard part."

"He'll say yes."

"What makes you so sure?"

"Because I know things," Mary replied.

"Oh really, and what, pray tell, do you know?"

"His boss' phone number."

Rich looked at her quizzically, "His boss' phone number?"

Mary took out her cell phone, scrolled through the address book and selected a name. She held the phone up for her husband to see.

Rich smiled as he read the name on the screen. "Of course, why didn't I think of that?"

"If you want things done, you go straight to the top."

CHAPTER THREE

Melody glanced down at the cell phone buzzing on her desk and checked the display. She picked it up and hit the button to connect the call.

"Hi, Mary."

"Hey, Mel, how's everything going?"

"Oh, the usual, I'm up to my butt in alligators. What are you doing?"

"I had to go to a luncheon out in Manorville."

"Oh sounds fun," Melody said sarcastically.

"Oh yeah, boat loads. I just thought I'd check and see if you were busy."

"No," she replied. "Certainly nothing that can't wait. What's on your mind?"

"I need your help on a couple of things, would you mind if I popped in?"

"Of course not, come on over. I'll let them know you are coming and have some coffee ready."

"Great, I really appreciate it. I'll see you in a little bit."

A half hour later Mary Stargold pulled her black Ford Explorer up to the wrought iron gate.

"Can I help you?" said a voice over the intercom system.

"Mary Stargold."

"Yes, ma'am, please watch the gate."

After the gate had opened, Mary proceeded up the driveway toward the house. Along the way she passed a security officer, in black BDU's, who was patrolling the grounds with a Belgian Malinois.

After the attack, life in the house had changed dramatically. It had not been easy for Melody and Genevieve to acclimate, but they understood the need. Eventually they became accustomed to the new normal for them, albeit grudgingly.

Melody was waiting at the front door as the car pulled into the courtyard. The two women had become fast friends, after they had first been introduced the previous May.

"Hey, girl," Melody said, as Mary stepped out of the SUV.

"Ugh, now I know why I hate coming out to Long Island," Mary replied in an exasperated tone. "Traffic sucks."

"Be glad it's November and not July."

"You have to be a special kind of insane to live here during the summer."

Mary walked up the steps and hugged Melody.

"Come on in, and take a load off."

The two women stepped inside, as the security officer closed the door behind them. The *men-in-black*, as they were affectionately referred to, were never more than a few feet away at any given time.

"So how was your luncheon?"

"It was boring, if you want to know, but rarely have I attended a fun one. What ever happened to people speaking honestly about stuff, instead of all this flowery crap that means absolutely nothing?"

"I don't know. No one wants to offend anyone anymore so they don't really say anything important or substantive."

Melody sat down on the couch, as Mary took the chair opposite her.

"So what's on your mind?"

"Well, you heard McMasters won the election right?"

"Yes, did Rich take the job?"

"Yeah, he did."

"That's great. I know James is going to be so glad to hear that. He really believes that Rich is going to make a fantastic police commissioner."

"Unfortunately, now we have the issue of moving."

"Why?"

"Residency requirement, the police commissioner has to live within the five boroughs or the adjoining counties. But realistically we need to find something in Manhattan."

"I didn't know that."

"They spring that on you after you say yes apparently. That is one of the reasons I wanted to talk to you. Do you know anyone here in the city, who handles real estate, that might be able to help us in a hurry?"

"Aw, honey I can do you guys one better. I have an apartment in Battery Park City that isn't being used. You guys are more than welcome to it."

"Are you serious?"

"Absolutely, it's a corporate apartment that we have for guests visiting the city, but honestly I can't tell you the last time we utilized it. I just could never seem to let it go."

"I don't know what to say, Melody."

"Oh please, don't say anything. You, Rich and the girls are family. I think you'll really like it. The apartment has three bedrooms, so the girls can each have their own space."

"I think I'm in shock."

"Good, I'll have Gen get you the keys. You and Rich can take a look at it. If it will work for you, move in."

"Thank you so much."

"My pleasure," Melody said. "What else did you need to talk about?"

"This might be a little more difficult for you to arrange."

"Hey, I'm on a roll, hit me with your best shot."

Mary picked up the coffee cup and took a drink.

"How's James doing?"

Melody looked at Mary quizzically. "James? He's doing fine. I wish sometimes he would back off this quest he's gotten himself caught up in, trying to find Banning."

"Are they making any progress?"

"Not really. It's like he just fell off the face of the earth and I'm fine with that. I know that James is driven to finding him, but honestly, I would feel more secure just having him here with me, instead of all the security in the house."

"What if I told you I might have an answer to that?"

"Oh really?" Melody said. "Then I'm all ears."

"When Rich agreed to take the job he said he would do it only if he had *carte blanche* to bring in his own people. They agreed and now Rich wants to begin that process."

"What are you getting at?"

"Rich wants James as his number two."

Melody took that in and began to digest it. She knew that even though he had made a name for himself in the private sector; there was a part of him that missed police work. But she also knew that he missed the street work, not the paperwork.

"Oh boy," she said pursing her lips together and let out a soft whistle. "Did I mention that the apartment also has three bathrooms?"

Mary let out a laugh. "Nice segue."

"You caught that huh?" Melody asked. "But in all seriousness, I think it would be great. The trick is getting him to see things the same way."

"Do you think it's possible?"

"Oh, honey, you know that when a woman puts her mind to something, anything is possible."

"I was hoping you'd say that."

"I'll tell you what; let me have a few days to work on James and see where I get. Why don't you bring Rich and the girls out this weekend? Come out Saturday for dinner and stay the night."

"Thanks, Melody, for everything."

"Don't thank me now," Melody said. "Thank me when he says yes."

CHAPTER FOUR

Midtown Manhattan, N.Y.
Friday, November 9th, 2012 – 1:57 p.m.

The man reached up, removed one of the backpacks from the rack and examined it. It was constructed of a fashionable, bluish gray colored *ripstop* nylon material and featured reinforced seams that were made of a high density rubber. They would certainly be able to handle the load and then some. He removed four more before he noticed the sign above the display rack that indicated they were on sale.

How considerate, he thought.

He reached up and removed an additional one. His son could use a new one for school books and no one would be the wiser.

He brought them up to the checkout and laid them on the counter, watching as the young, blonde haired salesgirl scanned each of the tags.

"That will be $183.97," she said.

The man reached into his pocket, removed his wallet and handed the woman a credit card.

"That's a lot of backpacks, Mister..... Hamadi," she said, reading the man's name off the card.

"Yes, my son's Boy Scout troop is going on a field trip and I thought it would be easier for them to put all their stuff in these. The idea of searching for missing lunch bags did not sound enjoyable to me."

The young woman laughed, as she swiped the card.

"No, I guess it wouldn't."

The machine took a moment to process and then began spitting out the receipt.

"Please sign here," she said. "Would you like a bag for them?"

"No, my car is parked around the corner," the man replied, as he signed the store receipt, "but thank you for asking."

She handed the man his card back along with the customer receipt.

"Have a great day," she said.

"You too, young lady."

The man gathered up the backpacks and made his way outside.

It was a typical, cold fall day and everywhere he looked he could see that the city was gearing up for the coming Christmas shopping season. Stores were decorating their windows, with festive holiday scenes, in the hopes of drawing in potential buyers. Every year it seemed to start earlier and earlier.

The man hit the button on the key fob and the minivan's rear hatch opened up as he approached it. He tossed the bags into the back and closed it, before turning around to look back toward 7th Avenue.

Are any of these back packs destined for this area? he wondered.

He quickly chased the thought from his mind; it wasn't his concern. He opened the driver's door and got into the vehicle. He still had a few things left to gather up before his part in all of this would be done.

Hamadi started the van and made his way westbound; toward the entrance to the Lincoln Tunnel. It was still early enough that he felt he would beat most of the commuters heading out of the city. He was partially right. He'd made it almost to the New Jersey side when he got caught in traffic inside the tunnel. He put the car into park and waited. The first few times he had been furious, but the longer you lived here, the more acclimated you became toward the incessant traffic congestion.

He stared at the tunnel wall, watching as water trickled down along the tiles. He thought for a moment what it would actually take to physically bring down the tunnel, flooding it with water from the Hudson River, which sat on top of it. Hamadi smiled at that thought. It would be a significant blow. Certainly not on the scale of the September 11th attacks, but one that would cripple the city and strike fear into the hearts of these infidels that walked around so smugly.

Hamadi wondered if he could do it. Did he possess the heart of the committed jihadist? Someone who could strap on a suicide vest and bring the fight to the enemy on a personal level?

He had immigrated to the United States from Lebanon fifteen years earlier. He had come with virtually nothing and now he ran his own lucrative IT business. He and his wife had two children and lived a very comfortable life in Lyndhurst, New Jersey. No, he reluctantly admitted, he was the logistics and supply officer, nothing more. At the end of the day, he would provide the others with the materials to wage war, while he took his son to soccer practice.

Up ahead traffic began to move and he dropped the car back into drive. Hamadi checked his watch, it was nearly three o'clock. He hoped there were no further delays. He needed to be at the school in an hour to pick up the children.

CHAPTER FIVE

James stared across the dining room table at Melody.

"Please tell me you're not serious?"

Melody played with the vegetables on her plate, like a six-year-old desperately trying to hide from the steely gaze of their parent, as she searched for the right words to promote her argument.

"I'm not sure why you seem so shocked; it makes perfect sense."

"Really? Well then, why don't you share those specifics with me?" he asked.

Melody looked up from her plate and glanced across the table into the penetrating blue eyes that had captured her heart so many months ago. She hadn't realized how hard a sell this was going to be. Maybe it was time to take a different approach.

"James, you have spent your entire adult life serving; it is a large part of who you are," she said. "The one thing you have always talked about was how your job was always made harder because the people in charge had no clue about what really needed to be done. Maybe this is your chance to change that."

Now it was Maguire's turn to look away from her gaze. He stared out the large bay window of the dining room. It was so unfair to hear his own words being used against him.

"I don't know," he said, half in response to Melody, the other in response to the battle that now seemed to be waging inside him.

What Melody had said was true. Whether it was his time in the Navy or when he had joined the NYPD, there always seemed to be one person up the chain of command ladder who had no

26

concept about how to effectively utilize the people under them. They had called it *reinventing the wheel.* The moment when you see a person taking something that worked fine and screwing with it simply because they wanted to leave *their* mark. To the men, having to do the work, it was often unnecessary and sometimes very deadly.

"Ask yourself why you encouraged Rich to accept the position and yet you are waffling on the same offer."

"That's different," he replied, but even he knew it was a lame attempt at an excuse.

It was the opportunity she had been waiting for. The words had barely left his lips before she pounced.

"James Patrick Maguire, don't you dare try to twist this around."

Maguire cringed and it was now his turn to stare sheepishly at the plate in front of him. What was it about being a woman that they seem to instinctively know the easiest way to take the fight out of a man was to use his full name.

"I'm just saying that Rich is in a better position to take the job. He's got the background, the connections, the whole nine yards. Besides, there are a lot of good people on whom he can rely."

"Yet, with all of that going for him, he still wants you with him."

He let that sink in for a moment. He and Rich had known each other for what seemed like an eternity. The truth was Rich and Mary Stargold were the closest thing he had to actual family. He loved them and the girls, and would do anything for them. Yet here he was struggling with this offer.

"You know I'm right," Melody said.

Maguire picked up the wine glass and took a sip. He knew she was right, but it wasn't making his choice any easier.

When Rich had first spoken to him about Alan McMasters' offer he had strongly encouraged him to accept. It was the opportunity of a lifetime and Maguire still believed that to be true. That being said, he had not anticipated that he would be drawn into it. Unfortunately, this was now the *put up or shut up* point in the game.

"You do realize that this will change things?"

Inwardly Melody smiled. The momentum had clearly changed, but she was not cocky enough to let it show.

"Why do you say that?"

"Well, for starters this is not a nine to five kind of job, Mel."

"Neither is the career you have now, James."

"You know what I mean?"

"No, I don't know what you mean," Melody said. "What I do know is that you miss it and now you have an opportunity to not only do what you love, but to have a positive impact on it."

"What if I can't make it better?"

"Is that what this is about? You're worried you won't be any good at it?"

"This is not the same as being a detective, Mel. There are over five thousand detectives in New York City, but there is only one first deputy police commissioner. You screw up in a squad and there are half a dozen guys who will cover your backside. Screw up as the 1st dep, and there are a dozen and half people who will be more than happy to watch you have your ass handed to you, in the hopes of taking your place."

"Then I suggest that you don't screw up."

"Damn it, Melody, this is serious."

Melody got up, walked around the table and sat down in front of him. She took his hands into hers and stared at him intently.

"I know it is, James, and yet I can't understand why you are second guessing yourself," she replied. "You were a Navy SEAL and an NYPD detective. You've run your own security consulting firm for major corporations. If I didn't have complete faith in you, do you think that I would have trusted you with mine and Gen's safety and well-being? I'm sorry, Rich thinks you're qualified and so do I."

He knew this was a losing battle, he felt it slipping farther away from him with each exchange. That being said, he didn't feel as if he was actually losing, as much as he was accepting what had already been *preordained* for him. It had never been his choice to leave the Department in the first place, that decision had been made for him by the powers to be at the Medical Section. Now here he was being given the chance to return triumphantly.

"Well I guess I'd better call Rich and tell him *my* decision," he said.

Melody smiled, as she leaned over and kissed him. "Don't bother, you can tell him when you see him tomorrow. I invited everyone out for the weekend."

"You are a conniving little minx, you know that?"

"Uh huh," said Melody. "That's why you love me so much."

Across the table, Genevieve Gordon had sat enrapt, as she watched the whole drama unfold before her.

"Hot damn," she exclaimed as she raised her wine glass up in a mock salute. "No more speeding tickets!"

CHAPTER SIX

Southampton, Suffolk County, N.Y.
Tuesday, January 1st, 2013 – 9:54 a.m.

Maguire stood in front of the bathroom mirror struggling to make the tie do what he wanted.

"This is stupid," he cried out to no one in particular, although he knew Melody was just down the hall having a cup of coffee in the kitchen.

"Do you want my help?" she called out.

"No," he said by way of protest.

"Are you sure?"

"Yes... I mean no. I don't know."

Melody got up from the table and made her way to the bathroom. She smiled inwardly as she got to the door of the bedroom, recalling the first night the two of them had met all those months earlier.

Maguire stood in front of the mirror dressed in a dark gray, two button suit, with a crisp white linen shirt, his tie hanging down under the collar.

"You're over thinking this," she said.

Melody reached up, took the ends of the tie and began working them until she had formed a perfect Windsor knot.

"Thank you," he said and kissed her on the forehead. "I don't know why, but I feel so out of my element right now."

"It's okay; you are going to be fine."

"Yeah today, but what happens tomorrow?"

"Do not worry about tomorrow, for tomorrow will worry about itself. Each day has enough trouble of its own," she said with a smile.

"That's so not fair, Melody," he replied. "You can't expect me to argue with Jesus."

"I had to shut you up somehow or we would never get out of here."

Maguire stepped back a bit and held his arms out. "How do I look?"

"Like a million bucks," she said. "So why are you stressing out so much?"

"Because, after we walk out of here today I won't have that option available to me anymore."

Melody walked up to him, wrapping her arms around his neck, and kissed him softly.

"James, over the last eight months I have learned that anything you set your mind to, you conquer. I have no doubt, not only will you make a great first deputy commissioner, you will set the standard for any that come after you."

Maguire looked down into the warm brown eyes that looked up at him.

"How did I survive before you?"

"Does it matter, cowboy?" she asked. "All that matters is that you are here with me now."

"I'm not going anywhere, angel."

"I know," she said, with a crooked little smile, then turned and walked out of the bathroom.

Maguire watched as she left the room.

He was still as enchanted with her today as he was the first day they had met at Peter Bart's annual *Spring Fling* charity event the previous May. He recalled how he had grudgingly showed up to the *soirée*. He had been hell bent and determined to leave as quickly as possible. That grandiose plan had ended the moment he spotted her across the room. Eight months later and she still took his breath away.

Maguire's revelry was cut short as he heard the door to the houseboat open.

"Hello," Gen called out as she stepped through the doorway. "Is everyone decent?"

"No, we're having sex on the coffee table," Melody replied from the kitchen.

"Good, I was afraid I was going to be late."

"You're incorrigible, Gen," Maguire said as he walked out of the bedroom and into the hallway.

"I know, it's just another one of the many services I provide," Gen said coming to a halt. "Damn, you look good."

Maguire just shook his head and laughed. He had long ago grown accustomed to Gen's quirkiness, but even so, she still managed to leave him speechless from time to time.

Melody and Genevieve had a complex relationship. The two women had met in college and were closer than biological siblings. When Melody's career had taken off, she had brought Genevieve along with her. It was a meteoric rise and Genevieve held the role of *majordomo*, Melody's second in command. She was herself a ruthless businesswoman, and yet, when the doors were closed, she was the life of the party.

"Where's Gregor?"

"He's probably inspecting the helicopter crew to make sure that the soles of their shoes are polished."

Maguire laughed, not because it was humorous, but because it was entirely plausible.

Gregor Ritter had been a member of Germany's elite federal border police, the *Bundesgrenzschutz*. During that time he had also served as a member of their anti-terrorism unit, the GSG-9. Even among other spit and polish military units, the Germans tended to take things to the extreme.

Maguire had known Gregor professionally for a number of years, ever since the man had taken over as the head of Peter Bart's security detail. The two men had become close friends since the night of the attack at Melody's. Gregor still ran Peter's security, but he and Genevieve had also become an *item*. So when he wasn't working, he was usually at Mel's house.

Melody looked up from the document she was reading on her iPad as Genevieve walked into the kitchen.

"Are we good?"

"Yep," she replied, as she took the seat next to Melody.

"The helicopter is waiting for us at the helipad. We'll land over at the South Street Heliport and the NYPD will have a car waiting to bring us over to 1 Police Plaza."

"I wonder if any other first deputy commissioners were flown in for their swearing-in ceremony?" Maguire asked as he took a drink from his coffee mug.

"I told you that you were going to raise the bar," Melody replied. "You ready for this?"

"As ready as I'll ever be. Shall we go, ladies?"

Melody stood as James held up the three-quarter length, dark gray, cashmere wool jacket for her. He then put on his black leather overcoat and they headed for the door.

"Do you think they'll let me play with the siren?" Gen asked as they stepped out onto the back deck of the boat and into the frigid morning air.

"I'm pretty sure that they'll do it just to shut you up," Maguire replied as they walked up the ramp.

The driver got out as they approached and opened the rear passenger door on the Mercedes Benz S600 for Melody.

"Thank you, George," Melody said to the man as she slid into the back seat.

Maguire took the seat behind the driver, while Genevieve got into the front. It was a short trip from the dock, across the road, and up the driveway to the helipad, where the big Sikorsky S92 helicopter sat, awaiting their arrival.

As the car pulled up to the helipad, the door of the helicopter opened and Gregor walked down the steps to greet them.

Inside the cockpit, the pilot, retired Marine Corps Major Robert Miller, began his preflight check. After everyone had boarded, Gregor raised the door, and locked it, before signaling to Miller that the bird was secure.

Miller and his copilot did a visual check of the immediate area outside to ensure that no one was near the helicopter. When they both confirmed it was clear, the engines came to life and the rotor blades began their slow, steady buildup until they became nothing but a blur.

A moment later the helicopter began its ascent and headed west, toward New York City.

CHAPTER SEVEN

Northern Maine
Tuesday, January 1st, 2013 – 10:41 a.m.

Keith Banning sat looking out the window of the enclosed porch, as the snow continued to fall outside, in the Longfellow Mountains of northwest Maine.

It was one of those images that made its way onto a postcard. Glimpses of green peeked out from beneath the new fallen snow that covered the branches of pine trees. On the ground below, a blanket of white covered everything for as far as the eye could see.

Banning closed his eyes and he could almost hear the sound of the wind as it rustled through the pines. It was a unique sound and one that was guaranteed to bring a restorative sense of peace to the soul, even during the most foulest of moods.

He had made a full recovery since the ill-fated attack back in May. It had taken him quite some time to come to terms with all of it. He had meticulously planned for every conceivable thing, only to be denied at the last minute. The fact that he had come so close to dying at the hands of his nemesis had done nothing to improve his thoughts when he had returned to the cabin several days later. An issue that was not lost on his current house guest, the wife of the late Sheriff Paul Browning and Maguire's former high school sweetheart.

Banning looked back on that time with some remorse. He knew that he had been particularly brutal to her, but he consoled himself with the thought that if he had stuck to his original plan she would have been dead long ago. Still, he knew that it could not have been easy on her.

After he had healed enough, he began to make regular visits to the secret room, that he kept her locked in, below the cabin. Each visit was a way to exact his revenge against Maguire. If he couldn't hurt him, then he would hurt his surrogate. But he knew that he had done more than hurt her, he had violated her both physically and mentally.

Human beings can endure the physical pain; they learn that it only lasts for so long. There comes a point when a person can lock themselves away mentally to keep safe. Banning had gone to great lengths to transition from the physical to the mental. It was a game for him. He made it personal, and over time he had broken her.

In the beginning he had enjoyed forcibly taking her. The exhilaration he felt, when he took from her what he wanted, was a high that was almost indescribable. Later on though, he discovered something even more insidious. Instead of taking what he wanted, he began to force her to comply. He made it her choice. Soon she was doing what he wanted and she had no one to blame but herself.

After a while, he even began to explain things to her. Telling her how she was lucky that he hadn't killed her. That she was only here because all of the others in her life had either failed her or, as in the case of Maguire, simply no longer cared. She was alone, except for him.

Yes they had gotten off to a bad start, but he was, after all, still the one who took care of her. He provided for her food and shelter, all while the others were off doing what they wanted, oblivious to her needs.

The weeks turned into months and soon Patricia Browning had emotionally surrendered. The experts referred to this as *Stockholm Syndrome*. It's a psychological phenomenon in which hostages can begin to express empathy toward their captors, sometimes to the point of defending them or, in some cases, displaying love and affection.

One of the most famous cases was that of Patricia "Patty" Hearst, the granddaughter of publishing magnate William Randolph Hearst. Patty Hearst gained notoriety when she joined the *Symbionese Liberation Army* after they had kidnapped her. On February 4, 1974, the 19-year-old Hearst was abducted from her Berkeley, California apartment and then, two months later, she was photographed wielding an M1 carbine rifle during an SLA bank robbery in San Francisco.

Banning's revelry was cut short as he heard her step into the room.

"I brought you more coffee, my dear."

He looked up at Tricia.

"That was so thoughtful of you," Banning replied as he watched her refill the cup.

Tricia turned, walked out of the room and went back to her chair in the kitchen. She knew her place and knew she was expected to be there, unless he called for her. But she thought it would be a nice gesture to show Keith that she had been thinking about him. It was, after all, just the two of them here and it didn't hurt to repay the kindness he had shown her in taking care of her all these months.

Banning leaned back in the chair and smiled.

Yes, things were working out quite well, he thought.

CHAPTER EIGHT

South Street Heliport, New York City
Tuesday, January 1st, 2013 – 11:13 a.m.

James stared out the window as the helicopter made its way over Coney Island in Brooklyn. They had spent the trip skirting the Long Island shoreline and all that James could see, from the left side of the cabin, was the endless expanse of the Atlantic Ocean. He took it as a good omen.

During his days as a SEAL, they had always said that if things went bad; make your way back to the water. The water had always calmed him, it was his element, and as he looked out into the vast dark blue ocean he felt himself growing more peaceful inside.

The helicopter banked to the right and began to make its way into New York harbor, cruising over the Verrazano-Narrows Bridge. Moments later they flew past the Statue of Liberty. To most people, the statue stood as a beacon of hope in the harbor. She had been the first to greet the countless numbers of immigrants to the land of opportunity. But it had always struck Maguire as odd at just how profoundly sad she looked.

What did she know, he wondered?

He had flown past her a number of times before when he worked in the Intelligence Division. Back then he had been a detective and was often assigned to *Huntsman*, the radio call sign for the aerial surveillance helicopter that was part of the Presidential Protection Detail. The difference between then and now was that the helicopters the NYPD used were not quite as comfortable, or quiet, as the one he currently rode in.

"Penny for your thoughts," Melody said.

Maguire turned away from the window and looked over at Melody who sat in the chair across the aisle from him.

"Just wondering what the future holds."

"For you, I think a lot," Melody replied. "Since Rich first brought this up I have been paying close attention to the goings on in New York City. It reminds me of a company where the management has lost touch with its workers."

"That is a very astute observation, Mel. I just wonder if they have caused too much damage."

"I don't think so, James. I've been in your spot, coming in to a company that is in upheaval. The employees want to work, they want to succeed. They just need to know that the people at the top have their back."

"Things haven't changed much since I left."

"Then go in and change them. Hold your people to a high standard, but have their back when they are doing what you ask. That is what you always said was lacking when you were on the job."

James reached out and took Melody's hand in his.

"How'd you get so smart, lady?"

"I did what I always do. I shut my mouth and listened. Now it's your turn."

An audible ping came over the aircraft's internal communication system.

"Ms. Anderson," Bob Miller's voice said over the intercom. "We're getting ready for our approach."

In front of them the lower Manhattan skyline came into view. Maguire looked out to where the Twin Towers once majestically stood, dominating the skyline. It had been over eleven years and still it felt like only yesterday. The helicopter banked slightly to the right and began its descent. A moment later, they felt the wheels of the helicopter touch down on the small helipad, which jutted out into the East River.

"Show time, cowboy."

As they stepped out of the helicopter they saw an unmarked Dodge Charger parked on the tarmac with a black Mercedes Benz parked behind it. A man in a dark blue suit approached them.

"Sir," the man said, extending his hand. "I'm Detective Brian Kane."

Maguire shook hands with the detective, "James Maguire."

"We'll take you over to the old Tweed Courthouse, which is where everyone is staging. I'll explain everything in the car."

"Lead the way," Maguire said.

They followed the detective over to the unmarked police car. He and Melody got in the back as Genevieve and Gregor headed off to the Mercedes. A few moments later, the two car motorcade made its way out of the heliport and headed north on South Street.

Detective Kane leaned around in the front seat and spoke to Maguire.

"Everyone is gathering in the Tweed Courthouse, sir," he said. "Once they are ready for the inauguration to begin, we will relocate you to the seating area in front of City Hall. You and Ms. Anderson will be up on the dais. I will stay with you and Detective Murphy here will stay with your guests. After the ceremony we will go inside where Mayor McMasters will swear in Commissioner Stargold. Once that is done we will head over to 1PP for your swearing-in, sir."

"Thank you," Maguire said. "Are you assigned to Intel?"

"Yes, sir," the detective replied.

"So was I."

"I know, sir, and it's good to have you back."

The cars meandered through the narrow streets of lower Manhattan as they made their way toward the inauguration venue.

The Tweed Courthouse is the second oldest city government building in Manhattan, after City Hall, and was originally used as the New York County Courthouse. Its name came as a result of construction funds provided by corrupt Democratic Party Chief William "Boss" Tweed, whose Tammany Hall political machine controlled the city and state government at the time. As a result, Tweed became one of the wealthiest New Yorkers of the day by using the construction of the building as a pretext to embezzle millions of dollars.

The two cars pulled up in front of the Chambers Street entrance. Kane led them into the building while Murphy relocated the vehicles to the designated waiting area across the street. Upon entering the building they were led into the reception area where the soon to be new members of the McMasters administration were gathered. Rich and Mary were standing off to the side, talking to another couple, when Rich spotted them and waved them over.

Mary turned around as they approached. She gave Melody a hug while Rich and James shook hands.

"James, I'd like you to meet Tippi Fisher and her husband Mark," Rich said. "Tippi is the incoming deputy mayor for operations."

James reached out and shook her hand. "It's a pleasure to meet you."

"Rich here speaks very highly of you, James," she said.

"He tends to exaggerate a bit."

"I've seen your file; I'd say you live up to every bit of it."

"Well that's very kind of you to say."

"I'm sure the two of you will have a lot to do in the coming weeks, but once the dust settles maybe we could get together for coffee and go over things."

"Sounds good," Maguire said.

Maguire felt Melody move in next to him and take his arm in hers.

"Hi," Melody said. "I hope I'm not interrupting anything."

"Not at all, I'm Tippi Fisher, this is my husband Mark."

"I'm Melody Anderson, pleased to meet you both. That's a very interesting name."

"Yes," the woman replied. "Mother enjoyed her Hitchcock a bit too much."

"Melody Anderson?" said Mark Fisher. "As in Anderson Global Investments?"

"That would be me," she said.

"Ladies and Gentlemen, may I have your attention," said a man at the front of the room. "The inauguration is about to begin so would you please proceed out this door and make your way over to City Hall."

"Mrs. Fisher, it was very nice to meet you," Maguire said.

Rich and Mary headed toward the door, with their security team in tow, as Maguire and Melody followed behind.

Tippi Fisher turned to face her husband.

"Who the hell is Melody Anderson?"

"You can't be serious?" he asked. "Don't you read anything in those papers you get besides the politics and gossip pages? She's one of the richest women in the United States."

"Please don't drool, Mark. It's so unbecoming," Tippi replied, before turning and heading toward the door.

CHAPTER NINE

Brooklyn, New York City
Tuesday, January 1st, 2013 – 12:56 p.m.

The man reached out his hand and slid the key into the lock, opening the front door that led to the interior vestibule of the small apartment building just off Atlantic Avenue in the Boerum Hill section of Brooklyn. His hands and face stung from the bitter wind, while his feet were frozen from the cold wet slush that had found its way into his shoes. As he stepped inside, his senses were assaulted by the heat that emanated from the old cast iron radiator that sat inside the doorway.

The weather outside reminded him of the harsh winters in the mountains of his native Afghanistan. Yet the interior was a match for the desert heat of Yemen where he had spent so many months. Deep inside, the man longed for the end of this journey to come.

Were there eighty thousand servants and seventy-two virgins waiting for him in paradise? he wondered. *Did it really even matter?*

He began to make the long march up the narrow staircase that creaked under his weight. Most days he felt a sense of empathy with the old wooden stairs. He felt the same pressure and his body also ached inside.

How much longer?

He laid the small brown shopping bag on the table next to the door. He placed the key into the lock and turned it until he heard a click. He held the door knob with one hand, then knocked three times, and paused, before knocking a fourth.

It seemed like a pointless act to him, most of this did, but it was not his position to make the rules. He just had to follow them like a good solider. He picked up the bag and entered the apartment, closing the door behind him.

One of the men sitting in the living room lowered the AK-47 back onto the small coffee table in front of him.

"What took you so long, Bashir?" said the other man who sat on the couch, watching a cable news show on *Al Jazeera*.

"Maybe you should try walking in that shit outside, Qaseem, and then tell me why it takes you so long," the man replied.

"No, I think you do a very good job," the young man laughed. "I don't want to rob you of your fun."

Bashir Al Karim hung up his coat and carried the bag into the kitchen, placing it on the table. He took the kettle from the stovetop and put water on for coffee. He then grabbed two small china cups from the cabinet above the sink.

Outside in the living room he could hear laughter from the men sitting there. At one time it would have bothered him, but now, as the time grew closer, he shrugged it off.

Besides, he thought, *they were young, stupid and came from easy lives.*

Qaseem bin Khalid was from Saudi Arabia and was a member of the House of Saud. He wasn't exactly a close member of the royal family, but his idea of roughing it was using his father's Jaguar to go to the clubs instead of the Ferrari. He had taken on the role of leader, primarily because he had always felt everyone else was subservient to him.

The other two in the living room were also from the Middle East. Nazir al Mahdi was from Iraq and Ramzi Sharif was from Syria. All three liked to pretend that they were real soldiers, but only Sharif had any real experience, fighting briefly in Damascus. Each man had their own reasons for being here.

Still, this was not exactly what he had imagined for his life.

How had this journey begun, he thought?

He hadn't always had this hardened heart. He recalled the days of his youth when he had lived in a small farming village in the Baghlan province, just north of Kabul. Despite all the political turmoil that seemed to rage in his country back then, to him the world seemed small and peaceful.

The Russians had changed all of that.

He came from a very well respected family. His father had been a highly revered tribal elder and, being the oldest male son, he had grown accustomed to certain things. That position ensured that most of the other families were hopeful that he would take one of their daughters for his bride, one of whom was Salimah. The literal translation of her name meant flawless and she was. He was smitten with her from the first moment he had laid eyes on her. He would have liked to say that he had chosen her, but the fact was he always believed that she was an angel sent to him by Allah.

He had inherited his farm lands when his father had died and established his life with his new wife. His younger brother, Hakim, had also taken a wife as well, but had moved to her family's farm, in a village about a day's journey away, to help her father who was ill. One day Hakim had sent word that he needed help constructing a new building for the sheep.

Bashir had packed up what he needed and promised Salimah, who was expecting their first child, that he would return by the end of the month.

He had kept his word, but his return home was bitter.

While large portions of Baghlan were accommodating to the Soviet occupation, and even housed the largest military supply depot in Afghanistan, there was still dissent. While many Ismaili leaders supported the communist regime, others did not. One such leader, from Bashir's village, led a partisan movement against the invaders. The Soviet response was swift.

Bashir came home to a village utterly decimated by elements of the 40th Army. What hadn't been burned to the ground, was demolished. As he walked through the remnants of what remained of his village, he discovered a literal ghost town.

No one had survived, not man nor animal.

Bloated bodies and the carcasses of dead animals dotted the landscape. By the time he reached what was left of his home he was physically and emotionally numb. Still, the scene that awaited him would be the one that completed his detachment from the rest of humanity.

As he walked into what remained of the small stone house he saw her body lying on the floor among the rubble. He dropped to his knees sobbing uncontrollably. Even through the physical destruction he could tell that she had not died from *mechanical* means. He would have preferred to think that her death had been the result of some anonymous bullet, but he knew that would have been a lie. No, the Soviet infidels were known as animals and the evidence of their brutal savagery remained visible for him to see. The image was seared into his mind. It was as if Allah himself was punishing him for not being there to protect her.

He felt a stinging pain in his hand and then heard the sound of the pieces of broken china clatter on the floor. The memories faded in an instant as Qaseem ran into the small kitchen.

"What the fuck, Bashir?"

The man looked down and saw the blood streaming from his hand as he clutched the remains of the china cup.

"I don't know what happened," he replied.

"Well clean this shit up and be more careful."

"Of course, of course."

Bashir ran his hand under the cold water and picked out the remaining shards of glass. When he was satisfied that he had gotten them all out, he wrapped a paper towel around it and applied some pressure.

It was hardly a significant injury. He had seen so much more on the battlefields of Afghanistan.

After his wife had been taken from him he had joined up with the *Mujahideen*, the Afghan guerilla fighters. With help from the west they had beaten their enemy and laughed as they watched them limp back to their Mother Russia. The sweet taste of victory, however, did not last. Bashir watched as these tribal groups then began to battle one another for control in the ensuing civil war. Repulsed by what he saw unfolding in his country, he fled. With the Soviets gone he needed a new enemy. He found that enemy in America, whom he blamed for deserting his country after they had gotten what they wanted.

Bashir reached up, removing the ground coffee and added it to the kettle of boiling water. While the coffee brewed he finished cleaning up the remaining pieces of china from the floor and then got a replacement cup. He then stirred in some cardamom and saffron to the kettle. When he was done, he put the cups and kettle onto a tray, carrying them down the hallway to the back bedroom.

In the small dark bedroom, Yusef Sayeed sat behind a wooden desk. The only source of light came from an adjustable magnification lamp that sat on top. Wisps of smoke rose up from the soldering iron he was using.

It had taken him several weeks to prepare all the circuit boards. It was a labor intensive project, both in terms of constructing and assembling everything, but he was just about at the end. It should have all been done already, but the cutout being used to purchase the materials had proven to be a bit more overly cautious than any of them had thought necessary.

Bashir closed the door behind him, setting the tray down on the small table next to the bed. He sat down on the wooden stool next to it and waited. He knew better than to interrupt his friend while he was working.

Yusef was not a physically imposing man. His relatively short size, coupled with his habit of wearing clothing that was rather ill fitting, belied just how dangerous he actually was. In his career, the master bomb maker, from Yemen, had certainly sent hundreds of infidels to an early death.

When he had finished soldering the last circuit the man placed the iron back into its cradle to cool down. All that remained was to attach the boards to the devices themselves.

He removed his round, wire rimmed glasses, setting them on the desk, and got up, walking over to where Bashir was sitting.

"Peace be upon you, my friend," said Yusef, using the traditional Muslim greeting.

"May peace, mercy and blessings of Allah be upon you," Bashir replied.

"You look tired; are you alright?"

Bashir poured some coffee into the two cups and then passed one to Yusef.

"I do feel tired," he said taking a sip of the strong coffee. "I have known only war for the last three decades."

Yusef smiled and nodded his head slowly. Bashir was about ten years older than he was and had much more battlefield experience, but the two men shared a common bond that was lost on the young men outside.

"Soon," he said, nodding toward the backpacks that were lined up along the wall, "it will be done and we will all be in paradise with our seventy-two virgins."

Bashir laughed.

It had become a source of humor between the two of them. Qaseem and the other two young men constantly spoke about paradise, along with their promised virgins. Bashir and Yusef were in agreement that none of those boys would know what to do with one virgin, let alone seventy-two.

"I do not wish for the touch of anyone but my beloved Salimah."

"And you will feel it again soon, my friend, Allah willing."

"*Allah* willing," repeated Bashir. "*Allahu Akbar.* God is Greater."

CHAPTER TEN

City Hall, New York City
Tuesday, January 1st, 2013 – 1:13 p.m.

Genevieve sat watching the spectacle of the mayoral inauguration as it unfolded before her. She had never been to an event like this before, not that she hadn't been invited. Melody had gone to a few, including the presidential inauguration in D.C. back in 2005. She had never understood why they were held in January of all months. She was a warm weather girl and did not feel inclined to sit out in the cold for anyone. The fact that she was here at all was a testament to her affection for James.

"Gregor, have you ever been to something like this before?" she asked.

"Yes, of course," he replied.

She loved to hear him speak. Something about his thick German accent sounded so sexy to her.

"I was on the *bundeskanzler's* protection detail in Germany for two years. You call this person the prime minister here I think. You know we also have a president, but it is not like the United States. In Germany, the chancellor runs the government."

"Do they have events like this?" she asked.

"Yes, but this is different," he said pointing at the towering buildings that surrounded City Hall Park. "*Das ist verrückt.* How do you say? Crazy?"

He had been amazed when they first walked outside and saw where the event was being held. He could see the members of the NYPD ESU Counter Sniper Team on the roof of City Hall, but the idea of trying to cover all of the buildings that overlooked the park seemed to be a monumental task.

"Is it really that dangerous?" she asked.

Gregor looked down at Genevieve and lied.

"No, of course for you it is very safe," he said. "I would never let anything happen to you, *meine liebchen*."

She laid her head on his shoulder as he wrapped his arm around her. As she looked up at the dais she spotted James and waved discreetly at him.

Maguire stared out across the sea of people that filled the seating in City Hall Park trying to pick up any indication that something was out of place. It was a force of habit that, after all these years, he still could not turn off. He caught Genevieve waving at him and smiled as he waved back at her. He noticed that Gregor was also scanning the crowd.

I guess it never really leaves you, he thought.

Despite the frigid temperatures outside it was a standing room only crowd. He and Melody sat in the seats on the main stage next to Rich and Mary. Behind them the Intel detectives assigned to protect them kept a watchful eye.

Directly in front of the general seating area was a large circular seal, featuring the New York City coat of arms and a podium, from which the inauguration ceremony was being held. Behind the stage, and evenly spaced between the massive fluted stone columns that stood at the entrance of City Hall, flew the flags of the five boroughs along with the United States and the New York City flags.

The weather had ensured that there were no overly long speeches today, as one after another, the assembled politicians found their voices affected by the extreme cold. After McMasters had been sworn-in as mayor, the ceremony broke up to the traditional strains of Frank Sinatra's classic song, *New York, New York*.

As they moved toward the entrance they were met by Detective Kane, who led them inside. A few minutes later they were rejoined by Genevieve and Gregor.

"Sir," Kane said. "They'll be holding each of the swearing-ins upstairs in the Blue Room. Everyone is gathering beforehand in the Governor's Room."

Maguire had been inside City Hall a number of times, but it still wasn't exactly familiar territory to him. He had spent his time in the Intelligence Division assigned to the Public Security Section. The Mayor's security detail, along with other city government dignitaries, came under the auspices of the Municipal Security Section.

"Lead the way," he said. He reached over and took Melody's hand in his as they followed Kane up the grand marble staircase.

The Governor's Room was as opulent, as it was massive. Two large chandeliers hung down from the elaborate plaster ceiling that soared twenty feet above the hard wood floors. Mahogany side chairs lined the walls along with other furniture from the 18th and 19th centuries. The walls were lined with priceless portraits of important figures from the Colonial era, American Revolution, and New York State government, including a portrait at the far end of George Washington that was done in 1790. In addition to the portrait, the room also housed the desk which Washington used, at Federal Hall, while he was President.

For most of those gathered here today, it was their first time in the room. Melody had attended several events here during the prior two administrations.

As they walked inside, Mary came over and grabbed Melody by the arm.

"I'm stealing her for a moment," she said to James.

"As long as you return her in the same condition that you got her."

Mary laughed and Melody rolled her eyes.

Mary led her over to the far end of the room where it was a bit more private.

"How's the apartment working out?" Melody asked.

"That's what I needed to talk to you about," Mary said. "I just wanted to say thank you again for letting us use it. The girls are in love with it, and I know that it has been a huge burden off of Rich's shoulders."

"Oh, I'm so happy to hear that."

"How is James doing?"

"You'd think he had never been a cop before."

"Oh God, I know. Rich has been driving me crazy. I can't wait for him to actually be gone out of the house and working again. If he asks me one more time if I know how important this is I just might shoot him."

"I agree," Melody said. "I think that once they get their feet wet again, they will be fine."

"I certainly hope you're right. I don't know about you, but I really could use a girl's night out."

"Just tell me when you are free and we'll make it happen," Melody said. "Gen doesn't need any additional urging to concoct her infamous piña colada's."

"Ooh, those are dangerous," Mary said as she thought back to the last time they had all gotten together. "Oh well, you only live once right?"

"That's the spirit," replied Melody as they rejoined the rest of them.

A short time later the swearing-in ceremonies began. At first Mayor Alan McMasters brought in all of his deputies to the Blue Room which is normally used for City Hall press conferences. There, the city clerk administered the oath of office and then each newly minted deputy mayor came up, with their families, to have a photo taken with the new mayor.

When that was done, the new agency heads were brought in and took their oath of office. McMasters had not changed all of them, only the ones he had deemed politically important. These included the Board of Education, Sanitation, Fire and the Police Department.

After the oath had been administered, McMasters presented Richard Stargold with the badge of the police commissioner. After the initial presentation photos had been taken, Rich called Maguire and Melody to come up and join them.

"I hear congratulations will soon be in order for you as well," Alan McMasters said to Maguire. "Please allow me to extend mine a bit early."

McMasters held out his hand and Maguire shook it, "Thank you, sir."

"I know Rich, and by extension myself, will be well served by your experience. I'm counting on the two of you to restore the luster back to the greatest police department in the world."

"I'll do my best, sir."

"Of that I have no doubt."

When the ceremony concluded, they walked back to the Governor's Room where their protection details awaited them and gathered up their jackets.

"You ready for this, James?" Rich asked.

"No, so you had better do this fast before I come to my senses."

"Well, then we better get this show on the road."

They made their way outside and found that the cars had since been relocated from the Tweed Courthouse to the Park Row side of City Hall.

For Rich the transition had already been made.

The regular unmarked car that they had arrived in earlier had now been replaced by twin black Chevrolet Suburban's. The two Intelligence Division detectives, who had been their escorts for the inauguration, now stepped to the side as they approached the motorcade.

A man approached them.

"Commissioner Stargold," he said. "I'm Sergeant Walcott. I'm the head of your security detail. If you would, please follow me."

The four car motorcade proceeded to make a U-turn and headed down Frankfort Street, turning left onto Gold Street, making their way under the Brooklyn Bridge. Ahead of them stood the large brick building known as One Police Plaza.

As they headed toward the building they pulled through a checkpoint where a uniformed officer stood outside and saluted as they drove past. Half way down the street the lead Suburban pulled to the side, in a blocking pattern, while the one Rich was in pulled down the ramp into the underground parking garage. The other vehicle then proceeded down the ramp, followed by the car Maguire and Melody were in, along with the Mercedes.

As they pulled into the basement a uniformed officer directed the Intel car and Mercedes into two vacant parking spots. New Year's Day was a typically quiet one and the basement garage was almost completely empty.

Maguire stepped out of the car and looked around. The last time he had been down here was the day he had been awarded the Medal of Valor.

"You ok?" Melody asked as she walked up to him, wrapping her arm around his, holding him tightly.

Maguire turned to face her.

"Yeah, I'm fine, angel," he said, kissing her cheek. "Let's go make this official."

Detective Kane led them over to the PC's elevator. It was a separate one used by the police commissioner, along with other high ranking commissioners and chiefs who were in charge of the various bureaus within the NYPD.

Rich and Mary had already gone up.

It was a short trip up to the 14th floor. As Maguire stepped out of the elevator it seemed to him as if he was setting foot onto some foreign soil.

"This way, sir," Kane said, leading them toward the end of the hallway to the large glass doors of the police commissioner's office.

The anteroom stood in stark contrast to the otherwise utilitarian construction of the other areas of the building. The dark red walls coupled with the oversized polished antique wood desk, which had always been a staple of New York City Police precincts, provided quite a first impression. The walls contained photographs of America's twenty-sixth president, Theodore Roosevelt, who had also served as police commissioner in New York City in 1895.

A member of Rich's security detail met them at the door.

"I'm Detective Owens," he said. "I'll take you back."

Despite the fact that he was a retired detective, and soon to be appointed as first deputy commissioner, there was still a procedure to be followed. Until he was officially sworn-in he would be escorted around.

"This is as far as I go, sir," said Kane. "Congratulations."

Maguire reached out and shook the man's hand. "Thank you Brian and pass my gratitude along to your partner."

"I will, sir," the man replied. "Good luck and stay safe."

Owens led them back to Rich's office and knocked on the door.

"Sir," he said. "They're here."

"That's fine, thank you," Rich said. "Come in, guys."

They walked into the large barren office. The previous police commissioner had obviously left and taken everything, but the furniture, with him. The only other items that remained were the United States, New York City and NYPD flags.

Standing inside the office was a department photographer and Chief of Personnel Rafael "Ray" Hernandez.

"Well, I guess we should make this official," Rich said. "Chief Hernandez, do your thing."

Maguire stood across from Hernandez with Melody at his side, while Rich stood next to him holding a case containing a gold badge.

James raised his right hand, recited the oath of office, and became the newest first deputy commissioner of the New York City Police Department. In the background, the sound of the photographer's camera broke the silence.

When the swearing-in was done, Chief Hernandez congratulated Maguire while Rich stepped forward and presented him with his badge.

"Well, it's official now," James said. "I guess I can't run away."

After a few more family pictures were taken the photographer excused himself and left them in the office.

"So what do we do now?" Mary asked.

"I don't know, but I'm hungry," replied Melody.

"Just for the record it is New Year's Day, people," Rich said. "Unless we want happy meals, our choices are probably going to be limited."

"Silly man," Gen said with a laugh. "We don't need reservations, we have Melody."

Melody took out her cell phone and scrolled through the directory, selecting a number and waited for the call to connect.

"Suzette?" she said. "It's Melody."

She listened to the woman on the other end for a few seconds.

"*Oui*, I am in Manhattan now with some friends can you fit us in," she said. "*Merci beaucoup, mon amie.* I will see you soon."

Melody ended the call. "See, all taken care."

"Whatever did you do before you found her?" Rich asked.

"Chinese take-out and beer mostly," Maguire replied.

"He's not kidding either," Melody chimed in. "You should see the plastic bowl collection he has under the sink."

As everyone filed out of the room, Rich grabbed Maguire by the arm and motioned him to wait.

"What's wrong?" he asked when they were alone.

"Christ, James I'm scared shitless," Rich replied. "Did I do the right thing?"

"Yeah, you did, don't sweat it. We'll worry about tomorrow when it comes, tonight let's enjoy the moment."

"Ok, if you say so."

The two men walked out of the room and rejoined the rest.

Melody caught Maguire's eye. He winked at her letting her know everything was alright.

"Ok, let's go eat," Mary said.

When they arrived back down in the garage, they were joined by Maguire's new security detail. The small unmarked Charger had been replaced by another black Chevy Suburban. The hierarchy of the Department was accustomed to traveling in comfort.

"This is going to take some getting used to, Rich," Maguire said as he walked toward the waiting vehicle.

"You're telling me," he replied.

After everyone had gotten in their respective vehicles, the motorcade made its way out of the garage and into the now darkening streets of New York City.

CHAPTER ELEVEN

Northern Maine
Tuesday, January 1st, 2013 – 4:13 p.m.

Banning stood at the kitchen table going over the photos spread across it. No matter how many times he looked at them he inevitably came to the same conclusion. The images were useless at best.

It had been his first trip back to Southampton since the night he and Maguire had done battle. After seeing Maguire's image on the security camera feed he knew that he would have to begin planning the next move. So back in October he had locked Tricia away with enough food to last a week while he made the drive south to scout things out in person. What he found when he arrived did not exactly please him.

His first disappointment came when he had gone to the marina where Maguire had previously docked his houseboat, only to find it gone. It had annoyed him, but the truth was that it wasn't entirely unexpected. It just meant that he would have to dig a bit harder. Next he began to probe the perimeter around Melody Anderson's house.

He knew that the stretch of road in front of the residence didn't particularly lend itself to easy observation. That was of course unless you fit in and nothing said *I belong here* more than a government vehicle. So he had *appropriated* an old Parks & Recreation truck and cruised down Meadow Lane toward the Shinnecock East County Park. The ride took him right past the front gate of the house, but no one paid any attention because they were so used to seeing these types of vehicles.

While security was nonexistent back in May, that certainly was not the case now. During the ride by, he had counted no less than a half dozen security cameras that scanned every aspect of the front of the property and roadway. He also observed several people walking along the grounds, including one with a dog.

Banning pulled into the parking lot and parked the truck at a random angle, facing the water. He pulled out a newspaper, laying it over the steering wheel and began eating the sandwich he had gotten, before he had stolen the truck. To the casual observer, he would appear to be just another worker, goofing off on the town's dime. But the placement of the truck gave him a fairly decent view of the edge of the property. There were cameras here as well, and he found it interesting that there was also a two man patrol on the beach with another dog.

They have certainly learned their lesson, he thought.

None of this made him particularly happy. Over the next thirty-five minutes he counted no fewer than a dozen different security personnel proactively roaming the grounds and they were good. There was no discernable pattern to their patrol routes or times. It was clear to him that the odds of a successful direct assault on the compound were slim. Still he needed more time to study things.

When he was done, he folded up the paper, tossing the remnants of his lunch into the brown paper bag and began to pull away. As he made his way back east along Meadow Lane he spotted something interesting off to his left. Across the road from the main gate was a dock and moored to it was the houseboat.

Tricky, Banning thought.

He knew that he was definitely going to have to take a closer look around. The only question was how.

When he got back to the motel he opened the laptop and pulled up the map for the area. He stared at it, looking for some type of inspiration. There had to be a way of getting a longer look at the location without setting off all the bells and whistles. Something in the middle of the bay caught his eye and he magnified the image for a better look. It was a fishing boat.

Over the next several days, he sailed on a half dozen different fishing charters. Some stayed in the bay, while others ventured out to the ocean. At various times he would set his rod down and pick up the Nikon camera he had brought along. The 600mm lens made easy work of the task at hand. If anyone asked, he told them he was doing a coffee table book on America's coastlines.

Now, nearly two months later, he stood looking at the pictures he had taken and realized that any attempt to infiltrate the house would be suicidal.

He picked up a photo that showed the houseboat. He could make out several cameras and these were all pointed out toward the water. With this many cameras in play, it would serve to reason that they had a dedicated monitoring system up and running as well.

Banning picked up a bottle of scotch and poured himself a drink. He sat down in one of the chairs on the porch and lit up a cigarette. Banning resigned himself to the fact that he was not going to be able to bring the fight to Maguire. No, he would have to provoke the man into action, force him to come out into the open. The only question that remained was how to accomplish it.

He took a drink, feeling the warm burn of the liquid as it went down his throat. He began to absentmindedly stroke the beard that he had begun to grow over the last few months. In a way it made him feel more connected to his current environment. Besides, it also helped to mask his real identity, something that could never be underestimated. He took a drag on the cigarette and looked out the window, watching as the last rays of the sun slowly slipped away behind the mountains.

Well there always was the tried and true method, he thought, as he looked back in the direction of the cabin interior. Maybe he needed to send him a more intimate reminder of what was at stake in this game.

CHAPTER TWELVE

Southampton, Suffolk County, N.Y.
Tuesday, January 1st, 2013 – 9:17 p.m.

The wheels of the helicopter came to a rest on the helipad. Up in the cockpit the pilot immediately began shutting down the engines. Outside, two cars sat idling, patiently awaiting the arrival of their passengers.

As the couples walked down the steps, and headed toward the cars, Genevieve broke the silence.

"I'm going to ride back to Gregor's place," she said. "I'll be back later."

"Ok, I'll see you in the morning," Melody replied.

"Goodnight," said Maguire. "And thanks again for coming guys."

"Wouldn't have missed it for the world," Gen replied, giving him a kiss on the cheek. "Congratulations again."

"Yes, congratulations, James," Gregor added, shaking Maguire's hand. "I wish you the best of luck."

"Thanks, Gregor, I appreciate that."

Maguire opened the door for Melody before walking around to the passenger side and getting in.

"Where to, ma'am?" the driver asked.

Melody looked over at Maguire. "I feel like a nightcap, cowboy," she said with an impish grin.

"You heard the lady, George, back to the house."

They drove up to the house and Maguire followed her inside.

"Go get comfy and I'll get us something to drink," she replied, and headed off to the kitchen.

Maguire walked into the salon and laid his leather coat over the back of the couch. He sat down, reaching into his suit pocket and removed the small case. He opened it and withdrew the badge, or shield as it is known in NYPD vernacular, and held it in his hand.

The gold starburst design glistened in the overhead lighting. On the top was an eagle, its wings outstretched and clutching oak leaves in each of its talons. Superimposed over the eagle where four silver stars. In the center, surrounded by a pool of blue enamel, was the seal of the city and the lettering, *City of New York Police*. Below that read the title: *First Deputy Commissioner*.

Maguire moved it around, watching the light dance across the highly polished metal. The shield bore a slight resemblance to the one he had previously carried as a detective, but the weight of responsibility that came with this one, far exceeded what he had been used to.

Melody came back into the room a few moments later with a bottle of red wine and two glasses.

"You look like a kid at Christmas," she replied, taking the seat next to him on the couch, "who just got a new toy."

"I wish," he said. "I'm more like Santa's number one elf that is responsible now for making sure all of the boys and girls have a good Christmas."

"Can I see?" she asked, looking at the shield.

"Sure," Maguire said and handed it to her. He reached over, picking up the wine bottle and filled the two glasses. He handed one to Melody and leaned back against the supple leather of the couch. Melody curled up next to him and took a sip of the wine.

"It's lighter than I thought it would be," she replied. "Not really sure what I expected. The big safety pin is a nice touch."

"Well that goes back to the old days when we wore the heavy overcoats in the winter," Maguire said, referring to the large traditional blue wool *reefer* coats with their distinctive double row of brass buttons up the front. "A regular pin back would never have worked. You needed the heavy lugs to go through the material and then the safety pin made it easier to secure the badge in place."

"But you won't be wearing a uniform, will you?"

"No, the highest uniformed rank is chief of department. Rich, myself and the other deputy commissioners are non-uniformed."

"I know you have been second guessing yourself lately. Are you still having some doubts?"

"Little too late for that now, isn't it?" he asked.

"Well, it's kinda of hard for me to imagine you having any doubts. You've always seemed to be so sure of everything."

"That's because most of the time I only had to take care of myself or those immediately around me," Maguire replied. "Now I have over fifty thousand cops and civilian employees to worry about."

Melody thought about that for a moment. She realized the significance of what he was saying.

She had made her way through the business world, climbing one rung of the ladder at a time. It hadn't always been an easy go. There were a lot of people who had tried to stand in her way, along with a few others who had intentionally gone out of their way to try and sabotage her. She wondered if the police department would be any different.

"Will anyone resent your appointment?" she asked.

"Oh sure," he replied. "The Department is no different than the rest of the world. You are always going to have people that think they were owed the spot and who will be resentful that someone, especially someone from a non-supervisory rank, got selected over them. Ego's tend to kick into overdrive by the time they pin that first star on your shoulder."

"How will you handle it?"

"Tomorrow will start the fun part for Rich and I. There are a lot of personnel changes that will be coming. Some will move up, some will retire."

"What happens if they don't want to retire?"

"Everyone above the rank of captain is a discretionary promotion," Maguire explained. "You serve at the pleasure of the police commissioner. So if you don't want to retire, you can stay, but you revert back to captain."

"Ouch," Melody said. "That has got to hurt."

"The Department has a long and storied history," he said with a laugh.

Melody set the wine glass on the table, turned around and climbed onto his lap. She held the shield up in front of him. Maguire placed his hand out and watched as she dropped it into his open palm.

"You know what?" she asked.

"What?"

"I'm thinking of something long and storied as well."

Maguire wrapped his arms around her and pulled her close to him. "You are so incorrigible you little minx."

"I know, I think Gen is finally rubbing off on me."

"Oh don't blame Gen for your proclivities."

"You need to take me upstairs before my proclivities take over and I attack you here on this couch."

CHAPTER THIRTEEN

Southampton, Suffolk County, N.Y.
Wednesday, January 2nd, 2013 – 5:15 a.m.

Melody stood in the doorway, dressed in a long white cotton robe, and held a stainless steel travel mug with black coffee in it.

Outside, the Suburban sat waiting in the courtyard, its windshield wipers keeping the blowing snow from piling up.

Maguire put on his overcoat and headed for the door.

"You have a great day at work, honey," Melody said with smile.

"You're enjoying, this aren't you?" Maguire said, giving her a kiss.

"Yeah, I am actually," she replied. "I'm digging this whole sending you off to work in the morning gig."

"Are you staying at home today?"

"Oh yeah," Melody replied. "After last night I think I owe myself a day of rest."

"What about me?"

"Duty calls, my love," she replied. "Now go keep the city safe. I'll be here waiting for you."

"Thanks, angel," Maguire said. He adjusted the collar of the jacket and took the mug, before stepping out into the frigid morning air.

"Love ya, sexy," she said and closed the door.

As Maguire walked toward the vehicle a detective got out and opened the rear door. Maguire knew the drill; it was one he had performed countless times when he had been a detective in the Intelligence Division. He didn't know if he would ever get used to being on this side though.

"Morning, sir," the man said.

"Good morning," Maguire replied, and climbed up into the vehicle.

When the detective had gotten back in, the truck began heading down the driveway.

"I'm Detective Mike Torres," the man said. "This is Detective Amanda Massi."

"Morning, sir," the driver replied.

"Please bear with me as I get used to all of this," Maguire said. "I'm more accustomed to being in your seat, than this one back here."

"Completely understandable, sir, anything we can do to help you, just let us know."

"Who is in charge of the detail?" Maguire asked.

"No one right now," Torres replied. "Our old sergeant retired last month and they didn't bring anyone in to fill the spot."

The man reached up, removing a manila folder off the dash and handed it to Maguire.

"Here's the Operation's printout for the unusual reports from yesterday's four to twelve shift and the midnight shift up to 0400 hours."

James reached up and activated the overhead light. He opened the folder and began to scan through the pages.

Unusual's, or UF-49's as they were officially known, were Department reports for any occurrences that were exactly that, unusual. The report was like a highlight reel of the previous hour's events throughout the city. A cop sustained a minor injury as the result of an accident in the eight-four precinct, there was a multiple shooting in the seven-three, which was in fact not all that unusual, and the one-oh-nine was investigating a potential hate crime at a local Korean church.

Maguire tossed the folder on the seat next to him and took a sip from the coffee mug.

"So you guys have the day tour coverage?"

"Yes, sir," Torres replied. "We cover from 0400 to 1200. Then your evening shift will take over and cover from 1400 to 2200. There's always someone at the office to cover the two hour difference if the need arises."

"Is this trip going to be hard on you guys?" Maguire asked. He knew the previous 1st dep had lived in Queens.

"No, sir, not at all," replied Torres. "Actually everyone on the team resides either in Queens or just over the border in Nassau. We store the truck over at Highway Three. The morning trip isn't bad; no one is on the road at that time."

Maguire recalled making the trip himself. Most of the time he had worked off hours so he hadn't gotten hit too bad with the daily traffic woes. On the days when he had court, well, that was a completely different story. Nothing ever goes smoothly when you're driving on Long Island. You generally just took the allotted travel time and multiplied that by two, three if there happened to be snow on the ground.

The Suburban pulled into the parking garage at 1PP just before seven. Even at this early hour it was already full.

The nice thing was that 95% of the spots were designated and parking in someone else's spot was highly frowned upon. In fact, the parking spots of the police commissioner and 1st dep were considered *sacrosanct*.

They took the elevator up to the 14th floor and got off. As they made their way down the hallway Maguire could make out the large wooden sign with ornate, gold gilt lettering which hung outside.

"First Deputy Commissioner"

He took a deep breath. Suddenly, this all became very real.

As he made his way through the door, someone called out "Attention!"

Everyone in the room rose to attention, causing Maguire to pause in his tracks. Normally, the call to attention was reserved for ranking uniformed members. However, this tradition is also carried over for the police commissioner and first deputy.

"At ease," he said looking at the men and women that comprised his staff. "Thank you very much. While I certainly appreciate the gesture, from now on we can dispense with it. I tend to move around a lot and you're not going to get anything done if you have to jump up and down every five minutes.

That elicited a few laughs.

"Give me a few minutes to get my jacket off, have a cup of hot coffee, and I'll be back out to talk to you."

Torres led the way back to Maguire's office. As they approached it, an older man in uniform stepped out of a side office and greeted Maguire.

"Deputy Inspector Martin," he said, with a trace of an Irish brogue. "Liam Martin. I'm the C.O. of your office, for now."

Maguire shook the man's hand. "Nice to meet you, Inspector, please follow me."

When they got to the office Torres stood to the side to let the two men enter.

"I'll be just outside if you need anything, sir."

"I really could use some coffee, Mike," Maguire said.

"Not a problem, sir, how do you like it?

"Black is fine," Maguire replied.

"Inspector?"

"No, Michael, I've already had my fill."

As Torres left, Maguire took off his overcoat and hung it on the coat rack next to the door.

"Please, Liam, have a seat."

Maguire walked over and sat down behind the large wooden executive desk.

"I assume you have had the opportunity to pull my jacket and take a look at the new boss' file," Maguire said.

"Indeed I have, sir, as I am sure you have read mine."

Once the announcement had been made that Stargold would be the new police commissioner a committee had been put together to make the transition as easy as possible, at least that had been the plan. What actually occurred was much different.

Almost from the very beginning the outgoing police commissioner, and his administration, refused to play nice. They went so far as to drag their feet on providing any personal folders or personnel to facilitate the transition, claiming that it was the holiday season and they were already too understaffed to waste time trying to bring amateurs up to speed.

The now former PC had enjoyed the luxury of being in the spot so long that he started to believe that it was his rightful position.

McMasters had known the man socially for many years. While he certainly had the *bona fides* for the position, McMasters wasn't looking for a yes man to simply placate him while he made his own political moves toward higher office.

The truth was, the Department was in a state of turmoil. Complaints and crime were both up, while morale and retention were moving in the opposite direction. The current hierarchy of the Department had been created by the former police commissioner and it mirrored his ideology. McMasters realized it was time for someone new which was the reason he had selected Stargold.

This veritable slap in the face was rewarded with an immediate managerial reprisal. Whole scale transfers were implemented, golden parachutes as they were called. People who had been languishing on transfer lists were pushed even further back as the administration rewarded their loyal minions. In addition, promotions were also made, flooding certain titles.

The reason for all of this was twofold. First, it allowed the outgoing PC to wield his power one last time, thumbing his nose at the incoming PC whom he openly mocked in the media, describing him as a "low level federal employee with minimal experience in *real* policing." Second, he put the new administration between a rock and a hard place. They were effectively stuck. If they tried to overturn transfers or promotions they would risk having the Department turn on them. If they did nothing, they would have key positions filled by those loyal to the prior administration.

In essence, they had been handed the proverbial bag of shit.

"The reality, Liam, is that no, I have not seen your folder. Not yet at least," he added, pulling a thick manila folder from the pile on his desk.

A knock on the door announced that Torres had returned with the coffee.

"Here you go, sir, can I get you anything else?"

"No, this is perfect, Mike," replied Maguire. "Thanks."

Maguire took a sip of the hot coffee and placed it on the desk.

"Besides, I'm not a big fan of personnel folders. I've found that evaluations don't tell you the real story. So please, tell me about you."

"Well, I came on the job in 1982. I worked in the two-eight until I got promoted to sergeant in 1990. Then I got shipped to the seven-seven."

"Out of the frying pan and into the fire," said Maguire.

Both precincts were notoriously busy. In New York City precincts were ranked as either A, B, or C houses, depending on how active they were. 'A' houses were the busiest ones, while 'C' houses were the relatively quiet ones. Although there were no truly *quiet* place's in New York. Both the two-eight and the seven-seven were considered to be 'A' houses.

"In 1994 I made lieutenant. I guess they felt sorry for me and shipped me off to the one-eleven. It was closer to home, but it was a bit too slow for my tastes. I called in a favor and got a transfer to Brooklyn North Narcotics. When I made captain in 1997, they assigned me as the executive officer of Transit District 34 in Coney Island. Later I was made commanding officer of the six-eight. I made deputy inspector in 2001 and in 2005 they put me here."

Maguire flipped open the folder. Everything the man had said was outlined in detail in the attached paperwork, along with his personnel evaluations and departmental recognition. All of his performance evaluations were stellar and he was highly decorated, including having been awarded the Combat Cross, the Departments 2nd highest award, for a shooting in 1993. He closed it over and pushed it to the side. He hadn't lied, it was his first time *seeing* the personnel folder, but he'd already had several phone calls about the man.

"So, Liam, how come you're still here?" Maguire asked.

"Well, I knew the former 1st dep from my Brooklyn North days. He's the one who brought me in, much to the chagrin of the former police commissioner, whom I also knew, but in a wee bit less hospitable way. The 1st dep tried to transfer me before he left, but the PC blocked it. I guess it was his way of getting the last laugh. He must have figured the new regime would come in and jettison me."

"That the reason you're still a D.I.?"

"The commissioner and I had a little go-round back in 1991. I forgot about it after it happened, he apparently didn't. I guess I should consider myself lucky that I still have my oak leaves," he said, referring to the rank insignia on his shoulders.

"So what is it that you would like, Liam?"

"You don't owe me anything, sir, but if you could put me someplace where I'm not spending half my day traveling, I would really appreciate it."

"You're right, Liam, I don't owe you anything, but I think the job does. So, if it's alright with you, I'd like for you to stay."

Martin stared across the desk at him, unsure as to what to say. When news had first reached them about who the new 1st dep was going to be, they had put out *feelers* to see what they would be dealing with. Every one of them had come back the same; Maguire was a cop's cop. In fact, no one had anything even remotely bad to say about him. He was a smart, streetwise, cop who knew his job and was good at it. He may not have had the supervisory experience, but he certainly had the street experience.

In the end Martin had held out that what they were saying was true and that Maguire would at least be fair. He hadn't expected to retain his spot.

"I don't know what to say, sir?" he said.

"Hopefully you'll say yes," Maguire said with a laugh. "I'd like to say that I was just being magnanimous, Liam, but I'd be lying if I did. I need someone who knows what he's doing and how this office runs."

"There are a lot of people who are qualified for this position."

"Yes there are, but you've paid your dues. A lot longer than most, I might add," Maguire said, taking a sip of coffee. "Truth is, I'm not making your life easier by asking you to stay. I fully expect that there are going to be those who will be resentful that I am occupying this seat. Being the C.O. here won't win you any friends. I need someone I can trust, someone I know will have my back. All I can promise you in return is I will have yours."

Maguire reached into his pocket and pulled out an envelope and slid it across the desk to Martin.

"What's this?" he asked, picking it up.

"Either a welcome, or going away, gift," Maguire said.

Martin thought about it for a moment.

This wasn't going exactly the way he had imagined it would. When he had left his house that morning, his wife, Siobhan, had walked him to the door and told him to put it all in God's hands. He knew she had been praying for the best, but despite all the assurances he had gotten, that Maguire was on the up and up, he couldn't imagine a scenario where he would remain as the commanding officer. That was until now.

"I'd be honored to stay, sir," Martin said.

Maguire stood up and extended his hand across the desk. "Thank you, Liam."

Martin stood up and shook his hand.

"So what's in the envelope?" he asked.

Maguire smiled, "Something long overdue."

Martin opened the envelope and removed the folded paper inside. It was a copy of a hand written note that read:

By order of the Police Commissioner

Effective 1000 hours, January 25th, 2013

Deputy Inspector Liam F. Martin is hereby promoted to Inspector.

Martin reread the last line twice before he looked up at Maguire.

"Sir?" he said. "What do I say?"

"Don't say anything, Liam," Maguire said. "The police commissioner and I both recognize that you have gotten the short end of the stick for the last few years. This is just correcting that wrong. It was never contingent on a yes or no, that's why I gave you the letter before you answered."

"Thank you for the vote of confidence."

"You're welcome, Liam. I'm going to finish this cup of coffee so if you could round up the troops in the conference room I'll speak to them next."

"Yes, sir," Martin said and headed out the door.

Siobhan is not going to believe this, he thought.

CHAPTER FOURTEEN

Northern Maine
Wednesday, January 2nd, 2013 – 8:43 a.m.

Keith Banning woke up, allowing his eyes to adjust to the relative darkness of the room. On the far side, a nightlight provided just enough for him to see faint details. Next to him, Tricia Browning remained sleeping beneath the heavy comforter.

He sat up on the edge of the bed and stretched. Banning reached down, grabbed his pants off the floor and put them on. He stood up and made his way around to her side of the bed, where a pile of discarded clothes lay on the floor. He bent down and grabbed her panties. Banning put them in one pocket and removed a set of keys from the other. He selected one and undid the lock on the leg shackle that kept her secured to the bed. When he was finished he made his way through the steel door, locking it behind him. He needed some time alone this morning and would come back to let her out later.

Banning made his way through the maze of converted shipping containers, buried underground, and up through the discreet staircase that led into the actual cabin. Once in the kitchen he turned on the coffee maker before grabbing the pack of cigarettes from the table and lighting one.

He walked over to one of the kitchen cabinets and opened it. He rustled through the boxes till he found what he was looking for and removed one of the resealable plastic sandwich bags. He placed the panties inside and sealed it up, laying the bag on the kitchen table.

Banning walked back over to the coffee maker and poured a cup. He sat down at the table, enjoying the cigarette and trying to wake up. As he stared out the window his mind was drawn back the activities of the previous night.

He found it amazing that, after all this time, he still felt *dirty* after having sex with her. He couldn't quite figure out why this one act haunted him despite all the other truly horrific things he had committed. It was easier in the beginning when she would fight back and scream; he would let himself get caught up in the act of taking her. It was angry, primal and he found great pleasure in physically violating her. Now it seemed as if she was almost enjoying it.

He struggled with that part a bit.

Banning closed his eyes and took a drag on the cigarette, breathing in deeply, before exhaling the smoke.

He often found himself wondering about what had changed. This had never been part of his plan. Tricia was only supposed to live long enough for him to draw Maguire into his trap, a useful pawn in a much greater game. But somewhere along the way he had allowed himself to get attached to her.

No, that wasn't it, he thought.

He grudgingly admitted that he had always been physically attracted to her, in the way the *class nobody* lusts after the *prima donna* cheerleader. In this case, that analogy happened to be quite accurate. It wasn't that she had been mean to him when they were in high school; it was that she never acknowledged that he even existed.

That had certainly changed.

He had fought hard not to give in at the beginning, but in the end, he simply couldn't control it. The first time had been so easy, she was sedated and in no shape to put up a fight. In fact, it was only supposed to be the one time, but once he had done it, he was hooked. That was when he had to alter the rest of his plans and that had not exactly made him very happy. It was as if she had become a drug to him and each time only left him wanting more.

It was after that when the anger had crept in. He resented the fact that he had been forced into altering everything he had strategically thought out. As a result, he took it out on her. He thought back to the day he had killed her husband. Of course he had first made him watch as he had his way with Tricia in front of him.

Now he did not know what the future held.

In a way, he was using the whole conflict with Maguire as an excuse to keep her around, but deep down inside he wanted her with him. Sure, for the first few months she had been difficult, but lately she had done a 180 degree turn. She had become passive, almost deferential toward him. At first he was taken aback by the sudden change and more than a bit skeptical to be honest. But she was consistent and he found himself allowing his own guard to come down a bit. That didn't mean that he let her wander freely, but he found himself spending more time talking to her.

It was ironic, he thought. *In the beginning, she was nothing more than an expendable piece that he had used to lure Maguire out into the open. Now, it appeared that she would be around long after he was gone.*

Banning took another drag on the cigarette before crushing it in the ashtray.

He got up and walked over to the small desk in the living room. He reached into one of the drawers, removing a pen and pad, before going back to the kitchen table. He sat back down in the chair, taking a sip of coffee and lighting another cigarette. He then began writing:

Jimmy, it was good seeing you up at the cabin last October. It has been awhile, so I just wanted to let you know that we have some unfinished business we still need to settle. In case you forgot, I'm sending along a trinket to remind you that you still have something to lose. I'll be in touch. Keith

He folded the paper over and placed it, along with the plastic baggie containing the panties, into a manila envelope and addressed it to Maguire, using the address for Melody Anderson's house.

He'd have to make a trip into New Hampshire to mail it off. There was a small town near the Canadian border. He was sure that it would cause them fits as they tried to determine whether he was crossing back and forth.

He chuckled at that thought and got up to get another cup of coffee.

CHAPTER FIFTEEN

Brooklyn, New York City
Thursday, January 3rd, 2013 – 2:21 p.m.

Hamadi walked up the stairs and paused in front of the apartment door, knocking in the prearranged manner. He had called Qaseem on the prepaid cell phone when he had left New Jersey to alert him that he was on his way. In this line of work, no one liked unexpected knocks on the door.

From what he could tell, the two older men were devout Muslims like himself, but the three younger ones troubled him greatly. The first time he had come to the apartment they were drinking and playing video games. The second meeting he had been forced to wait until the girls they were entertaining left the apartment. He was glad that this was the last time he had to meet with this particular group.

A moment later, he saw a shadow cross the peephole in the metal door before he heard the audible click of the lock. When the door opened, Ramzi Sharif stood in front of him.

"Peace be upon you," said Hamadi, in the traditional Muslim greeting. He placed his left hand over his heart and extended his right hand to the man.

"Qaseem," Sharif called out, ignoring the man as he entered the apartment.

Sharif turned his back on the man and locked the door. He then made his way back over to the couch and sat down, picking up the controller for the video game he was playing.

Hamadi was seething inside.

To show such disrespect to a guest was unconscionable. He struggled to hold his anger in check. It was not his place to judge and soon enough, he hoped, the man would have to explain his actions to a much higher authority.

He heard a door open and Qaseem stepped out into the hallway pulling a sweatshirt over his head. He saw Hamadi and motioned the man to follow him into the kitchen.

As the two men entered the kitchen, Qaseem pointed to one of the chairs. Hamadi didn't even bother with the greeting. He just wanted to get this done.

"Coffee?" Qaseem asked, holding up the pot.

"Please, thank you."

Qaseem poured two cups and set them down on the table. He then took the seat opposite from the man.

Hamadi held the cup in his hands and took a sip of the hot coffee. He felt the hot liquid chasing away the chill that seemed to perpetually grip him at this time of year.

"Thank you," the man said, placing the cup back on the table.

"You're welcome," replied Qaseem. "How are you doing?"

"I am fine, Allah be praised," replied Hamadi.

"Were you able to get everything?" asked Qaseem as took a sip of coffee.

The man reached into his inner jacket pocket and removed a large manila envelope and laid it on the table.

"Five different late model vehicles," Hamadi replied. "The tags on the key rings tell where each of the cars is parked."

Qaseem opened the envelope and dumped the keys onto the table. He sorted through them, noting the different makes.

"Any problems?"

"No, they all came from different used car dealerships in New Jersey," explained Hamadi.

"Then we are ready to move ahead."

Hamadi nodded sincerely and took another sip from the coffee cup.

"Each of the cars has a clean registration and is ready to go. They have a full tank of gas and the paperwork for each car is in the glove compartment, along with a set of keys and an address of an apartment. The rent has been prepaid for a year."

"What about the facility?"

Hamadi reached into his pocket and removed a piece of paper, sliding it across the table.

"Here's the address for the warehouse. Everything is waiting for you there."

"That is great news."

Hamadi's part was now done. He took another drink from the cup and stood up from the table.

"I wish you all well on your journey."

"Thank you, you have served Allah well."

Qaseem walked the man to the door and opened it. Hamadi turned around and shook hands with the man.

"*Ma'a Assalama*, Qaseem. Goodbye"

"Goodbye," replied Qaseem.

Hamadi stepped out into the hallway as the door closed behind him. He zipped up his jacket and pulled the collar up before heading toward the staircase. Behind him he heard the sound of the door being locked.

He was happy that his part in all this was completed. Supporting *jihad* had become a very lucrative business for him, but Hamadi didn't like coming to this part of the city. He had come a long way from his family home in Basrah, Iraq. Truth be told, he had grown accustomed to living in the west and with all the luxuries that came with it. Besides, it wasn't like any of these insignificant acts of *jihad* were actually going to bring about the end of western civilization anyway.

As he opened the front door he felt the sharp blast of cold air physically assault his face. He stepped into the frigid air and made his way quickly toward the car. There were some things he would never grow accustomed to.

Inside the apartment, Qaseem turned toward Sharif who was playing his video game.

"Gather everyone up," he said before heading back to the bedroom.

A short time later he exited the room with a petit brunette in tow. Qaseem attended New York University, in lower Manhattan, on a student visa. It still amazed him at just how easy it was to find any number of young radical women who were willing to go to bed with him simply because they viewed it as being the politically correct thing to do.

As they walked through the living room she glanced around at the four men sitting there.

Qaseem opened the door for her.

"Call me?" she asked, stepping out into the hallway.

"Yeah, as soon as I have time," he replied and closed the door on her.

He turned around and sat down in one of the chairs.

"We've got the cars," he said, opening the manila envelope. He reached in and pulled them out, handing each man a set. It was a diverse assortment of vehicles, but each had been selected because of their ability to blend in on the city streets.

"No way," said Nazir. "There is no way I'm driving around in this fucking piece of shit."

"Shut the fuck up," Qaseem yelled. "Is this a fucking joke to you?"

Nazir stared at Qaseem, his jaw clenching in anger. Qaseem held the other man's gaze until he turned away.

"No, it's not a joke," he said, leaning back in the couch and sulking.

"Tomorrow we begin," Qaseem continued. "After that there is no turning back. Once you get your car you will find an address for where you will be staying. You will not return to this apartment, nor will we have any contact with each other beyond this point. Understood?"

Each of the men nodded.

"Yusef, how long will it take?"

"Providing that all the materials are there, I would say no more than a day or two per vehicle."

"Ok, then in the morning you will leave and prepare for the first car. Call me when you are ready and I will send the first one over."

"As you wish," Yusef replied.

Qaseem looked around at the men assembled before him. Each of them, including himself, had a reason for being here. They had been chosen for this mission to once again strike fear into the heart of the great Satan. Too many years had passed without the blood of the infidels being spilled on their own land.

That would all change now, he thought. *Allahu Akbar*.

CHAPTER SIXTEEN

1 Police Plaza, Manhattan, N.Y.
Monday, January 7th, 2013 – 6:45 a.m.

Maguire looked up from the report he was reading and glanced over at the ringing phone on his desk. He saw the name on the display screen and picked it up.

"Good morning, Rich, what the hell are you doing in so early?"

"I could ask the same thing."

"I'm still trying to wade through personnel folders and figure everything out," Maguire replied. "At least this way I get some alone time before the office fills up and the phone starts ringing."

"I saw your car in the garage and thought I'd see if you had a few free minutes to go over a few things before we go to that command staff meeting we have this morning."

"Yeah, you got coffee on or do I need to bring my own?"

"Nope, I've got a fresh pot."

"Be there in a couple of minutes," he said, hanging the phone back on its cradle.

He closed the folder and placed it back on the pile waiting to be read. Maguire turned around in his chair and opened the file drawer in the credenza, behind his desk, and removed a folder before making his way out of the office.

"You need me, boss?" asked Torres, who sat at the desk just outside Maguire's office.

"No, Mike, I'm good. If you need me, I'll be in the commissioner's office for a few."

Maguire made his way down the hall. Over the course of the last few days things had settled down and the office personnel no longer jumped to attention when they entered the offices.

"Morning, sir," said the officer sitting at the front desk.

"Good morning," Maguire said as he went inside.

The interior office was just starting to come to life with the day shift personnel. James made his way to Rich's office, knocking on the closed door before opening it and looking inside.

Rich was on the phone and silently waved him in.

Maguire walked over to the serving table against the wall and poured himself a cup of coffee before taking one of the seats in front of the desk.

"Ok, I'll take care of it," Rich said, hanging up the phone.

"Problem?"

"Mayor's film office," Rich replied. "A film crew is getting grief from some of the locals over parking and street closures by Pier 17."

"Glad you took the job yet?" Maguire asked with a laugh.

"You didn't warn me about this kind of stuff."

"Fair enough, I'll take care of the film crew business. What else did you want to talk about?"

"The chief of transportation is refusing to step down."

The two men had spent countless hours going over the changes made right before they had come in. Mostly it was cheap politicking on the part of the prior administration and everyone knew it.

For their part, the two men agreed that it would be best to let the dust settle for a few months, before slowly beginning to reshuffle the deck. At least, as it pertained to the transfers between the ranks of captain through assistant chief.

Unfortunately, they didn't have the same luxury with the "super" chiefs, the three star ranks who were tasked with the day to day operations of the department's ten bureaus. These chiefs exercised too much control to have their loyalties be in doubt. On top of that they had to make sure that the chief of department, the four star chief who was the highest ranking uniformed member of the Department, shared their same vision.

Each of them had been interviewed extensively, starting with Chief of Department Anthony Ameche.

Ameche had joined the Department in 1980 and had worked his way up from the mean streets of Brooklyn North to the 14th floor of 1 Police Plaza. He may have worn four stars on his shoulders, but in his heart he was still a cop. The medals above his shield, which included the Combat Cross and Medal of Valor, served as proof that he was not afraid to throw himself into the fray. Tony Ameche was well liked but, more importantly, he was also well respected. In the end Rich had requested Ameche to stay on as chief of department and he had accepted. It was an important message to send to the troops that the new administration respected those who had served with distinction.

It would have been nice if the other interviews had gone off equally as well.

Of the ten chiefs who ran the various bureaus, only those from the Personnel, Patrol, Detective, Organized Crime and Transit Bureaus were being asked to remain. Of the other five, Rich and Maguire had indicated to them that their philosophical differences, in how the Department should go forward, were not consistent with this administration's position.

As a result, the chief of the Internal Affairs Bureau, who would hit the mandatory age limit in March, indicated that he would be taking his terminal leave effective immediately. Likewise, the chiefs of the Housing, Intelligence, Counter Terrorism and Community Affairs Bureau's also stated they would be leaving, most to take jobs in the corporate sector.

Chief of Transportation Jonathan Rogers apparently had other ideas however.

Rogers was the antithesis of Tony Ameche. At forty he was the youngest of his peers and he had what could best be described as nothing more than a *vanilla* career. It was well known that his meteoric rise was advanced solely on the coattails of others, most notably the former police commissioner who had elevated him to his position just several months earlier. It had earned him the nickname of "Chief Remora" a derogatory reference to the fish that attaches itself to sharks and goes along for a free ride.

During the interview with Rogers, he appeared almost bored and dismissive as they went over his career. At one time he even referred to Maguire as detective as he responded to a question. At the end Rich had informed him that it would be best if he retired to which Rogers had advised him that he would take it under advisement and get back to him.

Rogers had apparently come to his decision.

"You are kidding me, aren't you?"

"I wish I was," Rich replied, taking a sip from the cup of coffee that had gone cold sitting on his desk. "He informed me that he had thought *long and hard* about my recommendation and does not feel that he can acquiesce to my wishes. He went on to say that he has served admirably in his current position and that he enjoys the respect and support of his subordinates, to whom he believes he would be doing a great disservice to if he stepped down."

"What a pompous jackass," Maguire said.

"The question is what to do about it now."

"Demote him."

"That was fast."

"You don't have a choice, Rich," Maguire replied. "He fired a warning shot over your bow. The only choice you have is whether you get pulled into a pissing match with him or you go and blow the bastard out of the water."

"What about pushback?"

"Jonathan Rogers is not doing this on his own volition. This guy hasn't made a decision on his own since he first came on the job and I doubt he is going to start now. No, someone else is behind this and they are waiting to see if you blink."

"What do you recommend?"

"Right before the meeting call him in and demote him back to captain. Ship him off as the executive officer of Transit District 11. Trust me; he'll be gone by the end of the day. Then you go ahead and merge the Transit and the Transportation Bureau's into one. We'll do a press release and say it is part of your program to increase the overall efficiency of the Department."

"You think that will be the end of it?"

"It'll send a clear message that you are not going to tolerate bullshit games."

"Well, I made it six days before I upset the apple cart," Rich said with a laugh.

"That actually might be a record here," replied Maguire. "The bottom line, Rich, is that you have a helluva job in front of you, to rein things in. If you haven't noticed, we are a little top heavy in terms of people walking around with stars on their shoulders. We've got more chiefs and deputy commissioners than we have actual positions. Hell, they even have chiefs for assistants. No ship is going to sail straight and true with more admirals onboard than it has sailors. It's time to start promoting hard work and not peacocks."

"You're preaching to the choir, buddy. I'm still stymied about all this. I have more people to ask, and yet I still get fewer answers than you would expect."

"Time to start thinning the herd," replied Maguire. "While we have a moment I want to go over a few things with you, keeping in line with the 'reward the workers' theme."

"What's on your mind?"

"Have you had the chance to look at Nikki Ryan's file? She's a deputy inspector in Staten Island."

"To be honest," Rich replied, "no, not as of yet. I made it through Manhattan, the Bronx and Brooklyn over the weekend. I was planning on taking Queens and Staten Island home with me tonight. Am I missing anything important?"

"Yeah, I think so. Plus I got a phone call, which is what bumped it up on my list."

"What's her story?"

"Basically she was a newly minted D.I. working here in headquarters on September 11th when the attack happened. This place was a zoo. There was even a story going around about an inspector who was threatening the responding cops with disciplinary action for staging on the wrong side of the street."

"Get the hell out of here," Rich replied with a laugh.

"No, believe it. I heard that story from several different people who were there. The worst part was they went and promoted the guy to chief later on. Anyway, Ryan got assigned to a security checkpoint here at the building with a bunch of cops. After they had helped evacuate the civilians from the area they stood around with their thumbs up their asses without any direction."

"So what happened?" Rich asked.

"With nothing going on Ryan tried to get them cut loose to go work on the rescue efforts on the pile. After she had made several requests, I guess she got told to stop asking and was blacklisted by the powers that be. Next thing you know, she's in purgatory, transferred to Staten Island, working in the borough office. Problem is they forgot her there. She was doing the right thing, not hiding like a lot of others did that day. I think it is time to rectify the wrong."

"What do you suggest?"

"I'd like to promote her to Inspector and bring her back in. She did time in the Intelligence Division back in the day. I got some really good feedback on her. With our upcoming promotions and transfers I think we could put her in Counter Terrorism where she would be an asset. It also wouldn't be bad to have one of our own in there, especially since we are shaking things up a bit."

"Ok, let's make it happen."

Maguire opened up the folder, pulled out a piece of paper and slid it across the desk. "Here are all the names I have."

Stargold look over the list. "Ok, I'll pass this on to Ray Hernandez and have him draw up the orders."

Maguire got up and began heading for the door.

"Hey," Rich called out. "Don't forget that film crew problem."

"I'll take care of it personally."

"Thanks," replied Rich. "By the way, where are we having the chief's meeting?"

"Conference room in my office at nine," replied Maguire as he stood in the doorway. "Then we have the command staff meeting at ten in the auditorium."

"Okay, I'll see you at nine."

CHAPTER SEVENTEEN

Brooklyn, New York City
Wednesday, January 9th, 2013 – 8:43 a.m.

Qaseem handed the prepaid cell phone to Yusef Sayeed.

"After you get to the warehouse, call me and let me know that everything is ok."

"And if it isn't?" Sayeed said.

"If you see anything that doesn't look right, don't go inside."

Sayeed remained stoic.

He had been doing this nearly as long as Qaseem had been alive. If the situation was not so serious, he would have laughed in the young man's face. Sometimes he could not understand why they put idiots like this in charge, but considering the behavior of the others, he assumed that Qaseem was most likely the best suited.

For most of his career he had remained insulated from the operations side. His skills were deemed far too valuable to the cause to be needlessly risked. So he had never remained in one place any longer than it had taken him to construct the device and then move on. His sudden appearance before an event, coupled with his immediate disappearance, had earned him the nickname *Malak al-Mawt*, the Angel of Death.

He had secured his place on the most wanted list of numerous countries, including the United States, through his infamous explosive designs. As a result he had become increasingly aware of his personal security. He had been known to leave a location at a moment's notice simply because he had gotten a *feeling*. A practice which had served him well considering that he had missed a drone strike by a mere ten minutes. It irked him that Qaseem would even dare to instruct him on such matters.

Sayeed did not respect Qaseem, or the other two young men in the group. He did not know why they were here, nor did he particularly care for that matter. Like his friend Bashir, he had a personal reason. In 2003, his brother, Abdullah, had not been as lucky as he was and had been killed in North Waziristan by an unmanned, CIA operated, RQ-1 Predator drone aircraft. He had wanted to avenge his brother in a personal attack against the Great Satan, but was rejected every time by those in charge. His bomb making capabilities had been far too valuable to risk in a one-time attack.

Over time Sayeed had grown to accept his fate, even if he vehemently disagreed with it. All that changed a little over a year ago when he was diagnosed with pancreatic cancer. After spending several months training his replacement, the decision was made to include him on this attack.

"If I think the site is compromised I will call you and say 'the building will not meet our needs.' If the site becomes compromised while I am there I will call and say 'everything is as it should be, send the first person in an hour.' This should give you adequate time to get away."

"And if everything is okay?"

"I will tell you to send each person to me by name."

"Ok, I will wait to hear from you," Qaseem said. "Allah willing, all will go as planned."

CHAPTER EIGHTEEN

1 Police Plaza, Manhattan, N.Y.
Tuesday, January 15th, 2013 – 11:23 a.m.

"Dennis, how are things up in God's country?" Maguire said to the man on the other end of the phone.

"It's cold, nothing has changed," Monahan replied. "I understand congratulations are in order for you."

"I'm not sure whether congratulation is the word I would choose. I've been doing this for two weeks and I'm questioning my sanity for taking the job."

"Get used to it; my experience has been that it always gets worse before it gets better."

"Great, so you're telling me this is the quiet before the storm?"

"Welcome back to the wonderful world of policing."

"That'll make a great Hallmark card."

"I'd like to tell you I'm having better luck on this end, but all I've got are brick walls on three sides."

"That's what I wanted to call you about," Maguire said. "Now that I'm carrying a badge again, how about sharing the rest of the case with me?"

He heard Monahan laugh on the other end.

"I had a feeling you knew you weren't getting all the information," Monahan replied. "For what it's worth, the decision to exclude you from some of the stuff was above my pay grade."

"Trust me when I say that I don't take any of it personal. I've been in this game way too long for that."

"Well, you already know about seventy-five percent of what we have," Monahan said. "I wish I could tell you we were holding more close to the vest but the truth is we aren't. I'll have one of my tech kids work his magic and get copies of the rest of it zip-zapped and emailed out to you forthwith."

"Do you mind if I make a few calls on this?"

"I don't care if you call *Miss Cleo*; if it means that I get that little prick's head on a pike."

"I have a couple of slightly more reputable names in my rolodex," Maguire said with a laugh. "I just didn't want to step on your toes."

"At this point I'd be ecstatic if I could get a Boy Scout troop and a blood hound allotted to me."

"How bad is it?"

"I'm down to myself and two investigators," Monahan explained. "Hell they even took my Border Patrol guy."

"I told you they would."

"Each day that goes by, Albany loses more interest. In fact, they even pulled the plug on financing the witness protection arrangement for Lena Marx."

"What reason did they give for that decision?"

"State cited fiscal problems and the county isn't in much better shape. I spoke with the District Attorney, the State Police and the Sheriff's office. They all agreed to give the location *special attention*. Best we can do under the circumstances."

"It's better than nothing, but that's not saying much."

"The powers that be seem to believe that you're the only one he is interested in. Besides, I think she was much happier to get back home and to the gallery."

"I'd imagine life in *WitPro* gets old after a while," Maguire replied. "Get me those files and I will see what I can do."

"They'll be in your inbox by the end of the day."

"Sounds good," said Maguire. "Stay safe, Dennis."

CHAPTER NINETEEN

Northern Maine
Thursday, January 17th, 2013 – 5:13 p.m.

Banning sat in the living room watching the flames dance across the logs in the fireplace. He took a drag on the cigarette before crushing it out in the ashtray. Tricia came into the room carrying a whiskey glass.

"Thank you, dear," he said.

Banning took a sip and set it on the small table next to him.

He looked over at Tricia who was now sitting in the wood rocking chair near the fireplace.

"What's troubling you, Tricia?"

"I was just wondering why no one ever came looking for me?"

Banning reached over, and grabbed the pack of cigarettes. He lit one, taking a long drag, and slowly released the smoke as he formulated a response to the question.

In the beginning, the drug he had administered to her had been quite effective. Eight months later she was still unsure about what was actually real or something she had imagined. He had used that to his advantage countless times as he reinvented the story, weaving snippets of truth into a *mélange* of disinformation, half-truths, and outright lies. Over time he had explained that, while it had been his sole intention of luring Maguire out of hiding, he had been utterly shocked at the daily abuse that she had endured under her late husband Paul Browning. In fact he was amazed at the overall lack of interest that her disappearance had generated, including from her lover, Lena Marx.

Banning went on to explain in great detail how her husband had immediately suspended the search for her. He told her that, as each day passed, Browning had simply gone about his role as

Sheriff and ignored the fact that she was missing. He said he almost seem glad to have Tricia gone. He also said that Lena had taken over running Tricia's art gallery as if it were her own.

As time went on he slowly began to soften his approach to her, saying how sorry he was. Yes, he reluctantly admitted, his behavior toward her had been rather poor, but as time went by he had begun to realize that they were, in fact, kindred spirits."

Eventually she began to buy into it.

Tricia reasoned to herself that, while they had certainly had a rocky start, Banning had gone to great lengths to care for her. All he had asked for in return was affection. Yes there were times when he had been rough with her, but he hadn't actually hurt her. He was aggressive and strong; someone who knew what he wanted and took it. Didn't people celebrate that type of assertive man?

In fact he was the opposite of what she had grown accustomed to in her life. Everyone, it seemed, always wanted more from her than they were willing to give. Paul had been obnoxious and crude. He certainly was not what she would have considered a man's man by any stretch of the imagination. Just a malevolent little boy trapped in that poor excuse for a man's body.

And what about Lena?

Lena was a different story entirely. Of all people, she felt that Lena had betrayed her. She had given up everything for her, including Maguire. Would she even be in this place if it weren't for that fateful decision so many years ago?

Had it all been part of some master plan that Lena had? she wondered.

The more she thought about it, the more she came to realize that Lena had come into her life and systematically destroyed everything. She had destroyed her relationship with Maguire, had stolen her future, and even now, while she was still "lost", Lena sat in her seat, in her art gallery, and enjoyed it all.

Who knows? she thought. *Maybe she has even replaced me already.*

It all came down to her.

Maybe this was just a rude, but long overdue, wakeup call for her.

Over a hundred years earlier Sigmund Freud had explained this behavior by suggesting that bonding was the individual's response to the trauma of becoming a victim. By identifying with one's captor the ego is able to defend itself. When a victim believes the same values as the aggressor, they cease to be a threat.

"I've often wondered that myself, Tricia," Banning replied. "I admit that I knew your relationship with Paul was a ruse, but I expected him to put in at least some effort in locating you. But then I came to the harsh reality that everyone had abandoned you."

"Yes, they certainly did," she replied. "But you never did, Keith."

"I felt a responsibility to take care of you."

"I don't think I ever thanked you for that."

"Well, there is no need for you to thank me. I regret my earlier behavior toward you. It wasn't personal, but rather a manifestation of my anger toward those who had turned their backs on you. It took me a while to realize that you were as much a victim as I was."

Tricia turned and faced Banning.

"Was I ever mean to you in school?"

"No," Banning replied. "But to be honest, I don't even know if you knew I existed back then."

"That must have been hurtful to you."

"You were the cheerleader, I was the nerd."

"I'm sorry," she said. "I will make that up to you, I promise."

What had just happened? Banning wondered.

"We're both victims, aren't we, Keith?"

Inwardly, Banning smiled.

"Yes, Tricia, regrettably we are."

"Keith, I need your help."

"With what, my dear?"

"Revenge."

CHAPTER TWENTY

Georgetown, Washington, D.C.
Saturday, January 19th, 2013 – 2:09 p.m.

Thomas Moore looked away from the book he was reading and glanced down at the cell phone vibrating on the end table next to the recliner. He laid the book in his lap and answered the call.

"Shit must be real serious if you're calling me at home on the weekend."

"*Hakuna Matata,* Motherfucker," Maguire said in response.

"Easy for you to say, Paddy. I don't call you all the time with busy work."

"Please, spare me the violin solo, Saint. You're employed by NCIS, what do you know about hard work?" Maguire said with a laugh.

"Yeah, yeah, whatever," the man said.

"Sheesh, I should have let the *hajjis* haul your ass away when I had the chance."

"They'd have just returned me for a refund when they realized what a pain in the ass I could be."

"Isn't that the truth?"

Thomas "Saint" Moore had known Maguire since they had been teammates in Seal Team Four. They were part of a small fraternity of sailors who had completed, what is arguably, the toughest military training in the world. More importantly, Moore owed his life to the man on the other end of the phone in a mission that remained classified to this day as *Top Secret.*

"So how are you going to ruin my weekend *this* time?"

"I've got a ghost problem," Maguire said.

James spent the next half hour recapping what had occurred with Banning and what had been developed in the ensuing investigation. When he was done, Moore let out a long, slow, whistle.

"Damn, Paddy, you love pissing in people's Cheerios don't you?"

"It's just another one of the many services I still provide."

"So what has this got to do with me? I heard they pinned a badge to your chest again; can't your people look into it?"

"I don't know, Saint; I just got a weird feeling about this one."

Moore sat up in the recliner. For all the shit they gave each other, when another SEAL told you something didn't feel right to them you paid attention. When it came to hunches, lives often hung in the balance.

"How so?"

"Something's just not right with this guy, beyond the obvious," Maguire replied. "Everyone keeps assuming he's just nuttier than squirrel shit, but I'm just having a really hard time buying into that theory."

Based on what Maguire had already told him, Moore didn't buy into it either. There were just too many things in play. Crazed psychopaths were usually not well versed in tactical ambushes, improvised explosives, and identity theft. Not that they couldn't be. It was just that they tended to be more focused on being, well, crazed psychopaths. This guy appeared to know exactly what he was doing.

"What did the Bureau guys say?" Moore asked, referring to the FBI agents originally assigned to the task force.

"They lasted till the Fourth of July and then cited homeland security issues before pulling their people. From what I can see they didn't really bring much to the investigation."

"Gotcha," Moore replied. "Can you shoot me out an email with this guy's pedigree information and a list of those other names you've uncovered? I'll shake some trees and get back to you."

"Thanks, Saint, I really appreciate this."

"Fuck that appreciation shit, you're buying all the drinks at this year's muster."

"*Hooyah,* brother. I'll catch ya later."

CHAPTER TWENTY-ONE

Brooklyn, New York City
Tuesday, January 29th, 2013 – 12:21 a.m.

Police Officer William Maldonado of the Seven-Seven Anti-Crime Unit sat behind the wheel of the unmarked Chevy Caprice, as he drove east along Atlantic Avenue. Next to him, his partner Police Officer Thomas Dixon, was explaining, in graphic detail, his latest conquest at the wedding he'd attended over the past weekend.

"I'm telling you, Billy, you had to see her," Dixon said. "Damn she was fine."

"You say the same thing about every woman you meet, Tommy."

"No, this one's different."

"Uh huh," replied Maldonado. "I vaguely recall you saying the same thing about that stripper you met at Gonzo's party in August."

"She was a performance dancer," Dixon said in protest.

"Seriously? A performance dancer? That's the best you can come up with?"

"Hey," Dixon interrupted, pointing toward the car in front of them. "Check it out."

The two men watched as the late model Jeep Grand Cherokee, stopped in front of them at the red light, and then turned right onto Albany Street. In the overwhelming majority of major cities a red turn on right, after coming to a stop, was permissible. That was however not the case in New York City and provided for an easy moving violation summons.

"Yo, it's the end of the month, *Ese*," said Maldonado. "I'm low on movers."

"You're always low on movers, Billy."

"Hey, I just can't see the purpose of screwing people over when they are going to work or coming home," Maldonado replied. "If I wanted to be a ticket writer I'd have gone into the Summons Unit instead of Anti-Crime. Besides, it's not like the City is sharing any of the money we give them. Hell, they won't even give us a decent contract."

"Isn't that the truth," said Dixon. "I got a neighbor that's a Nassau County cop. Every time I turn around he's either adding onto his house or driving a new car. I think he makes more than the president."

"I don't think it's that much," Maldonado replied. "But I know they are making well over six figures."

"Shit, over a hundred grand to ride around in suburbia while I'm busting my ass in this goddamn war zone praying for some overtime so I can pay for my kid's friggin' braces."

"Like I always say, there's no *justice*, there's *just us.*"

They continued to follow the car, watching as it made a left onto Park Street and proceeded past the NYC Housing Authority, Albany projects.

"Get ready to bail," Dixon said, anticipating that the driver was going to pull into the projects and jump out.

As they watched, the car continued driving east bound.

Dixon picked up the portable radio.

"Seven Crime to Central."

"Seven Crime, go ahead," came the dispatcher's reply over the radio.

"Can I have a 10-15 on an occupied mover," Dixon said. "New Jersey passenger, William – Thomas – Henry – five – zero – one. Eastbound on Park from Troy."

"Standby, Seven Crime."

They continued to follow the vehicle as it made its way through the deserted streets of Brooklyn North.

"I'm not feeling any overtime love on this one, Tommy." Maldonado said. "Just going to be some idiot from Jersey who got lost."

"Well, at least you get your mover out of it. Then again, the way your luck has been running it'll be a nun who took a wrong turn looking for St. Pat's."

The radio broke up their banter.

"Seven Crime, your plate, WTH-501, New Jersey, comes back 10-17, no hit. Registered to a Paradigm Leasing in Passaic."

"Seven Crime, 10-4. Show us out on a car stop, Park and Utica."

As they pulled through the intersection, Dixon reached over and flipped the switch that activated the discrete emergency light bar above the rear view mirror. Ahead they watched the brake lights on the Jeep light up as the car pulled over to the side.

Maldonado pulled the Chevy Caprice up behind the Jeep and put it in park. Both men got out of the car, reaching into their jackets and removed their badges which were affixed to chains that hung around their necks.

Dixon reached inside his coat, withdrawing his Smith and Wesson 9mm, and held it down along the side of his leg. "Hey, look at the bright side. At least we didn't have to chase him through the projects."

Inside the Jeep, Ramzi Sharif sat physically shaking; his mind was racing wildly.

What had he done wrong, he wondered?

He hadn't been speeding and he knew there was nothing wrong with the car. In fact, he had checked the entire car, including all the lights, and then Qaseem had double checked.

He watched as the one cop approached the driver's side door. To his right he saw the flickering beam of a flashlight bouncing around the interior. There was no way they could have known, but that didn't mean they would not find out.

Sharif felt a wave of nausea wash over him. The reality of the moment was finally settling in. Up until this point it had all been a case of bullshit bravado. Talking about how badass they were, and how they were going to strike a blow at the enemy, was an easy thing to do sitting in front of a television set while drinking beer and playing video games. Now, that the moment had arrived, albeit prematurely, Sharif was faced with the fact that death no longer seemed very appealing to him. He was distinctly aware of the pounding of his heart in his chest and the extraordinarily loud roar of the rushing blood in his ears.

Sharif closed his eyes tightly and began praying. He heard the muffled knock on the driver's window and became acutely aware that he had pissed his pants. He opened his eyes and looked down at the simple little silver toggle switch that protruded from the dashboard.

When he had picked up the car at the warehouse Sayeed had walked him through everything. The vehicle itself was loaded with a variety of items, designed to increase its lethality. In the trunk area sat a box that held the primary explosive charge, which in this case was a military grade C-4 that came courtesy of a member of the U.S. Army who was also a Muslim brother. In addition to the explosive charge, there were four fully charged propane tanks coupled with nearly three hundred pounds of assorted screws and nails. The explosives were wired to a circuit board that was connected to a cell phone. When the time came, the operator of the vehicle would simply use the number set to speed dial in his prepaid cell phone to activate it. In addition, Sayeed had installed a toggle switch as a failsafe. Should anything go wrong, the device could be detonated by flipping this switch.

On the floor of the passenger side was a backpack which contained an explosive charge along with about twenty pounds of nails. The plan was that, on the dates each man had selected, they would park their respective vehicles at the chosen location and walk away. When they were sure that they were out of range they would detonate the bombs by remote. Each location was selected from a variety of different criteria, but most included symbolism and the potential for a high causality count.

After the car bomb was detonated they would head back to the area, getting as close as they could, and then detonate the backpack in an effort to take out as many first responders as possible.

After Sayeed had finished his part, Qaseem took over. Each of them was brought into a small office in the warehouse and given an envelope. Inside was a set of keys for the vehicle, a prepaid cell phone, a debit card, five hundred dollars in cash and an address.

"From this point, you are on your own," Qaseem explained. "You will not make any contact with anyone else from the apartment."

"What if there is a problem?"

"At the apartment you will find a phone book. On the inside cover will be a number written in pen. Call this number. When the person answers tell them you have a problem with your computer and that *Abdullah* recommended them. The person will say they are busy and ask for your number. Give them the prepaid number but reverse the last two numbers. On your phone it is 35, so tell them 53. The person who gets this message will know the correct procedure to contact you back."

Sharif nodded, "Ok."

"One other thing," Qaseem said. "Each of the apartments has been chosen for a reason. Each has an off street parking spot and is in close proximity to shops. There is no reason to drive anywhere. Park the car in the driveway and stay at the apartment until the chosen day. There is no reason to risk anything this far along."

"I understand," replied Sharif.

"Qaseem!" Sayeed called out from the warehouse.

"I'll be right back," said the man as he got up and headed back out to where Sayeed was working on the next car.

When he was out of range, Sharif began going through the other envelope until he found the car that had been assigned to Nazir. The two men had grown close during the past few months. He hated the thought of not having anyone around that he could talk to and, more importantly, play video games with. He powered up the prepaid cell phone and copied down the number before shutting it off. He wrote down the address where Nazir was staying and then returned it all to the envelope.

A few minutes later Qaseem returned.

"Ok, any other questions?"

"No," Sharif replied. "I think everything has been covered."

The two men stood up and hugged each other.

"*Ma'a Assalama*, Sharif. Goodbye"

"Goodbye," replied Sharif before turning and heading out the door of the office.

He made his way to the Jeep and got in. Sayeed was already working on the next car and he didn't want to disturb him. Sayeed had always made him nervous anyway, he was too religious for his liking, took things way too seriously. Besides, he always hung around with the other weird one, Bashir Al Karim, and there was really something seriously wrong with that guy.

Sharif pulled the car out of the warehouse which was located in the Maspeth section of Queens. From there he began making his way south, through the twisting back roads, toward the East New York section of Brooklyn where his apartment was located. On the way he drove through the Bushwick section where Nazir's place was located. He'd call him in a few days. The two men had talked about the dates they had chosen and he knew that they had time on their side.

He was brought back out of his memories by another knock on the window.

"Roll down the window," the cop was now shouting angrily.

"Fuck, there's some weird shit in the back here Billy," Dixon shouted.

Maldonado, sensing something was not right, drew his gun and smashed the driver's side window.

Sharif leaned over the center console as the spray of fractured glass cascaded down on top of him. Maldonado reached in and grabbed the man, trying to pull him upright fearing that the man was reaching over for a weapon. It was a misdirected fear. The fact was the whole car was a weapon.

As he was jerked backward, Sharif instinctively knew that the end had come prematurely for him. He could not be taken alive. He had heard the stories of the enhanced interrogations and he knew that he was not strong enough. He would break and all of this would be for nothing. It was not that he wanted to die, but the thought of spending the rest of his life in Guantanamo Bay seemed a fate worse than death. A coward, unwilling to die for Allah, would not fare well among the others.

He struggled violently as he reached out with his right hand to flick the toggle. From his right, the passenger window also erupted in a shower of shattered glass as the other cop smashed it with the large metal flashlight he was holding. He jerked the door open and was just about to lunge inside the passenger compartment when Sharif felt the cold metal switch against his skin and flicked it.

For a fraction of a second there was nothing and then all hell broke loose. The circuit, completed when the toggle was flipped, sent an electrical charge to the blasting cap detonators that had been pressed into the blocks of C-4.

As the primary charge exploded, gases heated up and expanded rapidly outward under intense pressure. The explosion sent out a shock wave, traveling at about 1,600 feet per second, which killed the three men instantly. This was followed, a split second later, by the explosion of the propane tanks. Shrapnel, in the form of nails, screws, and metal fragments from the tanks, and the vehicle itself, were expelled outward.

As the explosion continued to move outward, it ripped into the surrounding two story homes, reducing the closest ones to rubble. The cars that were parked along the street were lifted up and tossed backward, away from the blast, as if they were children's toys. The fireball, that followed immediately afterward, ignited everything in its path.

Three blocks away, Lieutenant John Adams sat behind the large wooden desk in the 77th Precinct making a blotter entry for a new arrest that had just been brought in. Without warning the building shook violently as if struck by an earthquake. Throughout the building, glass windows imploded and doors were blown open. This was followed a second later by a deafening roar.

The cops in the station house scrambled to their feet, guns drawn, their eyes scanning frantically for the unseen threat. Trying to come to terms with what had just occurred.

"What the fuck was that?" yelled one of the cops.

"Everybody out," shouted the lieutenant, who feared that the explosion had come from inside the building. As he headed toward the back door, he grabbed the portable radio from the desk.

As they made their way outside, they could see the orange glow of flames lighting up the night sky a few blocks south of them.

"Holy fucking shit," exclaimed one of the cops.

"Scagnelli, you and Rodriguez get down there and find out what the hell just happened," shouted the lieutenant.

Suddenly the portable radio in the lieutenant's hand came to life.

"In the confines of the Seven-Seven Precinct, receiving numerous calls for an explosion in the vicinity of Utica and Park.

Unknown injuries at this time. Seven Crime, are you on the air? Seven Crime?"

"Seven Adam responding, Central," came a reply over the radio followed a second later by another reply. "Seven Sergeant responding."

"Seven Lieutenant to Central, that's a confirmed explosion with fire, possibly residential, we can see it from here. Start FD, ESU and notify Operations."

"10-4, sir, be advised I'm also showing Seven Crime out on a car stop at that location and I'm getting no response."

"Try to raise them again, Central."

"Seven Crime, on the air? Seven Crime?" The dispatcher waited several more seconds. "No response, Seven Lieutenant."

Adams turned around to the cop standing next to him, "Ronny, get the temporary headquarters log out for me. Then get on the computer, print me out a copy of this job and the one Crime was out on."

"You got it, boss," said the cop who turned and ran back inside.

Adams stared back down Utica toward the orange glow of the fires burning brightly. In the distance he could hear the sounds of multiple sirens as units began converging on the scene.

CHAPTER TWENTY-TWO

Southampton, Suffolk County, N.Y.
Tuesday, January 29th, 2013 – 1:33 a.m.

Maguire awoke to the shrill electronic chirping of the cell phone on the nightstand. He had selected the most annoying ring tone he could, for this particular number, so it would immediately grab his attention.

It worked.

He reached over and picked up the phone.

"Maguire."

"This is Police Officer Miltenberg from Operations," the female voice on the other end replied. "Sorry to wake you, Commissioner Maguire, but we just had an explosion in the confines of Seven-Seven Precinct. The patrol supervisor is on the scene and preliminary indications are that it might be a bombing. He has requested a level one mobilization and the Duty Captain is already in route."

"Bombing?"

"Yes, sir, they think it might have been a car bomb. Seven Crime was out on a car stop at the location, they haven't been able to raise them since the explosion and there are no signs of the officers at the location," explained Officer Miltenberg. "Sir, according to the reports coming in this is a major explosion."

Melody, who had already been awakened by the call, now sat up in bed alarmed.

"Ok, has Commissioner Stargold been notified?"

"Yes, sir, he is on his way. Would you like me to contact your security detail to pick you up?"

"No, it'll take too long. Notify the Aviation Unit to send a helicopter to pick me up, they have the coordinates on file,"

Maguire said. "Notify the desk officer over at Highway Two to coordinate with Aviation for a landing at Boys and Girls High School. Have a marked unit waiting as an escort when I arrive. I'll contact my detail."

"10-4, sir, anything else I can do?"

"Yes, give me the number for the desk officer in the Seven-Seven," he said, getting up and walking over to Melody's desk.

Maguire listened as she read off the number, writing it down on the note pad.

"Ok, thank you," Maguire said and ended the call.

"What happened, James?" Melody asked.

"Looks like someone set off a bomb in Brooklyn North," he replied as he scrolled through the speed dial numbers and selected the one for Detective Mike Torres.

Melody let out an audible gasp, her eyes wide in horror.

The phone rang several times before being answered by a very groggy voice.

"Hello?"

"Mike, this is Commissioner Maguire. I need you to get ready we just had an explosion in Brooklyn, possibly a car bombing."

"Commissioner,…. Bombing? What?" came the startled reply on the other end as the man struggled to make sense of what he was being told.

"Not now, wake up and call Amanda. The two of you get over to Boys and Girls High School in Brooklyn. Coordinate with Highway Two on where to meet. Aviation is sending a bird to pick me up. I'll be there in about an hour. Dress down, it looks like it's going to be a mess."

"Roger that," said Torres. "I'll see you in an hour."

"My God, James."

"Yeah, and it also looks like we are missing some officers who were on the scene at the time of the explosion."

"What can I do?"

"I'm going to jump in the shower quick. Can you have the helipad lights turned on and get me a cup of coffee?"

"Yes, absolutely," she said.

James dialed the number he had been given for the Seven-Seven desk officer.

"Desk, Lieutenant Adams," the man said answering the phone.

"This is Deputy Commissioner Maguire," James said. "Do we have any updates on the explosion?"

"No, nothing as of yet," Adams replied. "The patrol supervisor is on the scene now, but it is still chaotic."

"Any word on our guys?"

"No, sir."

"I'm on my way in, so is Commissioner Stargold; get in touch with the patrol supervisor and have the latest information available when we get there. I also want the printout for the job Crime was on."

"Will do, anything else?"

"Defer all calls from the media to DCPI," Maguire said. "I'll see you in about an hour."

Maguire ended the call and headed off to the shower. Melody reached over, picked up the phone off her night table and called Genevieve.

"This had better be important," the sleepy voice on the other end said.

"Yeah it is, Gen. There was a bombing in Brooklyn. They're sending a helicopter to pick up James. Can you have them turn on the lights at the helipad right now? I'm running down to make coffee."

"Oh my God," exclaimed Gen. "Of course I will. I'll meet you downstairs."

CHAPTER TWENTY-THREE

Southampton, Suffolk County, N.Y.
Tuesday, January 29th, 2013 – 2:01 a.m.

Melody watched as the blue and white Agusta Westland AW119 Koala took off from the helipad and headed west toward New York City.

In the back of the helicopter, Maguire adjusted the headset.

"What do we know, guys?" he asked.

"Not much, Commissioner," came the pilot's reply over the headset. "The duty captain called a Level Four Mobilization about a half hour or so ago. The P.C. is in route."

"Highway meeting us at Boys and Girls High School?"

"Yes, sir, they already have a car 10-84, on scene."

"Any word on the number of casualties?"

"Nothing from the initial explosion site, so far. FD is on the scene trying to contain the fires, but it's pretty bad. They've removed a lot of injured to local hospitals already, mostly non-life threatening injuries."

Maguire sat back against the seat and listened to the muffled sound of the rotor blades. He stared out the window at the darkness below him. As they continued their westerly trek along the island, the landscape changed dramatically. The veil of darkness that had hung over the eastern end of Suffolk County was pulled away as they made their way through Nassau County. He could make out the street lights of towns and villages below him. By the time they reached the border of Queens the landscape was lit up like a Christmas tree. Soon they were close enough that Maguire could see the orange glow rising up in the distance.

"*Jesus H. Christ*," he muttered softly.

"It gets worse, boss," came the reply. "Looks like the initial blast ripped off the brick façades on the houses nearest to it. The fires are making quick work of the rest of them."

"Can we get in for a closer look before we land?" Maguire asked.

"Sure thing," replied the pilot. "They shut down the airspace around here. We're the only ones flying."

As they crossed over into Brooklyn, the pilot nosed the helicopter toward the site of the explosion. Slowly the pilot rose up on the collective, gaining altitude as they went. As they approached, the helicopter began making angled circles to allow Maguire to look down into the scene. It was an image that bore a closer resemblance to *Dante's Inferno* than it did of an actual city street.

"This is as close as we can safely get, sir."

The streets surrounding the site were flooded with police vehicles and fire trucks. Maguire couldn't tell if they were making any progress battling the flames. It was unlike anything he had ever seen before in a residential neighborhood. The first few houses looked like they had been completely leveled. He couldn't tell if it was from the immediate blast or the ensuing fire, but assumed it was most likely a combination of both. Houses further down the street were still standing, but appeared to be fully engulfed.

"OK, I've seen enough," Maguire said. "Thank you."

The helicopter came around and leveled off as it headed north toward the high school.

As it crossed over Atlantic Avenue it began its descent, coming to a hover just above the football field. To the west of the field, a marked Highway Patrol car and Maguire's suburban sat, their headlights lighting up the parking lot for the helicopter to land. A moment later the bird landed gently on the Astroturf field.

"I know you've been through the drill before, but wait until the co-pilot opens the door for you, and move toward the front of the aircraft, away from the tail rotor, sir."

"Got it," said Maguire. "Thanks for the ride, gentlemen. Fly safe."

A moment later Maguire was out of the helicopter and moving quickly toward the parked vehicles.

"What do we know, Mike?"

"Nothing good, sir," Torres replied, holding the door open for him. "I'll fill you in on the way."

As the two men got into the Suburban, the Highway Patrol car pulled out in front and the two car motorcade made its way toward the precinct.

Torres shifted around in his seat to face Maguire and handed him a container of coffee.

"Bless you, my son," Maguire said and took a sip.

"OK, here's what we know. I spoke to Operations, Seven Crime had a car stop on Park and Utica, moments later there were reports of a massive explosion at the location and no one has heard from them. Scene is still fully engulfed so no one has been able to get a good look around so far. You saw it from the air, it's even worse from the ground. Looks like at least a dozen homes destroyed so far, expecting casualties from those locations given the time of the blast. Right now they're using the precinct as the temporary headquarters since it's only a couple of blocks away, but Communications Division has a temporary headquarters vehicle in route."

"What about victims?" Maguire asked.

"EMS has a triage setup over on Bergen, between Troy and Schenectady. FD Rescue Two's quarters are over there so they have things squared away on that end. EMS is removing the injured over there first and deciding where to take them. They are trying not to overload any of the local hospitals, in the event they pull any critical injuries from the homes later on."

"Smart thinking."

"As far as our guys go, we have all the streets locked down surrounding the scene. From Dean Street south to St. Johns Place, and then from Troy Avenue, east over to Rochester Avenue. Commissioner Stargold was heading back to the precinct just as you landed. I also spoke to the office and Inspector Martin is on his way in," Torres looked down at his watch. "He should be there by now."

Just as he was finishing, the motorcade pulled into the parking lot of the precinct, next to where Rich's vehicle was already parked.

"Ok, you and Amanda hang out. If I need anything I'll call you," Maguire said as he got out of the suburban and headed inside the precinct.

"Attention!" shouted the young police officer sitting at the desk.

Maguire motioned for him to sit down as he walked up, "There's no need for that tonight, officer. Anyone says anything to you, tell them to see me."

"Yes, sir," replied the man.

Maguire made an entry into the command log, indicating that he was present in the precinct and turned to the cop. "Where's the desk officer?"

"Lieutenant Adams just went into the C.O.'s office with Commissioner Stargold."

"Ok, thanks," Maguire said and headed toward the office.

Inside he found Rich sitting behind the desk with the uniformed lieutenant sitting in front of him. Rich looked up as he walked in, and the lieutenant began to stand up.

"Sit down, Lou; we've got more pressing matters to deal with than to stand on formality. What do we know?"

"Nothing confirmed as of yet, but it looks like we lost two officers," Rich said. "The lieutenant was just bringing me up to speed. How does it look from the air?"

"Like a glimpse into hell," Maguire replied. "Anyone from Counter Terrorism Bureau here yet?"

"I don't know. I just got back from the scene myself."

"You speak to McMasters?"

"Spoke to him briefly on the way here. I told him I would give him an update when I knew more."

"Rich, if this wasn't planned, if this was just some sort of car stop gone bad, then we have a much bigger problem."

"Yeah, I know. Like are there any others out there that we don't know about."

It was a principle both men understood intimately from their protection days. If you have one, you look for two, if you have two, you look for three.

"Exactly," said Maguire. "I need to start making some phone calls. Lou, is there another office around here that I can use?"

"Sure, the X.O.'s office is just next door. He just retired so it's vacant."

"Ok, can you open that up for me?"

"Sure thing," he said. "Let me go and get the key."

"I'll meet you outside in a minute," Maguire said. When the man had left, Maguire closed the door. "Is Tony Ameche on his way?"

"No, I told him to head into 1PP to get Command and Control up and running. I told him to make sure all the Deputy Commissioners and Bureau Chiefs were on their way."

"Good call, at least we know things will get done properly with Tony calling the shots. Have you spoken to the Fire Commissioner yet?"

"No, I figured he had enough on his plate with his own people to deal with right now."

"Well, once things start to quiet down with the fire, the shit is really going to get stirred up," said Maguire. I'd reach out to him now and explain to him that it is imperative that we get in as fast as possible to figure out if we need to worry about more of these things going off."

"You're right; I'll do that as soon as we are done here."

"You deal with him and the mayor. I'll make sure everyone else is working together on this and get you the answers you need."

"So what do we say?"

"Just what we know. At approximately 12:30 last night, there was a report of an explosion at Utica and Park. The cause of the explosion is undetermined at this time and that we are investigating."

"Will they buy that?"

"Initially," Maguire replied. "Shit happens all the time. Residential hot water tanks are notoriously lethal. It could even be a natural gas leak. Bottom line is right now we have a hunch, but it's just that. Hell the crime guys could have just picked the wrong friggin place to do a car stop. We won't know till the experts get in."

"And if our hunch is correct and it turns out to be something more nefarious?"

"Then maybe we bought ourselves enough time to get a jump on the bad guys."

Rich looked at James for a moment then picked up the phone and dialed a number.

"This is Commissioner Stargold, switch me down to DCPI," he said. He waited a moment for the call to be transferred.

"Deputy Commissioner of Public Information, Police Officer Rodgers speaking, may I help you?"

"This is Commissioner Stargold; I'm out in Brooklyn at the explosion. Is Deputy Commissioner Cleary in yet?"

"No, sir, but he is on his way."

"Ok, I just wanted to call and give you a heads up. Until further notice, the cause of the explosion is undetermined pending further investigation. Since this is an ongoing event we cannot comment on any potential causes. We will update the press when we know more. However due to the fact that this is still an active fire, it might be awhile."

"Got it, sir."

"When the commissioner comes in have him call me on my cell phone."

"I will do that, sir."

"Ok, well that should buy us a bit more time," Rich said. "Now what?"

"Get some coffee and bring McMasters up to speed on what we think happened," Maguire said as he stood up. "I'll circle the wagons and get everyone digging as soon as they can. Anything new I hear I'll let you know."

Maguire went out to the desk. "You find that key, Lou?"

"Right here, sir," Adams said and handed the key to Maguire.

"Great, thank you very much. Hopefully we can move this circus out of your precinct soon and let you get back to some semblance of normal."

"No problem, sir. Let us know if there is anything you need."

"There is one thing, Lou; who were the two crime guys?"

"William Maldonado and Thomas Dixon, two of our best."

"Married? Kids?"

"No, not married. Dixon was, but he's divorced. He had a kid, daughter I believe."

Maguire frowned. It was never an easy thing to lose an officer in the line of duty. It was an inherent risk that they all accepted.

Lord knows he'd come close on any number of occasions throughout his military and police career, but he'd always been single. It had been his burden to bear alone. He couldn't imagine what lie ahead for Dixon's family, especially his child.

"Oh, I almost forgot, here is the printout for the car stop," Adams said and handed the computer paper to Maguire.

"Thanks, Lou," Maguire said, taking the paper and walked toward the X.O.'s office. He opened the door, steeped inside, and took off his jacket, tossing it onto the small couch that sat across from the desk. He removed his phone and called Torres.

"Mike, you and Amanda come inside. I need you guys to start making some calls."

A moment later Torres and Massi walked into the office.

"Grab a seat," said Maguire, pointing over to the couch.

"We're treating the origin of the explosion as unknown at this time pending investigation. Hopefully that will buy us some time to get to the bottom of this," Maguire explained. "Unfortunately that window is going to close really quickly so we need to jump on this. Mike, reach out to Counter Terrorism. Tell them I want them to start shaking the branches. See if there has been any chatter, any threats. Also, see if Inspector Nikki Ryan is in. If she's not in yet, leave a message for her to call me direct. Amanda, tap into Intel, same thing. Check to see if any of the known rabble-rousers are spouting off about local jihad."

As the two detectives began making their calls, Maguire picked up the phone and dialed a number.

"Chief Ameche," said the voice on the other end.

"Tony, its James."

"Hey, how bad is it?"

"Really bad and I don't see things improving very much as time goes by. We are going to have to get ahead of this as quickly as we can."

"What can I do for you?"

"Grab the representative from the Detective Bureau for me and tell him I want someone from the Arson and Explosion Squad sent over to me forthwith, same message to the Counter Terrorism Bureau."

"You got it," Ameche replied. "What are your thoughts on this?"

"If I had to bet my life on it, I think our guys stopped a car and the bad guy panicked. I don't think this was planned, which means something got screwed up. Now we need to figure out what that plan was before we start having other things going boom throughout the city."

"If we don't act fast, we won't be able to keep up with the panic that is going to set in."

"My thoughts exactly. The boss is going to try and buy some time in the press, but we have to move as quickly as we can on this one."

"Okay, I'll get on the horn and get you the people you want," Ameche said. "Let me know if there is anything else you need."

"I will, Tony," Maguire replied. "I'll talk to you later."

When Maguire hung up the phone, Torres was the first to speak.

"Spoke to CTB, they are working on it, but so far they have nothing. No chatter, no threats, nada. They also said the Joint Terrorism Task Force is responding."

"Outstanding, nothing like having the feds show up to turn everything into a circus," Maguire replied. "Ok, get back on the horn and tell them to have the FBI special agent in charge contact me direct. Give him my cell phone number."

"Will do," Torres replied and began dialing.

"Commissioner, I spoke to Intel. They've also got nothing. In fact they said things have been relatively quiet from the usual suspects. But they are continuing to look into it."

Maguire put his elbows on top of the desk and began to rub his eyes. He knew that it was going to get much worse before it got better. There was a slim chance that this was all coincidence. That there was some other plausible reason for the explosion, besides a bomb. But in his gut he didn't believe it. He looked down at his watch; it was just after three o'clock.

There was a knock on the door and Rich walked in.

"Just got off the phone with the mayor," he said. "They are going to do a press conference at seven. He's going to go with the whole 'it's a tragedy, but we are still investigating' story."

"That will at least buy us some time" Maguire replied. "As long as all the players from FD and the utilities are on board."

"Yeah, but will it be enough time?"

"No, probably not," Maguire replied. "So we better start praying that we catch a break."

The cell phone on the desk began to ring.

"One sec," James said and answered the phone. "Maguire."

"Commissioner, this is Special Agent Kurt Silverman. I'm the head of JTTF. I was told you wanted to speak with me?"

"Kurt, yes, I'm here in Brooklyn with Police Commissioner Stargold," Maguire replied. "Sorry we haven't had the chance to chat before this. I wanted to make sure that we were all on the same page with this thing."

"That's a refreshing thought," replied Silverman. "I'd just gotten used to being the last person to know with the previous administration."

"Trust me, there's going to be a lot of bridge mending going on."

"What can I do for you?"

"Not sure what they've told you, but things are pretty bad out here. All indications are it may have been a car bomb that was detonated during a car stop. But if that gets out, we are going to have mass panic on our hands. Not to mention we are going to alert the bad guys that whatever they might have in-play has been exposed. That's either going to drive them underground, or cause them to speed up their plans."

"Agreed," said Silverman. "What are you proposing?"

"At this point we are just going to confirm there was an explosion and that we are investigating. Try to downplay things and hide the car stop. Maybe it will buy us enough time to get a better idea about what we are dealing with."

"I'm okay with that. Tell me what you need from us?"

"Same thing my people are doing, just start digging and see what turns up. Maybe it's isolated, maybe not. If it isn't we have to get to them before they figure it out."

"That works for me, if I hear anything I will let you know."

"Thanks, Kurt," Maguire said and ended the call. "Well, JTTF is onboard."

"That's good to know," replied Stargold. "The last thing we need is a pissing match today. I'll reach out to the agent in charge of the New York Office as well. I know him from my Secret Service days. There shouldn't be any problems. I also spoke to the Fire Commissioner a few minutes ago. I explained our concerns and he assured me that as soon as they can safely get our people in, they will."

"Not much more we can do then, except wait."

"I'm going to head back in. I think it's best if I am there for the press conference."

"I agree."

"By the way, they've got the Temporary Headquarters Vehicle set up over at Bergen and Schenectady."

"I'll head over there in a bit and free this place up so they can get back to policing. Crime in Brooklyn North doesn't come to a halt for anyone or anything. I'll keep you updated."

"Okay, I'll talk to you later," said Rich.

Maguire leaned back in the chair. It had already been a long day and it was only getting started. He looked over at the two detectives sitting across from him.

"Well, I say we go grab some coffee and take a ride over to our new digs."

The three of them got up and walked out of the office. Maguire stopped at the desk, signing himself out of the precinct and then turned toward the lieutenant.

"Thanks for the hospitability, Lieutenant Adams. I wish it would have been under better circumstances," Maguire said and shook the man's hand.

"My pleasure," Adams replied.

"I'm expecting some people from Arson and Explosion as well as Counter Terrorism. If they stop by here first send them over to the THV."

"Will do, sir."

Maguire left the precinct and got into the suburban. A short time later he arrived at the THV bringing with him several large containers of coffee and donuts.

The THV was just an over glorified mobile home. It had been retrofitted to include communication and video equipment, along with an area where administrative logs and records could be kept. The purpose was to remove the chaos and confusion, caused by an event, from the precinct so that they could focus on providing necessary police services. It provided a few of the traditional amenities, such as a bathroom, and an area in which senior staff could conduct meetings in private.

"Good morning," he said as he stepped inside. "Anything new to report?"

"FD has made some progress on the initial scene and have started allowing in some detectives from the Bomb Squad and

AES," replied the duty chief who had been sitting down preparing his report.

Maguire took a seat in one of the leather swivel chairs.

"Casualties?" he asked.

"Nothing firm yet, but based on preliminary interviews of some of the neighbors the number we are looking at could be as low as twenty-five to as high as fifty. That number could of course change depending on what happens to those removed to the hospitals."

Maguire looked up at the clock on the wall. It was nearly five o'clock. Just then the door opened with a loud wintry howl and Inspector Nikki Ryan stepped inside.

"Well look what the cat dragged in," Maguire said.

"Morning, Commissioner," she replied. "I came straight from home when I got the call."

Ryan had first met him a few days earlier at her promotion. She knew he was responsible for it, but he never let on. Ryan hadn't known him beforehand, as she had left the Intelligence Division before he got there. But a mutual acquaintance had taken up her plight on her behalf. She had just been hoping to get out of Staten Island when the return call informed her that she was being promoted.

"Come on back," he said as he stood up and headed toward the conference room at the back of the THV.

Ryan followed him back and closed the door behind her.

"Grab a chair, Nikki, and I'll fill you in."

Ryan took off her coat and sat down.

"So what happened?"

Maguire filled her in on what they factually knew so far and what they thought had happened. He slid the printout of the car stop across the desk to her. Ryan picked it up and began reading it.

"You think these guys knew what they had?"

"I don't know," Maguire replied. "What I do know is that as of now you are working for me. You grab whoever you need, my authority, and I want to know anything, and everything, about Paradigm Leasing in Paramus by 0630. Keep Kurt Silverman over at JTTF in the loop as well. We are going to have to move on this really quick, Nikki."

"Then I better get going, sir," Ryan said.

As she stood up there was a knock on the door.

"Come in," Maguire called out.

The door opened and a man stepped inside. Immediately the room was filled with the heavy smell of smoke.

"Commissioner, I'm Sergeant Brendan Daly from Arson & Explosion," the man said. "I apologize for the smell, but I just came from the scene."

"Not at all, Sarge, please sit down," he said and pointed over at a chair. "This is Inspector Ryan from CTB."

"Morning, ma'am," the Sergeant replied.

"What can you tell us?"

"Judging from the damage and the blast pattern I'd say we are definitely dealing with a vehicle borne IED, and a rather large one at that" the man said somberly. "But I have a feeling you probably figured that one out already."

"The thought had crossed my mind," Maguire replied. "I need anything you can give me on this and as quickly as you can give it to me. If there is anything you need, you let me know."

"Will do, sir," the man said, before turning and leaving the room.

"I'm out of here as well," Ryan said. "As soon as I know something, I will give you a call."

"Thanks, Nikki," Maguire replied.

When the door closed he took out his cell phone and called Melody.

"Hey, cowboy," she said. "You okay?"

"Yeah, I'm fine. Are you watching the news?"

"Uh huh."

"What are they saying?"

"Not much, just that there was an explosion in Brooklyn. Conflicting accounts of what happened and how many injuries there are. How bad is it really?"

"Really bad," he said. "I'm just about to take a ride to the scene and get a look from the ground. I just wanted to call while I had the chance."

"I appreciate that," she said. "Now get back to work, slacker."

"Yes, ma'am," Maguire said with a laugh.

CHAPTER TWENTY-FOUR

Northern Maine
Tuesday, January 29th, 2013 – 5:53 a.m.

Banning sat in the living room enjoying the hot cup of coffee and cigarette. He couldn't sleep, which wasn't a bad thing.

Outside it had begun to snow hard and he watched as the wind swept flakes created near white out conditions. He closed his eyes and listened to the roar of the fireplace. He felt so alive.

So much had changed in the last two weeks and he was still coming to terms with much of it. It was a lot to take in.

For a long time he had been so angry. Angry at Maguire for not showing up all those years ago when his parents had died in the car wreck. Banning had put a lot of effort into making that happen, only to be denied when Maguire failed to return home for the funeral. Then the most recent debacle, that had ended with Maguire stabbing him and the explosive vest, which he had strapped to his girlfriend's chest, not detonating. He still wasn't exactly sure what had happened with that.

But now, everything had changed.

He thought back to that night when Tricia had first opened up to him. For some time Banning had begun to notice a change in her, as if she was brooding over her lot. At first it was subtle, but then gradually it became more pronounced. He was actually beginning to wonder if she was becoming a liability and then she had shared with him her feelings, and so much more.

There was something different about her now and that transformation had carried over into the bedroom as well. That first night it was as if something had been unleashed deep inside her. In the past she had just laid back while he satisfied his desires. That night was different.

They had talked for hours, over a bottle of scotch, and she had confided in him. She had shared her abuse under Browning and her twenty plus year love affair with Lena Marx. She shared her anger at being betrayed and her fundamental desire for revenge.

He recalled Tricia standing up and walking over to him. As she stood there, she began to undress. Banning watched as she removed her shirt, letting it drop to the floor, and then begin to seductively shimmy out of her pants. In a moment she stood before him wearing nothing but her bra and panties.

At that moment Banning ached for her more than he ever had. She was so beautiful, so perfect. Her long brown hair was draped over her shoulders; his eyes followed every sensual curve of her body. Even in this harsh environment she still managed to take care of herself, still found ways to maintain her muscle tone. As Banning watched her he became increasingly aware of the growing ache he felt deep inside. He wanted her, desired her, and lusted for her. He began to get up and she pushed him back down into the seat. He had no desire to protest, just to submit to her. She was intent on giving him something, and he was willing to sit back and allow her the moment.

Tricia reached back and unhooked her bra, letting it fall from her shoulders. She had large, firm breasts. He had always marveled at them in the past, but now he saw them from a completely new perspective. As he watched, Tricia playfully teased her nipples until they were hard and erect.

In the background the flames of the fireplace licked at the air behind her creating a surreal scene.

"Do you like this, Keith?"

Banning was at a loss for words. He simply nodded.

"Good," she replied, a smile spreading across her face.

Her face had taken on a different appearance now. The almost depressed look that Banning had grown accustomed to had been replaced by something new, something primal. It was as if the old Tricia had morphed into a new being. Gone was the innocence, the victim, and in its place stood a woman who was seductively dangerous.

She knelt before him and unbuttoned his pants, slowly removing them, and his underwear, until they rested on the floor around his ankles. She took his swollen shaft in her hand and lowered her mouth to him, teasing him gently with the tip of her tongue as her hand gently stroked it.

"Do you like that, Keith?" she asked, the words coming out in a low, provocative voice.

"Yes," was all he managed to say as he leaned back against the chair, his eyes closed.

"Mmmmm," she replied and took him in her mouth.

She didn't have much experience doing this, but judging from his response she must have been doing it fairly well. It had been a long time since she had been with a man this way. For months she had lay in bed as an uninterested participant and allowed him to have his way with her. In the beginning she had fought back against him, but as time passed, she began to wonder why. There was something strangely erotic in his brutish passion. She began to feel aroused. For Tricia, the last twenty years had been so much different. Her sex life was soft, gentle, and affectionate. Now she felt a fiery, lustful desire deep inside that was driving her.

Banning was moaning loudly now, she knew she had him. Tricia drew her mouth away from him, standing back up slowly. She watched as Banning's eyes opened, staring up at her.

"Not yet, Keith," she said.

She knew he ached, but tonight it was all about her desires.

Tricia sat on the small coffee table that was in front of the chair, positioning herself so that he had the best view.

He watched as she slowly pulled her panties to the side and slipped her finger inside.

Tricia moaned. She felt the wetness engulf her finger. Slowly she began to pleasure herself. Felt the hardness of her clit against her fingertip. It had been so long since she had embraced this side of herself. She wondered why she had punished herself all those years.

Across from her she watched as Banning slowly stroked his shaft.

Tricia closed her eyes tightly as she felt the orgasm take hold, her body convulsing. The intensity was unlike anything she had felt before. Wave after wave coursing through her body and she found herself fighting to maintain control. It was as intense, as it was liberating. She collapsed back on the table, her labored breathing coming in gasps. She fought her way back onto her feet, sliding off her panties.

She bent over the table, looking back over her shoulder at Banning.

"Now, Keith!" she said, the words coming out as sharply.

Banning leapt to his feet, eager to fulfill her wishes.

Tricia felt him inside her as she continued to pleasure herself. She knew he wouldn't last long, but she didn't need him to. From the moment she felt him enter her she began to climax. With each thrust, her body was wracked by waves of orgasms. She grasped the edge of the table with both hands, her knuckles turning white, and let it happen.

"Fuck yeah," she exclaimed. "Harder."

Behind her Banning was grunting as he thrust himself deep inside of her. He reached down, grabbing a fistful of Tricia's hair and jerked her head backward. She let out a scream as she came again and then felt him explode inside of her. For a moment in time they were locked together, both of their bodies surrendering to their most base needs. When it was over they collapsed to the floor.

Seconds turned to minutes as their bodies struggled to return back to normal. It was Tricia who spoke first.

"As steel sharpens steel, so one person sharpens another," she said. "I need you to help me, Keith, and in return I will give you everything you desire."

"Anything for you, my love," Banning replied.

CHAPTER TWENTY-FIVE

Brooklyn, New York City
Tuesday, January 29th, 2013 – 6:13 a.m.

"Paradigm Leasing is owned by Rafiq Hamadi," Nikki Ryan began. "Hamadi came here about fifteen years ago from Lebanon on a student visa."

Maguire tossed the pen he was holding onto the conference table and leaned back in the chair.

"What the fuck?" he asked rhetorically. "Do they just give these things away in the local Seven-Eleven's now?"

"Actually he really did attend school," Ryan replied. "He graduated with a bachelor's degree in IT management from Berkley. He's married to Sabah Abaid who he met here. They have two kids, a ten year old boy, Kassim, and a five year old girl, Mariam. They live in Lyndhurst but his IT firm is located in Passaic."

"So the business is legit?" Maguire asked.

"At face value it is," Ryan replied. "But under the surface things don't add up."

"Like what?"

"Like why Paradigm Leasing purchased five cars in the month of December, or six backpacks in November. There has also been a lot of cash flowing in an out of his business accounts in the last several months. Still trying to get the details, but that's going to take some time as the payments are being routed through half the world."

"Rich, are you getting all this?" Maguire asked.

"Yes," said the voice through the speaker phone on the desk.

"Kurt, where do we stand operationally?"

"I have six SSG teams set up on the house and surrounding streets," Silverman said, referring to the Bureau's Special

Surveillance Group who were tasked with clandestine vehicular and pedestrian observations.

"There's been no movement so far," he continued, "but we are ready in the event he leaves. I also have the FBI SWAT team standing by if something goes wrong."

"Nikki, what kind of outfit is this Paradigm?" Maguire asked.

"They do IT work, computer repairs, servers, etc."

"What about employees?"

"Seven full time and another half dozen part timers."

"Can anyone think of a reason why they would need five vehicles?"

"I have a team over at his shop," Silverman said. "There are three PT Cruisers in the lot, all marked with commercial graphics. No sign of the vehicles in question. My bet is we are dealing with something completely different."

"Rich, if we are going to do this we have to act really fast," James said.

"Agent Silverman, how much leeway are we going to have on this?" Rich asked.

"I just got off the phone with the Assistant U.S. Attorney in the Southern District. Since Hamadi is Lebanese they are prepared to approach this as an 'enemy combatant' scenario. But if we don't get any actionable intelligence I would count on that changing rather quickly."

"Where are we going to do the interview?" Stargold asked.

"We have a warehouse we use in Bayonne," Silverman said.

"James, I want you there," Stargold said. "You have the requisite skill set for this."

"Understood," James replied. "Kurt, we need to grab this guy before he gets to his office. This has got to be a picture perfect snatch and grab."

"He'll never see it coming," Silverman replied.

"Let's hope not. I'll call you from my car for the location of the warehouse."

CHAPTER TWENTY-SIX

Northern Maine
Tuesday, January 29th, 2013 – 6:21 a.m.

Banning drew himself back from his thoughts and lit another cigarette. In the days that had passed, their love making had actually intensified. Much to his surprise, it was Tricia who was the primary aggressor, not that it bothered him. He found it surprisingly erotic to be with a strong willed woman.

How did I not see that before? he wondered.

True to her word, she had satisfied every one of his desires, including a few he hadn't been aware he had. In turn he opened up to her, sharing his knowledge.

She was fine with his plans for Maguire, even though she personally harbored no ill will toward him. She admitted that she had feelings for Maguire, but those feelings were in the past and this was, after all, the present. She had, however, a few scores to settle, and at the top of that list was Lena Marx. For that she needed Banning's help. Something he was all too eager to assist with.

"Good morning, darling," Tricia said as she walked into the living room, stopping to kiss him before she made her way into the kitchen.

Banning watched as she walked away. He stared at her long legs, following them up and coming to rest on her ass that peeked out ever so slightly from the tee shirt she was wearing.

"Do you need more coffee?" she asked.

Banning looked over at the cup sitting on the table.

"Sure," he replied.

He didn't actually, but the thought of watching her walk back into the kitchen again was too overwhelming. Banning reached over and grabbed the T.V. remote.

Tricia came back into the room and refilled the cup. As he watched her walk back to the kitchen, he felt himself growing aroused.

Maybe we could make good use of the morning, he thought.

In the background he heard a reporter's voice.

"Jenna, authorities are not releasing any information at this time but reports are that a massive explosion, possibly caused by a natural gas leak, rocked this Brooklyn neighborhood in the early morning hours."

As Banning watched, the scene changed to earlier footage showing the night sky eerily lit up in an orange glow. Banning picked up the coffee cup and took a sip as the camera zoomed in for a close-up.

"Son of a bitch!" he exclaimed.

"What is it?" Tricia said, coming back into the living room.

Banning picked up the remote and played it back.

As Tricia watched, a figured appeared, coming around the black Suburban parked in the road. As she stared at the screen, the man turned briefly and looked back in the direction of the camera. Inside, her heart began racing as she gazed into the face of the man she had lost more than two decades ago.

"Well now, that certainly changes things doesn't it?" Banning said, taking a drag on the cigarette.

CHAPTER TWENTY-SEVEN

Passaic, New Jersey
Tuesday, January 29th, 2013 – 6:58 a.m.

Hamadi made his way north along River Drive. He had just been ready to turn onto Paulison when the SUV behind him slammed into his bumper. The force knocked the computer bag off the passenger seat next to him and sent the travel mug hurdling into the dash, bathing the interior in hot coffee.

"Fuck!" he yelled out, and put the van into park. He got out and walked to the rear of the car to inspect the damage. The rear bumper of the Honda Odyssey was pushed in.

He stood up just as the woman was getting out of the Ford Explorer.

"Are you crazy, lady?" he asked. "Didn't you see me turning?"

"I'm so sorry," the woman replied. "I thought you were going straight."

Hamadi was just about to rip into her when he saw the large, white Nissan panel van pull up next to them.

If Hamadi had any real world experience he would have known what was happening, not that it would have mattered.

It was a classic operation. While his attention had been directed toward the woman, he never saw the man who had gotten out of the passenger seat of the Ford. He had been too focused on the woman apologizing to him, to notice the vans fast approach. The passenger came up behind him and pushed him just as the van's door slid open. Hamadi was roughly grabbed by the two men sitting in the back of the vehicle and dragged inside.

As the van pulled away the woman got back into the SUV and her partner got into Hamadi's vehicle. The whole event took less than a minute.

Inside the panel van, Hamadi was thrown roughly onto the floor and physically subdued. He began to protest, but it was cut short by one of the men who taped his mouth shut. His hands and feet were also bound, and then a hood was placed over his head.

The men spoke Arabic, which only led to Hamadi's further confusion.

What had happened? he wondered. His mind was racing. *Was there someone at the house already? What about Sabah and the children?*

He was in a panic and there was nothing he could do to help them. Hamadi knew the people he worked for, knew what they were capable of and the lengths that they would go.

Tears streamed down his face as he imagined the fate that awaited his family.

CHAPTER TWENTY-EIGHT

Bayonne, New Jersey
Tuesday, January 29th, 2013 – 7:25 a.m.

The room was both large and sterile.

The walls and ceiling of the room were constructed of heavy gauge steel and painted a dark gray. The floor was bare concrete.

On one wall was a one-way mirrored window, made from thick ballistic glass. In the middle of the room sat an old steel industrial table, bolted to the ground. On either side of the table were straight backed chairs which matched the construction of the table. Above the table, mounted to the ceiling, were high output directional lighting fixtures.

Embedded discretely in the walls were tiny speakers and microphones that provided those on the other side of the glass with the ability to hear even the most muted conversations or whispers. The room was also equipped with temperature controls that allowed it to be cooled or heated to extremes. At the moment the room was being chilled to the point that its current occupant was shivering. A condition that was only exasperated by the sound of dripping water that was being piped into the room.

It was a depressing room, designed solely for the purpose of weighing heavily upon the mental state of the occupant, who in this case was Rafiq Hamadi.

Hamadi sat in the chair, his arms and legs restrained securely, still wearing the canvas hood that had been placed on him in the van. Through the hood's material he could make out a hint of light.

Upon their arrival here, he was physically dragged out of the van, and his body pulled violently along the floor. The men continued to speak Arabic, but he was unable to tell where they were from based on the dialect.

After strapping him into the chair they had removed the tape from his mouth. He had pleaded with them to let him go, that it was all some mistake, but they ignored his pleas. He heard the door slam shut and waited.

Water dripped from somewhere. He tried to listen for some other type of sound but there was nothing else.

He called out, pleading for help. First in English, then in Arabic.

There was no response.

As time passed the sound of the water seemed as if it was growing louder.

Drip.

Drip.

Drip.

Drip.

It was maddening, Hamadi thought.

For a moment he imagined that it was coming toward him and he began to panic. He tried to move in the chair, but it was secured to the floor. He struggled, trying to free his arms and legs, but it was futile.

Drip.

Drip.

Under the hood, despite the chill of the room, sweat streamed down his face.

The sound stopped and everything went black.

Silence filled the room.

Hamadi tried to listen intently, but there was nothing.

Time passed, but was it seconds or hours?

Then it began again.

Drip.

Drip.

He screamed, his body flailing wildly against the restraints.

His body slumped and he began to sob.

Behind the window, Maguire and Silverman watched the man. Maguire looked at the digital clock on the wall above him. The red LED display read 8:23 a.m.

"Where do we stand with the family?" Maguire asked.

"I have three teams watching the house where his wife and daughter are. Another team is watching the son, who is at school."

"I think it's time to have a chat with Mr. Hamadi," Maguire said, picking up the file from the desk in front of him.

"You sure?" Silverman asked.

"Yeah, trust me, he's done," Maguire replied. "Hit the lights."

The operator looked over at Silverman who nodded.

Maguire stepped out of the control room and opened the door to the interrogation room.

Immediately Hamadi's head snapped up.

"Hello?" he said. "Who's there? Please help me; there's been some terrible mistake."

Maguire walked over and ripped the hood off his head. Hamadi grimaced at the sudden harsh glare of the lights and shut his eyes tightly.

"Rafiq Hamadi," Maguire began. "Born April 11th, 1981, in Sin El Fil, Lebanon. Father is a baker, mother works in a textile shop."

"Who are you?"

"Came to the United States on a student visa in 2002 and graduated from Berkley with a bachelor's degree in IT management."

"What is going on?" Hamadi demanded.

"Married to Sabah Abaid, a first generation Lebanese American. You have two kids, a ten year old boy, Kassim, and a five year old girl, Mariam. You live in Lyndhurst and have a computer firm located in Passaic."

"I demand to speak with my lawyer," the man said angrily.

Maguire closed the folder and laid it on the table, taking the seat across from Hamadi.

"Who are you? Where am I?"

Maguire continued to stare at the man without any expression.

"I know my rights!"

Maguire let the silence take hold, watching Hamadi closely.

Without a word he opened the folder again and slowly pulled out the three grainy black and white photos, laying them on the table in front of Hamadi.

The man stared down at them and into the faces of his wife and children.

"What do you want?"

And in that moment it was over. All that was left was to ask the right questions.

"Rafiq you have a very big problem and only two choices," Maguire said. "The window is closing very quickly to save yourself and your family. Do you understand me?"

The man nodded his head slowly.

"Right now you are considered by the United States to be an *Enemy Combatant*. This means you have no rights, no protections. To the rest of the world you have ceased to exist. I can do anything I want to you, for as long as I choose. As long as you are telling me the truth, we are fine. If you lie to me, I will leave this room and you will disappear. You will not go to jail, or to

Gitmo, or to any place that fortunate. I will ship you off to the darkest corner of the world, where they *will* get the truth from you, and when they are done, you will be left alone in a cell with only your memories. Do I make myself clear?"

"Yes," Hamadi said quietly. In front of him, the faces in the photos seemed to plead silently to him.

"Right now I have people watching your family. If you tell me the truth, I will protect them. But, if you lie to me Rafiq, not only will you be on that plane this afternoon, but I will pull that protection and I will put the word out on the street that you are cooperating with us. I don't have to tell you what they will do to your family, both here and in Lebanon. That will be something you will have to live with for the rest of your life. Knowing that you could have saved them, but instead you chose to let them die."

"I will tell you what you want to know."

"I know you will," Maguire said.

Maguire started with questions that he already knew the answers to.

"How many cars?"

"Five."

"What's your role?"

"Logistics, supply."

"Who was your primary contact?"

Hamadi hesitated a moment.

Maguire reached down, scooped up the photos and began to get up.

"Qaseem," Hamadi shouted. "Qaseem bin Khalid, he is a Saudi."

Maguire sat back down. He placed the photos back on the table in front of Hamadi. Tears were streaming down the man's cheeks.

"If you hesitate again, the next photos I show you will be the ones taken by the crime scene photographer of what remains of your family."

Over the course of the next hour and a half Hamadi gave up everything. Names of the individuals involved. The locations they were staying at. Cell phone numbers for everyone and cut-outs.

The control room behind them was abuzz. While recording devices ensured that everything was digitally preserved, agents and officers with headphones on took copious notes. As each new revelation became known, names were plugged into computer databases, soon an image began to take shape of the actors involved, along with the breadth and scope of the threat they were facing.

In another room, computer experts had begun the process of going through the laptop Hamadi had been carrying. Hidden deep inside its hard drive was the proverbially mother lode of intelligence. Hamadi, it seemed, kept meticulous records of everything and everyone.

CHAPTER TWENTY-NINE

Brooklyn, New York City
Tuesday, January 29th, 2013 – 8:03 a.m.

Nazir al Mahdi sat down on the couch in the small apartment in the Bushwick section of Brooklyn and turned the television on.

He was just about to switch the feed to the video game console when he saw an image flash across the screen of a fiery inferno. He paused for a moment and raised the volume.

".... fire officials are saying the blaze is contained at this time, but it will not be until sometime later today when inspectors from Con Edison will be able to get in and assess the damage. Meanwhile, gas to the area has been suspended. The Red Cross has set up shelters where affected residents can go to get heat and food until they are allowed back in their homes. Now back to you in the studio."

"Nina, are officials saying what caused the explosion at this time?"

"The Mayor spoke earlier today and said that they were investigating whether a natural gas line had ruptured. So far we have not been able to get close enough to speak with any investigators. The police department has closed off the immediate area due to concern of structural damage to the surrounding buildings. Another press conference is expected to be held at 12:30 at City Hill."

"That was Nina Collins reporting from the East New York section of Brooklyn.

As he stared at the screen, Nazir had a bad feeling about what he had just seen. He got up and went to the bedroom. He removed the cell phone from his jacket pocket and selected a number from the call list.

"The number you have reached is unavailable at this time. Please try your call again later."

Nazir ended the call.

He didn't have any firsthand experience in bombs, but he had certainly seen enough in his native Iraq. What had been flashed on the television screen had looked to be a lot more significant than a gas leak. He wondered for a moment whether he should call Qaseem. He let *that* conversation play out in his mind. Qaseem was not what you would call *forgiving.* If he had learned that he and Ramzi had been getting together to play video games he would come unglued.

He reached up, putting the phone back into the jacket pocket and walked back to the living room. He would try to call Ramzi later on. Then, if he couldn't reach him, he would think about calling Qaseem. If something had happened to Ramzi, there was really no reason for both of them to get into trouble.

He switched the television feed and watched as the signal from the game console loaded up.

CHAPTER THIRTY

Northern Maine
Tuesday, January 29th, 2013 – 9:03 a.m.

Keith and Tricia were both hunched over the small kitchen table, staring at the screen on the laptop. Each was lost in their own thoughts, as they read the online article from the local New York City paper. It heralded the return of the *hero* detective who had just been sworn in as the NYPD's newest first deputy commissioner.

He had been right; there had been something different about Maguire. Now he understood just how badly he had underestimated his nemesis.

The article summarized his prior service with the department and also came complete with a photo from his swearing-in, showing him standing next to the new police commissioner. Tricia wasn't so much as interested in them as she was in the woman who stood to Maguire's side.

"So now what do you suggest we do?" Tricia asked.

Banning reached over, picked up the cigarette pack and lit one, leaning back slowly in his chair.

"We wait for the right opportunity," he replied.

"He's a cop now," Tricia replied. "He'll be surrounded by other cops."

"Have you ever read Frederick Forsyth, my dear?"

"No," she said. "Why do you ask?"

"Forsyth wrote a book called *The Day of the Jackal*. There is a passage in that book that reads '*All big men have bodyguards and security men, but over a period of years without any serious attempt on the life of the big man, the checks become formal, the routines mechanical and the degree of watchfulness is lowered.*' So now we wait and we plan, until the right moment presents itself."

CHAPTER THIRTY-ONE

Bayonne, New Jersey
Tuesday, January 29th, 2013 – 10:07 a.m.

Maguire walked out of the interrogation room and stepped inside the control room.

"Holy fuck," Silverman said.

"Yeah, how the hell did this slip under the radar and *nobody* had a clue?"

"I'd like to say that things got better with communications after 9/11, but I don't want to start this new relationship with you, on a lie," Silverman replied. "Truth is, the dysfunction that existed before, still exists, but now we have a really cool sounding agency to run everything."

Maguire took a deep breath; he knew it was all true.

"Nikki, Kurt, I need immediate *eyes on* at all four locations. If it breathes, moves, or blinks I want to know about it. They've got to be goddamn ghosts folks. I don't have to remind you of what could happen if any of our *would-be* terrorists get an inkling that they are being watched."

Both nodded and walked off to the side to coordinate the surveillance of the suspected locations.

"Mike, get me the CO of ESU on the phone. Amanda, get on the phone with Highway, I want a car waiting for us on the New York side of the Holland Tunnel. Tell him I also want twelve marked units sent over to the Special Operations Division forthwith."

As the two detectives made their respective calls, Maguire opened his phone and called Rich.

"Rich, it's bad," Maguire began. "This guy gave up everything. We have four more cars out there, and an equal number of back packs. The bumper sticker version is they were going to detonate the vehicles on random dates of their own choosing. The backpacks are for secondary suicide missions to take out first responders."

"Holy shit," Stargold said.

"Pretty much," replied Maguire. "We have to move and we have to move now. If we lose the cover story on the explosion we will lose this one opportunity to get them."

"I can't have four fucking terrorists running around the streets of New York City, James. Do what you have to do and tell me what you need to get it done."

Maguire looked over at Torres, who motioned with the phone to indicate he had the Commanding Officer of ESU on the phone.

"We have three locations in Brooklyn, one in Queens. We hit them hard and fast at the same time."

"Should we start evacuations?"

"There's no time, and even if there was I'd say no. The only element we have going for us right now is surprise. If any of them get an inkling that we are trying to evacuate people I don't think they'll hesitate to detonate the explosives. Last night showed me that we aren't dealing with people who are going to second guess their options."

"What about having emergency personnel on standby?"

"I'd call the Fire Commissioner and have him put the nearest fire houses on alert, just in case."

"Okay, I'll call him and fill him in on what we have, without giving away any operational details."

"Okay, I'm just about to get on the phone with ESU to get the teams in motion."

"Do you want me to meet you?"

"No, bring McMasters up to speed and run things from Command and Control," Maguire replied. "I'll handle things from the ground."

"Are you sure?"

"Rich, I'll be honest with you. We've gone from *FUBAR* all the way to *BOHICA* and we haven't even started the operation yet. If this goes south, and there is a really good chance that it will, you're going to need a fall guy."

"James…"

"No, Rich, I'm being serious."

"I'm not going to hang you out to dry for something you didn't cause."

James turned and walked toward the corner of the room, out of ear shot from the rest.

"Listen, you know I'm right. We've always know this. Success has a hundred fathers and failures an orphan. It sucks, but that's life and that's the reason they pay you the big bucks."

"Then you better not fail, James."

"If I fail, there won't be enough left of me to scrape into a thimble. I'll update you from the car."

Maguire ended the call, looked at Silverman and nodded.

Kurt leaned down and grabbed the portable radio from the desk.

"Anvil One, Olympus Base, do you copy?"

"Olympus Base this is Anvil One, go with message."

"Anvil One, green light has been given for immediate extraction. I repeat, you have a green light for extraction, over."

"Olympus Base, copy traffic. We are green lighted for immediate extraction. Executing now."

"Anvil Three, Olympus Base, do you copy?"

"Olympus Base this is Anvil Three, go with message."

"Anvil Three, same message. Green light has been given for immediate extraction. I repeat, you have a green light for extraction, over."

"Olympus Base, copy. Moving to extract now."

Maguire walked over and took the phone from Torres.

"Julie, this is Commissioner Maguire."

"Good morning, Commissioner, what can I do for you?"

Deputy Chief Julie Preston was a twenty-six year veteran of the New York City Police Department. She had originally been appointed to the New York City Housing Police and was a founding member of that agency's Emergency Medical Rescue Unit. When the Housing and Transit Police Departments were merged in the NYPD, she was assigned to the Emergency Service Unit. She was a *tough as nails* cop and a lead from the front supervisor. With each promotion she had been reassigned to patrol, but inevitably found her way back to the unit she loved. Now she had reached the pinnacle of her career, the first female Commanding Officer of the Emergency Service Unit.

"I'm about to ruin your day."

"I've heard that before, sir," she replied. "Just makes me work harder."

"Love the attitude, Chief," he replied. "This is an honest to God no shitter. We have four confirmed terrorists in four different locations. Three are in Brooklyn, one across the border in Queens."

"Are we looking at an imminent attack?"

"Don't know, the car last night was a premature detonation. There are four others out there and they all have secondary devices in back packs."

"When are we moving on this?"

"A half hour ago," Maguire replied.

"Understood."

"I need six teams, staged and waiting at SOD. I'm heading over there now."

"We'll be waiting for you, sir."

Maguire hung up the phone.

"Commissioner, Highway will have a car waiting at the tunnel," Massi said. "The CO is responding to SOD with the other units."

"Thanks, Amanda," Maguire said. "Kurt, you ready?"

"Yeah, his wife and kids are secure. I have teams locking down both the house and his business until we are done. We can sort the other players out later."

"Nikki ride with us, we can figure out the targeting priority on the way."

CHAPTER THIRTY-TWO

Southampton, Suffolk County, N.Y.
Tuesday, January 29th, 2013 – 10:15 a.m.

"Hey, whatcha doing?" Melody said, peeking into Genevieve's office.

Gen looked up from the papers on her desk. "Busy work," she replied. "Grab a chair."

Melody sat down in the chair.

"Would you like some coffee?" Gen asked.

"I'd love some."

She removed the carafe and poured a cup, sliding it across the desk to Melody.

"Yeah, I was doing the same. I just ran out of steam and focus," Melody said.

"I know. It's the not knowing that is killing me. Have you heard from James?"

"Got a text saying he was really busy and that things were moving very fast. He said he would call as soon as he could."

"Well I guess we wait then, don't we?"

"I don't know if I am cut out for this," Melody said as she took a sip of coffee.

"What are you saying, Mel?"

"I don't know. I guess that's the problem. I just don't know where I fit in."

"Seriously?"

"Yeah, am I just the girlfriend who gets to wait and wonder?"

"Hon, I don't think James thinks of you as just his *girlfriend*."

"How do you know?"

"Because I see the way he looks at you, the way the two of you are together. He loves you just as much as you love him."

"So what do I do? Just sit around and wait?"

"You talked him into taking this job," Gen replied.

"Ugh, please don't remind me."

"Listen, James does what he does, and you do what you do. But I don't think this has anything to do with waiting and wondering."

"He was supposed to be the 2nd in command, not running around like *Bruce Willis* saving the city."

"Mel, I hate to tell you this, but if anyone is going to save the city, it *is* going to be James."

"What if he can't?"

"That's what this is really about," Gen said. "You're worried about losing him."

Melody stared out the window. She didn't want to admit that Genevieve was right, but she was. For the last few months she was falling deeper and deeper in love with him and now, for the first time, she had to deal with the reality that she might lose him.

"So if you're right, what should I do?"

"Let James do the job that he knows how to do and is good at. You get your lazy butt back to what it is you know how to do."

"You're right," Melody said.

"I know."

Melody hated Genevieve at moments like this. She finished her coffee and put the cup on the desk. "Where do we stand on the *Dragon's Breath* trials?"

"We've got all the computer work sewn up. I was out there in November watching them do the in-house trials. We had one hundred percent functionality across the board on the software."

"How'd you pull that off?"

"Remember Senator Belinda Jones?"

"Yeah, doesn't she sit on the Armed Services Committee?"

"Yep, that's her," Gen replied. "She made a phone call over to the Commanding General at the Montana Air National Guard. They were kind enough to *loan* us an F-15 from the 120th Fighter Wing. We plugged the board in and did fifty simulations. We got target acquisition fifty out of fifty times and even broke the previous time record."

"Very impressive, chicky."

"We go live in March. The Navy is going to do a real time evaluation at the Point Mugu, Sea Test Range. We'll have a variety of aircraft, along with the guided missile destroyer, USS Stockdale."

"How do you feel about it?"

"Based on the results of the trials, I think we are poised to rewrite military history."

Melody took a deep breath and let that settle in. For all her quirky humor and party girl ways, when it came to business analysis, Genevieve was as cold and rigid as a bronze statue. It's why they worked so well together and had achieved so much.

"Where do we stand on the ground vehicle testing?"

"Actually we are even further along," Gen replied. "GDL already had most of the toys we needed on site. We've been running scenarios for the last couple of months. The only problem we had in the beginning was with the housing on the ground vehicles. They were taking a beating on the rough terrain."

"How did they fix that?"

"They up-armored them. The engineers went back to the drawing board. They came up with a titanium housing unit and sandwiched the unit inside it. They effectively created an armored box to put inside the armored vehicle."

"That worked?"

"Not one failure after the change. We went so far as to install one in a Humvee. Then had teams run it nonstop, on the worst terrain we could find, for three days. We then hammered it with test after test. One hundred percent target detection and transmission."

Global Defense Logistics had been their biggest acquisition to date, and their first military contracting firm. Melody had taken a step back and allowed Genevieve to take a more proactive role in the day to day operations. She was a techie at heart and enjoyed being hands on. This allowed Melody to focus more on their other interests.

"I know everything has been thrown at Dragon's Breath, but where do we stand with that reactive armor?"

It was a project that was near and dear to her heart since it had saved the love of her life that fateful night in May.

"It's been fast tracked to field testing," Gen replied. "Based on the positive results of James' *real world* test, the Pentagon has green lighted testing with select operational units in Afghanistan."

"I'd like to open it up to law enforcement as well."

"I know and I agree, but we will be in a better place with solid military reviews."

"Yes, I know," Melody replied. "It's hard to be patient when I am passionate about something."

Genevieve peered over the top of her glasses at Melody, arching her eyebrows dramatically.

"You, impatient? No, I'm shocked........."

Melody got up from the chair and headed for the door, turning just before she left the room.

"I'm going down to the gym, care to join me?"

Genevieve opened her mouth; the smartass answer forming on her lips almost immediately but abruptly stopped. She hated the gym. She hated sweating, hated exercising, in fact she could not think of anything that could even remotely be considered positive about that room of horrors. She had been blessed with a hyperactive metabolism and had never had to watch what she ate or drank. That was at least until she had met Gregor. Now, every time she *saw* him she began to be a little more self-conscious.

"Yes," she replied, much to Melody's surprise. "I'll meet you downstairs."

"Seriously?"

She closed the laptop as she got up from the desk and looked over at Melody. "Hey, a girl's got to do what a girl's got to do."

CHAPTER THIRTY-THREE

Lower Manhattan, New York City
Tuesday, January 29th, 2013 – 10:23 a.m.

Amanda Massi steered the Suburban south on West Street, through the early morning traffic, following the marked NYPD Highway Patrol car that was leading the way. Despite the flashing lights and blaring sirens, some drivers remained lost in their own world, forcing the two vehicles to weave back and forth between the three lanes of traffic.

As they passed Vesey Street, all eyes subconsciously looked to the left where the Twin Towers once stood and where the Freedom Tower now rose majestically into the sky. Even after all this time it was still difficult to comprehend the magnitude of the loss. As they passed by, the two vehicles moved into the left lane and turned toward the entrance to the Brooklyn Battery Tunnel.

"Rich, we're going to be going into the tunnel," Maguire said into the phone. "If I lose you I will call you back. But we've prioritized the targets based on the intelligence we have been getting. The primary is going to be Yusef Sayeed. Secondary is Bashir Al Karim. These are two who we have identified as the true believers. The A-Team will be hitting Sayeed's place. He's the bomb maker and I have a bad feeling that he is going to be the hardest to take down."

"What are the odds?" Rich asked.

"Ask me that question when we are done."

"I've got to call McMasters," Rich replied. "He's going to want to know."

"Tell him the truth Rich. We'll be incredibly lucky if we end up batting .750% today."

On the other end of the phone Rich lowered his head into his hand. Across from him sat Michael Stone, the Special Agent in Charge of the FBI's New York City field office.

"Is there anything else I can do for you?"

"A prayer or two couldn't hurt, aside from that I think we are good to go."

"Do what you have to do, James," Rich replied.

"I'll call you back when we are in-route to the location."

"I'm heading down to Command and Control," Rich replied. "Happy hunting."

"Will do."

Maguire put the cell phone back into his pocket.

"How are we doing people?"

"The FBI SWAT team is already heading over to Floyd Bennett Field," Silverman replied.

"Good," Maguire said. "Are we in agreement that they should take down Al Karim?"

"I'm okay with that. I spoke to the SAIC before we left and he just wanted the Bureau to be part of the entry."

"Good," replied Maguire. "I think this thing is already a cluster fuck Kurt, so the less complicated we make it the better. We'll let each entry team maintain unit cohesion and not worry about mixing & matching."

"That work's for me," Silverman replied.

"Nikki, how are we doing with the Bomb Squad?" Maguire asked.

"Spoke to Lieutenant Weir, he's recalled all his guys and directed them to report to the SOD. He'll put the teams together to go in immediately after everything has been cleared."

The two vehicles emerged from the tunnel. Directly ahead, a Triborough Bridge and Tunnel Authority vehicle sat at the toll plaza, an officer stood outside waving them through.

"Are we missing anything?"

"Damn if I know," Silverman said.

"Anything you'd like to add, Nikki?"

"What if Hamadi lied? What if there's someone else? Or what if there is a call that needed to be made and wasn't?"

"I've considered that," Maguire said. "I don't think he has the backbone for it. I think the fear of losing his family overrode his conviction to the cause. Besides, deep down inside he knows he would never be able to withstand a CIA black site interrogation."

Nikki Ryan looked out the window at the commercial buildings that dotted the landscape as they headed down the Brooklyn Queens Expressway lost in her thoughts.

So much had changed in the world since that fateful morning of September 11th. The battles had always seemed to be *over there* and then, in the blink of an eye, they were here, in our own backyard. She remembered the choking dust that filled the air, the look of panic and bewilderment as they helped to evacuate civilians from lower Manhattan, the rubble that remained of what had once been the most iconic buildings in the New York City skyline. She remembered friends that would never see the light of day again.

Now, to prevent future attacks, we were, in a way, having to become like our enemy. Enhanced interrogations, black sites, enemy combatant status, torture. Where did it end?

The truth is, there is sometimes a very fine line that separates the two sides. But when you are confronted by evil, sometimes the only response is to respond in kind. It amazed her that so many people couldn't understand this concept. Some did, she corrected herself. She remembered a quote by Lieutenant General James Mattis, USMC: 'I come in peace. I didn't bring artillery. But I'm pleading with you, with tears in my eyes: If you fuck with me, I'll kill you all.'

Wasn't that us?

America wasn't the enemy; America was a place that anyone could come to and be anything they pleased. Sure the talking heads on TV always seemed to enjoy taking potshots at her, but at the end of the day, if America was so bad how come people would risk anything and everything to come here?

She took a deep breath. No, we did not start this fight and it was not our obligation to acquiesce into a subservient role for the sake of political correctness. America was a country that was slow to anger, but those who would mistake kindness for weakness deserved to meet their fate. Today, God willing, four men would learn that lesson.

"Nikki?" Maguire said. "You alright?"

"Huh?" she replied. "Yes, Commissioner, I'm fine. I was just lost in thought for a moment."

The two car motorcade had pulled off the Belt Parkway and arrived at Floyd Bennett Field, home of the NYPD's Special Operations Division.

"Well, get your game face on, folks, we're here."

CHAPTER THIRTY-FOUR

Northern Maine
Tuesday, January 29th, 2013 – 11:03 a.m.

Tricia reached over and picked up the coffee cup, taking a drink as she looked out the window. Outside, the wind whipped the falling snow into a frenzy, peppering it against the glass. Just beyond the cleared area, the majestic pine trees were covered, their boughs bending under the weight of the newest accumulation.

This is such a beautiful place, she thought.

Tucked away in the mountains, unspoiled, tranquil, and yet she knew that reality lurked just beyond and it would have to be dealt with eventually.

"What are you thinking, my love?" asked Banning.

Tricia looked back at him. He was kneeling in front of the fireplace, adding another log onto the fire.

Their roles had solidified over the last few days. What had once been was no more. She had become his partner, and in return walls had come down. It was kind of odd the first night that she hadn't been chained to the bed. It almost felt uncomfortable. She remembered how she had woken up several times during the night feeling that something was wrong. But it had been his way of showing trust and she had rewarded him for it. It was clear to her that Keith had never experienced anything like her before.

For so many years, her life seemed simultaneously upside down and backward. She had traded Maguire in for Lena Marx, because she thought she had been in love. Was it real or did she just want it to be real?

How long ago had it been? she wondered. *Almost twenty-five years ago?*

Besides Maguire, the only other man she had physically been with was Paul Browning and that was when he had raped her. She should have killed him when she had the chance. That fat little drunken pig had fallen asleep almost the moment after he was done, not that it had lasted long anyway. She remembered being in the shower for what seemed like an eternity trying to scrub him off of her body. She had thought about getting one of the shotguns, but in the end couldn't do it. Ultimately she had threatened him with enough conviction that he had never tried it again, but it had always haunted her. Mentally she endured the shame of not being able to strike back at him.

That was until now. In a way, this was so liberating to her. It was as if she had become someone new. She thought back to the other night and smiled inwardly. For the first time in her life she had done what she wanted, acted as if no one else's opinion mattered. The truth was, she no longer cared what anyone thought. She no longer had to pretend that anyone else's feeling mattered to her. *What had changed*, she wondered? It was as if a new Tricia had come out, pushing back the meek little girl that had once been. This new woman was strong, aggressive, and dangerous. More importantly, she liked this new her.

"I hate my name," she said.

"What did you say?"

"I hate my name, Keith," she replied. "It's not me, it's never been me. Tricia,...... it sounds so pathetic, so weak. Do you think that I'm pathetic and weak, Keith?"

For a moment he was caught off guard, unsure how exactly to respond.

"Uh, no, Tr.....," He stammered. "I mean no, I don't think that way about you at all."

"I'm not the old me anymore. I need something different, something new. Something that reflects who I am now."

She turned and looked back out the window. The snow had subsided and the sun was now shining brightly. The icicles clinging to the edge of the roof sparkled brilliantly in the sunlight. It reminded her of some far away exotic place, like the winter scene in *Doctor Zhivago*. As a young girl she had always preferred books and movies that transported her to faraway places. They always seemed to enchant her and help break the boredom of her life out in the country.

"Tatiana," she said.

"Tatiana?"

"Yes," she replied and turned to look back at Banning. "Don't you think it suits me now?"

"I love it. I honestly do. It really does reflect the new you. It's strong and seductive. "

She thought about that for a moment. It did fit the new her. She *was* Tatiana and she knew what she wanted. She no longer needed anyone's approval or permission.

She laid the coffee cup on the table and untied the belt that was cinched around her waist. She slid out of the robe, letting it fall to the floor.

Banning gazed longingly at her naked body. It was the first time he had ever seen it in this light. She was exquisite and the curves of her body were accentuated by the sun shining through the living room window.

"Do I excite you, Keith?"

"You most certainly do, Tatiana."

The name hung in the air for a moment, as if to mark the occasion.

Yes, something had changed, she thought. Even standing here naked before him she knew who was ultimately in charge. She felt young, vibrant and alive. Now she was going to live the life she had been denied for too long.

"Show me how excited I get you, Keith," she said in a low, seductive voice. "And when we are done we will begin plotting our revenge."

CHAPTER THIRTY-FIVE

Floyd Bennett Field, Brooklyn, New York City
Tuesday, January 29th, 2013 – 11:10 a.m.

"Alright people, listen up," Chief Julie Preston said to the group of officers gathered in the large conference room.

"We don't have much time so I am going to make this as quick as possible," Maguire began. "There are four confirmed terrorists within the confines of Brooklyn and Queens. In addition to these individuals, each of them is in possession of a vehicle and a backpack, both of which have been outfitted with explosives. The vehicle is remote detonated by a cell phone; the backpack has a plunger detonator. We will be hitting all four locations at the same time. That gives us about forty-five minutes to formulate our tactical plans and be on scene."

The room erupted with murmurs and hushed conversation.

"I know this is a shitty situation, but the explosion last night was a premature detonation. The longer things go on the more likely the story about the gas leak will collapse and the greater the risk that we will lose these individuals. We are going to keep this simple people. The entries will all be coordinated to take place at the time when all four men should be engaged in afternoon prayers. It will give us the greatest opportunity to potentially catch them off-guard. The code word I will give to initiate entry will be *Leap Frog*."

"Do we even know if they are going to be there, sir?" someone asked from the back of the room.

"We have eyes on the locations and will know if anyone has come or gone. But when we pull up you are going to be going in blind."

Around the room officers exchanged looks with one another that ranged from grimaces to uneasy acceptance.

"Truck Seven," Maguire continued. "Hook up with Chief Preston, she has your information. Truck Eight, see Inspector Ryan. A-Team, you're on me. FBI SWAT, see Agent Silverman. OK people, this is the job we have been given so let's get it done."

As the assembled officers began to break into groups, a figure approached Maguire.

"Commissioner, I'm Sergeant Patterson from the A-Team, what are we looking at?"

Maguire spread the folder, and its contents, on the table in front of him. Among the papers was a grainy 8x10 photo of Yusef Sayeed.

"This is our target, gentlemen," Maguire said. "Yusef Sayeed is a bomb maker from Libya and has been on numerous countries' watch lists. For the moment, ignore the fact that he somehow still managed to get into this country undetected. Right now you men have been tasked with him because, of the four targets this morning, he is the biggest threat we are facing."

Unlike regular ESU trucks, whose daily duties include responding to a wide variety of emergency calls, the A-Team's sole focus is to execute high risk entries and apprehension. In that respect they are like the highly honed tip of the ESU spear.

"Our source says Sayeed has constructed each of the devices in play. He is highly proficient in his trade and has survived this long without being caught or blowing himself up. In the parts of the world he normally frequents that speaks volumes about the man."

"What about a layout of the location?" asked one of the cops.

"All we know is that it is residential. The informant's information on the locations is sketchy at best. He'd only been to each place once and seemed confused about the layouts. The best thing you will have going for you is surprise, speed and violence of action."

"Weapons?"

"The informant has seen AK's in the past, so I don't have anything that would lead me to believe that they are not armed with conventional weapons. Those pale in comparison with the bombs that will be sitting right outside. Remember, these are all remote detonators and there is also the potential that the backpacks might be close by as well. Bottom line is if they have something in their hands take the shot, if it turns out to be the remote for the television, oh well, it sucks to be them. The Commissioner and I already have to go to two funerals, we don't want to go to anymore, understood?"

"Crystal clear, sir," replied the sergeant.

"Ok, Sarge, gather your equipment and mount up."

Throughout the room the various teams were alone in discussion, formulating where each man and woman would be in 'the stack' for the dynamic entry.

Maguire walked over to where Nikki Ryan was talking to Kurt Silverman.

"Well?" he asked.

"Everyone's as ready as they can possibly be," said Silverman.

At that moment they were joined by Julie Preston.

"We ready, Chief?"

"Yes we are, Commissioner," she replied.

"Okay, each of you goes with your respective teams. Highway will lead the motorcades to the staging point. After that, God help us all. Good luck people, see you on the other side."

Outside, the ESU and FBI SWAT officers began to suit up. Ballistic armor vests and Kevlar helmets were removed from their storage compartments and put on. When they were done, they removed their weapons, which in this case were predominantly Heckler and Koch MP-5 submachine guns along with a few M-4's. Magazines were checked and secured, before each of the officers began mounting up in their vehicles.

When everyone was ready the Highway Patrol cars began moving out. The massive motorcade began making its way through the streets of Brooklyn. As they drew nearer to each destination, a segment of it would break off to continue on to their respective target destination. Finally the last of the original motorcade was alone and heading toward the Brooklyn / Queens border.

Maguire stared out the window of the Suburban watching the houses pass by. His thoughts reflected back to the images of the previous night.

Was there another tragedy out there awaiting them? he wondered.

He shook the thought from his mind.

It would be different if he was going in with them, but his role was relegated to the sidelines and it just didn't suit him. He was used to being the one going through the door, just like the men in the truck in front of him. He knew what they were thinking; everything else had shut down for them and the only thing that mattered was the target that lay ahead.

"Two minutes out, boss," Torres said.

"Thanks, Mike," Maguire said and looked down at his watch. It was five minutes till twelve.

At least we won't have to wait long to see how this plays out, he thought.

His was the last motorcade and the furthest target. He knew the three other teams were already waiting. They would all be pre-staged four blocks away from the targets so that when the order was given they would have the same amount of time to get to the locations and hit them simultaneously. The observation groups would be on site and direct the responding officers to the exact location.

The motorcade made its way east on Atlantic Avenue and a moment later crossed over into Queens. They pulled off the main thoroughfare and began weaving through the local streets before coming to a stop.

Maguire looked down at his watch, the second hand moving in a steady countdown. He removed the phone from his pocket and called Rich.

"You ready?" Stargold said.

"On scene and just about to give the order," James replied.

"Good luck and God speed. I'll be waiting for your call back."

James ended the call and picked up the portable radio. For this operation they were on their own encrypted channel. He watched as the second hand silently edged its way toward the top. When it hit twelve he keyed the transmit button.

"Car Two to all units, *Leap Frog, Leap Frog, Leap Frog.*

CHAPTER THIRTY-SIX

Washington Navy Yard, Washington, D.C.
Tuesday, January 29th, 2013 – 11:59 a.m.

"You have reached James Maguire. I'm sorry but I can't come to the phone right now but if you leave your number I will get back to you as soon as possible."

"Paddy, it's Saint, hey call me when you get this. Heard you guys are up to your eyeballs in shit right now, but I have that information you asked me about."

Special Agent Tom Moore sat in his office in the Russell-Knox Building on the Marine Corps Base in Quantico, Virginia.

Word had already spread through government Intel channels that the 'gas explosion' in New York City was just a cover story. Then a series of phone calls were made requesting any and all information on a series of foreign nationals. It didn't take a rocket scientist to figure out something bad was going down.

Moore laid the cell phone down on his desk. He hoped everything was going well for his old friend, but he resigned himself to the fact that, whatever it was, he would have to wait just like everyone else. He reached over, removing the newly assigned case folder from his in-basket and began reading it.

Lovely, he thought. *Paddy's chasing terrorists and I'm investigating a Navy chaplain ministering to women of the night.*

CHAPTER THIRTY-SEVEN

Southampton, Suffolk County, N.Y.
Tuesday, January 29th, 2013 – 12:00 p.m.

Genevieve was lying on a flat bench, staring up at the ceiling and desperately trying to catch her breath. She could feel the sweat pooling on the vinyl bench beneath her.

She couldn't remember the last time she had been in the gym with Melody but, judging from the pain she was currently in, it had been awhile.

Suddenly she found herself staring into the face of Melody who was looking down at her with concern.

"You're not going to die on me are you?" she asked.

Okay, Gen thought. *Maybe it was just sarcasm masking itself as concern.*

"Go away, I hate you."

"You'll love me when Gregor is drooling at you in your bikini this summer."

"What does it matter if I am paralyzed?"

"Okay, you're fine," Melody said. "Let's go chicky, ten more reps."

"I'm going to die."

"That's nice; you'll make a very attractive corpse. C'mon, wimpy, give me ten more."

Genevieve reached up, taking hold of the Olympic barbell and slowly lowered it to her chest, before raising it back up.

"ONE," Gen screamed out.

Melody fought the urge to laugh at her friend. She always had a flare for the dramatic. Deep down inside she envied her, the girl never seemed to gain an ounce, while all Melody had to do was *look* at a cookie and she gained a pound.

Genes could be so fickle, she thought.

When she was done spotting Genevieve, the two women moved over to the heavy bag that hung in the far end of the gym. She helped Melody put her gloves on, then stood and held the bag as her friend began her routine. At this point she needed the rest.

"So do you have anything coming up that I need to know about?" Gen asked as she watched Melody pummel and kick the bag.

"Charity fund raiser with Mary next month," Melody said before driving her forearm into the bag and then kneeing it hard enough to move Genevieve backward.

"Oooh sounds fun," Gen said with a laugh.

"I thought you'd think so," Melody replied. "That's why I got you a ticket as well."

Genevieve rolled her eyes. "I'm busy."

"You don't even know the date. Besides, you need to give Gregor at least *one* night of rest."

"Oh, he doesn't seem to mind," she said with a smile.

"I bet he doesn't."

As Melody continued to work out her frustrations on the helpless bag, she couldn't help but think back to when she and James had first met. She understood completely what she was going through, but that didn't mean she wasn't going to have some fun at her friend's expense. Especially since this was only payback for what Genevieve had put her through.

"Yeah, but I miss you too. It seems like forever since we had a girl's night out."

"Okay, fine," Gen said. "It's so hard being this popular sometimes."

Melody's body twisted and she struck the bag with a roundhouse kick that violently snapped it loose from Genevieve's hands.

"Yes, but you make it look so easy," Melody said with a laugh.

When she was done, she leaned back against the wall trying to get her breathing back under control. "Alas, poor Gregor is just going to have to spend the evening with himself."

"Eh, knowing him and James, I bet they wind up spending the evening, over at Peter's range, shooting things."

"Boys and their toys," Melody replied.

"Oh, speaking of *toys*," Gen said. "I got an email from Pope. He said that they were getting ready to go into full development on the prototype equipment for the infantry version of *Dragon's Breath*."

Melody got up, walked over and grabbed a bottle of water from the table.

"Do you know if they have a trial date set yet?"

"Nothing firm as of now, but realistically I'd say we are looking at late summer. They just worked out the ammo issues on the weapons system."

"That's great news," Melody replied. "I need to schedule a trip out to Wyoming next month. I've spent too much time in Maryland doing paperwork. What I really need to do is get out there and go see the things I am reading about."

"Tell me when you want to go and we can get the hell out of Dodge and go have some fun."

"Sounds like a plan. Now what I really need is a hot shower."

The two women made their way to the door and stepped out into the hallway where they were immediately met by the two security men.

"Ah, back to reality," Melody said as they headed toward the elevator.

CHAPTER THIRTY-EIGHT

Queens, New York City
Tuesday, January 29th, 2013 – 12:01 p.m.

Maguire watched as the unmarked, dark blue truck pulled up in front of the target location and stopped. Even before the truck had come to a full stop he could see officers disembarking from the rear. Ahead of them, a plainclothes detective from the Joint Terrorism Task Force was directing the ESU cops toward the door.

The seven man team moved down the long driveway, preparing to stack up at the door that led to the basement apartment. As they went along they passed by the grey Nissan Pathfinder which, they were all too aware, held enough explosives to end their day very quickly.

From the other side of the street, two officers made their way over the backyard fence, taking up positions that gave them access to one of the apartment's rear windows.

One of the JTTF Detectives had managed to gain access to one of the neighboring homes and had relayed a rough description of the layout. The rear room would most likely be the living room and provide the most open area for prayers.

In the backyard, an officer stood with a large sledge hammer while the other held a flash bang. When the signal, *Geronimo*, was given by the entry team leader, the officer would break the window with the sledge hammer and the other officer would toss in the flash bang. The small black cylindrical device weighed in at just over 8 ounces. But what it lacked in size was made up for in sheer power. When detonated, the device emitted an intensely loud *bang*, in excess of 170 decibels, along with a blinding flash of light that clocked in at over one million *candelas*. The immediate effect to anyone in range of the detonation would be disorientation, confusion, loss of coordination and balance.

At that point, their part of the mission would effectively be over and their immediate fate would be in the hands of the entry team. They would remain at their location and maintain the rear security in the event someone managed to sneak out.

At the doorway, one officer held the screen door open while another stood by with the battering ram, a 50 pound steel tube with handles, which, when applied properly, would breach the old wooden door and reduce a large portion of it to splinters.

One by one, the members of the entry team clasped the shoulder of the man in front of them with their left hand, indicating they were ready.

When Sergeant Patterson felt his shoulder being gripped he knew the team was ready. He reached up and keyed the transmitter for the radio.

"Geronimo."

For a moment time stood still and then all hell broke loose.

As the one officer swung the sledge hammer into the small basement window, the other officer followed just behind, rolling the device through the still shattering glass. It was a routine they had practiced regularly and today that precision paid off. They each turned away, anticipating the concussive blast that would follow.

Around the side of the residence, the battering ram came down on the door just as the glass was shattering in the back. The old wooden door shattered under the force, sending a shower of splinters and metal shards, from what used to be the lock, in every direction. At that same moment the flash bang went off, and the house rocked violently. Even as the ram was coming backward, the officers were already through the doorway and making their way down the stairs, into the narrow hallway.

Clearing a known location is hard. Clearing one, in which you do not know the physical layout, is excruciatingly slow. But it is times like this that training takes over and the ESU officers began making their way down the long narrow corridor in one fluid movement.

As they approached each room, one officer would go through the door, turning left, and followed by another going right. The remaining officers would move forward. When they cleared the room they would rejoin the stack as it proceeded along. It was like a well-choreographed, deadly ballet.

As the leader officer reached the end of the hallway he caught motion to his left.

Yusef Sayeed had been kneeling in prayer when the device had come through the window. Instinctively he knew what was happening and had turned toward the cell phone lying on the small coffee table. It was a fatal miscalculation as it put his face directly in front of the device when it went off.

The concussive force threw Sayeed violently back against the living room wall. He tried to find the phone again but, since he was temporarily blind and deaf, he did little more than flail aimlessly on the ground.

He knew it would only be a matter of seconds before they would be on top of him. He remembered setting the small backpack next to the television stand and lunged for it. Sayeed knew he had only one chance and as his body collapsed against the floor, he felt the familiar material brush against his hand.

He desperately tried to orient himself to the position of the bag, his hands furiously struggling to locate the small plunger discreetly hidden in the side pocket. He felt the cold metal of the zipper brush against his fingers and shoved his hand inside.

The .9mm bullet plunged into the base of his head, where the spine meets the bottom of the skull. As it tore through the skin and into the vertebrae, the bones shattered, ripping into his spinal cord and severing it. The signal running from Sayeed's brain to his hand, instructing him to depress the plunger, abruptly ended at that moment. A fraction of a second later his life would also end as the bullet made its way into his brain where it lodged deep within his frontal lobe.

The entry teams that entered the apartments belonging to Qaseem Bin Khalid and Nazir al Mahdi both met with a much different outcome.

Qaseem bin Khalid was taken without a struggle when he was caught, in what could best be described as *in flagrante delicto*, with a nineteen year old Middle East and Islamic Studies major from NYU.

When the officers had come through the bedroom door Qaseem's true colors came out and he tried to shield himself with the naked woman's body. It ended with her being led out of the bedroom screaming while he lay on the floor, curled up in a fetal position, two darts embedded in his back, their wires dangling from the Taser held by one of the officers.

On the floor of the bedroom closet they found the backpack, and on the shelf they located the cell phone in a yellow manila envelope hidden behind some clothing.

Nazir al Mahdi was still sitting in front of the television set playing a video game when the flash bang came through the window. When the device went off, the concussion shattered the television screen which peppered Nazir's face with glass fragments. Later, while being treated at the hospital, it would be determined glass had shredded his left eye leaving him partially blind. If there had ever been any inclination on his part to fight back it was lost in an instant.

A search of his apartment discovered the backpack and cell phone secreted in the suspended ceiling in the bathroom.

In the end, it appeared that neither man was as devout a Muslim as Yousef Sayeed. Fortunately, for all concerned, it also seemed that neither of them had the same operational security knowledge that the other man had regarding keeping the explosives close at hand. Or maybe it had just been that neither of them was overly eager to leave this world in the pursuit of their seventy-two virgins.

A mile away, the story was playing out slightly different.

Bashir Al Karim had just turned the corner when he watched the large, matte black, armored truck come to a stop in front of his house. A group of men in green tactical uniforms exited the vehicle and began heading toward his apartment.

The man instinctively dropped to his knee, setting his grocery bags on the ground, as he pretended to tie his shoe. As he watched, the men stopped just outside his door. Bashir adjusted the collar on his jacket, pulling it up higher and lowered the brim on the hat he was wearing. He grabbed the bags and stood back up, turning slowly, before heading away in the opposite direction.

What had gone wrong? he wondered. *Had someone been caught? Had they talked?*

So many thoughts were running through his head now, but he knew he needed to get away, to put distance between himself and the apartment. He moved quickly, but with a sense of purpose.

Do they have my picture?

Bashir had hated this location to which he had been sent. He didn't fit in and he hadn't felt safe. Not in the physical sense but in the way that he wasn't around his own people. Now he realized he was alone, cut off from the rest. He needed a place to go that he could fit in and give him time to figure out what had gone wrong.

Where do I go now?

He made his way south toward Fulton Avenue. He spotted a fast food restaurant and went inside. After ordering his food he took up a spot near the front window where he could see the entire street, in both directions.

It struck him as odd that he wasn't so much afraid as he was angry. This had been his opportunity to avenge her death and it had been snatched from him. He needed to find out what had gone wrong. Was it just him, or were the others in the same position? He wished he could get in touch with Yusef, he would know what to do. The others were idiots but Yusef had been in situations like this before. The only problem was he had no way to contact him.

He had gone out for a walk early that morning. He grown tired of being cooped up in the house and needed some time to think and reflect. He had long ago stopped praying when his wife had been taken from him. Instead he walked and had a conversation with *Allah*. It wasn't that he was being disrespectful it was just that he struggled with it all. In his heart he felt it would be disrespectful to pray without meaning it. As a result, the cell phone, his only method of communication, was now lost.

Fortunately for him he carried the money in his wallet so he had the means necessary to make his way back to Boerum Hill, where they had been previously staying. He didn't dare go back to the old apartment, but there were other options available to him. With its large Muslim population he felt at home. He also knew there were others who would be sympathetic to his situation and would provide help to him.

Bashir stayed in the restaurant for about an hour watching the street. When he was sure that there was no surveillance going on he left and made his way west on Fulton. He had walked about a mile when he flagged down a passing cab.

"Atlantic Avenue and Bond," he said and sunk back against the seat.

The trip was not long, but what it lacked in distance it made up for in culture. From where he had begun, the local food stores had advertised *Jerk Chicken* and the strains of reggae music could be heard. It was all uncomfortably foreign to him. Now, as they moved west he began to see the familiar Arabic script begin to appear more frequently on the shop windows. Before long it appeared in the majority of businesses and he felt himself begin to relax.

The taxi came to a stop. Bashir leaned forward and paid the driver. Once again he stepped out into the cold, but at least this time he felt as if he was not alone.

As the taxi pulled away, Bashir crossed the street and headed directly toward the *Al-Haffah* Bread Shop.

CHAPTER THIRTY-NINE

Tatiana rolled over onto her stomach, lifting herself up onto her forearms.

"So tell me, Keith, where do we go from here?"

"Well, my love, it depends on what you mean by *we*," he replied.

"Don't go and pull a Clinton on me. I think I have made myself perfectly clear as to what my feelings are on all of this."

Banning smiled. It certainly had been an interesting turn of events. One he had never imagined or could have planned. He had to admit, it was nice having someone like her to not only pass the time with, but to have a kindred spirit with as well.

"Maguire is not vulnerable now," he said. "Nor are the ones closest to him. We are going to have to approach that issue with a bit more care and planning."

"What do you have in mind?"

"He is clearly focused on other issues right now. It might not be a bad idea to shake him up a bit. Play some mind games with him for the time being while we redirect our attention elsewhere."

Tatiana perked up at that. She raised herself up onto her elbows and brought her hands up so she could rest her chin on them. She began to playfully cross her ankles back and forth.

"Ooh," she said mischievously. "And where, pray tell, would that take us?"

Keith stared at her for a moment, his eyes slowly looking downward to gaze between her arms at her breasts. He felt mesmerized by her at times. As often as he had seen her naked body, he was still amazed at the physical effect she had on him.

"I'm up here," she reprimanded him.

"Sorry, but you seem to bring out the worst in me, my dear."

"Oh I wouldn't go that far," she replied. "I kind of like bringing out the bad boy in you. It has the most *wonderful* effect on my body."

"I'm so happy that I can tend to your needs, Tatiana."

"So where do we go from here, Keith?" she asked.

"Now we begin to play a game of misdirection."

"This sounds intriguing. Go on."

"A while back I liberated a pair of your panties."

"You know, I had wondered about those. I was going to ask you what the reason was, but I had begun to sort of fill in the blanks on my own."

"I'd be lying if I told you the thought hadn't crossed my mind, but I actually did have other plans for them."

"A souvenir?"

"Yes, in a way. But not for me," he replied. "I thought I would give Jimmy something new to think about."

"How exactly does that help us?"

"Well, it reminds him that this isn't simply a matter of him against me any longer. In a way I think he struggles with not knowing your fate. This will cause him to have to become more cautious in his pursuit of me."

"Why do you think that?"

"I've always felt that he would just prefer killing me outright, and that could be done effectively at a distance with a well-placed snipers bullet. However, knowing that you *may* be alive, he is going to have to dismiss that thought and settle for something a bit more up close and personal.

"Interesting idea," she replied. "But how do we accomplish this without alerting him to exactly where we are?"

"We go on a road trip."

"I'm liking the sound of this more and more. Not that I don't think it's beautiful here, but I'm starting to give the trees names."

"Well, first I thought we would take a ride over to New Hampshire and drop off our little care package. Then from there we take a trip back home and see if we can't convince your old flame to take a ride with us."

She thought back to the last night she had seen Lena.

It had been the opening night for her art gallery in Keenseville. It had been such a wonderful night for her. So many well-known artists and supporters had attended that it was almost packed to capacity. It was probably one of the few times in recent history that a business in Keenseville had that many people inside it at one time.

After everyone had left, the two of them had collapsed onto the couch with a bottle of wine. They sat like two school kids as they shared their individual recollections of the evening. She remembered laughing and just feeling her entire body relaxing after the long months of preparation.

Lena had been more than just the manager of the art gallery. The two women had been *discreet* lovers ever since high school, even before James had left. In fact it was that relationship that had caused everything in her life to go wrong. She had lost James over it and had been blackmailed into a relationship, and ultimately marriage, with that bastard Paul Browning.

Keith had fixed the Paul Browning issue rather well, she thought.

Although any end for that miserable prick should have been just as long as the hell he had put her through. Now only one score remained to be settled for her, and that was Lena.

The issue with James was between Keith and him. She didn't have any hard feelings with what had happened with James. No, her issues began and ended with Lena. She had come into her life at an awkward time. She was vulnerable and Lena had used her. In fact Lena had latched onto her and reaped the benefits of her success.

Now Lena had it all. Everything that had once been hers was now in the hands of the woman who had turned her back on her and now it was time for a day of reckoning.

"Tatiana?"

"Hmmm, yes," she said. "I'm sorry, my mind just wandered off for a bit."

"Are you sure you're alright?" he asked.

"Oh, I'm better than alright, my dear, I'm positively giddy in anticipation of what's to come."

"Oh, and what might that be?" he asked.

"Why, revenge, silly," she said with a smile.

Banning smiled back at her.

"Well, we will have to move quickly on this," he said cautiously. He watched her face trying to see if there was any change.

"Not too quickly, Keith," she replied. "As much as I am giddy with anticipation of my impending reunion, I don't exactly think that I would go unnoticed in Keenseville."

"We'll go at night," he replied.

"I think we should, but I also think I need to work on my appearance a bit. Don't you?"

Banning hadn't given any thought to altering her looks. Still, her idea had merit.

"What do you suggest?"

"I've always had a thing for blondes," she replied. "Maybe it's time for me to cross over to the *wild* side. I think we go wherever it is that you want to and I get a new look along the way."

'Wait a second," he said suddenly. "What do you mean impending reunion? I thought you just wanted to get revenge."

"Honey, you have a lot to learn about women," Tatiana replied. "You have your ideas of revenge and I have mine. Personally, I have decades for which to make up. But don't worry; you'll be happy to know that I'm a girl who loves to *share*."

He had been worried. Worried that something had changed in her. He couldn't help but wonder if the mention of her former lover might have triggered something deep inside her. Banning didn't think he could handle losing her now, not after all this. But he didn't detect any of that now.

"I love your thinking," he replied.

"Mmmm, if you love that then you're going to love this. Remember when I said I liked bringing out the bad boy in you? Right now I need the bad boy back inside me."

"Anything you desire, my love," Banning said as he watched her climb back on top of him.

CHAPTER FORTY

Southampton, Suffolk County, N.Y.
Tuesday, January 29th, 2013 – 1:17 p.m.

Melody looked down at the phone buzzing on the desk and snatched it up when she saw James' name appear on the screen.

"Is everything alright?" she asked.

"Yes," James replied. "Well, almost everything. We only got three of the four."

"So there's another car bomb out there?"

"No, we have all the cars and the backpacks," James explained. "The fourth guy just wasn't there when the team hit the apartment."

"What are you going to do now?"

"Well, we have two in custody to interrogate, so we will start there."

"Two?"

"Yeah, one of them apparently wasn't the surrendering type."

"Oh my God, are all your people alright?"

"Yeah, all the ops went off flawlessly. I'm really proud of them."

"I take it you probably won't be home for dinner."

"No, I think it's safe to say that I'll be burning the midnight oil."

"I can't even offer you a place to stay," Melody said. "I gave up my only apartment in the city."

"No, don't worry about it," he said. "I'll be fine. I have the couch in my office."

"I hate the thought of you sleeping there," she replied.

"It's okay, angel. Trust me, I have slept on worse."

"I bet you have," Melody said with a laugh.

"Besides, just think how happy you'll be to see me when I get back."

"Oh I'm counting down the minutes as we speak."

"I figured as much. Anyway, I just wanted to give you an update. I'm getting ready to go and have a discussion with one of our new *guests* so I might not get a chance to talk for a while."

"Go have fun, cowboy. I'll talk to you later.

Melody ended the call and put the phone on the desk.

She stared out the window, looking at the waves crashing against the shoreline.

So this is my life now? She wondered. *Casual conversations about interrogating terrorists while one of my companies begins field testing a better way to wage war?*

Things had certainly taken a much different direction than she had ever imagined. As a young girl growing up in Queens she had dreamt of normal things like friends, love and family. Making friends for her was never really a difficult task. The love and family thing hadn't quite worked out nearly as well.

Early on, she had decided that she needed to find a suitable replacement for those things and so she began focusing on her education, a move that had the unlikely benefit of introducing her to Professor William Oswald Thomas. It was Professor Thomas who had not only recognized the gift she had, and steered her along the best path for her to achieve her dreams, but who also took on the role of surrogate father. A role cut entirely too short by his untimely death while she was away at the Wharton School of Business.

Here she was, an inner city kid whose counsel was now sought out by both presidents and global business leaders alike. But all of that no longer mattered to her. The only thing she was focused on was the man who had stolen her heart so many months ago.

It had seemed so easy to her before, encouraging James to take the job. She knew that he loved police work and she wanted to see him happy. The private security consulting he had been doing was fine, and it did keep him busy, but Melody loved watching his eyes light up when he would talk about his days spent *on the job*, as the cops called it. So when the job had come up she thought it was the perfect way for him to return to something he loved. Now she wondered if she was cut out for it. She would always support him, but today brought the reality of being in a relationship with a cop crashing down on her doorstep. At the end of the day, they might not come home.

Melody chased the thoughts away. She picked the phone up and called Mary.

"I was just about to call you," Mary said, when she answered the phone. "I just realized that this is your *first* big incident."

"Yeah, I just got off the phone with James."

"How are you handling it?"

"Honestly? I don't know, Mary," Melody replied. "Things seem so surreal to me. In the past, stuff like this always happened somewhere else, to someone else. I hate to admit it, but I have led a fairly sheltered life."

"It isn't easy and I would be lying to you if I said it would get better. You always worry, it never really goes away."

"I was hoping you'd have more encouraging news for me."

"Well, if it's any consolation it does validate how you feel about them, because if you didn't love him you wouldn't put up with this."

"I hadn't thought about it that way."

"When James got shot I thought that was the end. I wanted Rich to get out. We had some, how do I put this? Extremely *colorful* exchanges."

Melody chuckled at that mental image. Her, Mary and Genevieve had shared quite a few 'girl's nights' fueled by Gen's now infamous piña colada's. After a couple of drinks Mary's *wild child* side definitely came out. She was after all half Sicilian on her mother's side.

"So how did you resolve that?"

"James did," she replied. "When he first got out of the hospital he stayed at our house. One day we were talking and I asked him what he planned to do. He looked at me like I had three heads. He said he was going back to work."

"He is stubborn."

"I thought that was it at first, but then he said something that made me rethink everything. He looked at me and said 'Mary, it's what we do.' For people like him and Rich it's not a job, it's a calling. I can't understand it, because I could never do it. I'd be terrified of having to face my own mortality on a daily basis. But for men like James and Rich, they do it in spite of the risks."

This was something Melody had never considered before. Cops were only something that you hated to see in your rearview mirror, or were never around when you needed them.

"So how did you come to terms with it?"

"Would you leave the operations of your business empire to the care of your gardener?"

"No," Melody replied quizzically.

"Why?"

"Well, not to be rude, but the truth is they wouldn't have the first idea about what to do."

"Think about it this way, Melody, there are people that are walking around today that would have died in those terror attacks if it hadn't been for our men. Not everyone could have done what they did and I'm glad that they are out there doing that job."

"What if one day their luck runs out?"

"I won't lie to you," Mary said. "It is something I wonder about every time Rich leaves the house. But he and James both rushed to the Towers when they were attacked. They both came home, while a lot of others didn't. I guess at the end of the day that is something that God only knows."

Melody couldn't argue with her. She had known a lot of those lost and none of them had been first responders. Mary sensed her dilemma.

"Let me ask you a question, Melody. Do you think he knows what he is doing?"

"Yes, I do."

"Then kiss him goodbye in the morning, say a prayer, and know that he is good at the job he does."

"Thank you, Mary."

"No need to thank me, hon," Mary replied. "Cops have each other to lean on, and so do we."

"You need to go into motivational speaking."

"Hey, I'm a mom. I can fix anyone's problems other than my own children's. To them I'm just an idiot that they have to humor."

"Please, I don't think I would ever be able to be a parent."

"Good Lord, girl, can you imagine just how gorgeous yours and James' baby would be?"

"Oh stop it," Melody said with a laugh. "I swear you and Gen really need to stop spending so much time together, she's rubbing off on you."

"Speaking of my *sister-in-crime*, did you tell her about the charity event?"

"Oh yeah, she is absolutely ecstatic."

"Uh huh, I figured she would be. Did she already have an excuse as to why she couldn't make it?"

"Yeah, she said something about her being busy in February."

"Girl is quick on her feet."

"The girl is something, that's for sure," Melody replied. "But I told her she didn't have a choice."

"It actually should be a really good night."

"I've already reached out to all my contacts, most of the ones who are local have indicated that they plan on attending. Those who had scheduling conflicts said they would be making a sizeable donation."

"That is fantastic," Mary said.

"Well, I think a lot of them understand that providing quality shelters for women and children is an important issue that is unfortunately grossly underfunded."

"I spoke with one of the board members, they were wondering if we might get together to tour one of the facilities and do a photo op for them."

"Sure, just let me know when you want to do it."

"Alright, as soon as I get more information I will let you know."

"Thanks again, Mary, for the pep talk, I needed it."

"I'm here for you anytime."

"Okay, talk to you soon. Give my love to Rich and the girls."

"Will do, bye."

Melody ended the call and laid the phone back down on the desk.

It had helped her to hear Mary's take on all of it. She did love James and she would do anything to support him, even if that meant accepting his new role. She didn't have to like it, but she would do it. After all, like Genevieve so often pointed out, behind every great man was an even greater woman.

CHAPTER FORTY-ONE

Bayonne, New Jersey
Tuesday, January 29th, 2013 – 3:16 p.m.

Maguire watched the interrogation of Qaseem bin Khalid through the other side of the window. Hamadi had indicated that he had been the group ring leader, although Maguire had a hard time believing that this man, kid really, could shave by himself let alone lead a terror cell. Still, Maguire reminded himself that he had also been young once as well, and he certainly knew what he had done for *God* and *Country*.

The man doing the interrogating was clearly CIA. His long brown hair and thick beard gave Maguire the impression that he had only recently returned stateside from the *sandbox*. Right now the man was explaining to Qaseem the perils that awaited him, should he decide that he was *stronger* than they were.

"Here's the thing, Qaseem," said the man sitting across from him. "You *are* going to talk; it's just a matter of how much pain you want to put yourself through before you do."

Immediately behind him, two other men stood wearing balaclava masks. They had already been in the room when they had brought Qaseem in. Maguire knew all the psychological tricks. If this had been Yusef Sayeed he doubted whether they would have had an effect on the man, but on Qaseem bin Khalid they were taking a toll. The kid was unhinged by it all. He repeatedly looked back trying to see what the men behind him were doing.

"I demand to speak with someone from the Saudi government."

"Yeah, well sorry, sport, that's just not going to happen."

"I am a member of the Royal House of Saud, I have rights."

"I don't give a flying fuck if you're the king's piss boy; right now the only people who know you are here are the people in this room. None of whom I think are going to give two shits if your sorry ass ends up on a C-130 with a one way ticket to the *Dark Prison*. I hear Kabul is lovely this time of year, although I doubt you'll ever actually see it."

The kid looked on the verge of tears. Clearly this is not how he had envisioned things. It was one thing to come to the United States with thoughts of Jihad, but often those thoughts passed quickly when one began to enjoy the freedoms and amenities of the west.

However, those same freedoms and amenities were now nothing more than fleeting memories for Qaseem. The fate that awaited him was much more ominous. If he continued to play hardball he would more than likely get shipped off some place for enhanced interrogation. That was normally the first trip in what would eventually end at Guantanamo Bay, Cuba. It wasn't a matter of if the kid would talk; it was just a matter of when he would talk. Maguire didn't give him much of a chance.

"I demand to see the Ambassador; I demand to be sent back to Saudi Arabia."

"Yeah, well you be sure to remember that wherever you wind up. It's always nice to have happy memories to fall back on," the man said mockingly. "Unfortunately for you, Qaseem, the odds of you ever seeing palm trees and sexy, burkha clad women again are between zero and never."

"I demand to……."

The interrogator made a dismissive gesture with his hand. The two men who had been behind the kid suddenly moved forward and placed a hood over the kids head. When they had secured it they dragged him, and the chair he was in, backward toward the far wall.

The chair itself was lifted up and placed on top of an inclined bench that had been brought into the room. Qaseem was screaming frantically now, begging.

"You're gonna want to shut up now, kid," the man said.

Whether Qaseem had not heard the man over his own screaming or simply chose not to listen was immaterial. The only thing that mattered was that he only succeeded in aiding his captors.

One of the men stood behind Qaseem, holding the hood down firmly, while the other picked up the water jug and began pouring it over the hood, into the man's mouth and nose. Qaseem's body spasmed and he began making gurgling noises as the water cut off his screams.

While the term *water boarding* is a relatively new one, the actual act itself dates back to the Spanish Inquisition. The key to any interrogation technique is learning that it is a double edge sword. No one can withstand torture indefinitely. But there is a fine line between getting the truth from the person you are interrogating and being fed information that is useless simply because they are trying to make the pain stop. That is where the individual interrogator comes into the picture.

After fifteen seconds the man had Qaseem's chair lifted up and the hood removed.

The kid sat there, wide eyed and gasping for air.

"Okay, Qaseem, let me try to explain this to you so that you understand. That was your introduction to our upcoming question and answer session. What you just experienced was what I would call *mild discomfort*. If you didn't like that, you are really not going to like where we go from there. Are you following along with me?"

Qaseem vigorously nodded his head in the affirmative, still trying to regain his breathing.

"Excellent," the man replied. "Then we are off to a good start. So tell me, Qaseem, do you know who Khalid Sheikh Mohammed is?"

Again Qaseem nodded.

"Great. Well let me just tell you that the good Sheikh went through that nearly two hundred times and in the end he still gave up everything. Hell he gave up stuff we didn't even ask him about. What I'm trying to get at is, you can either be a hero or you can be smart. If you want to be a hero we can just pack your ass up, ship you over to Kabul or Kosovo and water board your ass till you tell us what we want to know. Or, you can be smart, sit here like a gentleman and talk to me. Maybe you'll get a trip to a Shangri-La prison in Kuwait and have one of your uncles buy your freedom. Are you getting where I'm going with this?"

"Yes," replied Qaseem nervously.

"Outstanding, boys bring Qaseem here up to the table."

The two men lifted the chair up causing Qaseem to immediately tense up, a terrified look gripping his face. The men carried the chair back to the table and set it down.

"How many others were there in your cell?"

"Four," Qaseem replied.

"Who was your contact?"

"Hamadi. That's all I know, I swear."

"How did you contact him?"

"I didn't. We met when we first got here, at the apartment in Brooklyn. We told him our needs and he took care of it all. He came back when he was finished."

"What was the plan if there was a problem?"

"We had a number to call. We'd give them our name and then Hamadi would call us back."

"What was the number?"

"I don't know, it's written inside the phone book at the apartment."

"I'm going to ask you about the others now. First, who is Bashir Al Karim?"

"I don't really know, only that he is Afghani," Qaseem answered. "He never spoke much, only to Sayeed. He is the one you should ask."

"Yeah, Sayeed's having a conversation with some other gentleman right now," the man said, lying to Qaseem. "So Bashir never said why he was there?"

"No. the only thing I know about him was a conversation I overheard between him and Sayeed. He said something about his wife being killed. Russians, I think."

"So why were you there?" the man asked. "You look like you have a bit more on your shoulders then the normal jihadists."

"Honor," the kid replied.

"Oh, I've got to hear this story."

At that moment the door to the control room opened suddenly.

Maguire turned from his chair to see three men in suits enter the room. They had the look of feds.

"Kill the audio now," said the first man. "Who's in charge?"

Silverman stood up. "Who the hell are you?"

"I take it that this is your op?"

"Yeah, and you didn't answer my question."

The man turned to one of the others who had accompanied him into the room. "Go and secure the prisoner."

"You touch that man and you'll be in jail after they release you from the hospital," Silverman said.

"Easy there tiger," the man replied. "I'm Dean Oliver, State Department, Diplomatic Security Service. I'm the Special Agent in Charge of the New York Office."

"I hate to break the news to you, but this is a criminal investigation, so why don't you just head back to New York and I'll send you a memo when we are done."

"I'm not going to get into a pissing match with you, junior. The man you are holding is a member of the House of Saud, as in the Saudi Royal Family. Your interview, or whatever the hell you think you're doing in there, is over. He has full diplomatic immunity."

Maguire felt the cell phone in his pocket buzzing. He reached in and removed it, scrolling through the messages. The newest one was from Rich.

"State Department is heading to your location to take custody of suspect. Someone tipped off D.C."

"Are you fucking kidding me? This cocksucker is a terrorist!" Silverman said.

"It's above my pay grade, and I know damn sure it's above yours. Let him go."

"Ain't gonna happen. He's our only source...."

"I suggest you call your boss," the man replied, cutting Silverman off.

Maguire stood up and walked over to Silverman, putting his hand on the man's shoulder.

"Let it go, Kurt."

"I'm sorry, who are you?" Oliver asked?

Maguire turned and looked at the man. "Sorry, that's above your pay grade as well, Agent Oliver."

James turned around and grabbed his jacket from the back of the chair, making his way outside.

When he was clear of the warehouse building he removed his cell phone and called Rich.

"Where are you?"

"Right now, standing in the parking lot," James said. "Mind telling me what that was all about?"

"We're still trying to figure that out ourselves," Rich replied. "Not sure if it was someone from the Bureau or if one of the record checks popped in some database. Bottom line is the bells and whistles started going off somewhere."

"For them to grab this kid that quickly means that the call came from pretty high up. Not to mention that the *SAC* made this little house call personally."

As Maguire watched, Dean Oliver escorted Qaseem bin Khalid from the warehouse toward a group of Suburban's that were gathered in the parking lot. Before he got into the vehicle the kid raised his hand up and waved, a smug smile on his face.

"Well, whoever he is, he has pretty influential friends."

"Something's not sitting right with me on this one, Rich."

"What are you thinking?"

"This kid is a little pissant. He's so far down on the list of royals that his only shot at a wearing a crown is when he goes to Burger King for his birthday. Someone didn't want this kid talking to us. More importantly, they knew he wouldn't last."

"I can't argue with that assessment," Rich replied. "So where does that leave us?"

"Out in the cold with very limited options."

"That's not really what I wanted to hear James."

"I didn't say we were out of options, I just said they were limited."

"Do I want to know?"

"I couldn't tell you even if you did," James replied with a laugh. "Well, actually I could but then…"

"Yeah, I know, but then you'd have to kill me, right?"

"For now I'd suggest having the folks over at Counter Terrorism and Intel start beating the bushes. We know Bashir Al Karim is on the run with limited resources. I'd suspect he is going to try to locate someone to provide him sanctuary. They are going to need to start listening for anything that can help us track him down."

"I'll have them get on it right away. I also have to talk to McMasters and let him know what just happened."

"I'd recommend he start bitching and moaning to some of his politician friends and see what happens. Some of the local ones aren't going to be too happy that the feds just waltzed a terrorist out of an interrogation."

"He's got a 4:30 press conference at which he's going to come clean on the car bomb."

"They'll rake him over the coals a bit. The Press Corps never likes to be shut out of anything. He'll weather it okay."

"Yeah, I'm just hoping they don't turn us into piñatas."

"That's why you get paid the big bucks now."

"Let me know if you hear anything."

"Will do," James replied and ended the call.

He paused for a moment, and reached into his jacket pocket and pulled out the other cell phone he carried and dialed a number from memory. The phone rang a few times and went to voice mail. There was no greeting, just a beep.

"Mother, this is Paddy. I need some help."

CHAPTER FORTY-TWO

Northern Maine
Tuesday, January 29th, 2013 – 6:36 p.m.

Tatiana sat across the table from Keith, as the two ate dinner. Outside the wind was howling, but the snow had finally subsided. The clouds that had lingered for the past few days had passed and the moonlight reflecting off the snow bathed everything in a bright eerie glow.

"So tell me when we get to take this road trip you are planning, Keith."

"Well," Banning said, as he looked up from the plate. "I thought we would head out at the end of the week, give the roads a chance to clear up a bit. I checked the forecast and it looks like we should have clear weather for at least the next ten days."

"You know what I would love to do?" she asked.

"No, what?"

"I would really love to stop at an old bookstore along the way. I miss reading. I've thought how wonderful it would be to curl up on the couch, in front of the fire, with a good book."

"I'm sure we can find a place."

"That would be really nice," Tatiana replied. "By the way, have you given any thought to how we might go about snatching Ms. Marx?"

"Oh, I imagine that shouldn't be too difficult," Banning replied. "So much time has passed, that I would think that old habits have begun to kick back in once again."

"How do you know so much about things like this, Keith?"

"My parents," he said. "I guess you could call them the original *preppers.* I grew up being taught everything about survival. It was a wonderful learning experience and yet, at the same time, a very lonely one."

"Why do you say that?"

"Well, they were what I would call introverted, to say the least. They used to say the less people knew about us, the safer we were. I think the only reason they let me go to school was because they didn't want the truancy officer knocking on the door."

"Was it a hard life?"

"I didn't really think so. I learned a lot. Wilderness survival, weapons, improvised explosives, self-defense, languages, you name it, and I learned it, even chess. I rather enjoyed it, it made me feel different, better. But then my father warned me never to let anyone know. He said in weakness there is strength."

"What do you mean?"

"In the face of a formidable foe, everyone prepares their defenses. They don't let their guard down. But with a weak opponent, no one bats an eyelash. They don't see the threat, don't take it seriously. Before they know it, they have allowed their opponent to get too close and it is over."

"That's a very interesting point of view. It must have been a very challenging, but fulfilling, childhood. Where are your parents now?"

"Dead," Banning said, matter-of-factly, as he cut off a piece of steak and ate it.

"What were they like? Anything had to beat mine."

"My father was a hard man, but it was just the way he was raised. He was from Idaho. He had served in the Army in Vietnam and was wounded. He had met my mother while he was convalescing at a military hospital. She had volunteered there as a *candy striper.* I think that's what they used to call it. After he was discharged they got married and they moved to Keenseville. He took the money he had saved, bought a little farm and they did their own thing.

"Sounds glorious to me," she replied. "I don't think my parents knew I was even around half the time. Daddy was too busy with all his clubs and trying to be a big shot in a small town. Mom, well, she was too busy being the perfect little housewife. I wonder if that's why I even got involved with Lena, cause it was the wrong thing, the bad thing."

"Parents serve a useful purpose for a time. Then you move on, learning new things for yourself so that one day, if the opportunity presents itself, you can pass it along to someone else."

"Can you teach me?"

"Anything can be taught, my love, as long as the student is willing."

"Oh, I think you know just how willing, and able, I am, darling," Tatiana replied. "I want to know how to do it all. I don't want to be a hindrance; I want to be an asset."

"Well then, after dinner I suggest we start with the basics and progress from there."

"Okay," she replied. "But getting back to my original question, how are you planning on getting her?"

"After you went missing, she continued to operate the gallery. I would venture that it is something that she will not give up doing. So that actually presents two possibilities. We either snatch her when she is coming or going from the gallery or the apartment."

"Well, there is a spare key for the door to the apartment. I had a bad habit of forgetting my keys in the store, so I had an extra one made and put it in those little holders with the magnet. It's on the underside of the metal staircase."

"I like how you think," Banning said with a smile. "Go on, tell me your idea."

"If she is still operating the gallery, she'll be in there early in the morning, around eight. Most of the other businesses in the area don't open till nine. Once she is in we can slip into the apartment and wait for her to come back."

"A man and a woman going in through a side door are too noticeable," said Banning. "But a woman going in, especially an attractive blonde haired woman, would look absolutely normal."

Tatiana knew where he was going. Lena was blonde and the two women were about the same height. To the casual observer she could easily pass for her, especially with the right hair coloring.

"That's a great idea," she said. "Only problem is I don't see too many stores around here to pick-up what I need."

"Which is precisely the reason why I stock up on such things," Banning said. "You just never know when a need will arise."

"You do think of everything, don't you?"

"See, another lesson for you. Always remember to think long term. Not what you need now, but what you might need a year or two from now. This way you minimize the chances of being caught off guard."

"What would I ever do without you?"

"I suggest you pay very close attention, dear, because the learning curve can be deadly if you make a mistake."

"Well then it is fortunate I have a great teacher," Tatiana replied. "Now that we have the entry figured out, what do I do once I am in there? Don't get me wrong, I am sure at first she will be positively thrilled at the little homecoming reunion, but I don't imagine she'll stay that way for very long. How do you suggest that I deal with that?"

"Sumagethonium," he replied.

"What's that?"

"A little something I picked up on one of my shopping sprees at a veterinary office a while back."

"So what does it do?"

206

"It's a variation of a drug used to treat humans. It is a short term muscle relaxation and paralytic that enables a doctor to perform an intubation of the trachea. However, this version is used by vets to euthanize horses. The general difference is that it is administered intramuscularly, as opposed to an IV drip in humans, and the paralytic action is much quicker, maybe 10 seconds. Here is your first lesson my love, never risk getting caught stealing from a people hospital that which you can easily liberate from an animal hospital."

"What do I have to do?"

"Wait till the moment is right, and then inject her with it. As long as you don't overdose the patient, it's fast but short lasting. Once you administer it, I'll come in. Then we'll get her tied up and remove her."

"Mmmm, sounds downright *delicious*."

"My love, you sound like you're getting excited."

Tatiana smiled coyly as she played with the remaining food on her plate.

"Let's just say that you have opened my eyes as to just how fun being bad can really be."

"And does that include being bad with your *former* lover?"

"Are you jealous?"

"Maybe a bit," he replied. "I guess I am more curious than anything else."

Tatiana laid the fork down on her plate and took a sip of wine. She stood up, walked over to Banning and sat in his lap. She wrapped her arms around his neck, and stared into his eyes.

"There is nothing for you to be jealous of," she said softly. "You know exactly how to satisfy every deep desire I have and then some. Just think of this as a sort of *foreplay*. I get to play, you get to watch and then, if you are so inclined, you can even join in."

Banning smiled at her.

"You know what, my love, you were right, it does sound *delicious*."

CHAPTER FORTY-THREE

Southampton, Suffolk County, N.Y.
Tuesday, January 29th, 2013 – 7:54 p.m.

Genevieve walked into the salon zipping up her fleece coat.

"Where are you heading off to?" Melody asked.

"I'm just going over to spend some time with Gregor," Gen replied. "He had to work late, so I figured I go over there and watch his beloved *Fussball* with him. His hometown team is playing tonight."

"And you're wearing only that little jacket?"

"I'm only walking out to the car, *Mom,* I'll be fine. What are you going to do?"

"Probably read for a bit and then go to bed early. James is working late so he is going to stay in Manhattan tonight."

"Want me to cancel?"

"Are you serious? I'm a big girl, I'll be fine. Besides I should probably get to sleep early, anyway. We have that meeting tomorrow."

"Yeah, I won't be too late. Having him only a few doors down does have its advantages."

"Go have fun," Mel said. "I'll see you in the morning."

"Oh I will," Gen said with a wink.

She made her way out the front door and into the cold. The wind had picked up, and it was one of the few times she was happy about the security arrangements. As she climbed into the back seat of the waiting car, she was hit by a blast of hot air.

"Are you still going to Mr. Ritter's house?" the driver/security man asked.

"Yes, Mark," Gen replied.

A few moments later the car pulled up to the gate outside Peter Bart's house. The driver lowered the window on the Mercedes and pressed the intercom button.

"Yes?" a voice, with a heavy Nordic accent, asked.

"Ms. Gordon to see Mr. Ritter," the driver replied.

"Wait for the gate to open fully before proceeding. Follow the lighted pathway."

Once the gates opened and the bollards in the roadway ahead of them lowered, the car made its way up the driveway. Other bollards remained in place preventing the vehicle from traveling anywhere else on the property. Despite the frigid temperatures outside, she could still see the security patrols walking along the perimeter of the building.

As the car pulled up, the front door opened. A man stepped outside and opened the car door for her.

"Good evening, Ms. Gordon," the man said, extending his hand to help her out.

"*Guten Abend,* Kurt," she replied.

"Ah, your German improves with each day."

"I have a good teacher."

The man laughed. "He's from south Germany, he speaks like a farmer."

Like Gregor, Kurt Schiller was a former policeman who had served with the Berlin *Spezialeinsatzkommando*, the German capital's police SWAT team.

When the team members weren't needling each other as to who the best operator was, they picked apart one another's nationality, agency, favorite drink or sports team. It was like a frat house filled with stone cold killers.

Once inside the house, Genevieve took off her jacket to reveal the red sports jersey she was wearing with the large 1FCK on the front, the logo of the *1. Kaiserslautern Fussball Club.*

"*Ach du lieber, Gott im Himmel,*" the man cried out. "I cannot believe he has corrupted such a fine young woman. When you want to watch a real team, you come over and we can watch *Hertha Berlin.* Then you will see a real team."

"Ha!"

Genevieve and Kurt turned to see Gregor walking down the stairs.

"If you think *Hertha Berlin* is a real team then I need to immediately remove you from duty tonight because the cold has made you delusional."

"Ja, ja," Kurt said, waving his hand dismissively. "Good night, Genevieve."

"Good night, Kurt."

Gregor walked up and hugged her.

"I've missed you, *mausi,*" he whispered in her ear.

She could feel his arms around her, holding her tight. It felt so good to her, made her feel so safe and secure. She had a reputation as a formidable businesswoman and yet with him, none of it mattered. To him she was just Gen or *mouse,* as he had affectionately begun to call her. She had the most adorable way of scrunching her nose that made him envision one of those cute little mice in the cartoons.

"Would you like something to drink?"

"A glass of wine would be nice."

"I have some upstairs I think you'll enjoy."

He led her upstairs to his room and opened the door. Each of the men on the security detail had their own rooms in the house. But like most places, there was a caste system here. All of the junior members of the detail had their rooms in the basement while senior ones had rooms on the first floor with a view. The second floor was reserved for the officers, of which Gregor was the head. In accordance with his position he had two rooms, one of which served as an office/living room.

Genevieve sat down on the large leather sofa while Gregor went to get her drink.

"How long has the game been on?" she asked.

"Only a few minutes," he replied. "Where did you get this shirt from?"

"You like it?" Gen asked.

"Of course, but I didn't expect to see you wearing something like this."

"Well, I figured if I was going to get into the spirit of watching your team play, I should go all out."

"I think you will soon become the number one fan for Kaiserslautern."

He walked back over and handed her the glass before taking the spot next to her.

"Mmmm, this is really good."

"I thought you would like it," he replied. "It comes from a small vineyard near where I grew up."

"I'd love to go there one day," she replied. "I think it would be so interesting to see it with someone who grew up there."

She set the glass down on the coffee table in front of her. She curled up on the couch, laying her head on his chest and felt his arm wrap around her shoulder.

"Oh I think you would really like it."

"Tell me what it is like."

"It is quite beautiful," he replied. "It's a small town called Bernkastel-Kues, on the Moselle River. Rolling hills, mountains. It's a very nice place to grow up. Most of my family is still there."

"Do you miss it?"

"Sometimes, yes," he replied. "Then I think of you and realize if I was there I would not have you in my life."

Genevieve looked up at him and rolled her eyes.

"You're just saying that."

"No, it is the truth," Gregor said, as he leaned over and kissed her head.

Genevieve closed her eyes and smiled. Inside, she knew he was telling the truth. It made her feel special to think he felt that way about her. She'd never made the time to have a man in her life. It wasn't something she had ever felt she was missing out on. Now, she was happy that she hadn't because she would get to experience all of the important *firsts* with him.

"You said that most of your family is still there. Do you stay in touch with them?"

"Yes, the computer makes that very easy."

"What are some of your favorite memories?"

"In the summers my friends and I would climb the hilltop to explore the ruins of Burg Landshut, the castle that overlooks our city. We would pretend we were knights. At Christmas my mother would take me to the *Weihnachtsmarkt* in the old town. It has small holiday shops and everything is lit up. It is very special."

"You have a real castle? Is it an old city?"

"Bernkastel? Yes, very old. The first *Lord of Bernkastel* was in the early 11th century. Before that, there was a Roman fort in the 4th century. The earliest known people lived there around 3000 B.C."

"Oh my God, I didn't realize it was that old."

"Yes, a bit more history than the United States."

"I guess when you compare five thousand years to two hundred, there really is no comparison."

"Yes, in many places in Germany today you can still see remnants of fortifications from Roman times. One of the most famous is the *Porta Nigra*."

"It would be neat to see some of those historical sites."

"Perhaps one day we can run away for a few days when no one is looking," he replied with a laugh.

She felt his body tense up and he pumped his left fist in the air.

"What happened?"

"The Red Devils just scored!"

Genevieve stared at the screen, watching several men celebrating on the field.

"That's their nickname, the Red Devils?"

"Yes, it's actually *die Roten Teufel*."

"Wait a minute, what time is it in Germany?"

Gregor looked down at his watch. "Just after three o'clock in the morning."

"So you mean they're not playing right now are they?"

"No, this was from last night in Germany."

"So you can tape this and watch it later?"

"Yes of course, but I thought you wanted to watch and learn about soccer."

"Oh I do want to watch the *Roten Teufel's*," she replied, as she got up from the couch.

She turned around to face him, straddling his legs, and sat down in his lap. Genevieve wrapped her arms around his neck, and stared into his eyes.

"I just thought you might be interested in a different kind of *Red Devil* tonight," she said, playfully shaking her head and letting wisps of her auburn hair fly around.

Gregor looked up at her and smiled.

"You know that you are much more interesting to me than anything on television, *mausi*."

He had never felt this way about anyone before. He thought he had been in love once and had rushed into a marriage that was destined for failure. In retrospect he realized that it wasn't really love that he had felt, more like *friends with benefits*. When the friendship part of the relationship ended, he had hoped that they could have an amicable divorce since there were no children involved. However, that was not to be.

A vindictive ex-wife and an angry ex-father-in-law, who was also a high ranking member of the German judiciary, did not make for a good combination. He could have handled the private issues, but when it began to affect his assignment with the *GSG-9,* he knew the handwriting was on the wall. He could not have his operational status disrupted because his ex's father wielded influence with high ranking members of the *Bundespolizei.* While his officers knew it was not right, there was little they could do to help him.

In the end, he decided that leaving Germany was the best move personally and for his career. So when the opportunity came up to work for Peter Bart he had jumped at it. Little did he know how that decision back then would lead him to this place.

He thought back to that first night he had met her. How he brushed the hair away from the injury to her head and treated her. He had never left her side since. Every time he saw her, she made his heart beat faster. Now, for the first time in his life, he knew what it meant to be in love.

Gregor wrapped his arms around her, and pulled her close to him. He felt her lips on his, felt the warmth of her touch. He moved his hands slowly across her body, caressing her gently.

With each passing second the intensity grew. Playful kisses turned into a passionate embrace. She turned her head slightly and he pulled her hair to the side, kissing her neck. He heard her moan softly, pressing her body hard against his.

Genevieve leaned back slowly and stared at him. She took in everything, as if seeing him for the first time. From his close cropped blond hair, to his captivating blue-gray eyes, to his chiseled jaw.

She reached down, grabbing the edges of his tee shirt and lifted it up over his head. He raised his hand up and let her pull it free. She laid it down on the couch and stared at his chest. She had seen men who worked out before, but he was different. He didn't have *show* muscles. His were the result of training for something potentially deadly. Like a modern day gladiator. It was simultaneously sensual and terrifying.

He opened his mouth to say something, but she held a finger up to his lips and slowly nodded her head. There was nothing to say at this moment.

Genevieve reached down and slowly removed the jersey, dropping it onto the couch next to his shirt. She then removed her bra and laid it on top of the shirt.

She lowered herself down to his chest, feeling the warmth of his skin against hers, and wrapped her arms tightly around him.

Gregor stood up, lifting her in his arms, and carried her off to the bedroom.

CHAPTER FORTY-FOUR

1 Police Plaza, Manhattan, New York City
Tuesday, January 29th, 2013 – 8:36 p.m.

James sat at his desk looking through the latest reports on the initial explosion and the subsequent raids.

Overall the operation had been an incredible success, all four remaining car bombs and the suicide packs had been recovered. Three of the four terrorists were no longer an immediate threat, although Maguire didn't think that they had seen the last of Qaseem bin Khalid, and the remaining one had gone underground.

Still, while the majority of those involved in today's operations were patting themselves on the back, Maguire found no reason to celebrate. The funerals for the two anti-crime officers were scheduled for Monday.

Just then, Nikki Ryan poked her head through the doorway.

"Got a minute, Commissioner?"

Maguire glanced up from the papers.

"Nikki, sure come in, grab a seat."

Ryan took a seat across from the desk.

"What's on your mind?"

"I just wanted to check-in with you and see what else you wanted me to do."

"Unless you have something pressing to do back at CTB, I'd like to keep you here with me for a bit longer to act as my intermediary in this. You've been there since the beginning and I don't see any reason to change something that is working well."

"No, I'd be happy to stay on."

"I want you to keep on top of the search for Bashir Al Karim, keep everyone on point. I'd like to be able to do it myself, but I have too many other fires to deal with. So tag, you're it," he said with a laugh.

"My pleasure."

"If you have any issues with anyone you let me know. If you need any people, make the phone call and have them transferred under my authority. When you're done, give the names to Chief Hernandez and have them do a personnel order to make it official."

"Yes sir, anything else?"

"Well, I'd like to tell you that you did a helluva job today," Maguire said. "It could have gone wrong in so many ways and yet it went off as if we had the luxury of planning for everything. That couldn't have happened without you, so thank you."

"I really appreciate that, sir," Ryan replied. "It was refreshing to see someone at the top actually taking the lead for once."

Maguire smiled. "I might get accused of a lot of things, Nikki, but not being present when the shit hits the fan, will never be one of them."

"Well, if you don't mind, I think I'm going to call it a day and try to get some sleep."

"No, that sounds like a fantastic idea. If I'm not around and something pops up, you have my cell number; call me anytime."

"Will do, sir," she replied and stood up. "Have a good night."

"You too, Nikki," he replied.

When she had left the office he pulled out his cell phone and called Melody.

"Hey, cowboy," she said.

"Hey, angel, what are you doing?"

"Sitting in bed reading. What about you?"

"Sleeping at my desk reading," James replied.

That elicited a laugh from her.

"It's not too late to come home."

"I would, but I still have a ton of stuff to sort through and a bunch of calls to make."

"Anything you need me to do?"

"Clone me?"

"Funny you should mention that," Melody replied. "I vaguely remember Gen once suggesting we do that."

"Do I even want to know?"

"Probably not, although right now it seems like a splendid idea to me. I miss you."

"I miss you too, angel. I figured you two girls would be enjoying the evening."

"I got dumped for Gregor."

"Were we that bad?"

"Probably," Melody said. "Do you need me to send you anything? Clothes? Food?"

"No, I'm okay. I think I'm going to order in Chinese."

"When do you think you are going to be back?"

"I'll most likely be home tomorrow afternoon. I just want to be here in the event anything pops up between now and the morning."

"I understand," Melody said. "I have to go to a board meeting in New Haven tomorrow. I should be back before dinner."

"Gen going with you?"

"Yep, and the wonderful security team," she replied sarcastically. "I have so many people running around here I'm thinking about starting a softball team next summer."

"Ok, Gen *junior*, gotta go"

"Love ya, cowboy."

"I know you do," Maguire replied. "Love you too, angel."

Maguire set the phone on the desk and began going through the notes he had taken during the interrogation of Qaseem bin Khalid. Just then, the phone on the desk rang.

What the hell is this, Grand Central Station? He wondered.

Maguire looked at the phone and saw it was Rich.

"Shouldn't you be at home?" he said, answering the call.

"I could say the same about you. I'm not paying you overtime, am I?"

"I'm dedicated," James replied. "Actually I keep getting the feeling that I'm missing something in all of this."

"I'm too friggin' exhausted to even think, you wanna crash over at......, well I guess in reality it's your place, isn't it?"

Maguire laughed. "No, it's Melody's, and I have a comfy couch here."

"Speaking of which, when are you going to put a ring on that?"

"Seriously? We just disrupted a terror plot and you're quoting relationship advice from Beyoncé?"

"Just keeping it real."

"You need to go home and get some rest *old* man," Maguire said. "And for the love of God, stop listening to the music on Sophie's iPod."

"Good night," Rich replied. "Call me if you need anything or something else happens."

"Will do."

James stood up and stretched. He walked out of his office and into the main room. Most of the regular staff was long gone.

"You need anything, Commissioner?" asked Detective Luke Jackson, a member of the evening security detail.

"Actually yes, I could use a recommendation for a good Chinese food place."

"No problem," the man said, opening the file drawer on the desk. He pulled out a manila folder that held an assortment of menus and selected one, handing it to Maguire. "House of Beijing, my personal favorite."

"They deliver?"

"I'll go and pick it up."

"Shouldn't you be getting ready to head home?"

"I volunteered to stay, just in case you needed to go anywhere."

"I appreciate that, but I'm probably just going to be camping out here all evening."

"Not a problem," Jackson replied. "I got my patrol guide and I'm studying for the sergeant's exam."

"Smart man," Maguire replied as he looked over the menu. "I'll take the #10 and a coke. Get whatever you want."

He handed the menu back to the man along with a fifty dollar bill and headed back to his office. He sat down and once again began going through the papers on his desk.

After a while he realized that he was just going through the motions. He needed to walk away and get back to it when he had fresh eyes. Maguire remembered the phone call he had missed earlier and called Moore back.

"What do you know?"

"More than you apparently," the man replied. "How'd that shit work out this morning?"

"It's a cluster fuck, Saint."

"Then you should feel right at home."

Maguire laughed. "It does feel like *déjà vu*, all over again."

"Well, I hate to rain on your memories, but you might have more problems on the horizon."

"Banning?"

"If that's what we are calling him, yeah."

"What did you learn?"

"I had a secret squirrel buddy of mine do a bit of digging on those names you gave me, seems like your little friend might have a sick sense of humor."

"Go on."

"Theodore A. Zinchenko."

Maguire remembered seeing the name on the list associated with a credit card.

"Ok, I'll bite, who's Theodore Zinchenko?"

"My source thinks the name is an *homage* to Feodor Alexeyevich Zinchenko, who was the son of Alexi Zinchenko. Daddy Alexi was decorated three times, Hero of the Soviet Union, under *Uncle* Joe Stalin. Anyway, Alexi sired a bunch of kids, including a son, Feodor. Zinchenko also had a friend, Nikita Khrushchev. It seems that during the battle of Stalingrad, Alexi saved the old man's ass."

"Interesting story."

"Oh, it gets better," Moore said. "Seems Comrade Khrushchev had a little 'get to know your western military neighbors' program back in the early 60's. They shipped out families to keep an eye on *interesting* military bases. One of the participants was…"

"Feodor Zinchenko."

"Give that man a cigar," Moore replied. "At that time Feodor was a junior Lieutenant in the Army and had himself a wife, Yulia. Alexi, who was now a Major General in the KGB, saw the political hand writing on the wall. Khrushchev was beginning to lose his grip on the power reins, so Alexi put a bug in the old man's ear. Next thing you know, Feodor and his wife are put into the program."

"Where did they end up?"

"Charming little town called Plattsburgh, home of a United States Air Force, Strategic Air Command Base."

"*Sonofabitch!*"

"Pretty much sums it up."

"So what happened to them?"

"I guess when Khrushchev had the rug pulled out from under him by Brezhnev a lot of the program participants thought they'd get yanked back as well, so most of the Indians went rogue and left the reservation. It didn't take long for the feds to round the majority of them up. But a few, like your friend Banning's folks, were a bit more resilient."

"You're just a little ray of fucking sunshine today, aren't you, Saint?

"Just another service I provide to old, washed up, frogs."

"Washed up, my ass," Maguire said with a laugh. "If you hear anything else get back to me."

"Will do, brother," replied Moore, "and, Paddy,.."

"Yeah?"

"Watch your six."

"*Hooyah.*"

Maguire ended the call just as Detective Jackson knocked on the door.

"Food's here, Boss."

"Let's eat in the conference room, Luke," Maguire said. "I need a change of scenery."

CHAPTER FORTY-FIVE

Northern Maine
Tuesday, January 29th, 2013 – 8:41 p.m.

Tatiana sat in front of the long bench down in the bunker and slid the top cover back on the AK-47 rifle, hearing the audible click as it locked in place.

"Very good," Banning replied. "Honestly, I've never seen anyone pick that up so quickly."

Tatiana set the rifle on the bench and removed the blindfold.

"Not to be rude, but it seems so simple to me."

"Well, it was designed with the Soviet soldier in mind. Remember, they needed to be able to use the weapon and repair it in severe conditions, like arctic weather or in rugged mountainous terrain. With the large gas piston, bigger clearances between moving parts, and the tapered cartridge design, the gun can endure large amounts of foreign matter without failing to cycle. But you must also remember that this reliability comes at a cost of accuracy. Know your weapon, know your target."

"Going under the principle that *nothing* is infallible, what if the gun should fail?"

She was smart Banning had to admit. He would never have guessed in a million years that the refined woman he had brought here would turn out to be this person sitting in front of him. She seemed a natural to this lifestyle, this mindset.

"Then you have to be prepared to transition to a side arm."

"What do you recommend?"

"That depends on what you plan on doing with it and whether you can conceal it."

He walked over to the storage cabinet and removed a small plastic box, setting it on the bench in front of her. Tatiana opened it up to reveal a small Walther PPK.

"It's so small," she replied as she picked up the handgun.

"It's a .380 caliber, what the Germans called a 9mm *short*. Always think of it as a backup weapon. It does not have the power of a 9mm, so keep that in mind. If you have the option of carrying something larger do so, but if you need to have something that is discreet, it will do the trick."

"How does it operate?"

"Lower the lever to the down position. That's the safety. Then press the small button on the side which will release the magazine," Banning explained. "When you are done, draw the slide back."

Tatiana did as she was instructed, setting the magazine on the bench and drawing the slide back. A small brass round ejected from the barrel and landed on the bench.

"If you are firing the weapon and the magazine is empty, the slide will lock back. Put another magazine in, pull the slide back and let it go forward on its own."

Banning picked the rifle off the bench and walked back to the storage unit to put it away.

Tatiana picked up the magazine, slapped it into the handgun and racked the slide back. She flipped the lever into the safety off position.

When he turned around she was standing there, holding the gun in her hand. They stared into each other's eyes for a long moment until a smile crossed her face.

"God that's a helluva feeling," she said as she flipped the safety into the off position. She removed the magazine, laying the gun on the bench and topped off the magazine with the loose round. When she was done she turned and put it back in the box.

"Did you like the way it made you feel?"

"Oh yeah," she replied, a smile on her face. "It's very, empowering, and that gun is sexy as hell."

"Not as sexy as you," Banning said. "But the two of you are a very fine match."

He reached up, removed a box of ammunition and set it on the bench. He took the gun from the box and removed the rounds from the magazine, along with the one in the chamber.

It had, after all been a test.

The rounds were dummies, made to look and feel exactly like regular factory rounds, but the primer and powder charge were both inert. Even though he believed in *his* heart that her affection was real, he needed to know, once and for all, where *her* heart was. Now that he knew, he handed the gun back to her.

"Silver tip hollow points," he explained. "They are much better in terms of stopping power. Load it up, it's yours."

Tatiana looked at him. "Are you serious?"

"Yes, you'll need to be able to defend yourself. Keep it on you at all times."

"At all times, Keith?" she smiled. "Couldn't that get a bit dangerous?"

"Love, that body of yours is *always* dangerous."

Tatiana laughed and sat down on the stool. "So when do I get to shoot?"

"Tomorrow," Banning said. "In the morning we'll take the snow machine and head down into the valley. Then afterward you also get to learn the joys of cleaning your weapon."

"So, what's next?" she asked.

"Now you study," he replied.

"Something fun, I hope."

"First aid," he answered. "If you are learning to shoot, you better know what to do if something goes wrong. Inevitably it will, and when it does, it will be at the worst possible time."

Banning reached up on the shelf, removing a thick binder, and laid it on the bench. Tatiana looked down at the cover. It read: *US Army First Aid Manual FM 4-25.11.*

"It's a bit dated, but the basic principles never really change."

He walked over and pulled a large green bag off a shelf.

"Medical kit; if you need anything more you should be at a hospital. Start to become familiar with everything so that if the need arises you don't panic."

"Can't we just go back to guns?" she asked.

"Once you start moving forward, you can never go back."

CHAPTER FORTY-SIX

1 Police Plaza, Manhattan, New York City
Tuesday, January 29th, 2013 – 9:28 p.m.

"Thanks for the company, Luke," Maguire said, as he put the take-out tray into the plastic bag.

"No problem, Commissioner," the man replied. "Actually it's the first time I've ever eaten in here. The last 1st dep didn't socialize with the *help*."

Maguire laughed. It was something he had experienced enough in his previous time with the Department. It was the mentality of some, who by virtue of a few good test scores, felt that they were somehow superior to those below them. Maguire knew that it was a flawed mindset.

"A boss, I used to work for a lifetime ago, once said to me 'remember that the toes you step on as you go up the ladder will be attached to the asses you have to kiss on your way down'. I always thought that was pretty sound advice."

"It would be nice to see that gain a foothold in the Department."

"Give us time, Luke, we've only been here a month," Maguire replied. "Now crack open those books."

Maguire made his way back to his office, stopping to grab a cup of coffee on the way. As he sat down at the desk his cell phone began to vibrate. There was no name or number displayed.

"Maguire."

"You rang my, son?"

"Mother, it's good to hear from you."

Mother was the term of endearment given to Special Warfare Operator, Senior Chief Petty Officer (SEAL) Roy K. Gentry, US Navy – Retired.

SCPO Gentry was a legend in the SEAL community and had once been Maguire's team leader. Gentry had served in both the east and west coast teams. He'd also had several combat deployments everywhere from Panama to Afghanistan, along with a number of places that remained nameless for security reasons.

After leaving the Navy he went to work for another government agency. Most people are familiar with the various national intelligence agencies like the CIA, NSA or DIA. The *agency* that SCPO Gentry worked for did not appear on any official government roster and did not report to the normal chain of command. They were a *black budget* agency, funded by six hundred dollar hammers and toilet seats, which reported directly to the West Wing of the White House.

"Sorry I couldn't get back to you sooner, I was otherwise *preoccupied*," the man said. "What can I do for you?"

"I have a bit of a problem and I need to get a peek, under the radar."

"Who's causing you stress?"

"I take it you know what happened here today?"

"Yep, we've been watching."

"I've got two thorns," Maguire said. "First is an Afghani national who goes by the name Bashir Al Karim. Word is that he might be an original Mujahideen. I need to know what's making him tick. Second may be a bit trickier."

"How so?"

"He might have some flags on his folder."

"Then it's a good thing we don't share the same folders as those other guys."

"This guy's name is Qaseem Bin Khalid. He's a Saudi. Alleged ties to the royal family. How deep is anyone's guess, although I don't recall too many royal family members being eager suicide bombers."

"How'd they slip you?"

"First guy managed to elude an FBI snatch and grab."

"Shocking," Mother replied.

"Eh, we were all playing against the clock with the shit end of the stick."

"Don't be going soft on me, Paddy."

Maguire laughed.

"Second guy was just getting introduced to the benefits of full disclosure when a bunch of suits from State Department showed up squawking about diplomatic immunity. They scooped him up and rode off into the sunset."

"Jesus Christ," Mother replied angrily. "What the hell has happened to this country? We're letting fucking terrorists walk, and giving them a courtesy ride to the damn airport."

"Political correctness runs amok. Can't violate our enemies' Allah given right to kill us."

"And people wonder why the folks don't trust the government anymore."

"So, you can see why I would prefer to operate outside the normal channels."

"Give me twenty-four hours and I'll see what I can shake loose for you."

"*Muchas gracias*, Mother," Maguire said and ended the call.

He reached up and ran his hands across his face. He felt tired. *Maybe Mother was right*, he thought. *Maybe I am growing soft.*

He thought back to his days in the teams, they seemed to be able to go for days without sleeping and then, when the op was over, go out and party for days afterward. It must have been the training. Back in BUD/S, during Hell Week, they went through five and a half days of continuous training. At most, he remembered only getting about four hours of sleep during the entire week. Yet during that same period, they ran more than two hundred miles and went through more than twenty hours of physical training each day.

Maguire picked up the coffee mug from the desk and took a sip. He began to gather up the reports and put them back in the folder. The last one was the grainy photo of Bashir Al Karim.

Where are you now? Maguire thought, as he stared at the photo.

CHAPTER FORTY-SEVEN

Brooklyn, New York City
Wednesday, January 30th, 2013 – 10:23 a.m.

Bashir Al Karim sat waiting outside the office of Imam Ali ibn Muhammed in the Al Azhar Mosque. Inside his friend from the bread shop was speaking on his behalf.

He could hear the muffled sounds of the two men conversing on the other side of the door. In the corner a clock ticked off each passing second.

The previous day he had returned back to this section of Brooklyn and sought out his friend Faisal Hakim. He had often stopped at the man's shop and they had become friendly over the past few months that he had been here. They came from different parts of Afghanistan, but a friendly face here was worth a lot.

After what seemed like an eternity, he heard the sound of the door opening. Faisal stepped outside and greeted his friend.

"He will speak to you now."

"Thank you," Bashir replied and walked into the office.

Imam Ali ibn Muhammed sat at the small table. He was an older man, certainly older than Bashir, and his face bore a hardness that Bashir had seen countless times in his native land. The lines were etched deep in the skin, as if done with a chisel, and he had a long beard that was now grayer than it was the natural color.

"*Salaam alaykum*," Bashir said to the man.

The man looked up at Bashir. "*Walaykum salaam*. Please have a seat. Faisal has explained your *delicate* problem to me. How may I help you?"

"I seek advice because I am lost and need direction."

"Do you still wish to continue your journey?"

"Yes, more than ever, but I lack the means that had been provided to me before."

"What you seek is not about the means, but about your desire to achieve the ends. Remember, jihad is an exerted effort in the struggle for self-improvement. What is it that drives your efforts?"

"Revenge," Bashir said.

The Imam looked at him for a moment longer, watching him, gauging the man's words.

"You have been wronged, I can see this clearly," he replied. "Revenge is allowed in Islam, but Allah prefers forgiveness. If you must act, you should seek justice, not revenge. In taking revenge you may find yourself being unjust."

"How will I know if my actions are just or unjust?" Bashir asked.

The Qur'an teaches us that 'retribution for an evil act is an evil one like it'. Whatever it is you seek, it must only be equal to the wrong you have suffered."

Bashir sat quietly, taking in what the man had said.

"Remember, Anger is from *shaytan*, the devil. If you must pursue jihad of the sword, then wait until you are no longer emotional and then think it over properly."

"Thank you," Bashir replied and stood up. "You have helped me to see the path I must now undertake. Before I was lost, because my journey was not a just a one. But now, *Allah* be praised, I understand what I must do.

"*Insh'allah*, all shall be well with you soon," the man replied. "It rests with Allah alone to show you the right path. I shall pray for you."

Bashir left the office and met his friend outside.

"Have you found your answers?" Faisal asked, as the two men made their way down the long hallway, toward the exit.

"Yes," replied Bashir. "Now I must pray and ask Allah to show me the path he has chosen for me."

"Well, while you wait for his answer you are welcome to stay with me."

"You are a good friend, and I am honored by your generous offer. But I cannot accept unless you accept my offer to work in exchange."

"What do you know about bread and baked goods?"

"Nothing about making them, but I know the ingredients come in big containers and I am not troubled by hard work."

"Then I think we have a deal," replied Faisal as he opened the door which led out to the street.

Bashir stepped outside and adjusted the collar of his coat.

Would it ever get warm again? he wondered.

CHAPTER FORTY-EIGHT

Northern Maine
Wednesday, January 30th, 2013 – 10:51 a.m.

"Have you ever driven a snow machine before?" Banning said, handing a key to Tatiana.

"Only during the winter months," she replied with a smile.

"You'll find it out in the shed. Get it warmed up and ready to go. I'll get the guns."

"Yes, sir," she replied and headed toward the front door.

Tatiana grabbed an old heavy duty canvas work jacket, that was a size too large, along with a fur lined hat and a pair of work gloves. She opened the door and stepped out into the snow.

The sun was shining brightly up above; the sky was clear and blue. It was the kind of blue reserved for picturesque mountain locales. She made her way to the shed and opened the door. Inside sat a two passenger snow machine. Tatiana walked around and thoroughly examined the machine. She got on, put the key in the ignition and turned it over. The engine roared to life and she pulled it out of the shed.

As she drove up to the front of the cabin Banning was just coming out carrying a rifle bag and an ammo box.

"You want to drive?" she asked.

"No," he replied. "You need to learn it all and that means everything."

He handed her a pair of goggles and strapped the ammo box to the small rack on the back of the machine. He then slung the rifle bag over his shoulder and sat on the back, wrapping his arms around her waist.

"Head out past the drive, where those pine trees are," he said, pointing in the direction he wanted her to go. "You'll see the path through the trees, just follow it."

"Hang on," she replied and hit the gas.

They headed down a sharp, *narrow* pathway, which was a nice way to say that there was enough space for the machine to navigate its way through the trees. At one point in the trip she had to slow down as she crossed a mountain road that ran up to the city of Rangeley. Fifteen minutes later the ground leveled off and they found themselves in an open area that sat adjacent to a small mountain lake.

"Do we shoot targets?" Tatiana asked.

"Not today," Keith replied. "Today is about just getting accustomed to the weapon."

"Couldn't we have done that back at the cabin?"

"Only if you wanted to run the risk of drawing attention to us," he said.

Banning removed the rifle case and laid it on the seat. He then opened the ammo box and removed one of the preloaded magazines which he handed to Tatiana.

"Remember how to load the gun?"

"Yes," she replied.

She unzipped the rifle bag and withdrew the AK-47. She inserted the magazine into the rifle till it locked in place and then racked the bolt carrier back, chambering a round.

"Very good," Banning replied, handing her a set of ear plugs. "Leave the goggles on and put these in. When you're done, pick out a tree, line up your sights, and begin."

"That won't make the environmentalists very happy."

"Don't worry, they'll find another tree to hug."

Over the course of the next hour Tatiana went through two dozen 30 round magazines and managed to *chop down* a medium sized birch tree.

"That was awesome," she said, after she had fired the last round.

"It was a good start," Banning said. "How did you like it?"

"It was pretty easy to fire, recoil wasn't as bad as I thought, but it can get a bit heavy after a while."

"Well, next time we will work on target shooting," he said, as he put the rifle back into the case and slung it over his shoulder. "But for now, let's go home and get some lunch. Then you get to learn how to clean it."

"And then what shall we do?" Tatiana replied as she got back on the snow machine and started it up.

"Then we plan our road trip, love."

CHAPTER FORTY-NINE

Maguire was sitting in the salon, going through some of the reports that Monahan had sent him, when Melody came through the door.

"Hey, cowboy," she said, tossing her coat onto one of the couches and taking a seat next to him. "Ya miss me?"

Maguire lowered the papers into his lap and looked over at her.

"More than you know," he replied.

Melody could see the seriousness in his face. Something was clearly troubling him.

"Aw, you're so sweet," she said, giving him a kiss. "What are you doing?"

"I was just going through some paperwork."

"Oh no, you're not going to start bringing stuff home with you now."

"Actually, this is from the state police. It's all the paperwork they have on Banning."

"Oh," she replied.

He could see the visible change in her. It was still a wound that had not healed. A wound Maguire was sure would not heal, as long as Banning was still alive.

Melody cuddled next to him, wrapping her arms tightly around his. She found comfort and security being next to him. She looked down and saw the papers in his lap, the top one was a photo of Banning, in uniform, standing with several other deputies, laughing.

238

"What's going through your mind right now," she asked.

"Honestly? The banality of evil," he replied.

"The *huh*?" Melody said. "You know better than to use big words on me after I have spent the day in board meetings. Pretend I'm Gen right now."

Maguire laughed for a moment, but his disposition turned serious again just as quick.

"During my life I have had the opportunity of seeing people at their absolute worst, *man's inhumanity to man*, to paraphrase Samuel von Pufendorf. There were times when I had to deal with someone who had lost all regard for human life. It is a very interesting experience, to say the least, and probably the reason why psychiatrists get paid so much money."

"You know how much I love history," he continued. "Every time and generation has their notable sociopaths, but I think Nazi Germany has a slight edge here. I remember once reading about the *Wannsee Conference* and how, over cognac, the fate of the Jews in Europe was decided. Aside from the actual act, what struck me as so incredible was the detachment from the topic the attendees actually had. It was as if they were discussing nothing more than reallocating resources. And yet, what it shows us is that human life can be reduced to that point."

"Well, that's what happens when you elect a madman to run a country," Melody replied.

"When most people think of Germany, during WWII, they assume that Adolf Hitler was the architect of the evil that pervaded the country. While I agree that he certainly holds a top spot, for me, Reinhard Heydrich was the real face of evil."

"Who was that?" Melody asked.

"Heydrich was an SS general who was in charge of the *Reichssicherheitshauptamt*. It would be the equivalent of the Department of Homeland Security, with a socially integrated, highly intelligent, sociopath in charge. The RSHA ran the state security apparatus, along with the criminal and secret police, the infamous *Gestapo*. He was also one of the architects of the final solution and earned the nickname *'the man with the iron heart'* from, of all people, Adolf Hitler.

"Sounds like quite a guy," Melody said sarcastically.

"You would think," James replied. "But there was another side of the man. You see Heydrich came from a well-to-do family. They had both social standing and were well off financially. His father was an opera singer, who had also founded the Halle Conservatory of Music, and his mother was a piano teacher. In fact, Heydrich himself was an accomplished violinist, exceptional student and athlete. By all accounts young Reinhard was a normal, if not a bit shy, young man."

"So what happens in a person's life that causes the switch to turn off?"

"Therein lies the question." Maguire replied. "How does a seemingly normal person, a husband and father, kiss his wife and children in the morning, and then head off to work to try to figure out the mathematics of killing an entire race?"

Melody shuddered. Trying to even begin to comprehend that was frightening in itself.

"And that's what you think Banning is, a socially integrated sociopath?"

"I think the bodies at his house were the ones he wanted to be found. I think the actual number is probably staggering. Yet you saw him, standing there in uniform, and a respected, well liked, member of the community."

"How could someone like this simply slip under the radar?"

"I remember when I was back in Intel. I had gone to a training session and there was an FBI agent there from the Serial Crime Unit. He said that at any given time, there are anywhere from 35 to 50 active serial killers in the United States. If they're lucky, they'll catch roughly five of them a year. But the remainder of them go undetected, and unrestrained, by the rest of society, until they either die of old age or just lose interest in killing."

"How do these murderers get away with it?" Melody asked, incredulously.

"First, you have to realize there is a difference between someone who kills in the moment, and someone who kills methodically," Maguire explained. "In truth, very few murderers actually get away with it because there is generally a motive involved. It can be fueled by a myriad of things such as money, love, or revenge. Then it just becomes a case of piecing together the puzzle. But in the case of the serial killer, the murders are often just random opportunities that present themselves. The pieces that connect them exist only in the mind of the killer. They can stop for a week or they can stop for years, and there is no discernable rhyme or reason why. It is probably the most frustrating aspect for law enforcement."

Melody didn't want to think of Banning loose out there. She'd often awake in the middle of the night terrified from some dream in which he was back in the house. She knew it also bothered Genevieve and, despite all the grief that they gave James, they were both happy for the added security around the house.

"Do you think you will ever find him?"

"Yes," Maguire replied. "But only because he will never let this go. He has found something more enjoyable than the act of killing. To him this is a game and he likes it. In fact as long as this is holding his focus, he probably won't kill again."

"Sort of like what I do in the business world?" she asked.

"Hadn't thought about it that way before," he replied. "But yes. Money is no longer the driving factor to you. You enjoy playing the game itself. The reward comes from the means, not the end."

"So if killing you would be the end of the game, then it is reasonable to assume that he would like to prolong that as long as possible," Melody said. "Which means something else becomes the target."

"Or someone," James replied. "Hence the reason for all this security."

"I love you," she replied. "But I miss my boring old life."

"So do I, angel," he said, kissing her head softly. "I promise it will return to normal soon."

"I'm going to hold you to that."

CHAPTER FIFTY

The small alarm clock on the table next to the bed went off and Bashir Al Karim grudgingly awoke.

The bedroom was small in size, about ten feet long by eight feet wide, but more than adequate for his needs. A single bed sat against one wall with a small night table next to it. Across from the bed was a small writing desk with a lamp. In one corner of the room was a closet and, next to it, a small sink.

Faisal had asked if he would like a television set, but Bashir had declined the offer. There was nothing he liked on it. He remembered that the younger men in the group always had the television on. He thought that most of the shows were decadent and offensive. When he had watched the propaganda, that was supposed to be the *news,* he found that it was slanted to portray the west as some type of victim. His own experiences had taught him differently.

Bashir got out of the bed and turned on the desk lamp. The room had a small window that faced out into the courtyard behind the shop. It was still dark outside, not that it would have made much of a difference. The years had built up a layer of grime on the window that made viewing out of it nearly impossible. He made his way over to the sink and splashed cold water on his face.

For most Muslims the day would have started with prayer. But for Bashir the day began with struggles, as it had every day since the death of his beloved Salimah.

"Why do you continue to torture my soul, Allah?" he asked, as he stared into the faded mirror above the sink.

In his mind Bashir heard the voice of the Imam.

"It rests with Allah alone to show you the right path."

Bashir turned, opening the door of the closet and began to get dressed. It was the start of his first day working in the bread shop and he did not want to be late.

He made his way down the narrow stairs and found Faisal sitting in the back.

"Did you sleep well my, friend?" asked the man as he looked up from the small ledger in front of him.

"Yes, for the first time in a quite a while," replied Bashir.

"Sit down. We shall have some coffee together and I will explain how you can help me here."

CHAPTER FIFTY-ONE

Northern Maine
Friday, February 1st, 2013 – 7:37 a.m.

The Ford Explorer crossed over into New Hampshire as it made its way west, toward New York. They could have shaved an hour and a half off the trip by crossing back and forth through Canada but, being a wanted man, it was ill advised. Not that it couldn't be done; it was just that Banning hadn't seen the need to waste his time planning it. Besides, he had some stops to make along the way and he rather enjoyed his new traveling companion.

Tatiana slept in the passenger seat next to him. She had a big day ahead of her and he wanted to be sure that she was well rested. Everything hinged on her being able to accomplish the task at hand and he didn't want to leave anything to chance. They had spent the night before going over the procedure to follow.

She would get into the apartment in the late afternoon and wait for Lena to come back home. With it being Friday it was unlikely that anyone would miss her until Monday when she failed to open the gallery. By then they would be long gone.

There would be no forced entry into the apartment and nothing would be missing. Everything would be locked up as if nothing had ever happened. The investigators would rightfully assume it was him, but with no prints or anything else to go on, it would seem as if she had simply disappeared.

Of course there were no absolutes, but the odds of this little adventure meeting with success were actually quite high.

Banning looked out on the road ahead. It felt good to be out of the cabin. He admitted that he probably would have gone stir crazy a while ago if it had not been for her. There was something about her that made everything seem new and *wild*. Granted she was no longer the same person that he had first brought to the cabin with him.

His mind wandered back to when they were in school. She had always been an anomaly to him. She was the head cheerleader and yet she dated one of the geeks. She was smart, yet she never participated in any clubs that would have showcased that intelligence. He had fantasized about her so many times and had always felt guilty about it. Yet now, the woman who sat next to him far exceeded anything he had ever dreamt up in his fantasies.

He reached over and put his hand on her thigh, caressing it softly.

"Don't start anything you can't finish, mister," she replied, her eyes remaining shut.

"I thought you were still sleeping, my love."

"I was," she replied. "And I was enjoying the most wonderful little erotic dream."

"Oh do tell," Banning replied.

Tatiana opened her eyes and looked over at him, a devilish little smile appearing on her face. "I'd much rather show you."

"Now?" he asked.

"No, silly," she replied. "But I will, when the time is right."

"You are the most amazing creature."

"Yes, I am, and don't you ever forget that."

"Yes, ma'am."

"Where are we?" she asked.

"New Hampshire," Banning replied. "We just turned toward Belkin."

"Can we get something to eat?" Tatiana asked. "I'm starving."

"Whatever your little heart desires, my love."

"Don't tease me, Keith. I can't have what my heart desires right now."

"Well, I meant food wise. I'm going to pull into town and mail off our little package. Once we are done we can go find somewhere to get a bite to eat."

"Then I will let you surprise me," she said.

Belkin was one of those big, small towns. It had some of the creature comforts of the larger cities, like a Wal-Mart and a few large chain restaurants, on the outskirts of town, but the interior was virtually unblemished. As they drove down Main Street Banning spotted the small post office and pulled into the angled parking in front.

As he started to get out Tatiana stopped him.

"Do you really think that's wise?" she asked.

"What do you mean?"

"Well, I doubt that you have much to worry about, but what happens if you walk in and find yourself face to face with your photo hanging on the wall?"

Banning thought about that for a moment. She was probably right that the odds were against it, but why take the chance that someone might remember seeing him.

"You are learning," he said.

Banning reached over the seat and removed the package, handing it to her.

Tatiana took a rubber band out of the console and pulled her hair up into a pony tail.

"How do I look?" she asked.

"Absolutely delicious."

She smiled and took the package from him.

"Money, sweetheart."

"Ah, the end of my fantasy arrives. Now you're asking me for money."

"Well, I do have a bunch of thongs back at the apartment. If it would make you feel better I could put a pair on and you could slip bills into them."

Banning handed her a twenty. "You can keep the change."

"You didn't seriously think you were going to get any," she said with a laugh and headed toward the post office.

Tatiana opened the door and stepped back in time. A small bell affixed to the door rung as she walked in, announcing her presence. The place hadn't seen a renovation since the 50's. Yet it still looked remarkably clean and presentable. From a small desk an elderly woman got up and walked up to the counter.

"What can I do for you today, dear," she asked.

"I need to mail this," Tatiana said, her voice breaking and her chin quivering a bit. She handed the package to the woman.

"Are you alright, honey?"

"Yes, I'm breaking up with my fiancé," she lied.

"Oh dear, I'm so sorry," replied the woman as she put the package on the scale. She hit a button on the machine and a label printed out, which she then affixed to the package.

"That will be $2.07," she said. "Do you need anything else?"

"No," Tatiana said, sniffling as she handed the woman the bill.

When she received the receipt and the change she turned, heading for the door. At the last second, she stopped and rushed back to the counter.

"No," she called out. "I can't do it. Please can I have that back."

"I'm sorry," the woman replied. "I can't give it back once it's been paid."

"You don't understand," Tatiana explained, tears running down her face. "I can't lose him. If he gets that package it's over."

"I could get into big trouble," she said.

"Have you ever been so in love that the thought of losing that person made your heart ache?"

The woman stared out Tatiana for a moment. "Yes I have, dear."

Silently, the woman handed the package back to her.

"Thank you so much."

"It'll be our little secret."

"Forever," Tatiana replied. She stuffed the envelope back inside her jacket and headed out the door.

"Was there a line?" Banning asked when she got back in the car.

"No," she replied and lowered the visor to check her eye out in the mirror. "It's freezing out here and the old geezer had the fan going. I got something in my eye and can't stop crying."

"She probably had the heat turned up high as well, right?"

Tatiana turned to look at him. "Yes, it was like a sauna in there."

"Your federal tax dollars hard at work," he said, and backed the car out of the spot.

"I got you a receipt though. I didn't know if this was a deductible business expense," she said with a laugh.

As they headed through town she looked out at the quaint little stores. It reminded her of Keenseville. As they turned a corner to head back out she spotted an old used book store.

"Keith, can we stop there?" she asked, pointing to the store.

"Sure," he replied and pulled into a spot out front.

"I'll only be a minute. I just need something other than medical manuals to read."

"Take your time."

She got out and headed toward the door. Banning had to admit that the view was quite enjoyable. As if on cue, she looked back over her shoulder and smiled at him.

Stepping inside she was hit with that immediate smell of old books. It was a familiar scent that you instantly recognized. The store itself had been repurposed from its original use. Makeshift shelving now lined the length of both walls and used racks lined the center. The ceiling was clad in old fashioned tin plate and had a well-worn wooden floor.

"I'll be right there," said a voice from the backroom.

A moment later a woman emerged and walked toward her.

"How can I help you?"

"I'm looking for some good mysteries," Tatiana replied.

"Oh come right this way, dear," the woman replied, leading her down one of the aisles.

She came to a stop near the back of the store.

"Mysteries begin here," she said, pointing to a section of the shelves. "And they continue on to the back wall. All the paperbacks are seventy-five cents each, unless marked otherwise."

Tatiana began looking through the books, which were alphabetical by author. She took her time, looking through the rows and selecting books that seemed to have an interesting storyline.

As her fingers scanned the rows she stopped on one particular one. Frederick Forsyth's *The Day of the Jackal.* She selected the book and added it to the small pile.

When she was done she headed up to the register.

"Will that be all for you today?"

"Yes it will," she replied.

"That will be $6.75," the woman said, placing the books in a plastic bag.

Tatiana handed her the money and took the bag.

"Enjoy your books."

"Oh, I will," she said and walked out.

"Are we all set?" Banning asked, as she got back in the car.

"Yes, and thank you for indulging me," she replied. "Now all we need to do is get something to eat and arrange the long awaited reunion."

"Are you sure that you are ready to do this?"

"I've never been surer of anything in my life."

Banning smiled and put the car in gear and headed back out of town.

CHAPTER FIFTY-TWO

1 Police Plaza, Manhattan, New York City
Friday, February 1st, 2013 – 10:12 a.m.

"So you're telling me that this little prick is a spy?" Monahan asked.

"No, not in the literal sense," Maguire replied. "However, a great deal of what we are dealing with now probably came as a result of the training his parents had."

"Outstanding, as if this couldn't possibly get any more surreal."

"Well, I think they gave him the foundation, but he clearly went off the reservation."

"I don't suppose the feds would want to reconsider giving us help in finding him?"

"I wouldn't count on it," Maguire said. "Right now this is all conjecture, based on possible name recognition alone. However, I am sure they would be more than happy to show up and take credit when you catch him."

"Between you and me, I'm hoping he's not the surrendering type."

"Oh, I think that's a pretty safe bet. Just don't underestimate him, Dennis. It's not like he just started doing this. He's been at it for a long time. That means that he not only likes what he is doing, but he is also very good at it."

"I'm going to try and drum up some additional help from Albany. Maybe now they will see that this has the potential to be something really serious and give me back the investigators they took from me."

"If it will help I'll reach out to the Superintendent."

"Can't hurt, especially coming from you," Monahan replied. "Those guys with stars on their shoulders only seem to listen to other folks with stars on their shoulders."

"Well, I'm only pretending. I still think like a working man," Maguire replied. "Speaking of which, you might want to reach out to the surrounding areas. See if any of them have any unresolved homicides or missing persons. Not that I think you need more work, it's just that I think he's been active beyond Keenseville."

"Don't lose that trait. It will serve you well."

"Thanks, but right now the only thing it is doing is causing me to lose sleep at night."

"That's why you get paid the big bucks now."

"I've heard that before," he said. "It's not true, but I've heard it."

"Well, if you hear anything else, be sure to give me a call."

"I will, Dennis," Maguire replied. "Stay safe."

Maguire hung up the phone and got up from the desk, heading over to Rich's office.

"Got a minute?" he said, peeking into the office.

"Please, come in," Rich replied. "At least I know you're not looking for a piece out of my ass."

"Huh?"

"Deputy Mayor for Operations, Tippi Fisher, wasn't exactly happy about being kept out of the loop."

"Wow, I didn't envision her ever being a pain in the ass," James replied sarcastically.

"Yeah, well she is," said Rich. "Not as bad as some of those idiots down in D.C., who think that just because they work for the President that they have the same authority as him, but she's a close second."

"You speak to McMasters about it?"

"I mentioned it to him. He basically said to just ignore her. If she started getting mouthy he'd have Tom Murphy talk to her. Right now he's so damn happy that nothing else went *boom* in the city that he could care less."

"Yeah, I caught the video of the press conference. It was a veritable love fest. I at least expected them to be a bit pissy about being lied to."

"You and me both, it was like he had them mesmerized. Maybe it's the honeymoon phase."

"Are we talking about the same New York media?" Maguire asked incredulously. "The honeymoon phase is over with them even before the '*I do's'* are said."

"I know, but whatever he was selling they were hungry to buy. I have to admit he did go out of his way to give the Department a good plug."

"It is a nice departure from what used to be the norm. Still, I think that there's got to be a way to smooth things over with Fisher."

"If you can think of anything, I'm all ears."

"Aren't Mary and Melody going to that charity function this month?"

"Yeah, why do you ask?"

"Why not ask Mrs. *Witchy-Poo* to attend the event with them? Sort of like a guest of honor befitting her omnipotent*ness*."

Rich sat and thought about it for a moment. It wasn't a half bad idea. It's not that he was actually worried about Tippi Fisher; he just didn't need to get into a pissing match with her so early on in the administration.

"I'll talk to Mary tonight and see if she can make it happen," Rich said.

He stood up and walked over to the credenza and poured a cup of coffee.

"You want one?" he asked.

"Sure," replied James.

Rich poured a second cup and handed it to James. He looked at the mug which had the logo of the NYPD on one side and a facsimile of the gold and platinum Police Commissioner's badge made by the Tiffany Company in 1901.

"You know, you friggin' feds are so damn buffy," James said, as he took a sip of coffee.

"Pens will be in next week, want one?"

"I'll hold out for the cuff links."

"Hey, that's a good idea."

"I think I created a monster."

"Did you just come down to harass me or was there something else you wanted to talk to me about?"

"Yeah, we have the funeral on Monday."

Rich let out an audible sigh. He'd been putting off having to think about it. Ever since he had first accepted the job in the back of his mind he knew that he would one day have to deal with a line of duty death.

When he had worked for the Secret Service losing someone in the line of duty was rare. In 2001 the New York Field Office had lost a special officer in the September 11th attack on the World Trade Center, and in 1995 they lost four agents in the Oklahoma City Bombing. But you would have to go back over thirty years since the last agent was killed by gunfire. In fact heart attacks and vehicle accidents were the biggest threat faced by the agency.

Now, as Commissioner of the largest police department in the United States, officer deaths were an all too common occurrence.

Especially now, as even more continued to lose their battles to illnesses brought on from the September 11th attacks. While twenty-three NYPD officers had died on that day, over a decade later that number had more than doubled and there was no sign that it would end anytime soon.

"I got the notification someplace here," Rich replied as he went through the papers spread out on the desk. "Where is it being held again?"

"The families agreed to hold the wake and the funerals together," Maguire said. "Saturday night is the wake out in Hicksville and then the mass is being held Monday morning at St. Malachi's in Plainedge. When they are done they are taking Maldonado's body to a cemetery in Hempstead and then Dixon is being buried in Ronkonkoma later in the afternoon. It will give the members of the command time to get to both places."

"How are they going to cover the command?"

"We'll *fly* people in from other commands and the Task Force for the day tour and the four to twelve shifts," Maguire replied.

"Mary said she wants to go."

"Yeah, Melody said the same. I figured we would all just meet at the church."

"That sounds like a plan to me. Are you going to the wake as well?"

"Yes, and I suggest that we should go early. It will be a madhouse as the night progresses and the last thing they need is us making it worse."

"I agree," Rich said. "Not to change the subject, but are we getting any noise about our missing terrorist?"

"No, he disappeared. I'm still waiting on a call back from my sources. However, considering the bullshit State Department pulled with the one guy, my people will tiptoe around things so as not to set off any other alarms."

"That's smart thinking."

Rich and Maguire both realized that whoever had alerted the State Department had been plugged in at a very high level. Otherwise there would have been no way that they could have monitored the real time inquiries that were being conducted and moved on things so quickly. It wasn't that Qaseem Bin Khalid was that big of a fish, but more likely that some big fish didn't want Qaseem Bin Khalid talking.

"You think the threat is over?"

"This threat? Yes, at least in its original form. I don't think they'll revisit this one for a long time. It was a spectacular plan, but they know that they won't be able to put all the components together for a repeat attempt for some time to come."

"That sounds wonderfully *dire*."

"It should be, because it is. We both know the game we are playing. It's no different than when we were doing protection. We have to be right one hundred percent of the time; they have to be right once."

"Yeah, but back then we had one target, not the population of an entire city."

"Hey," Maguire said as he stood up to leave. "If it were easy, anyone could do it."

CHAPTER FIFTY-THREE

Keenseville, Upstate New York City
Friday, February 1st, 2013 – 3:07 p.m.

Banning pulled the truck up to the curb and Tatiana got out, quickly heading toward the wrought iron staircase on the side of the building. She reached under the third step and located the small box containing the key. She made her way up the rest of the stairs, opening the door quickly and stepped inside. Before heading up the interior staircase she reached up and removed the coaxial cable from the camera perched above the door.

She took a deep breath and began walking up the steps. It was like stepping back in time.

Tatiana recognized the apartment, but it didn't feel right. This had all belonged to Tricia and she no longer existed. She walked around the apartment trying to acclimate herself back to it, but she could not shake the feeling that she no longer belonged here.

The apartment itself was an open floor plan but as she looked around, she realized that so much had changed since she last walked down those stairs. The brick walls, that had once been stripped down to expose their natural red color, were now painted a pale cream. The exposed wood ceiling beams retained their natural color, but now the old tin plate ceiling and duct work that ran above it was painted a flat black. She felt like one of those people on the home improvement show that went back to their old house. It looked familiar, but it wasn't hers.

You certainly have moved on with your life, haven't you, Lena? she thought.

Tatiana made her way into the kitchen and opened the fridge. There was an open bottle of red wine inside and she poured herself a drink. She walked over to the couch, removing her jacket, and draped it over the back, before sitting down. The last time she had sat here having a drink the night had ended so horribly for her.

Tonight, Lena would experience the same fate and learn just how quickly life can change for someone. She looked down at her watch, it was 3:17. She knew that she had almost two hours before Lena would close up the shop and come upstairs. She got up and walked back into the bedroom. She was relieved to find that nothing here had changed. In the center of the room was a king sized, four post, bed. Matching end tables flanked either side. She walked around to her side of the bed and opened the top drawer. It was empty.

Tatiana stared at it quizzically for a moment.

Surely I must have kept stuff inside, she thought.

It had been over eight months and she began to wonder if her memory was playing tricks on her. She walked over to the dresser, opening the top drawer, and began to go through the lingerie that was inside. None of it looked familiar.

She began to feel panic setting in. She rushed over to the closet and opened it, frantically searching through the garments hanging inside. Again, none of it was hers.

Suddenly she felt weak and tried to brace herself against the wall as she slid to the ground. Was she in the right place? Had Lena moved out? Rented it to someone else?

She felt the plan beginning to unravel, felt sick to her stomach. She reached into her pocket, grabbing the cell phone that Keith had given her, and began to dial the number.

She stopped and put the phone back into her pocket.

This is no way for you to act, she chided herself.

Tricia would act this way, not Tatiana. Inside the sick feeling dissipated and was replaced by something angry, something much darker. She got back to her feet and began to explore the room, this time with a more discerning eye.

The room had changed. There had been a photo of the two of them on the night table that was missing. That was the first sign. She began going through the closet again, Lena was a size seven but as she sorted through the clothes on the left side, her side, the clothes labels read ten.

The gears were spinning now.

Who gains weight when they have lost someone? she wondered.

She went back to the dresser and again found that the sizes didn't match up. She removed a bra and looked at the label 36D.

"Ha, not in this lifetime, sweetheart," she blurted out.

Tatiana left the bedroom and walked to the storage room in the back. She turned the light on and saw several boxes stacked in the corner. She pulled the top one down and opened it. Inside were all her clothes.

You fucking cunt, she thought.

Keith had done the best he could when he removed her clothes from Paul Browning's house. But those were just ones she hadn't really cared about. The clothing in these boxes were the pieces that meant something to her and now they had been discarded like she had never even existed.

"Well, they say that *karma* is a bitch, and I guess you're going to find that out first hand, Lena."

She looked around the room and saw a small black suitcase. Tatiana laid it down on the floor and began going through the boxes. She selected a variety of clothes and undergarments, packing them away neatly. In the last box she also found her old vibrator.

Well, you never know when this might come in handy, she thought.

She slipped it into the suitcase and zipped it up. When she was done, she brought the suitcase out and set it next to the couch, just out of view.

Suddenly she remembered the package in her jacket pocket. She removed it and buried it in the bottom, between some jeans.

She knew Banning was trying to draw James out, to continue their fight. But she was enjoying her life right now and she didn't need a battle going on around her. That could happen later, but only when she was ready to allow it.

Tatiana continued to go through the apartment, searching for other clues.

In the bathroom she opened the mirror and went through the medicine cabinet. She picked up a prescription bottle from the shelf and read the label: Klonopin. She looked at the patient's name.

"Just who the fuck do you think you are, Susan Hadley, putting your meds in *my* bathroom and why are you taking benzos?"

She opened the bottle; there were about a dozen pills inside. She put the bottle in her pocket as she continued looking through the cabinet. She found a bottle of Vicodin along with a bottle of Valium, all in the same woman's name.

"Christ, Lena, could you have found someone with a few more issues?"

When she was done she walked back outside. She removed three of the Klonopin and then put the three bottles into the suitcase. When she was done, she went back to the kitchen and crushed the pills, and then placed them in one of the wine glasses.

She continued her tour of the apartment, seeing all the *changes* that Lena had done. Each one subtly reinforced Tatiana's desire for revenge.

As she passed the small desk she noticed the light blinking on the answering machine. She pressed the play button and waited for the message. When it began playing she heard a female voice.

"Hey, honey, just called to let you know I got rerouted to Albuquerque. I won't be back till Monday. Tried your cell, but got no answer. Call me tonight. Love ya."

"So sorry," Tatiana said to the phone, as she hit the delete button. "Lena's going to be *tied up* for quite a while."

She checked her watch again. It was 4:46.

She went into the bathroom and looked herself over. She liked the new her. The dye had worked out perfectly. Gone was her dark brown hair, replaced by an almost honey blonde color. It wasn't exactly as blonde as she would have liked, but she could work on that later. For now it was the perfect contrast between the old and the new.

She walked out and lit the candles on the coffee table and turned the lights down low. It was just about time for their reunion.

CHAPTER FIFTY-FOUR

Eastbound Grand Central Parkway, Queens, New York City
Friday, February 1st, 2013 – 4:59 p.m.

Maguire sat in the back of the Suburban, going through a folder of reports that required his signature, as it made its way east toward Long Island. He found that the commute home was the only time that he actually got to review the majority of them without being constantly interrupted.

As if on cue, Luke Jackson turned in his seat to face Maguire.

"Hey, boss, what time do you want us to pick you up tomorrow?"

Maguire looked up from the papers.

"Thanks for the offer, but I'm not going to ruin your day off."

"Sorry, you're stuck with us, boss," said Detective Peter May from behind the wheel. "We pulled the weekend coverage."

"Don't you guys ever get tired of seeing me?"

"I worked in the two-eight for six years, Commissioner," Jackson replied. "I'll take the commute to Southampton over gun runs any day!"

"Well, you do have a valid point there, Luke," Maguire said with a laugh. "I'll be going to the wake tomorrow evening. I'd like to be there when it starts at five."

"We'll pick you up about three-thirty then," May said. "With it being the weekend we will have plenty of time."

"That will work," replied Maguire.

Just then his cell phone went off.

"Maguire."

"Can you talk, Paddy?" Mother asked.

"You know me, Mom," James replied. "I'm a great listener."

It wasn't that James didn't trust the two members of his security detail; rather it was a courtesy to the man on the other end of the phone. Discussions like this were always undertaken with the knowledge that everything that was said was an entirely private matter. It was something that people in these circles took very seriously.

In government work there are several levels of security clearances. They start out with *Controlled Unclassified*. This level does not require any form of background check and generally involves information that should not be redistributed to those not involved at an operational level. It is the most basic form of security. Next would be *Controlled*, followed by *Secret*, clearance. Clearances of this type require background checks lasting from weeks, in the case of the former, up to a year.

Top Secret clearance, or TS for short, allows the holder to access data that can directly affect national security, counterterrorism, and counterintelligence, as well as other highly sensitive data. This type of clearance generally required up to eighteen months for the background checks to be done.

But there was another classification to Top Secret and that was the addition of *Sensitive Compartmented Information*, or TS/SCI. Information at this level routinely involved sensitive intelligence sources, methods, and means. Not only did you know the intelligence, but you knew from where it originated and how it was obtained. This was the level that Maguire, and the rest of his teammates, had operated in.

Mother's security exceeded even that. His White House assignment also carried the additional classification of *Yankee White, Category One*.

"Then I'll give you the bumper sticker version now and I can fill you in on the nitty gritty stuff later."

"That sounds ideal."

"First, that little federally funded abduction of your suspect was sanctioned from Foggy Bottom."

"Any particular reason?"

"His *ammy* called and said it was all just a big mistake. He claims junior just got caught up with the wrong kids at school."

"It happens to the best of them," Maguire said dismissively. "Just for shits and giggles, did he give a reason why?"

"The oldest," Mother replied. "Sex, drugs and rock and roll, brother."

"No shit," said Maguire. "I guess I should have known."

Of course it didn't involve any of those three subjects. They had taken to using it as a euphemism for *God, guns and money.* Something that was never in short supply in the Middle East

"Just out of curiosity, what floor did the elevator stop on?"

"The top," Mother replied. "On both sides of that particular conversation."

"Outstanding. I can't wait to hear the whole story. Do you have any other good news?"

"So far your misplaced book isn't getting rave reviews; in fact some have said it's pretty boring."

"What's the dust cover read like?"

"Local boy meets girl, falls in love with girl, loses girl to the bad guy, and goes on a quest to successfully vanquish his foe. But so far it's only been published in its native language."

"I wonder if they could be looking to translate it?"

"Perhaps," Mother said. "Unless of course they've decided to do a remake."

"That's an interesting premise."

"Yeah, well let's hope it doesn't have the same success as the original."

"Agreed," said Maguire. "Either way it sounds like a book I would love to discuss with you at length mom."

"You have my number."

"I'll call you when I get some free time. By the way, do you recall who played the female lead in that?"

"Yeah, hold on a sec."

Maguire heard the sound of papers being shuffled on the desk.

"Here it is," Mother replied. "Salimah, looks like she was a one hit wonder. Don't forget you need to visit and take your mother out to dinner."

"Thanks. Dinner sounds wonderful. You get that senior discount now, don't you?"

"That's not gonna sound half as funny when you're getting your ass kicked by an *AARP* member."

"Gotta go, love you too."

Maguire smiled and ended the call. Things had certainly taken an interesting turn of events. From the call he had put together that his misplaced book, Bashir Al Karim, wasn't a known player, hence the term local. The vanquished foe was the Russians, who he blamed for the demise of his woman. But until now he'd only been active in Afghanistan, hence the reference to the local language. Until now, being the operative words.

There were a variety of reasons why people chose jihad and Bashir would not be the first to have engaged in it because of the loss of a family member. Pain and anger was an enticing motivator. But what was the reason for bringing the fight over here? That was something he would have to think about.

Equally troublesome was the news that the orders to grab Qaseem Bin Khalid had emanated from the top of the State Department. Foggy Bottom was a metonym for the U.S. Department of State because its headquarters, the Harry S.

Truman Building, was based in that neighborhood in Washington, D.C., a few blocks away from the White House.

The fact that the order came from the top floor meant that it was either ordered by the Secretary of State, Eliza Cook, or her Deputy, G. Prescott Linehan.

Eliza Cook was a career politician who had served in both the House of Representatives and the Senate before being sworn in as Secretary of State. She had a significant amount of connections around the world and carried a lot of clout. Still, it seemed strange to him that she would personally order the release of a potential terrorist. He could however envision her having a cutout assume that role.

Politics was not for the faint of heart.

What was more curious to him right now was who had actually made the call on the other end. Mother had said that the kid's *ammy*, or uncle, had called. The only problem was that the kid probably had a ton of well-connected *uncles*. He would have to put in a private call to one of the connections he had in the Saudi Royal Guard Regiment. However, that little mystery was going to take a bit more time to unravel and was not as pressing as the current one he was facing.

He needed to find Bashir Al Karim before the man had a chance to formulate a plan B.

CHAPTER FIFTY-FIVE

Keenseville, Upstate New York City
Friday, February 1st, 2013 – 5:01 p.m.

Lena shut down her computer and turned off the light that sat on the desk. It was generally slow this time of year and she didn't need an excuse to close the art gallery on time.

Most of her time now was focused on getting confirmations for the inaugural show in April. It was something that she dreaded, but, deep down inside, she knew she had to do. So far the responses had all been positive. Everyone on the art scene seemed inclined to mark the occasion, everyone that was except for her.

Outside it was dark and dreary. She didn't look forward to going out in the cold, even though her *commute* only amounted to a walk around the corner.

She put on her black wool, thigh length jacket and grabbed her purse. Above the desk she opened the electrical box door and turned off the galleries interior lights. When she was done she keyed in the code for the alarm and made her way toward the front door.

The wind had definitely picked up and she felt a chill on her neck as she fumbled with the key to lock the front door. She adjusted the collar as she made her way around the building and up the stairs. She'd have just enough time to change, have a bite to eat and then leave to pick up Susan.

I hope it doesn't start snowing, she thought.

Lena opened the door to the apartment and stepped inside. She took off her jacket, hanging it on the coat hook, and began walking up the stairs. She was going through a laundry list of things she needed to get done this weekend. Even though the opening was still nearly three months away, trying to locate new pieces for the show would take up every free moment of that time.

She made a mental note to reach out to that psychotic little sculptor in Lake Placid tomorrow. The guy gave her the creeps, but his work was incredible.

She made it to the top step and was just about to toss her purse onto the desk when she heard a voice.

"Hey, sexy, did you miss me."

Lena looked up and dropped the purse, its contents scattering on the floor at her feet.

She let out a scream.

It took a moment for the realization to hit, but when it did she rushed forward and into her arms. Tears were streaming down her face and she wrapped her arms tightly around Tatiana.

"Oh my God, you're alive!"

Tatiana held her tightly, it had been so long since she had smelled her scent and it was having an unexpected effect on her.

"Yes I am," she replied. "I'm back now."

Lena pulled back. Suddenly the look of shock was replaced by one of fear and apprehension.

"Where have you been? How did you get here?"

"Come, sit down, it's a long story," Tatiana replied and led her over to the couch.

"I don't understand, what happened to you?"

"Here, take a sip of this," she said, handing Lena the glass of wine. "I'll explain everything."

Tatiana took the seat next to her, holding Lena's hand tightly.

"They rescued me yesterday," she began. "I was being held some place in the mountains. Not sure if it was New Hampshire or Maine. They wanted to let you know, but I said no. I needed time to get myself together and be a bit more *presentable*."

"I wouldn't have cared," Lena replied.

"I know you wouldn't have, baby, but I don't exactly look like I did nine months ago."

Lena had noticed the new hair color and saw that she was a bit thinner as well, but not in a bad way.

"Actually, you look pretty damned good to me."

"Eh, there's really not much to do when you're being held captive," she explained. "I passed the time doing whatever I could, even exercising."

"So what happened?"

"I'm really not sure. I spent most of my time held in an underground bunker. Then yesterday I heard this big explosion, followed by some gunfire. The next thing I knew these guys in black burst through the door and rescued me."

"What happened to *him*?" Lena asked, not even daring to mention the name.

"Banning? He's dead. They killed him in the raid."

"Oh thank God," she replied. "I've lived in fear since you were abducted, always wondering if he would come after me next."

"Well it's over now," Tatiana said, looking Lena directly in the eyes. "Now we can start over, move ahead with our lives."

Lena stared back at her and she could see the panic setting in.

"Are you alright?" she asked. "Anything I need to know?"

"Uhm," Lena stammered. "Well, you were gone for so long and..."

"And what? Did you get lonely, Lena?"

"Yes, but it's not what you think," she said.

Lena reached down and picked up the glass, finishing off the remainder of the wine.

"It's okay, babe, I already knew. I saw that there was a message on the answering machine. Susan said she wouldn't be back this weekend."

"I'm so sorry."

"Don't worry, we have time to sort this all out," Tatiana replied as she stood up and grabbed the wine glass. "Would you care for your own or do you just want to keep drinking from my cup?"

"I'll take a glass, thank you."

Lena watched as she walked into the kitchen. She was dealing with so many emotions, so many thoughts running through her brain. She was having a difficult time processing it all.

Yet considering everything that she had been through, Tricia appeared to be taking everything in stride. As if nothing mattered.

Maybe something about the experience has changed her, she thought.

She certainly appeared calm and steady, even in light of the admission that there was now another woman in the picture.

"Here you go, babe," she said, handing Lena the glass. "To new beginnings and awesome adventures."

Lena took the glass and sipped the wine. She had so many questions; she didn't know where to begin. Still she knew they were going to have to come to terms with *their* relationship and Susan.

"I don't even know where to begin," Lena said. "There's so much I want to know and so much I need to tell you."

"Well, we have plenty of time for all of that later. Right now I'd much rather enjoy this moment before we tackle anything too *heavy*."

"Oh really?" Lena replied with a playful grin. She swirled the wine around in her glass and took another drink. "And what exactly would you to like to enjoy at this moment?"

Tatiana smiled back at her. "Well, this is *my* homecoming isn't it?"

She put her glass on the coffee table and leaned back against the couch. Slowly she began to unbutton her blouse until the navy blue lace bra she was wearing was completely exposed. She then began to play with her breasts, feeling the nipples become erect beneath the material.

As she watched, Lena began to feel herself becoming aroused and felt herself biting her lower lip. She brought the glass up to her lips and swallowed the remaining wine, setting the glass down on the table in front of her.

Lena stood up and walked over to where Tatiana was sitting. She reached down, hiking up her skirt, and then sat down, straddling her thighs. Her hands reached down and gently pushed Tatiana's away as she took over caressing her breasts.

Tatiana moaned as she slid her hands around and grabbed Lena's ass.

"Is this the moment you want to enjoy?" Lena asked.

"Oh yeah, babe, every last minute of it," Tatiana replied.

Lena reached up and took Tatiana's face in her hands, kissing her passionately.

She was so aroused now, could feel herself grinding down on top of her. Slowly at first, but building in intensity, until it became almost primal, aggressive. Lena could feel the rough material of the jeans rubbing against her panties.

She wanted more, wanted to feel the satisfaction that came with surrendering to her desires. She could feel the taste of lips against hers. The sweetness of the wine was erotically intoxicating.

Desire was overcoming her and she struggled to keep pace with it. She was so hot, felt like she was on fire. She moaned loudly.

Inside her mind was racing, screaming. Lena wanted her now, here on the couch. She wanted to feel her touch, to taste her. She broke free from the kiss.

"I want you," she said, the words coming out in a low seductive tone. "I want all of you."

Tatiana smiled at her. "Do you think you can handle all of me?"

Lena leaned back, her hands reaching up to unbutton her own blouse. The room was spinning now. She couldn't believe how excited she was and the effect it was having on her. She felt like a kid that had drank too much.

Her hands weren't cooperating with her. All she wanted was to get undressed and to feel her hungry lips on her hard nipples. She tugged harder at the button.

Her vision seemed to be getting blurry. She focused harder and watched as the button popped off of the blouse, falling slowly until it landed in her lap. She looked up, wanting to ask what happened, just as someone turned out the lights and everything went black.

Tatiana grabbed her just as Lena's body collapsed onto her.

"Fuck," she exclaimed angrily.

She hadn't expected to get as aroused as she had, or to have the drug work as quickly as it had. Now she was left feeling overly horny and extremely angry.

Tatiana pushed Lena's body off of hers, watching as the woman slumped backward and crashed into the coffee table, before falling to the floor.

Tatiana stood up and began to button her blouse.

"Did you really think you could handle me, bitch?" she said rhetorically to the body of the now unconscious woman. "Oh and just for the record, I'm really *not* okay with Susan."

When she was done she picked up the jacket, reaching into the inner pocket and removed the cell phone.

"It's done," she said when he answered the phone.

She made her way down the stairs and opened the front door. Banning had pulled the truck around so that the front faced the street and rear was backed up right next to the exterior stairs.

"Okay, we have to be quick about this," Banning said as he walked inside.

There was still a very real threat that someone might notice the truck or even that a patrol car could drive by and decide to investigate.

When he got upstairs he saw the body on the floor.

"What the fuck happened?"

"I don't know," Tatiana said. "I did what you said. She stood up and her body spasmed. Next thing I knew she fell back into the coffee table."

Banning bent over and secured Lena's hands and feet with flex-cuffs. He then used a piece of duct tape to cover her mouth. It was a long trip and he didn't want to listen to a screaming woman. He noticed a cut over her eye. It wasn't too bad and he slapped a piece of duct tape over that as well.

While Banning secured Lena, Tatiana cleaned up the mess. She scooped up the broken glasses from the floor, placing it in a plastic bag and repositioned the coffee table.

"Okay, we need to get her out of here," Banning said. "I'll carry her, you get the door."

Tatiana put on her jacket, grabbing the suitcase and plastic bag as she headed to the stairs.

"What the hell is in that?" Banning asked as he lifted Lena off the ground.

"Some stuff I missed."

"I hope it's worth it," he replied.

"When you see me in it you'll know better than to ask such dumb questions."

"I stand corrected my, love," Banning replied as he slowly navigated the staircase with Lena's body draped over his shoulder.

Tatiana opened the door slowly and scanned the street. A light snow had begun to fall outside.

"I'll go down and open the back," she said.

Banning watched as Tatiana walked to the back of the truck and opened it. She moved around to the passenger side where she opened the door. Tatiana tossed the suitcase in the back and paused to get a better look at the street.

When she was sure that it was clear she motioned him to come. Banning moved quickly down the staircase, unceremoniously dumping the women in the back and shut the rear hatch.

As Banning went around to the driver's side, Tatiana ran back into the apartment. She grabbed Lena's purse and jacket, and then made her way back out, locking the door behind her.

"What's that for?" he said as she got in.

"She said that she was supposed to be picking up her girlfriend at the airport. I thought it would throw things off if it appeared as if she had left on her own."

"Good idea," Banning replied and started the truck. "She has a girlfriend?"

"*Had*," Tatiana corrected him. "Now she has us."

CHAPTER FIFTY-SIX

Manhattan, New York City
Saturday, February 2nd, 2013 – 10:23 a.m.

Mary picked up the phone and began to dial the number written on the piece of paper in front of her.

"I can't believe you're asking me to do this, *Richard*," she said.

Stargold inhaled deeply, feeling her eyes cutting into him like daggers. He recalled the same sense of dread when his mother had said his name like that.

Was there a special class in school that taught women how to use something as simple as a person's name as a weapon? he wondered.

"Yes, dear, I know I owe you big time."

"Oh you have no idea….., Tippi, hi, it's Mary Stargold," she said, glaring at Rich.

"I've been meaning to reach out to you and ask if you would be interested in attending a charity event with me and Melody Anderson this month?"

She listened for a moment as the woman on the other end spoke.

"Well, it's being held on February 13th at the Marriott Downtown. It is for the Lamplighter House. They provide counseling for at risk women and children, along with temporary housing for victims of domestic violence. This event is to promote awareness as well as providing an opportunity for the community to come together and raise funds to support their operation."

Mary looked over at Rich, her face readily showing her displeasure with being put in this position. She moved her lips silently, mimicking the woman on the other end of the phone running her mouth off.

"Really?" she said with feigned enthusiasm. "That's wonderful; I can't wait to see you again. I'll get in touch with the organizers tomorrow and I will have them send you out an invitation."

She listened for another minute.

"Oh that sounds lovely. I think that would be a fantastic idea."

Mary looked back again at Rich and rolled her eyes.

"Ok, Tippi, well it was very nice speaking to you and I can't wait to see you again. I'll have them send that out tomorrow."

She paused again, waiting for the women on the other end to finish speaking.

"Great," she said. "Talk to you soon, bye."

Mary hung up the phone and turned to face Rich.

"I wonder," she began. "Did any other police commissioners have to be saved by their security detail after they were beaten by their wives?"

"The things we do for love," Rich said.

"I own you," Mary said. "In fact you owe me so much you can't even die."

"I love you."

"I sorta like you," she said as she got up from the desk and walked toward the living room. "Don't blow it now by getting on my last nerve."

"Thank you, dear," Rich called out after her.

CHAPTER FIFTY-SEVEN

Plainview, Nassau County, New York
Monday, February 4th, 2013 – 9:53 a.m.

Hicksville Road was awash in a sea of blue uniforms.

Thousands of police officers lined the western side of the street, for as far as the eye could see, as they awaited the arrival of the funeral procession. While the majority of those in attendance were from the NYPD, there were representatives from just about every federal, state and local agency in the tri-state area. In fact there was even a uniformed officer from the Garda Siochana, the national police force of the Republic of Ireland, who had been visiting the city on vacation.

The neighborhood was a mix of residential homes and businesses. At the moment it seemed as if they had all laid aside whatever they were doing and donned their winter coats to stand among the uniformed officers and pay their last respects.

Across the street from St. Malachi's Church, officers stood in their winter dress uniforms. Their somber faces seemed to match the cold gray sky above. Standing among them were Rich and James, along with the Mayor and the rest of the Department's hierarchy.

This was an *Inspector's Funeral*, one that was generally afforded to high ranking members of the department and for any officer who had died in the line of duty. It was a solemn occasion, yet one that was steeped in tradition and symbolism.

As they stood waiting, a procession of motorcycles from the Highway Patrol made their way up the street silently, two abreast, followed by a marked radio car. As the motorcade passed by them a silence fell over the assembled crowd. Suddenly the faint sounds of muffled drums could be heard in the distance.

As Rich watched the members of the NYPD Emerald Society Pipes and Drums, clad in their dark blue kilts and jackets, with long gold capes, slowly approached. The black bearskin hats that each man wore gave them the appearance of Celtic giants.

With each step they took the sound grew stronger as if to announce the impending arrival of the funeral procession.

Immediately behind them were the two black hearses carrying the remains of the two fallen officers. Each was escorted on either side by pall bearers from the Ceremonial Unit. The vehicles came to a stop just opposite from where he stood.

It was at this moment that the weight of his job came crashing down upon him.

These were not officers from some other agency or some faceless names he had read about in a bulletin. These were *his* cops, his responsibility, and they had been lost on *his* watch.

As the pallbearers opened the back of the vehicles, the bagpipers began to play, the first strains of *Amazing Grace* filing the air.

"Attention!" a voice cried out.

On command, the entire gathering of uniform officers came to order.

"Present Arms!"

In unison, each officer brought their right hand up smartly, the tips of their pointer fingers coming to rest on their hat's visor. Those wearing civilian clothes covered their hearts.

Slowly the two coffins, draped in the blue, green and white flag of the New York City Police Department, were drawn out and lifted up onto the shoulders of the pall bearers. One by one they were brought into the church, followed by the fallen officer's family members.

"Sir," said a uniformed Sergeant from the Ceremonial Unit. "Please follow me."

Rich and James, accompanied by the Mayor and the other chiefs, followed the family into the church. They were escorted to the front were they rejoined Mary and Melody who were already seated inside.

It was a large church that could easily accommodate the needs of the local parishioners every Sunday, but today it was packed to overcrowding with both family and members of the command.

Melody took James' hand in hers.

"Are you okay?" she asked.

"Yes," he said. "I'll be fine. Where's Gen and Gregor? I thought they were coming."

"They were, but as we were getting ready to leave Gen started to feel sick so I told her to stay home. Gregor is looking after her."

"Flu?"

"I think so," replied Melody. "I just hope it doesn't get passed around. It is that time of year."

Maguire felt the cell phone in his pocket vibrate. He peeked at the display and saw that it was a missed call from Monahan. He'd call him back later.

When the service was over and the coffins were being brought back outside, a representative of each of their respective security details gathered them up and brought them out a side entrance where their vehicles were waiting.

"Did you come alone?" James asked.

"No, George is with the car," she said. "He's in the parking lot across the street."

"Call and tell him that you're riding with me."

"Okay."

James walked over to Rich who was talking to a Lieutenant from the Ceremonial Unit. As he approached the officer walked away.

"You alright, buddy?"

"No, not really," he replied. "I don't know what I had expected, but all of this just got a lot more real for me."

"If it's any consolation, it will never get easier."

"I told the lieutenant that I wanted to go to each of the gravesites for the services. I know that's not the norm, but I think the families deserve it, and I sure as hell owe it to those cops."

"Lead the way, *Sir*," James replied.

The two men left to attend the first of the two graveside services.

The service is similar to a military funeral in that the flag is removed from the coffin and folded before being presented to the respective family member. Traditionally it was presented by a ranking member, generally the commanding officer of the officer's command.

Today, that tradition changed.

As the flag was being folded, Rich walked up, taking possession of it when it was handed to him by the uniformed officer. He then walked over to Officer Maldonado's mother and presented it to her.

"On behalf of a grateful city," he replied, handing her the tightly folded flag.

When they were done, they proceeded to the cemetery where Officer Dixon was being buried. There, Rich presented the flag to Dixon's fourteen year old daughter, Layla Rose, who sat with tears streaming down her face and being supported by her mother.

As the two men walked back to the vehicles it was James that broke the silence.

"That was an incredibly gracious act, Rich."

"Christ, James, I need a drink," Stargold replied.

"I think we all do today."

CHAPTER FIFTY-EIGHT

Northern Maine
Monday, February 4th, 2013 – 5:11 p.m.

Banning stood outside the room and stared through the small viewing slot at the figure lying on the bed.

Lena was chained to the bed by her ankle. There was just enough chain to allow her to move around in proximity to the bed, but not enough to get close to the door. This made bringing in food a bit easier for him.

She was sedated now. It was easier this way as she was still a bit combative. He had learned with Tricia that it was easier this way. She had been quite truculent, and very vocal, but after a while even the strongest of opponents broke. It was a mental game, breaking a person's spirit, and one that he found he actually enjoyed playing. The first few days were the hardest, the ones where the hostage honestly believed that they were going to be rescued. As those days passed, the reality would set in. Then they would become depressed and withdrawn.

It was the period that followed that he enjoyed the most. Establishing that, while he was in fact the master, it was actually their choice that decided how things would progress. Good behavior and submission brought reward, while bad behavior and rebellion brought punishment. It was always hard for them at first and he understood that, but eventually they all began to submit.

At first there was a detachment. As if the mental and the physical became two different entities. *It was probably a defense mechanism*, he thought. He remembered this with Tricia when their relationship had first turned physical. She would just lay there and let him do what he wanted. Granted, it wasn't the relationship they shared today, but at the time it certainly satisfied *his* physical needs.

She rolled onto her back and the sheet that had been covering her body slid to the side exposing her naked upper torso.

Like Tricia, it was obvious that Lena took good care of her body. She wasn't as tall as Tricia was, but they had a similar build.

That's odd, he thought. *Why do I still remember her as Tricia, even though that personality no longer exists?*

There was a part of him that missed that innocence. He no longer felt dirty when he and Tatiana had sex. In fact, most of the time, he felt as if she was the one in charge. It wasn't that he didn't enjoy it, but it was a completely different feeling.

When she had been Tricia she had been pure. Even though she submitted to him, he knew it wasn't something she wanted to do. There was pleasure in making her do it. He got off on that power, he admitted to himself.

Can I recapture that with you, Lena? he wondered.

Tatiana appeared suddenly behind him, draping her arm over his shoulder.

"Do you like her, Keith?" she asked seductively.

"I was just checking to see if she had awoken," he replied.

Tatiana reached down and ran the palm of her left hand over his crotch.

"Uh huh," she replied. "Sure you were."

"Well, I can't help it. Tell me that doesn't get you aroused," he said and pointed to the slot.

Tatiana peeked inside.

"Mmmm, I do see what you mean," she said playfully. "It is quite a nice view."

"Yes it is."

"I bet you'd like to do more than just stand here and be a pervert."

"What are you suggesting?"

"You're a grown man, you don't need my permission."

"Well, I just assumed that with the past you two shared, that it wouldn't be right."

"I'm flattered by your consideration, Keith," Tatiana replied.

She peeked back through the window at Lena.

"It has to be hard on you though," she said. "No pun intended of course. I mean she's never been with a man before. That has to be pretty high up on any guy's fantasy list, being the first real cock in a lesbian."

Tatiana looked at him and smiled. "I just came down to tell you that I'm going to make myself a drink and curl up in front of the fireplace with a good book."

"You're an amazing lady," Banning said as he looked back at her. "I hope it's a book that you can really sink your teeth into."

"Time will tell," she replied, tapping the paperback she was holding against her open hand as she turned to walk away.

As she reached the staircase she heard the lock open on the door behind her.

CHAPTER FIFTY-NINE

Bashir hung the white apron on the hook near the back door of the bakery. He then made his way up the staircase, to the small apartment on the second floor.

He was tired, but he felt good. It had been a long time since he had worked hard. The ache in his muscles was like an old familiar friend he had not heard from in a while.

He stepped into the small room and turned on the desk lamp. He then opened the closet, selecting a change of clothes and made his way down to the communal bathroom at the end of the hall.

At the turn of the twentieth century it had been an old tenement building. A series of unused, one room apartments lined the hallway. Inside the bathroom were a toilet, sink and shower.

Bashir shut the door behind him and hung his clothes on the hook behind the door. He reached behind the shower curtain and turned on the water. He began to undress, neatly laying the clothes on the toilet seat, as the steam from the shower began to fill the small room. He stepped inside, feeling the hot water stinging his skin and bringing soothing relief to his aching muscles.

The conditions were poor by western standards, but for Bashir they were like a five star hotel. He allowed himself the luxury of taking a long shower. Most westerners had no clue as to what they had right at their fingertips. It infuriated him the way they took things for granted and wasted simple things, like water. Westerners walked around thinking that they were superior to everyone else and yet, they were not.

Most had never known what it was like to not have running water or indoor plumbing in their home. They were dependent on just about everything. The past summer there had been a transformer fire that knocked out power for a few hours. People became outraged and that outrage had immediately turned to violence. Several blocks away they had begun to loot stores, smashing windows and taking what they wanted. They hadn't ventured down to this area because they knew that such lawlessness would never be tolerated. It disgusted him and only served to steel his resolve that these people did not deserve any mercy.

When he was done he grabbed the towel from the rack and dried himself off. He wiped down the mirror and stared at his reflection. His skin looked weathered and bore the scars of old wounds suffered in the mountains of his homeland. This had been a hard life for him, but soon, Allah willing, he would be reunited with his beloved Salimah.

Again he heard the voice of the Imam; *it rests with Allah alone to show you the right path.*

Bashir finished getting dressed. He gathered up his work clothing and made his way back down the hallway to his room. He walked inside and found a tray sitting on the desk. It held a covered bowl with lamb stew and a piraki, the traditional Afghani flat bread. On the side was a cup of black coffee and a Qur'an.

He picked up the book and opened it. As he leafed through the book he stopped at a spot where there was a hand written note stuck inside.

Bashir, In order to understand the path Allah has for you; you must first have a relationship with him. Faisal.

He laid the book down on the bed and sat down at the desk. He uncovered the bowl and began eating. It was hot, and the first spoonful burned his tongue. But it was very good and it reminded him of home. He took a sip of coffee and laid the cup back down on the desk.

He felt a sense of uneasiness as he ate. As if someone or something was calling out to him spiritually. He glanced back over his shoulder at the book lying on the bed. He reached over, picking up the book and began reading.

CHAPTER SIXTY

Southampton, Suffolk County, N.Y.
Monday, February 4th, 2013 – 5:42 p.m.

James and Rich sat in the salon having a drink.

It had been a long and emotional day for the two men. While they talked, Melody and Mary went upstairs to check on Genevieve. In the dining room, the members of the two men's security detail sat having dinner.

"You ever go to a funeral for someone you knew?" Rich asked. "Not just someone from the job, but someone that you actually knew?"

"Yeah, I have," Maguire replied.

Rich swirled the scotch around in his glass.

"I've never attended a funeral for someone I knew professionally who died in the line of duty," he said.

"Unfortunately it's part of the job that we choose," Maguire said. "No one forces us to do it."

"No, but you know, like I do, that when you're young, and full of piss and vinegar, mortality is not a word that is part of your lexicon."

"To an extent you're right," James replied. "It's always something that happens to someone else. But deep down inside of us we all know the inherent dangers of this job. The difference is, despite that knowledge, we still suit up then go out and do it. But that's not what this is about."

Rich leaned back in the couch and stared up at the ceiling.

"I guess I got so caught up worrying about the whole 'the buck stops here' part of the job that I got my priorities screwed up."

"How's that?" James asked.

"I became so focused on doing the job for the people above me that I lost sight of all those people that do the job *for me*."

"There's nothing wrong with being conscientious and wanting to do the best possible job you can. We all have our superiors and we get hired to do the job to the best of our ability. If we don't then we shouldn't be in that spot."

"But those guys died because they were doing that job, it killed them."

"Yes, it did. And if they hadn't, if they had looked the other way for a moment, just imagine how many others who would have perished."

"I guess it is something that I am going to have to come to terms with," Rich said.

"A wise man once said 'Death smiles at all of us, all a man can do is smile back'," replied James as he took a drink from his glass.

"Doesn't make it sound like we have too many options."

"The men and women that work for you don't want your sympathies, Rich, they want your leadership. They want to know that you have their back and won't let their sacrifices be forgotten. Troops didn't follow Patton because he was a *nice guy*, they followed him because he was a leader who wouldn't ask anything of his men that he wouldn't or hadn't done himself."

"You missed your calling; you should have been an inspirational speaker."

"It's just another service I provide."

"Speaking of that, did you ever hear back from your contacts about our missing terrorist?"

"I did," James said. "However I didn't get anything that is going to help us. Actually, it makes this guy more of a mystery."

"What makes you say that?" Rich asked.

"According to my sources, this guy has never been on any radar. He appears to be just a local player who spent all his time in Afghanistan. If he had any beef, it looks to have been with the Soviets."

"So what brought him to New York City?"

"That's the million dollar question."

"Are we getting anywhere with the one in the hospital?"

"No, in his case a suicide bombing would be a mercy killing. All he could tell us about Bashir was that he basically hung around with Yusef Sayeed."

"The guy we killed, great."

"Whoever put this team together was either scraping from the bottom of the barrel or is a psychotic genius who apparently knows something that we don't."

"What makes you say that?"

"There's no rhyme or reason with any of this. You have a hardcore element with Sayeed and Al Karim, and then you have the Middle East version of the *Three Stooges* thrown in."

"Hardcore? I thought you said Al Karim was just a local?"

"He was, but he was also a member of the Mujahideen. They are battle hardened vets."

"So you think there is more to this than what we are seeing?"

"I do," Maguire replied. "Unfortunately we are left with more questions than answers."

"What are the folks over in the Bureau saying?"

"There too busy patting each other's back and talking about what a fantastic job was done disrupting this terror plot, everyone that is except Silverman. He still seems pretty miffed about the game State played with Bin Khalid."

"What do you think?"

"I think someone's covering their ass and that there is a lot more to that story."

"Why does it feel as if we are in the middle of a battle with ourselves?"

"Because we are," James said. "You and I both know that they created DHS to *streamline* intelligence sharing after 9/11 so that things *wouldn't* slip through the cracks. Here we are more than a decade later and not only is the intelligence problem not fixed; now we have our own agencies cutting them loose."

"Should I make a call down to Washington?"

"If you want my opinion, I'd tell you not to."

"Really? You don't think it would do any good?"

"I think we need to focus on the priority, which at the moment is Al Karim. Once we have resolved that issue I think we need to revisit the other one. I just have this strange feeling that there is something more here and I wouldn't tip my hand just yet."

"What hand?" Rich replied. "I don't even have a lousy pair of two's."

"Yeah, but they don't know that."

Rich was just about to respond when Mary and Melody rejoined them.

"How's Gen?" James asked.

"Eh, feeling a little bit better, but still whiney," replied Melody. "But she's Gregor's problem now."

"What are you guys talking about?"

"Saving the world," Rich said.

"I learned long ago the world doesn't want to be saved," Mary replied and took a sip of Rich's drink.

"Amen to that," James said and held his glass up in a mock toast.

"You're so cynical sometimes," said Melody.

"Oh crap," Maguire said and took the cell phone out of his pocket.

"What's wrong?" Melody asked.

"When we were at the funeral I got a call from Monahan. I forgot all about it. I have to call him back."

Maguire got up and walked away, leaving the three of them to their conversation. The phone rang several times before it answered.

"You're not going to believe this," the man said.

"What's wrong?" James asked.

"Lena Marx is missing."

"What? How?"

Suddenly the conversation behind him stopped as they waited to hear what was happening.

"We don't know yet. But I'm guessing you're thinking the same as I am."

Maguire was angry inside. Not at Monahan, but at the bullshit politics that had led to the decimation of the task force and the dropping of protection for Lena Marx for financial reasons. It seemed like he and Monahan were the only voices of reason left in this investigation. Sadly, Rich was worried about the two men he had lost while the powers that be in Albany had all but forgotten about their fallen officers.

"How did you find out?"

"Lena's girlfriend called me. Said she had called Lena last week to say that she wouldn't be back till Monday. When she got back today, she said that Lena was gone and the gallery was closed. Her purse and jacket were missing, but her car is still there."

Maguire was trying to piece it all together in his mind.

"Wait, what girlfriend?"

"Well, I guess she met someone, a stewardess from Keenseville named Susan Hadley."

"Could she have gone somewhere?"

"After they dropped the protection detail she said that she would check in with me and let me know if she was going to be out of town for any reason. I tried calling her number but no answer."

"You try pinging the cell?"

"Yep, it's dead. Battery must be out of it."

"Last location?"

"Home, or close to it. Then it went dark."

"When?"

"Around 1830 hours on Friday."

"You guys check the apartment?

"Yeah, nothing seems missing except for her. I have the apartment sealed up and awaiting the arrival of a forensic team coming up from Albany tomorrow. They'll do their CSI magic on it and see if anything pops."

"I appreciate the heads up, Dennis. Keep me posted and let me know if there is anything I can do."

"I will," Monahan replied. "Talk to you later."

"Bye."

Maguire hung up the phone and turned around. Melody was now standing behind him.

"What's wrong, James?" Melody asked.

"Lena Marx went missing from upstate. No signs of foul play at the apartment, but her cell phone went dead on Friday night."

"Banning?" Rich asked.

"That's who my money's on."

"Fuck!" Melody cried out.

Instantly, the members of the two security details flooded into the room, scanning it for any threats.

"It's okay," Rich said. "Everything's fine."

Maguire took Melody in his arms and held her.

"It's okay, angel," he said. "I promise he won't get near you again."

Melody looked at James, her eyes pleading, and silently mouthed the words "*kill him.*"

CHAPTER SIXTY-ONE

Northern Maine
Tuesday, February 5th, 2013 – 10:17 a.m.

Tatiana looked up from her book as Banning walked into the living room and sat down in the recliner.

"Good morning," she said. "Sleep well?"

"Like a rock," he replied. "I can't believe I slept so late. How long have you been up?"

"I got up around six," she replied. "I didn't sleep well, tossed and turned. Lots of weird dreams. I decided to just get up, do some cleaning and make the coffee. Care for a cup?"

"I'd love some."

Tatiana laid the book down on the couch, picked up her own cup and went to the kitchen. She had the fire already going in the fireplace. It was nice to wake up to an already warm living room.

A few moments later she returned with two cups, steam rising up from them. She handed one to Banning before going back to the couch and sitting down.

"Ah," he exclaimed as he took a sip. "I needed this."

Outside the sun shone brightly through the cabin windows. The winter weather was sometimes hard to get used to. They'd endured weeks of gray, foreboding, skies so any break, even if just for a day, was a welcome respite.

"What are you reading?"

Tatiana held up the book so that he could read the cover.

"*The Day of the Jackal.* So you were paying attention!"

"Always," she replied with a wink.

"What do you think of it?"

"I like it. It has a much better premise than the movie."

"Hollywood never gets it right," he said. "They always have to remake movies, thinking they know better. As if adding technology and over the top action is best. All they wind up doing is ruining a classic."

"Do you think you could get away with it today?"

"Anything can be accomplished as long as you have the desire to achieve your goal and you couple that with the right amount of planning."

She thought about that for a moment.

"But you cannot plan for everything," she said.

"No, you can't," Banning replied. "But you have to remember that you always have the advantage because you know the when and the where, your intended victim doesn't."

"But what about someone who is always on guard?"

"The odds are that they cannot maintain it. Remember, they have to be right one hundred percent of the time and you only have to be right once. So if you have the luxury of watching and waiting, you will eventually find a weakness to exploit."

"In the book there were a lot of attempts, wouldn't this normally wear security down?"

"It depends," Banning replied. "There are a lot of variables to consider."

"Such as?" Tatiana asked.

"Training and force composition for starters. Take the Secret Service. They are at the tip of the spear in terms of training and they have a large cadre of personnel to draw from. It would be very hard to bait them. However, history has shown that attempts can be successfully made. Usually it is the person who is completely off the radar who has the best chance. A one time, one opportunity event, that no one sees coming."

"What about someone with 'normal' security? Like a celebrity?"

"Most of their bodyguards are *wannabes*. Occasionally someone will hire a former Secret Service agent or other person, who has actually done protection, but the very nature of the *celebrity* status is to be exposed and often they are their own worst enemy."

"Why do you say that?"

"Celebrities or businessmen only like to look important. It's all a façade. You see them walk out of a store with their big strapping bodyguard who is carrying packages or they are holding an umbrella over their boss' head. If their hands are occupied they are already out of the fight, even before it began. They are there only for show. Over time the bodyguards become accustomed to being nothing more than a servant and stop being vigilant. Someone who *takes* their security seriously, *treats* their security seriously."

"What about Maguire?"

"I'm working on that," Banning replied. "In that case, he needs to be separated from his security. That will require a bit more planning."

"Well, that just means I have more time to train."

"That's my girl, always focusing on the positive."

"You taught me well," she replied. "Speaking of which, I'm thinking of doing some target practice, since the weather is nice."

"Want me to come with you?"

"No," she replied. "I know you have things to do and I need to learn to be self-reliant. There might come a time when you have plans and it would be wrong to alter them just to babysit me."

"You really have embraced the pioneer spirit."

"I like being able to take care of myself. It is very empowering to know that I can carry my own weight."

"Then far be it from me to stand in the way of self-improvement, love."

"What are you going to do?"

"I'm sure I can find something *fun* to occupy my time," he replied, his thoughts turning to the woman locked away.

"Oh, I'm sure you will," Tatiana replied with a laugh. "And since we're on the subject of *wood*, make sure you find the time to restock the fireplace holder. I light, you load."

"Yes, my dear," he replied, taking a sip of the coffee before returning back to his thoughts.

CHAPTER SIXTY-TWO

Manhattan, New York City
Tuesday, February 5th, 2013 – 1:54 p.m.

Mary hung up the phone and let out a long slow sigh. Deep inside her she was fuming. It had only been three days since she had grudgingly *invited* Tippi Fisher to the charity event and the woman had already started causing problems.

She had just spent the last half hour listening to Deb Perez. She was venting about how *that* woman was inserting herself in the final planning of the event.

"The woman is driving me mad," Deb said. "It's not as if I'm not busy enough to begin with, but now she is *asking* that we include more ethnically diverse foods at the event. She says it will highlight the wide spectrum of community involvement in this cause."

"I'm so sorry, Deb," Mary replied. "I wish I could go back and withdraw the invite."

"It's okay. Do you know this woman really well?"

"No, that's the worst part of it. In title, she is in charge of the police department and Rich thought it might be a nice thing to include her."

"He knows he owes you right?"

"Oh he most certainly does and I'm willing to loan him out at this point."

Deb laughed. "It's okay; we all have our crosses to bear."

"What can I do to make it up to you?"

"Oh don't be silly. I just needed to vent to someone. It will be fine."

"How much work is this going to involve?"

"Not too much really. We will just include some extra sides and desserts. I have already talked to the caterer and he is going to handle it all. They will just include it with the primary dishes."

"I still feel horrible."

"That's okay, she's sitting with you," Deb laughed.

"What?"

"It's not my fault. *Ms. High and Mighty* requested a place at your table."

"That's not going to happen," Mary said defiantly.

"What do you mean?"

"I'll still be in jail. After I kill Rich I doubt they let me out on bond to attend."

"It's only one evening. We will all get through it."

"She had better be making a huge donation for all the trouble she is causing."

"I have to admit, having a deputy mayor in attendance will almost certainly gain us a lot more media attention. So it might be worth it, in the end."

"Boy, is that the power of positive thinking or what?"

"This is charity, Mary; all we have is positive thinking."

CHAPTER SIXTY-THREE

Northern Maine
Tuesday, February 5th, 2013 – 3:31 p.m.

Tatiana came up the hill, trudging through the snow. She had the rifle case strapped to her back and carried the ammo box in her hand.

Banning ran out of the house and met her out in the field in front of the cabin.

"Are you alright? What happened? Where's the snow machine?"

Tatiana stopped, dropping the ammo box, and rested her hands on her knees. It had been a long walk and she felt physically spent.

"I was on my way back and all of a sudden the engine started acting funny. It felt like it was choking and then it just died."

Banning grabbed the rifle bag from her and picked up the ammo box.

"I'm so sorry. It's probably a gummed up carburetor. How far away was it when it broke down?"

"I'd say about a mile or so. Mile and a half tops."

"It's too late to fix it tonight. I'll go out in the morning and figure out what's wrong with it. Come inside and I'll get you some hot coffee."

"I'm sorry, Keith. I tried to figure it out. I thought that maybe I hit something. But I didn't see anything in the snow. I didn't want to make anything worse."

"No, you did the right thing," he replied. "Tomorrow we'll go take a look and see what is wrong with it."

As they walked through the cabin he dropped the rifle case and ammo box on the table in the kitchen. It felt warm inside as they made their way into the living room. Banning moved the rocker closer to the fireplace. He removed her jacket and had her sit down.

"You just relax and I'll get your coffee."

Tatiana felt the heat on her face and it stung. She rubbed her hands together, trying to warm them up quicker. She'd thought she had been dressed well enough, but she would have to make sure that if she ventured out again that she had better gloves and one of those balaclava hoods that covered her whole face.

Keith returned a moment later with a hot cup of coffee that she clasped with both hands.

"Drink slowly," he said as he knelt down and stoked the fire, adding another log on it.

"I feel so stupid," she said. "Like there was something more I could have done."

"No, these things happen and you just don't have the experience that I have. When I get it back here, I'll sit down and show you the basic things to check for in the future. Plus I'll strap a tool kit on it. This way, when you're out, you will at least have something to work with if you have any mechanical problems again."

Tatiana took a sip of the coffee, tasting the slight burn of whisky in it.

"That's what I call a cup of coffee," she said, saluting him with the mug.

"I thought you could use something to take the edge off quicker."

"It was a wonderful thought."

"How'd your shooting go? I noticed the ammo box was much lighter."

"That part went great," she replied. "I did what you told me and got it sighted in with five shots."

"Fantastic! How'd the target shooting go?"

"It went extremely well. Even at 100 yards I was able to keep them in a fairly respectable grouping. I even loved the little Russian *hand-warmer* they included on the front stock."

"You won't in the summer time," he said with a laugh.

"So how has your day gone? I see you found the time to stock up some wood."

"I managed to keep myself busy doing chores," he replied.

"Oh really?" Tatiana said. "I'm pleasantly surprised. I figured you would have found some free time to play."

"Well, I might have *thought* about it." Banning replied.

Tatiana laughed.

"Boys will be boys," she replied. "Maybe after dinner you can have a special dessert."

CHAPTER SIXTY-FOUR

Brooklyn, New York City
Tuesday, February 5th, 2013 – 4:53 p.m.

Faisal sat at the small desk, writing on a note pad, as he held the phone to his ear.

"I hope it's not too short of a notice for you?" the man on the other end of the phone asked.

"No, that is not a problem at all," replied Faisal. "We can accommodate your needs. Do you have any ideas about what you would like to have?"

"I'd like to have a plate for each table. Maybe like a sample platter with some baklava, ma'amoul, cashew assabe, basbousa, and Kanafeh?"

"Yes, we can do this easily. Would you like different types of ma'amoul?"

"Yes that would be wonderful."

"Ok, please tell me the information for the event."

"Do you have a fax machine? I can send you the flyer with all the information."

"Yes, that will be fine," Faisal said and gave the man the fax number.

"Thank you so much, Faisal. If there are any problems please call me. My number will be on the fax sheet."

"Very good, sir," Faisal replied and hung up the phone. He began writing out his notes onto an order sheet. A few moments later the fax machine began to chirp and printed out the flyer for the event. When it was complete, he stapled the flyer to the order sheet. He tried to stand up but his back ached severely, the result of a fall he had taken earlier in the day.

"Bashir?" he called out.

A moment later the man poked his head out from inside the store.

"Yes," he asked.

"Please be so kind to give this to Halimah," he said and handed the man the sheet.

"Yes, of course," Bashir said and took the papers.

As he walked toward the front of the store, he examined the order sheet. He flipped it up and looked at the flyer underneath, reading it as he walked.

Lamplighter House Annual Charity Fundraiser
Guest of Honor - Mary Stargold
Wife of the New York City Police Commissioner

Bashir stopped dead in his tracks, the voice of the Imam once again resounding in his head, *"It rests with Allah alone to show you the right path."*

"*Allahu akbar*," he said softly. "God is greater."

CHAPTER SIXTY-FIVE

Northern Maine
Tuesday, February 5th, 2013 – 6:17 p.m.

Tatiana stood at the sink doing the dishes from the evening meal.

Banning walked up behind her, grabbing her by the hips and kissing the back of her neck.

"Mmmm," she said, lowering the plate back into the sink and tilting her head slightly to give him better access.

"If you're trying to butter me up to get your dessert, it's working," she said.

"I was actually wondering if you wanted to join me?"

Tatiana turned around to face him, her arms crossed over her chest and her lips scrunched up in a smirk.

"How sweet of you to ask me if I wanted to have a threesome with you and my girlfriend," Tatiana replied.

Banning stepped back and raised his hands up in mock surrender.

"No, no," he stammered defensively. "I just meant…"

"Oh stop, I'm just kidding," Tatiana replied and went back to doing the dishes. "You go down and get warmed up. I'll come join you in a minute."

Banning kissed her on the back of the neck and slapped her ass.

"You're the greatest!"

"Damn straight, and don't you forget it."

Banning made his way down into the bunker and walked to the back room where Lena was. He opened the door and stepped inside.

She was lying on the bed. Banning kept her in a semi sedated state. It was easier in these early stages. She knew what was going on, but lacked the ability to put up much of a fight. It was as if her brain was working a few seconds too late.

He stared at her for a moment, appreciating the beauty of the woman in front of him. It wasn't that he was growing tired of Tatiana, but he liked having something different from time to time.

Even if you love steak, every once in a while you still want chicken, he thought.

Lena certainly satisfied that role. He wondered what it would be like when she was off the meds. Would she be a fighter? Tatiana never was. Maybe he would enjoy a bit of roughness with her. He'd have to be careful of course, he was after all *sharing* her and he wondered if Tatiana would allow him to be too aggressive with her.

Banning began to get undressed.

Lena tried to focus, but it was so hard. She could see the figure in front of her. It was hard to make out features, everything always seemed blurry to her.

Was it him again?

She wondered if she was dreaming.

No, this is not something I would dream about, she thought. *This is not a dream, this is a nightmare.*

She steeled herself in anticipation. She could close her eyes and just drift off.

What had happened to Tricia? Was she alive? How had Banning found them? Wasn't he dead?

The thoughts went through her mind faster than she could comprehend them all. It was a weird feeling. It was like she was standing still but everything around her was racing by at a hundred miles an hour.

Suddenly she felt pressure on top of her and then inside her. Hands began grabbing her body roughly.

She closed her eyes and began to disconnect from her body. It would end soon and she just needed to occupy her time until it did.

Lena tried to focus on the room. It was hard to make out the details in the room. The light shifted a bit and she saw a shadow walk into the room.

Was there someone else here? Were they watching?

The shadow drew closer.

"Having fun, baby?" Tatiana asked.

Banning looked back at her sheepishly.

"Do you want me to stop?" he asked.

"No, I'm sore from the walk, I'm going to sit over there and watch if you don't mind. Make it a good show and make it last."

"Yes, ma'am," he replied eagerly.

Tatiana sat down in the chair.

It was a surreal image to watch him with her. Erotic, but surreal nonetheless. Her mind drifted back to her prior life with Lena. Their nights were passionate, sensual. She remembered the warmth and taste of her skin on her lips. The way she moved and how easily it was for each of them to please one another. She missed her touch now, missed the innocence of the relationship. It was lost now, both of them were tainted.

The old saying is true, you can't go back, she thought.

Watching Banning with her was voyeuristic. She felt dirty as she *spied* on them, but at the same time she found herself drawn to it and growing more aroused with each passing moment. She decided it was time to have her fun.

Tatiana got up and walked over to the bed.

"Keith," she said. "I want you to do her from behind, for me."

Banning stopped and pulled out of her.

Lena was chained to the bed so Tatiana leaned over and unlocked the ankle chain allowing Banning to turn her over onto her stomach. He lifted her limp body up by her hips and slid himself back inside her.

"You like watching?"

"Oh yeah, baby," Tatiana replied. "Are you having fun?"

"Uh huh," Banning said, grunting harder now as he thrust in and out of Lena.

"I hope so, baby," Tatiana replied. "I wanted this to be special for you."

"Oh yeah, why is that?" Banning asked.

"Because it's your last time in the saddle, big boy," Tatiana replied and drove the syringe into his ass, depressing the plunger which injected the drug into his body.

Banning screamed as he lunged forward. He tried to get away, putting some distance between him and the danger. He crashed to the ground, but he knew it was already too late.

Tatiana stood in the center of the room. In one hand she held the empty syringe and in the other was the small Walther PPK, just in case the drug took longer than she anticipated.

"Why?" was all he was able to say, his eyes wide with terror, as the effects of the drug took hold. His body collapsed to the floor.

The drug wouldn't last too long, but long enough for her to get him dressed and tie him up.

Tatiana walked over and stood over him.

"Did you really think that I was just going to roll over and play your little game, Keith? Men are so friggin' pathetic. Be the perfect subservient woman, give them a little piece of ass and they'll do anything you want. Every time you fucked me, you didn't realize that you were actually just fucking yourself, Keith."

Banning could only stare at her as she took his clothes and began dressing him. When she was done, she rolled him onto his chest and hogtied him. She then used zip-ties to secure his ankles and wrists.

After she was finished she walked over to where Lena was laying on the bed. She grabbed the sheet and wrapped her up.

"Oh, baby, I'm so sorry that you had to go through this, but it was the only way I could think of to get us free."

She helped Lena up off the bed and guided her toward the door, which she locked as they went out. When they got upstairs she led her into the living room, sitting her down on the couch and held her tightly.

"It's okay, baby, everything is going to be fine," she said and began rocking her gently.

It took a while for the sedative to begin wearing off. When it did Lena began to sob uncontrollably. She held her tightly and let the emotions run their course.

"What the hell is going on?" Lena asked.

"It's a long story, baby. Trust me I know this has been tough on you, but this has been my life for months. I had to go along with it to gain his trust. You wouldn't believe what I have had to do, what I had to let him do to me."

Lena began crying again.

"It's okay. Let it all out. It's all over now."

Suddenly Lena snapped upright.

"We need to get out of here!" she exclaimed, panic stricken.

"Don't worry, I have a plan. But first we need to get you cleaned up and dressed."

She helped Lena up and led her to the bathroom. She turned the hot water on, then watched as Lena dropped the sheet and got in.

"I'll get you some clothes, honey," she said and walked out of the bathroom.

Lena began to scrub herself hard with the bar of soap as she desperately tried to wash him off of her. When she was done she stepped out and dried herself off with the towel that was set out for her.

The door opened and Lena turned to see Tricia walk in with new clothes in her hands.

"You all finished, babe?"

"Yes," Lena replied, taking the clothes. "We have to call the cops."

"Don't worry, I told you I have a plan," she said. "Get dressed and I'll explain everything to you."

When she was done, Lena walked out into the living room to find Tricia sitting on the couch.

"Feeling better?"

"A bit," Lena replied. "I have a headache."

"Here, this should help?" she said and handed her a drink.

Lena took the glass of whiskey and drank half of it.

"Tell me about this plan you have, Tricia," Lena said as she set the glass down on the table.

"We can't call the police, Lena," she began. "I don't know about you, but I can't take the chance of him getting off on a technicality and spending the rest of my life in fear. Even if he did go to prison, do you ever think we could have a peaceful life? Or would you worry like I would, that he would get paroled or escape?"

"I agree with you, but agreeing and doing something about it are two different things. What do you want to do?"

"There is enough of that drug left that we can drive out to the road. I know this place where we can drug him, put him into the driver's seat, and then let the car go over the cliff."

She could see Lena processing it all. Despite what she had been through over the last several days, the concept of murdering another human being, even a despicable one like Banning, was a tough thing to come to terms with.

"Can't we just leave him down there?"

"We need certainty. We need to know that we are not going to wake up one morning and find him standing over us, or turn the aisle in the store to see him standing there. I can't live that way can you?

"I don't think I can kill him, Tricia."

"You don't have to do anything, Lena. Just help me get him there and into the front seat. Then just walk away, I will do the rest. I don't have a problem with it."

Lena reached over and took the glass, finishing off the other half.

"Give me another glass for courage."

"Take as much as you need," Tricia said, and handed her the bottle.

Lena poured another drink, gulping it down to get it into her system quicker.

"What do we do afterward?"

"Get on with life."

"Then let's get this over with."

They stood up and made their way back down into the bunker.

Banning was thrashing about the floor, desperately trying to get free.

"You fucking cunt!" he cried out as she walked back into the room.

"Aw, poor, Keith," she replied condescendingly. "Evening not going the way you thought it would?"

"I'm going to fucking kill you," he screamed, spitting as the words came out. "And when I'm done, I'm going to skin, gut you and feed your fucking entrails to the animals."

"Ooooh, someone has unresolved anger issues," she said, taking his face in her hand. "Unfortunately for you, it's not going to be the *happy ending* you thought you were going to get."

"Fuck you!"

"No, Keith, tonight it's all about *me* fucking *you*," she replied and wrapped Banning's mouth with duct tape.

"Well, that'll make the trip a lot more pleasant," she said.

She grabbed a tarp off the shelf and laid it on the floor.

"Grab his legs," she instructed Lena. The two women picked him up, carrying him over and dropping him in the center of it.

She ran a length of nylon cord through the grommets and cinched him into the tarp.

"Okay, Keith, hold on," she said.

It was a struggle with his thrashing, but the two women managed to physically haul him through the bunker system. Then they hoisted him up, his head banging violently along the way. Dragging him across the snow was a bit easier, and they lifted him up, laying him in the back of the truck.

"How far away is this, Tricia?"

"Not far, I saw it earlier in the day," she said. "It's a pull off that drops off into a deep ravine. We set the truck on fire, if the fall doesn't kill him the fire will."

Fifteen minutes later they arrived at the spot. She turned the lights off and the two women got out of the car. Then they went to the back of the truck and popped the hatch. Tatiana untied the cord and opened the tarp. The look of sheer panic in Banning's eyes was quite evident.

"Last call, Keith," she said as the needle slipped through the material of the shirt and depressed the plunger.

Lena glanced back and forth along the dark deserted road waiting for the next car to come and catch them in the act.

"Calm down, baby. Everything's going to be just fine."

"I don't know how you can be so calm," Lena replied. "We're about to kill another human being."

"He's not human," she replied. "Let's just get this over with."

From inside her jacket she withdrew a buck knife and cut the zip-ties from his ankles and wrists. Then they dragged him from the back of the truck and put him into the driver's seat, strapping him in place with the seatbelt.

"There's a gas container in the back, Lena, I need you to dump it into the back seat."

Lena walked around and climbed into the back of the truck.

"Tricia, I don't see it," she called out.

Lena turned to get back out only to see her standing at the tailgate.

"Not sure why you keep calling me that," she replied. "My name is Tatiana."

Lena looked down to see the gun she held in her hand.

"What's going on?"

"Sorry, babe, really I am, but things have changed," Tatiana relied. "Remember how you moved on with your life while I was missing? So have I, and my life doesn't include you anymore."

"I don't understand."

"I needed you to close this chapter of the book. The story ends with Banning kidnapping and killing you, before he then tragically dies in a crash trying to dispose of the body."

"But..."

"Don't worry, babe, you won't be alone for long. I plan to arrange a get together for you and Susan in the hereafter real soon."

"Tricia…"

Tatiana shot her twice, center mass, just as Banning had taught her.

Lena clutched her chest, her eyes wide open as the life drained out of her. She gasped, trying to speak, but instead collapsed onto the bed of the truck. Tatiana pulled her body just to the edge of the tailgate.

When she was done she walked around to the back door where the gas can was and poured it over the back seat. She closed the door and then struck the window with the glass shattering pike on the knife. She walked over to the driver's side door and opened it.

"How ya doing, Keith?" she asked. She reached over, removing the cigarettes and lighter from his shirt pocket.

Tatiana grabbed his face and turned it so that he could see her. Fear raged in the man's eyes.

She lit the cigarette and took a long drag, exhaling the smoke.

"Bet your wondering why, right?" Tatiana asked. "Actually, you only have yourself to blame. You should have never recommended that book to me."

She took another drag on the cigarette, this time blowing it in his direction.

"You see, I read the whole book. When you first quoted it to me I thought I understood, but there's more to it, Keith. Great men do have bodyguards, but over time the security can become mechanical and lax. That's when the assassin's bullet is effective and, more importantly, that's when the assassin can escape."

"You had a great plan, but unfortunately you failed at the very moment when you had your target in your sights. Now there is no letting down of the security. In fact the only way to lower that security is to make the assassin go away. You see, they're looking for you, not me. My desire for revenge with Lena was two-fold, I got even, but you get the credit for her death. If you killed her, then they are going to conclude that Tricia is most likely dead as well."

"I'm sure you can appreciate the work I have had to put into fixing your screw-up. I'd love to go into detail about my plans, but I'm afraid the drug won't last much longer. Be proud of the monster you've created, Keith; unlike you, I won't fail."

She leaned in and pressed her left foot down on the brake pedal, putting the truck into drive. Tatiana then kissed Banning hard on the lips while reaching down and slowly rubbing his crotch.

"Once more, for old time's sake, eh," she said.

She took her foot off the pedal and closed the door, watching as the truck slowly began inching its way toward the edge.

"*Bon Voyage*, Keith," she called out.

As it passed by, she flicked the cigarette into the back seat and watched as the gasoline erupted into a fireball just as it went over the edge.

Tatiana turned and made her way across the road and back up into the woods.

A moment later the silence of the night air was interrupted by the sound of the snow machine's engine roaring to life.

CHAPTER SIXTY-SIX

Southampton, Suffolk County, New York
Tuesday, February 5th, 2013 – 7:17 p.m.

Maguire walked into the salon and found Melody sitting on one of the couches in front of the fireplace reading a book.

"Hey, cowboy," she said, laying the book down on the coffee table in front of her.

James laid his jacket over the back of the couch and kissed her on the forehead.

"Good evening, angel," he replied. "You need a refill?"

Melody picked up the wine glass and handed it to him.

"Why, thank you kind, sir."

Maguire walked over to the dry bar, pouring her another glass of *pinot noir* and got himself a scotch on the rocks.

"So how was your day?" he asked, handing her the glass and taking the seat next to her.

"Quiet. I just spent the day going over some updates from GDL. I'm going to have to leave at the end of the month for about ten days."

"Is there anything wrong?"

"No, I just have to deal with some issues at corporate. Then I'm going out to Wyoming for a show and tell."

"Sounds like fun."

"You want to come? I have my own cabin."

"I wish I could, but with everything going on with our missing terrorist, I can't leave."

Melody snuggled up against him, feeling his arm wrap around her.

"I hate this," she said. "I hate feeling this way."

"What's wrong?"

"I despise leaving this house, James," she said. "I feel as if it is the only safe place and it has become my fortress."

Maguire took a drink and set the glass on the end table next to him.

"What are we talking about? The terrorist, Banning, or all of it combined?"

All of it," she replied. "But more than anything else, I worry about you."

"Me?" he asked. "Why do you worry about me?"

"Because I love you, stupid."

Maguire laughed. Even when she was being serious she could still manage to find a way to take the edge off.

"I love you, too."

Melody sat up and turned to face him.

"No," she said. "I *love* you, James."

Maguire stared into her eyes. This was different. She was different. Her normal playful side was gone, replaced by something much more serious.

"I've come to realize that, for the first time in my life, another human being means more to me than everything else I have worked all my life to achieve. It's as if I hold my breath when you leave in the morning and I can't let it go until you're back home, at the end of the day. There are days when I would give anything to go back to my old life. Then I remember that I wouldn't have you and it wouldn't be worth it. My life's just not worth living without you."

Maguire sat listening to her as she shared her most intimate thoughts and fears.

"I could say that it is the reason why I have never let anyone else in before. But the truth is, until I met you, I never needed anyone else. I had Gen to keep me company and make me laugh. I had my work to challenge me and get lost in. I loved it and I could control every aspect of it. Then I met you and from that very moment everything else just faded away. Now I'm terrified that I have been blessed with something so wonderful and I don't how I could survive if I lost you."

This was a conversation Maguire had never anticipated having. Truth was he knew exactly how she felt. For over twenty years he had put all of his time and energy into the pursuit of his career. The women that had come into his life were there for only a brief moment. That had all changed the day he met her. Something about her was different and he could not imagine what his life would be like without her.

It wasn't a matter of surviving. Anyone could survive even the worst tragedies. The question was, what was the purpose of surviving when you had lost your reason for living?

Maguire took Melody's hand in his.

"You know the reason I call you angel is because that's what I think you are. From the very first moment I saw you, you took my breath away. The night with Banning, when I had to face the thought of losing you, I realized I had never felt that way about anyone before. The truth is, I love you too Melody, with all my heart and soul. I don't want to imagine a life without you in it. I do understand the fear you are trying to come to terms with and I would give up everything if it would make you feel better."

Melody got up, sat in his lap, wrapping her arms around his neck and kissed him gently.

"No," she said, staring into his eyes. "I would never ask you to stop doing what you do. I know you would walk away from it for me, and I hope you know I would leave it all for you as well. I'm being a silly little girl, just put up with me when I get like this."

"You're not going to lose me," he replied, holding her tightly. "I know you worry about me, but you have to understand that it would be like me worrying that you would go broke."

"So it's true, you're only with me for my money?" she asked playfully.

"Yep, you finally figured me out," he replied. "Well, your money and the way you do that little thing with your…"

She pressed a finger up to his lips.

"I don't know what you're talking about, mister. I'm a *good* girl."

He moved her hand away.

"You're a *great* girl."

She lowered her head onto his shoulder, feeling his arms wrap tightly around her. For a moment she wished they were away from all of this, someplace far away from the work, the stress, and the threats.

"Don't ever let me go," she whispered.

"There's nothing on Earth that would ever keep me away from you, angel."

Melody felt a sudden wave of emotion come crashing down upon her. She closed her eyes tightly as the tears streamed down her cheeks.

CHAPTER SIXTY-SEVEN

Northern Maine
Thursday, February 7th, 2013 – 7:01 a.m.

Tatiana stretched out across the bed.

She stared out the window and watched the snow falling outside, the white flakes contrasting against the dark gray clouds. Despite the foreboding skies outside, she felt more rested and content then she had in months.

It was her first morning alone in the cabin and she was thoroughly enjoying it. That might change after a while, but for now the solitude was a welcome friend. She needed time alone with her thoughts. So much had changed in such a short time that she needed to re-evaluate what was truly important to her. On top of that she needed to take stock of what mysteries this cabin held.

She had often seen Banning going through piles of documents and photos. Tatiana knew where some of them were, but she surmised that there was more in the cabin somewhere; she just needed to find them. Banning had been a very secretive person and it would not surprise her to uncover a variety of things as she went along.

She got up, putting on her robe and made her way out to the living room. It was kind of Keith to stock the wood for her. She'd have to start doing that for herself soon. But today was her *liberation* day and it was going to be treated like the holiday it was.

Tatiana placed some small pieces of wood into the fireplace and grabbed a handful of the pine needles that were stored in an old metal pail. She knelt down and began blowing on the embers that remained from the previous night. Watching them glow brightly before igniting the needles. It wasn't long before the fire roared back to life.

She grabbed a cup of coffee from the kitchen and curled up on the couch, her hands wrapped around the hot mug as she stared out the window.

It was funny how something she had seen hundreds of times could take on a new feeling. Maybe it was being in the mountains, with only nature to surround her and protect her from the rest of the world. She felt like she could live here forever.

Could I? she wondered. *"Could I just stay locked away up here?"*

It was an interesting question. While she was intent on enjoying the quiet for a little bit longer, she knew that she would eventually need company. The real question was what type of company.

Tatiana had to admit that she rather enjoyed his touch. He was, of course, a bit rough in his approach, but there was something wonderfully primal about it. She had found herself turned on by his grunting and groaning during sex. He certainly got into it and there was an intensity about being with someone who could just take her whenever he wanted. However, she could not forget how quickly she had gotten aroused by Lena's touch back at the apartment.

If she was going to have a dilemma, this was at least a good one to have.

One thing she did not have a dilemma about was her future. Something had changed in her. She found that she had developed a taste for this life. There was a liberating feeling not having to actually care about another person. That she could use them, exploiting them for her interests and desire, yet not have to invest in any relationship, was appealing to her. It was like the best of both worlds, all the pleasure without any of the drama.

She hadn't been sure how she would actually handle the *disposal* part of her plan. In the end it wasn't as difficult as she had thought it would be. Lena, having cheated on her, had made things easier. That being said, she had wondered how it would *feel* when the time came to actually pull the trigger. When the moment arrived she found that she had no qualms. It was all rather mundane.

With Keith, it was a bit different. It wasn't personal like it had been with Lena. Despite how she had come to be in his company, she felt no animosity toward him. In fact she felt that in some way she owed him for setting her free. It was, after all, Keith Banning who had created her, at least who she was today. She would never forget him for what he had done and how he had impacted her life.

There was a cold reality with this life. Accomplishing ones goals and desires was the only real concern. Unfortunately for Banning, his failure to achieve his original goal had created the situation where the security would never be pulled back, as long as he was alive. Therefore, it only made sense to address it and she had. There was no regret, no emotional difficulty.

She planned. She executed. She achieved.

In terminating Banning's life she got the opportunity to achieve what he had not. It also removed the restrictions she would have had with him. Everyone was looking for Keith Banning; no one was looking for Tatiana....

Tatiana who? she thought.

That was something she would have to eventually contend with. Hopefully there would be something in this cabin that would aid her in completing her transformation.

CHAPTER SIXTY-EIGHT

1 Police Plaza, Manhattan, New York City
Thursday, February 7th, 2013 – 7:29 p.m.

"Did you see that piece last night on the bombing?" Rich asked over the phone.

"I didn't see it last night," James replied. "I was preoccupied. But I did get a copy of it this morning from Operations and watched it."

"I'd like to kill that *sonofabitch* Rogers."

"Listen, that was to be expected. I told you, Rogers doesn't do anything without being instructed. I'm sure that your predecessor is pulling those strings. They will do anything to make you look bad."

"What do you suggest I do?"

"You don't do anything; it's beneath you to respond. That's what you have a DCPI for. Tell Cleary to prepare a press release addressing the comments. Something to the effect: 'in light of the tragic deaths of our two officers, and the acts of heroism on the part of the members of the NYPD and FBI, the Department is saddened that former Chief Jonathan Rogers would seek to besmirch them or this Department. We however will not respond to such scurrilous attacks and will allow the facts to speak for themselves.'"

"I like it," Rich replied. "Where did you learn to come up with that line of BS?"

"When I had to explain to people, why all the Secret Service agents needed Intel detectives to babysit them around New York City."

"That's not funny."

"I can stop by your office at noon, if you need help finding a good restaurant for lunch?"

"I gotta go, talk to you later," Rich said.

Maguire laughed and hung up the phone.

There was a knock on the door.

"You have a minute, Commissioner?"

"Sure, come in, Nikki," Maguire said. "Do you want some coffee?"

"No, I'm fine."

He got up, refilling his mug and sat back down.

"What do you have for me?"

"Well, I wanted to let you know that our blind terrorist is heading to the Caribbean for some quality one on one *talk therapy*."

"Eh, I don't expect them to get too much from him. If that kid had a brain cell it would die of loneliness."

"Yeah, but even a broken clock is right twice a day."

"You need to stop hanging out with those folks on the 12th floor."

Ryan laughed at the reference to the Internal Affairs Bureau.

"I'll try to remember that," she said. "Silverman is sending down two of his JTTF boys just in case. If they come up with anything he'll let us know."

"I'm more concerned with Al Karim," he replied. "Are we picking up any chatter?"

"Nothing at all," Nikki replied. "I'm wondering if he didn't flee the country."

"No, he's still here."

"What makes you say that?"

"Call it a hunch. My feeling is that, of the five, he's the most dangerous, after the bomb builder. He's not going to let this get in his way. He's already adapting his plan. We just have to pray we figure it out in time."

"Any suggestions?"

"If I were him I'd hide in plain sight. Tell them to start beefing up the surveillance of the mosques. Have the U/C's start taking a second look at new arrivals in the community. He has to eat and sleep, we need to figure out where he is doing that."

"I'll let them know."

"Hamadi said they originally stayed in Boerum Hill. I'm sure they are already looking into it, but tell them to expand out as well, Bay Ridge, Bed-Stuy, Harlem, and Jackson Heights. If I were him I'd look for friendlies, any areas with Afghani communities. They won't give him up, but maybe we can put enough pressure that we can catch him on the move."

"Will do," Ryan replied. "Anything else?"

"Other than you're doing a great job and I really appreciate it? No, I think that about covers it."

"Well thank you, I appreciate that. I'll let you know if anything develops from the interrogation and I'll make sure they are combing the woods for our missing Afghan."

"Thanks, Nikki," Maguire said.

He took a sip of coffee and continued going through the reports on his desk. He had a busy day ahead of him including lunch with Assistant Chief Bob Parker, the Manhattan North Borough Commander, and his staff.

As a cop, he had spent most of his time in Brooklyn North. While he had a strong working knowledge of that part of the city, he had begun meeting with the borough commanders in the other parts of the city to determine what their specific needs and issues were. It also helped for them to see that the new administration was interested in helping them to combat crime in their respective neighborhoods.

This morning he began going over the Compstat figures for the last year. Compstat was the Department's computerized crime statistic program. Data was entered that allowed crimes to be tracked geographically. As a result, trends were identified which led to improved personnel and resource management. Theoretically this would reduce crime and improve the overall quality of life for the residents.

At least that was the original concept.

The program had originated in the former New York City Transit Police and had been wildly successful, reducing crime by nearly thirty percent. When William Bratton had taken over as police commissioner he implemented it in the NYPD. By 2003 the murder rate in New York City had dropped to a low it hadn't seen since 1964.

Unfortunately, the program was a victim of its own success. Once crime began to effectively be reduced, increased pressure was put on precinct and borough commanders to continue the reductions. As a result, the program deteriorated to the point that it was now being used to bully those same commanders into continuing the crime reductions. In order to not look bad at these meetings, commanders began to creatively *adjust* crimes. Aggravated assaults became simple assaults, and simple assaults were downgraded to harassment.

Everything came down to semantics.

Maguire was trying to get things back to their pure purpose, which was the effective targeting of crime, instead of fudging numbers to not look bad. However, it was going to take a lot of time and reassurance for some of them to tread back into the deep end of the pool.

The cell phone on the desk began to vibrate. He looked down at the number and answered.

"Hey, Dennis, I hope you have some good news."

"Yes and no," the man said.

Maguire could hear the stress in his voice.

"What's wrong?"

"We got a call early this morning from the Maine State Police," he replied. "Banning's dead, so is Lena."

Maguire took a deep breath and exhaled slowly. He had wanted desperately to hear those words, and yet now he realized how heavy the price for that was.

"What happened?"

"The investigators there tell me that the vehicle he was driving went off a cliff," Monahan explained. "It was up in the mountains and they'd had a lot of snow recently. Anyway, it goes over and rolls a bit. He was trapped inside and Lena's body was ejected."

"We have a positive ID?"

"On Lena yes, Banning was apparently trapped inside and burned in the crash so they couldn't do a visual. I'm flying out later this morning and bringing the DNA samples I have of Banning for comparison. They are going to expedite it for us. I hope to have confirmation by the weekend."

"I trust you, Dennis, but I need to know it's him."

"I agree with you, that's why I'm going personally. I want to make sure that prick is dead."

"Lena died from the crash?"

"No, gunshot apparently. The working theory they have is that he killed her, and was on his way to dispose of the body when the truck went over the side. There was a gas container in the truck and they think it ruptured during the crash. They're going under the assumption that he might have been smoking and it ignited it."

"So you're telling me that last night all the fucking stars were in perfect alignment and I missed out on playing lotto."

"It's *their* theory."

"I'll buy into it if it turns out that Banning really was behind the wheel. Where did this all happen?"

"All they said was that it was up in the Longfellow Mountains. I've got a helicopter coming up from the Aviation Unit at Saranac Lake at nine o'clock. I put the Aviation guys in contact with the State Police in Maine and they are coordinating the arrival. Then they are going to drive me to the accident scene. I'll let get back to you, once I know more."

"What about Lena's body?"

"I don't think she has any family left."

"Find out where they are keeping the body and give them my number. Once they clear her for release I'll make the arrangements to have her brought back to New York."

"I'll do that," Monahan said.

"Thanks, Dennis. Let me know if you need anything."

"I will. I'll call you when I know more."

Maguire ended the call as he stared at the photo of him and Melody that sat on his desk. He wanted it to be true, for her sake. To be able to finally put the nightmare to rest. But he would have to wait to tell her. He needed to be absolutely certain that the person behind the wheel was actually Banning, and not just another one of his tricks.

He wasn't sure how he felt at the moment. There was always a part of him that had envisioned pulling the trigger. To know with absolute certainty that he had put an end to Banning's reign of terror. Now he would have to come to terms with the fact that the man had met his end by another means, if it were truly Banning occupying the tray in the morgue.

The reality of Lena's death was much more difficult for him to face because it revived the question of where was Tricia. The fact that Lena was dead after being kidnapped only a few days earlier was not a good omen that Tricia was still alive. Even if she was, it would seem that her last chance at survival had died in the mountains of Maine.

Everything he had learned about Banning taught him that the man was nomadic. His appearance in any place could be significant or completely coincidental. Being in Maine could have simply have been the result of a program he had watched the day before.

Maguire rubbed his eyes, he suddenly felt very tired.

CHAPTER SIXTY-NINE

Northern Maine
Thursday, February 7th, 2013 – 3:56 p.m.

Tatiana had begun to methodically make her way through the subterranean bunker. She was only midway through the first room and already had a sizeable amount of material stacked in the middle of the floor.

Banning, it seemed, was an even better planner than she had originally thought.

She hadn't thought it would be as difficult as it had proven to be so far. After all, these were steel containers and there was only a finite amount of hiding space. Or was there?

Some things were easily discovered, such as the box of materials pertaining to Maguire. Banning had poured over them so frequently that he had taken to just leaving them on a shelf.

The first hint as to the complexity of her search came when she had accidentally dislodged a shelf support from one of the cabinets above the work bench. As she was removing an oversized box it had knock it loose and, out of the corner of her eye, she saw the back *wall* pop out. It had been just barely perceptible.

When she had cleaned out the cabinet she found that the wall itself was just a thin piece of laminated luan plywood. Moving it from left to right had popped it free from the mortise joint that held it in place. This action caused the wall to drop down a quarter of an inch, which allowed the ceiling panel to move backward, revealing the cache of fake identity documents and money hidden behind it.

It was the first of four such, Japanese *puzzle box* inspired, hiding places that she had discovered, so far.

The documents and the money would come in handy, but the one that intrigued her most so far had been found in the false bottom of the bench itself. Sandwiched in the middle of the shelf were two dozen identification cards. They ranged from drivers licenses to student IDs.

Tatiana laid them out on the bench, perusing each one of them. The people depicted covered just about every sex, race and age, from all along the north east seaboard. She recognized a couple of the names from the Keenseville / Plattsburgh area, but most were unknown to her. The ones she knew however all had one thing in common, they had all been reported as missing persons. It didn't take her long to come to the conclusion as to why he had all these IDs.

Keith Banning, it seemed, was a serial killer and these were his *trophies*.

Tatiana decided to call it a day. She had plenty of time to continue her search. She didn't want to miss anything because she got tired and lazy. She left most of the stuff in the center of the room, but she took the IDs, along with the box containing Banning's paperwork on Maguire, and went upstairs.

She set the box on the floor, next to the coffee table in the living room, and poured herself a cup of coffee with a shot of bourbon. The snow hadn't let up and she was happy that she had executed her plan when she did. Good fortune had certainly smiled upon her.

She began flipping through the IDs like a young boy would go through baseball cards. The first pass she took in everyone's information.

There was an elderly woman, Ingrid Hoffman, who, according to her date of birth, had been sixty-eight. Ingrid had lived in Scranton, Pennsylvania. She had kind eyes and she struck Tatiana as a matronly woman. She was probably a grandmother, the kind who made cookies for her grandkids on cold winter days like this. She wondered if anyone missed her.

The next was a student ID, from a community college in Vermont, for a Jerome Mitchell. This one didn't have a date of birth but she surmised he was probably only nineteen or twenty. He had on a striped polo shirt and glasses that made him look nerdy, like that kid from the 90's sitcom with high-water pants and suspenders.

She continued going through them until she was finished. Then she *shuffled the deck* and went back through a second time. This time she separated them into two piles. One pile was for ones that did nothing for her, while the other was for ones that she found *interesting*.

She found that she apparently had more discerning tastes than Keith did. No offense to Grandma Hoffman.

When she was done there were only seven cards in her keep pile. Most were women, for obvious reasons, but two were men. She held the last card up as if this was Rome and she was Caesar, sitting in the Coliseum and engaging in a modern day act of *pollice verso.*

The only questioned that remained was whether it would be a thumb's up or thumbs down.

Tatiana flipped the card toward the table, watching as it hung in the air briefly before landing face up on the keep pile.

After all, didn't every girl fantasize about taking a nerd's virginity? she wondered.

She laughed as she gathered up the IDs, stacking them in a pile and laying them back on the floor. When she was done she got up and went into the kitchen. She went through the cupboards, removing a box of spaghetti and a jar of sauce. She put on a pot of water to boil and poured some of the sauce into a smaller pot to heat.

She went back to the living room and poured herself an actual drink this time. She took a sip, set the glass on the table and headed off to the shower.

Tatiana reached in, turned on the water and got undressed. She stepped inside and felt the hot water running down her skin. It stung, like the sensation of a knife's tip being dragged slowly along the skin, but in a good way.

Pleasure and pain.

As she showered, she wondered what had motivated Keith.

Was his pleasure achieved in the hunt, the capture or the kill? she thought.

No, if that were the case why would he let me live when the game he played with Maguire had progressed beyond that point?

He got something from her, beyond the physical satisfaction. Was that what it was about? Power? She admitted that she felt it when she had devised her plan. Knowing each and every move that was needed to be played, each sacrifice required, in order to move to the next level. At first it had been hard for her to let him have Lena, whom she had viewed as being *hers*. But she had come to terms with the fact that someone else had already spoiled her so there really was no reason to hold onto those past feelings.

Watching Keith was actually cathartic for her. She surrendered those old feelings, realizing that letting such antiquated emotions control her was weakness. As she watched she actually felt herself growing stronger, as if the sex only served to fuel her thoughts and plans.

Had Keith figured that out?

No, he hadn't, she thought. *He had still been in the process of trying to figure it all out.*

If he had figured it out he would never have let her live, especially when she had *changed*. He would have recognized the immediate threat to his plan and to himself. His problem was he was too narcissistic. He believed that he was good enough to control the creature he had created. His downfall came when he began to personalize the game. Had he just struck when the opportunity presented itself, instead of trying to create a moment, he would have prevailed.

Of course she would be dead, but he would have succeeded.

She had to learn from that lesson. Take what she wanted and immediately dispose of it when she was finished. Emotional attachments made you act stupid, like the thoughts she had about going after *Susan*. There was a time and place for everything. Right now wasn't that time and she accepted that.

She turned off the water, grabbed a towel and dried herself off. She stepped out of the shower and looked at her reflection in the mirror. Admittedly she had an advantage over Banning. She was still a very attractive woman and would have no problem finding willing suitors of either sex.

Tatiana hung the towel up and put on her robe. She walked into the bedroom and spied Lena's purse sitting on the chair next to the dresser. A smile crept up on her face. She bit her bottom lip as she went over to it and rummaged through the contents. When she was done she walked over to the dresser and opened one of the drawers. After a moment she found what she was looking for. She headed back out to the living room and sat down on the couch.

She picked up the glass from the table and took a sip. Tatiana examined the two items in her hand. Staring back from the licenses were the images of Keith Banning and Lena Marx.

They were her first trophies.

CHAPTER SEVENTY

Southampton, Suffolk County, New York
Saturday, February 9th, 2013 – 3:12 p.m.

"It's him," Monahan said.

"That was fast," replied Maguire.

Across from him, Melody and Genevieve sat going through stacks of papers. Gen was finally feeling better and trying to get caught up with everything before the work week began.

"Probably didn't hurt that I camped out at the State Police Lab and asked 'do we know yet' every five minutes."

"How positive?"

"Unless the fucker had a twin brother he kept hidden away it's a positive match."

"*Sonofabitch.*"

Melody looked up from the papers at him quizzically. Maguire held up one finger, motioning her to wait a moment.

"Yeah, I didn't see this one coming either. It's sort of anti-climactic. I had really wanted to see that prick spend the rest of his life in prison."

"This is probably for the best, Dennis."

"I guess you're right," the man replied. "Anyway, I thought you'd like to know. Also, I spoke to them about Lena. They said that they'd release the body whenever you had made the arrangements."

"Okay, I'll get on that Monday. Email me the information and I'll have the funeral home take care of it all."

"You're a good man, Maguire. In spite of the circumstances, it was a pleasure working with you. I wish you the best of luck and if there's anything you ever need from the state police, give me a call."

"Same here, Dennis. I'll be in touch."

Maguire ended the call and looked over at Melody.

"Banning's dead."

Melody closed her eyes and let out a long sigh, the nightmare had come to a final conclusion.

"Good fucking riddance," replied Gen.

Melody looked at him. "What was that about a funeral home?"

"Lena Marx is dead," he explained. "Banning killed her and was most likely going to dispose of the body when his vehicle went off the road up in Maine."

"Oh my God," Melody exclaimed. "That poor woman."

"Yeah," Maguire replied as he stared out at the ocean.

"You don't seem as happy as I assumed you'd be," Melody said.

"Monahan was right, it all seems very anti-climactic."

"You expected a different ending?"

"Actually, yes, I did expect it to play out much differently."

"What bothers you about it?"

"I guess the ordinariness of it," James said. "It would be like that guy in the horror movies with the mask. He racks up this amazing body count and then, at the end of the movie, he slips on a banana peel and gets impaled on his own knife."

"Well, if you ask me, I couldn't give a rat's ass how he died as long as he is dead and gone," opined Gen.

"You do have a valid point, Gen," Maguire replied.

Melody got up and walked over, sitting down next to him.

"I know what you are thinking," she said. "More importantly I know what you wanted to do. The fact that you were willing to do it says a lot. However, I am grateful that you didn't have to."

"I know and you're right, all that matters is that it's over."

"Does that mean we can finally get back to normal here, folks?" Gen asked. "I mean, don't get me wrong, I have developed a bit of affinity for the *men in black* running around here, but I'd occasionally like to go to the store without the motorcade."

"I'm with Gen on this one. Although I do agree that we need to be aware and have some security around here, I don't think we need to continue the *siege* mentality."

"What a shock," Maguire said. "I'll think about it."

"Thank you, cowboy," Melody replied. "Besides she has Gregor and I have you, what more could two women ask for?"

At that point Maguire realized the decision had already been made. The only question that remained was how long he would continue to argue a losing proposition. In the end he reached the only viable conclusion that remained.

He agreed with her.

CHAPTER SEVENTY-ONE

Brooklyn, New York City
Saturday, February 9th, 2013 – 6:12 p.m.

Karim Al Bashir opened the metal access gate that led down the small exterior walkway between the two buildings and into the small backyard of the bakery. He unlocked the back door and made his way upstairs to his room.

He closed the door and removed his jacket, hanging it on the coat hook. From his pocket he removed a small package, setting it on the desk and turned on the small coffee pot that sat on the edge. It had been a gift from Faisal who said that he should have something on hand since he rarely left the building. With the cold weather he had gladly accepted it.

The euphoria that had first gripped him when he had seen the flyer had left him now. It was replaced by an uncertainty that he was struggling with. Yes, he still had a need for revenge, but the killing of a woman?

Is this something I can really do? he wondered.

He had spent the last few days scouring over the Qur'an, seeking out guidance in knowing Allah's will for him. It was justified, but it didn't feel right to him.

Bashir took the package from the desk and began to open it, peeling the paper edges back. Slowly the polished deep blue color of the small revolver emerged. This gun had come from a friend of a friend for the very *reasonable* price of nine hundred dollars.

The original seller had obtained it after it had taken a *Brooklyn Bounce*. Police slang for a gun that was dropped by a criminal who was being chased by the police and then picked up by someone else before the officers could recover it.

The gun was an old Smith & Wesson .38 caliber revolver. He opened the cylinder and removed the bullets, inspecting each of them and then setting them aside.

Bashir closed the cylinder, hearing it snap shut, and held the gun in his hand. The barrel was small, jutting out just over an inch from the frame of the gun. It had checkered wood grips and some of the bluing was worn away at the edge of the barrel. He pulled the trigger slowly until the hammer fell with an audible click.

It was basic, but it would adequately do the intended job. Its small size would make it very easy to hide. He opened the cylinder again, replacing the bullets, before rewrapping the gun and putting it under the mattress.

Bashir removed his shoes and set them under the desk. He poured himself a cup of coffee and took a sip. He then picked up the pillow, propped it up against the wall and sat back on the bed. He began to question whether he should delay his plan and wait for some sign from Allah as to what he should do.

He leaned over, picked up the Qur'an and laid it on his lap before taking another sip of coffee from the mug. When he was done he placed the mug on the desk, looked down at the book which had fallen open, and began reading the verse.

"Fighting has been enjoined upon you while it is hateful to you. But perhaps you hate a thing and it is good for you; and perhaps you love a thing and it is bad for you. And Allah knows, while you know not."

Bashir closed his eyes and silently accepted the path that Allah had chosen for his life.

CHAPTER SEVENTY-TWO

Northern Maine
Monday, February 11th, 2013 – 4:26 a.m.

The coffee table had been moved against the wall and Tatiana now sat in the middle of the room, the papers from the box spread out all around her.

The nice thing about living alone was that she could do whatever she wanted, whenever she wanted.

Admittedly she had been angry when she had first gone through the paperwork and realized who the *blonde* woman actually was. She would have preferred to have had someone at hand to lash out against but she had managed to bring herself under control relatively quick. She forced herself to detach the emotions and focus on the analytical side.

While she had originally held no enmity against Maguire, that had changed when she realized that he, like everyone else, had moved on with his life. So now she could achieve Keith's goal, as well as to satisfy her own need to get even, all at once.

Tatiana picked up the photo and stared at it. She grudgingly had to admit he had good taste in women. She laid it back down and went through the surveillance photos from the house. While the security appeared impressive, she was unsure whether or not it had changed. The photos were over three months old already and a lot could change in that period of time.

The news had reported that two people had died in an accident, but there were little other details being given. She wondered if they had even identified the bodies as of yet. Tatiana thought about powering up the laptop to do some research, but dismissed that idea. She'd have to get away from the cabin before she would do that. No sense in getting caught at home because of something stupid.

She would have to take a road trip.

Unlike Banning she didn't have to worry about being spotted. Her new hair color gave her a freedom that Banning had not enjoyed. She was glad that she had gotten up early now. If she hurried she could get dressed, grab a bite to eat and be on the road in time to get to Southampton before it got too dark. With any luck, she would be able to take a peek, then find a hotel and begin to plan.

She gathered up the papers, placed them back in the box and set it on the kitchen table. She went to the bedroom and got dressed, throwing some extra clothes into a travel bag. From the small night stand next to the bed she removed the Walther PPK and put it in her jacket pocket. Next she went down into the bunker and selected several items; including a small cigar box which contained about five thousand dollars inside. The box was one of several she had found during her initial search yesterday. Each had contained money, except for one, which was filled with gold and silver coins.

Tatiana returned to the living room. The fire had subsided and she closed the glass doors. She turned on the small electric baseboard heater. It would keep the cabin just warm enough that the pipes wouldn't burst. When she was done checking the interior she put on her jacket and gathered up everything before heading out the door.

Behind the cabin was an old run down barn. Banning had said he had never bothered to work on the exterior of it because it helped give the place the look of not being worthy of a second glance. Inside however was an entirely different story. He had replaced all the internal beams so that, while it appeared unstable from the outside, it was structurally sound on the inside. The weathered wood planks of the barn door were actually tacked onto a reinforced plywood frame. Inside, the interior walls were clad in three quarter inch plywood and the barn could easily be used as a fallback position, should the cabin ever become compromised.

In the middle of the building, under a faded tan tarp, was the reason why she had come here. Tatiana pulled the cover away to reveal a 1993 Land Rover Defender 110. She got in, turned the key and the vehicle roared to life. Tatiana pulled out of the barn, then returned to secure the door, before getting back in and making her way off the mountain.

CHAPTER SEVENTY-THREE

Southampton, Suffolk County, New York
Monday, February 10th, 2013 – 8:41 p.m.

"Let's get away," Melody said, as her and Maguire sat on the couch in front of the fireplace.

Okay, where would you like to go?"

"Paris."

"Paris?" he asked. "You mean Paris, France?"

"Well I don't mean Paris, Illinois," she replied.

"When?"

Melody turned to face him.

"Thursday," she said, "for Valentine's Day."

"Are you serious?"

"Yes, let's make it a long weekend. We can leave Thursday morning and be there by dinner. We can spend Friday and Saturday walking around the city, then we can come home Sunday."

"Why not go Wednesday?" he asked jokingly.

If Melody had heard the humor, she chose to ignore it.

"I have that charity event to go to."

Maguire stared at her.

"You're certifiable, you know that don't you?"

"Don't you think we deserve it?"

He was about to put up an argument when he realized he didn't have one. Melody was right. They did deserve to get away for the weekend. The only thing that was actually odd about it was the destination. But for as long as they had known each other he had never seen her do anything *small*.

"Okay."

"Really?" she asked. Now it was her turn to be shocked.

"Why not?" Maguire replied. "If I'm going to be anywhere with you on Valentine's Day it might as well be in the *City of Light*."

Melody squealed, the look of amazement quickly changing to one of sheer ebullience.

"I can't wait. I'll make all the arrangements."

"Here's a thought," he said. "Why don't I just hang out in the city with Rich on Wednesday evening? Then I can pick you up after the event and we can leave for the airport. We can sleep on the plane and have the whole day there to spend together."

"Thank you, honey," Melody said. "This is going to be the best Valentine's Day ever!"

She leaned over and kissed him.

CHAPTER SEVENTY-FOUR

Brooklyn, New York City
Wednesday, February 13th, 2013 – 4:41 a.m.

Bashir Al Karim lay in bed staring at the ceiling above.

The day had finally come.

Sleep had eluded him for most of the night. He had given up trying to fight it and instead focused on seeing the details of a room he knew he would never see again.

He had enjoyed his time here, but he knew that once he left he could never return. It pained him to think that his friend would suffer as a result of his actions, but following Allah's path was something he had to do.

For it was written in the Qur'an *"Let those fight in the way of Allah who sell the life of this world for the other. Whoso fighteth in the way of Allah, be he slain or be he victorious, on him We shall bestow a vast reward."*

Bashir got up and began to prepare himself. It would be the last chance he had if everything went according to his plan.

For the first time in many years he got down on his knees and began to pray.

CHAPTER SEVENTY-FIVE

Southampton, Suffolk County, New York
Wednesday, February 13th, 2013 – 5:01 a.m.

The Land Rover drove slowly along Meadow Lane, taking in the spectacle of the multi-million dollar homes. As she went past Melody Anderson's house she glanced over at the fortress like façade that was lit up against the black sky.

"You did well for yourself, James," Tatiana remarked. "Too bad it's not going to last."

She made her way back east to the small parking lot at the intersection of Halsey Neck and Meadow Lane. The lot served as an access point for the beach, but it also provided a discreet and unobscured view of any vehicles coming from, or going in, the direction of Melody Anderson's house. This time of the morning she would be able to see any headlights long before they would see her. Not that it really mattered.

The late model Land Rover actually fit in rather well in the area. It was an iconic vehicle, like a vintage model Mercedes Benz or Jaguar, and people tended to ignore them, assuming they just belonged in the area. Besides, people were so self-conscious about being seen that they had gone to great lengths to put up barriers to shield their homes from view. She couldn't see them, but then, they couldn't see her as well.

Tatiana didn't know how he had managed to access it, but Keith had obtained a printout from the Department of Motor Vehicles listing all of the vehicles owned by the woman. Most were high end luxury cars that she couldn't imagine being driven during this time of the year, so she had a general idea of what to look for. Now it was only a matter of watching and waiting.

As she sat drinking her coffee she saw a pair of headlights coming down the road, approaching at a fast rate of speed. As she continued to watch, a Chevy Suburban, with blacked out windows, drove through the intersection and proceeded north on Halsey.

Never a cop around when you need one, she thought.

She had spent the day here yesterday watching for patterns, but had not seen any of the cars registered to Anderson drive by. She decided to come a bit earlier today to ensure that she didn't miss out on an opportunity. Fortunately she had found a local hotel on the main road so the drive was fairly short.

Tatiana had no idea what the woman's days were like. From the material that Banning had gathered she was wealthy enough not to do anything, but she doubted that she would stay cooped up inside the house. Eventually she would need to get out.

Last night she had gone online using the hotel *Wi-Fi* signal and did some research. She found an article about a charity event in Manhattan, which was being held this evening. It listed some of the attendees and Anderson's name had figured prominently in the piece. If she didn't see any movement today, at least she knew where the woman was scheduled to be later in the evening.

Tatiana adjusted the seat and settled in. She had a feeling it was going to be a long day.

CHAPTER SEVENTY-SIX

Brooklyn, New York City
Wednesday, February 13th, 2013 – 4:37 p.m.

Bashir stood in the back room on the verge of tears. His plan was crumbling to pieces before his very eyes.

Earlier in the day he had approached Faisal and volunteered to help with the delivery. Much to his dismay Faisal had turned him down saying that he had been working so much that he needed the rest. No matter how much he protested Faisal refused to budge going so far as to say it was an *order* although it was clearly said in jest.

Bashir could not tell his friend what his plan was and now he was watching it slip slowly from his grasp.

How could Allah show him the path and then steal it away from him?

No, Allah would not do that to him, not now. There had to be something he could do, something to correct this situation. The path was clear to him, but Allah never promised that it would be easy. A believer found a way to overcome all obstacles for His glory.

Ibrahim Abbas walked through the back carrying one of the large covered serving trays for the event. He was an arrogant young man who had grown up accustomed to all things western. Bashir knew the only reason the boy had a job here was because he was the youngest son of Faisal's sister, Halimah, who ran the bakery. The boy's father had been killed in 2003 during fighting along the Afghanistan / Pakistan border. Faisal had tried to take on the role as a father figure, but in the last ten years the boy had continued to become more and more rebellious.

Faisal had often lamented to him that he believed the boy needed to be sent back to live with relatives in Afghanistan to learn hard work and respect. Halimah, however, would not hear of it. She defended the boy at every turn.

"Hey, old man," Ibrahim called out. "How about getting the door instead of standing around doing nothing?"

The blood in Bashir's veins boiled as he walked over and opened the steel security door. The kid smirked as he walked out and headed toward the waiting truck.

The success of any plan is not determined by whether they proceed as you originally thought, but what you do when they don't. It was like being a tree in a storm. The unmovable ones, those which could not deviate from what they had planned, snapped easily under the unrelenting winds. The supple ones, those who could reevaluate and adapt, swayed back and forth easily until the storm had passed.

The kid came back through the door and Bashir called out to him.

"Ibrahim, Faisal needs us to get some trays out of storage upstairs."

The kid turned and walked toward where Bashir stood at the back staircase.

"Really, you can't manage some trays on your own?" he said mockingly, before heading up the old staircase.

On the second floor the two men headed down the hallway to the storage room. Ibrahim opened the door and stepped inside, Bashir following behind.

"How many?" he asked, his voiced tinged with annoyance.

"None," Bashir responded.

Ibrahim turned to confront Bashir.

The boy's mouth opened to speak, but he never had time to formulate the words. Bashir drove his fist into his throat, shattering his windpipe. Ibrahim reached up to grab at his throat as his eyes went wide in fear and he dropped to his knees. Try as he might he could not get air to flow into lungs.

Panic set in. He needed help, needed to get away and find his mother. He looked past the man in front of him, at the door they had just come through. He had to get to it.

Bashir stepped to the side as the kid moved forward. One hand supporting his body, as the other held his throat. Bashir reached down, grasping the boys head with his left hand as the right hand drove the short, broad knife into the base of his neck and twisted.

The body immediately went limp and he lowered him to floor. He removed the knife and wrapped the wound with a towel, tying it tightly around the neck. He then lifted him up, dragging the body over to the closet and stuffed it inside.

It had taken less than two minutes to get his plan back on track.

Bashir closed the door and walked to the bathroom. He washed the blood from his hands, along with the knife. When he was done he made his way back down the stairs.

"Bashir!"

He saw Faisal standing at the back door.

"Yes?"

"Have you seen Ibrahim?"

"A few minutes ago," he replied. "He took a tray out the back. I held the door for him. Why do you ask?"

"He hasn't returned. Could he have gone upstairs?"

"No, I just came from the bathroom, I would have seen him."

"I cannot believe this. We have to leave for the event tonight."

"Children have the attention span of squirrels."

"Yes, but we don't have time for this now. I am afraid I must take back my order. I will need your help tonight."

"Of course, my friend," Bashir said. "Let me go and get my jacket, then I will be ready."

Faisal stood staring out the back door.

"One day I am going to kill that boy," he muttered softly to himself.

CHAPTER SEVENTY-SEVEN

Southampton, Suffolk County, New York
Wednesday, February 13th, 2013 – 4:43 p.m.

"We're going to be late," Melody called out from the bottom of the stairs.

While she waited for her tardy friend to appear, she slipped on the black three quarter length mink coat, over the sapphire blue evening dress she was wearing.

"You can go without me," Gen cried out.

"Not on your life, chicky."

Genevieve came out of the bedroom and made her way down the staircase. She was wearing a shimmering black evening dress with matching black high heels. Her auburn hair was pulled up off her neck.

"Where is your empathy for a sick woman?" she asked.

"You don't look like a very sick woman in that dress. In fact where is the rest of it? "

"It's because I'm feverish and can't wear anything that covers me up."

"I told you that you should have worn a heavier coat."

"*Youshouldhavewornaheaviercoat*," Gen replied sarcastically, then stuck her tongue out at Melody.

"Oh that was mature. Besides, you're playing that sick card into the ground. Save it for Gregor, he seems to have fallen for it."

"I can't believe you're making me go out in this weather."

"Where's your sense of adventure?"

"I'd rather write a check and spend the night thinking of other ways of being adventurous."

"Give our little *Teutonic* friend a night off, will ya."

"I guess this is your idea of getting even with me?" Gen asked.

Melody stopped at the door to the garage, turning to face her friend.

"*Moi*?" she said. "Whatever would possess you to think I would want to do that?"

"Because I would do it," Gen replied. "And let's admit it; you know you want to be just like me."

"Ha! I'm only dragging you along because I need a designated driver."

"I thought that's what you had James for."

"Get your mind out of the gutter and into the car," Melody said.

"If I get any sicker, it's your fault," Gen replied as she got into the Mercedes.

Melody backed the car out of the garage and headed down the driveway.

"Since your abandoning me tonight for Paris, can I leave early?"

"Fine," Melody replied. "Just don't let Gregor drive my car. He'll start having flashbacks of driving through the Alps and the next thing I know you'll be calling me from atop some sandbar."

"He's going to teach me how to shoot this weekend."

"Well that doesn't scare me."

"Oh stop that," Gen chided her. "Besides, now that we are out from under all the heavy security I think it's a good thing for us to have some protection."

"I hate to admit it, but you might have a point," Melody replied.

"When you and James get back from Paris why don't the four of us go out to Wyoming and have some fun. I know the boys would love to play with all the toys out there."

"I talked to him about that the other night, but he's all worried about leaving while that other terrorist is still on the loose," she replied. "But maybe we can get away for a weekend. Grab my phone out of my purse and see what my schedule looks like in March."

Genevieve leaned back over the arm rest, stretching to reach the purse on the back seat.

Tatiana had been watching the clock, worried that she had missed something. As the minutes ticked away she backed the car out of the parking spot and had headed west on Meadow Lane. It would be getting dark soon and she decided to take one more look before her ability to see the location was diminished.

As she neared the house she watched as the silver Mercedes Benz pulled out of the driveway and headed toward her. She looked straight ahead, but out of the corner of her eye she glimpsed the woman's unmistakable blond hair.

Finally, she thought. *Now at least I know what to look for.*

She waited until she had gotten to the end of the road before making the U-turn. There was no need to screw anything up by being too aggressive. She knew which car the woman was driving now and where she was heading.

CHAPTER SEVENTY-EIGHT

Midtown Manhattan, New York
Wednesday, February 13th, 2013 – 5:59 p.m.

Event coordinator Édouard Michel stood in the center of the Grand Ballroom of the Sheraton Hotel like a symphony conductor, directing the activities of over two dozen staffers, designers and food service personnel as they put the finishing touches on the table settings for tonight's event.

"How is it going, Édouard?" asked Deb Perez.

"Absolutely fabulous," the man replied. "You know I don't do anything less than that."

Deb swallowed hard, suppressing the laugh that fought to come out.

The man was extraordinarily *flamboyant*, from his personality to his wardrobe, but he was also renowned for his masterful skill in putting on world class events. In fact, he had earned a reputation for accomplishing the impossible, which only added to the mystique.

Need to replicate the Amazon Rainforest for an intimate group of a hundred, in the middle of New Mexico? Édouard was your man. When a west coast hip-hop producer thought he'd try and stump him with an arctic themed soiree set in Los Angeles in August, Édouard had it so cold inside that at the last minute they had to import fur coats for the guests to wear.

Normally he was booked two years in advance, but Deb had known him since he was just *Eddie*. The two of them had shared the same stoop, in front of the old Soho apartment building they both lived in, along with their dreams for the future. The two were closer than brother and sister.

"I didn't expect anything less, my dear," she replied. "I'll let you get back to work."

As the woman walked away, a man approached Édouard.

"Mr. Michel?"

"Yes," Édouard replied.

"I'm Faisal Hakim," we spoke on the phone.

"Ah yes," the man said. "I'm grateful you could fit us in on such short notice."

"It was no problem. Where would you like us to set everything up?"

"You can bring your trays up through the kitchen entrance. They have a food elevator that goes from the garage to the kitchen," Édouard explained. "I'll need the bread baskets on each table before we begin and the desserts to be served after dinner."

"As you wish, sir," Faisal replied. "Everything will be perfect."

"Thank you, Mr. Hakim."

Faisal turned and headed back through the main door he had just come through.

Such delightfully respectful people, Édouard thought before returning his attention back to the iPad in his hand.

"Okay, everyone," he called out. "Let's start wrapping up."

CHAPTER SEVENTY-NINE

1 Police Plaza, Manhattan, New York
Wednesday, February 13th, 2013 – 6:17 p.m.

Rich and James sat in the conference room, stacks of reports piled on top of the table in front of them.

With Mary and Melody both attending the charity event they had taken it as an opportunity to get in some afterhours *quiet time* to go through the numbers. Each pile represented the Compstat reports for a particular borough. Each pile was then further broken down by individual precincts.

"This is nuts," Rich said.

"That's one way of classifying it," James replied. "The sad thing is that it ever got to this point. I remember someone once telling me that in the old days, if a precinct commander said he had identified a gang problem it was career suicide. After Compstat was implemented they would beat you up if you said that you *hadn't* identified the gang activity in your precinct."

"How'd your meeting go with Bob Parker the other day?"

"Good, but I could tell that he was being cautious, choosing his words carefully."

"I have to believe that most of them are going to fall into the category of *once bitten, twice shy*," Rich replied.

"That goes without saying. I don't blame them in the least. It's going to take some time before they figure out whether we are playing it straight or we are just another, in a never-ending line of politicians, who say the right words to them, right before they plunge the knife into their backs."

"This is something that I am going to rely heavily on you for, James. You know firsthand about street crimes and the best ways to address it. We didn't have to worry about this in the Service."

"Well, we're not reinventing the wheel here," James replied. "The job has always had great ideas to addressing crime. You can go back to the old Tactical Patrol Force days. When there was a problem, they sent in TPF. Problem solved. Of course then you had complaints about their methods, but I never really lost much sleep over how criminals felt. You also had a slew of other programs like TOPAC, NSU and Impact. They worked, but then when the reductions in crime leveled out they began using them in the wrong ways. We have to find a way to keep whatever program we institute *pure*."

"But will it survive the politics?"

"The effective ones usually don't," James replied. "And the politicians never seem to go after the *ineffective* ones. Maybe doing nothing is something they are more comfortable with."

"Spend a week in D.C. and you'll find out just how true that statement really is."

"The biggest issue we as cops face, is proving to the citizens, that when no crime occurs, it really is the result of us being present. It's something that can't be quantified and therefore they want to dismiss it. I have never understood that mindset."

"So what do you recommend?"

"That's a loaded question. My recommendations would have you booted out of office by the end of the month."

"And what would that be?"

"Our personnel numbers are too low and the reason we can't increase them is because no one wants to take this job for what we are paying them. Not when they can go next door to Nassau or Suffolk County and make double the money."

"I don't see that changing anytime soon. What else do you have?"

"It's like I said before. No crime means something different to those folks across the street. The problem is you have been dealt a really shitty hand. For years everyone has been lying about crime, fudging the numbers. No one wanted to get caught talking about the real numbers. It's been like the dirty little secret of the city, like some crime stat *ponzi* scheme. Question is whether you want to be the police commissioner who watched the numbers rise under his watch?"

"I didn't take this job to feed my ego, James."

"Then I would set up a meeting with McMasters and go over the numbers with him. Tell him the reductions were not made as a result of effective deployment of resources, but through manipulation of the numbers. He won't like it, but he needs to know. Everyone aligned with the former administration will take pot shots and wag their fingers. When that happens the response has to be swift. If he tries to play political nice-nice because he has higher aspirations this will bite him, and ultimately you, in the ass."

"What about you?"

"Hey, I'm just the piano player in this gin joint."

"What's the plan going forward?"

"Get the borough commanders in here and tell them to spread the word to stop fudging. What we have going for us is they will be semi reluctant. So the increase won't be as sharp as it should be. It'll give us some time to start hitting it harder, go after the real quality of life stuff that gives the criminal element a good foundation."

"And when the usual suspects start screaming about racial profiling?"

"You know I keep hearing about this nonsense. Yet, when you get beyond the media hype, no one seems to be able to explain why exactly it is racial profiling when the cops have reasonable suspicion. We train our cops right, they know what they are doing. If they get a radio run for a reported crime and they stop someone who fits the description that's not racial profiling, that's good police work. The rabble rousers are always going to try and stir shit up.

That's how they make their living. But the answer to rhetoric should be fact. One of the ramifications of having these *amazing* reductions in crime is that folks begin to think there is no more crime and begin to think you're just harassing innocent people. Maybe if the folks who produce junior's 2nd grade honor roll photo, spent more time making sure that they were still on the honor roll in the 12th grade, we wouldn't be having these discussions."

Rich took a drink from the coffee cup and leaned back in his chair.

"When I get fired do you think you can get me a job in the private sector? Mary and the girls have grown fond of having food in the fridge."

"You didn't hire me to piss down your back and tell you it's raining."

"Is that a yes?"

"I'll see what I can do."

CHAPTER EIGHTY

Midtown Manhattan, New York
Wednesday, February 13th, 2013 – 6:51 p.m.

Melody pulled the car up to the valet station in front of the Sheraton.

"Lamplighter event," she said to the young man as she got out of the car.

Genevieve joined her a moment later on the sidewalk.

"Happy face," Melody said.

"This *is* my happy face," Gen replied sarcastically.

"You're such a *Debbie Downer*."

"You'd be too, if you were sick."

Melody took her friend's arm in hers and led her up the front steps of the hotel entrance.

"If you pretend to enjoy yourself tonight, I'll talk to Mary and maybe the three of us can swing a girl's weekend in Cabo."

Genevieve stopped at the entrance and turned to look at Melody.

"St. Bart's and it's for a *long* weekend."

"Deal," Melody replied.

A smile slowly appeared on Genevieve's face.

"This is going to be such an awesome night!"

"You're easy, but you're certainly not cheap."

"Sun, sand, and *Bahama Mama's*!"

"Come on, *Jamie* Buffett, we're going to be late," Melody said and pushed her friend through the door.

Across the street Tatiana pulled the Land Rover over to the curb. She watched as the cars pulled up, their passengers exiting and the valets getting in, then quickly pulled away. Each of the cars then pulled away from the curb and drove to the corner where they made a left turn. She waited for the light behind her to change red and she pulled away from the curb, cutting across all three lanes. She pulled up right behind one of the vehicles that had just left the valet station. When the light turned green the car proceeded around the corner and she watched as it went halfway down the street and into the underground garage.

Tatiana followed the vehicle inside, stopping when it was her turn to take a parking ticket. As she drove through the different levels she kept an eye out for the vehicle. Two stories down she spotted it, parked along the back wall. She continued driving down another level until she found an available spot and pulled in. From the back seat she removed a small black plastic case, setting it on the seat next to her and opened it. Inside the case was a dense foam insert that held a small black rectangular metal device.

She removed the device from the box, slipped it into her pocket and exited the Land Rover. Tatiana walked back up the ramp slowly, watching for movement. As she approached the back of the Mercedes she paused and dropped to one knee as she pretended to tie her shoe. When she was sure no one was watching she slipped the tracking device under the bumper hearing the loud pop as the magnets grabbed hold of the metal frame.

The device was a self-contained real time tracking unit that was equipped with a GPS transmitter and powered by lithium ion batteries. It sent information to a computer program and would update its location every ten seconds.

When she was done she got up and headed back toward the car. She backed out and headed for the exit, paying the twenty dollar fee to the attendant. It was a small price to pay for the reward she planned to reap later.

She was happy to leave Manhattan. It was much too busy for her tastes. There were too many people and way too many cars, especially those damn yellow cabs. She liked the suburbs with their tree lined streets and quaint homes. This place was like being in hell with neon lights.

Tatiana made her way east, back to Southampton. She had time to pick up something to eat, go back to the hotel and take a shower. She knew that once she received the alert that the vehicle was moving that there would be no time for her to rest until she got back to the cabin.

CHAPTER EIGHTY-ONE

Midtown Manhattan, New York
Wednesday, February 13th, 2013 – 8:21 p.m.

Bashir looked at the seating chart posted on the wall in the kitchen.

It would soon be time for them to begin serving the desserts to the tables and he wanted to ensure that he knew exactly where he had to go.

Table number two was on the far side of the room, close to the windows that overlooked 7ᵗʰ Avenue. He memorized the seating positions so he would know exactly where his target would be sitting.

The waiting was the hardest part for him. He reached inside his pocket and felt the cool metal against his warm skin.

Soon, he thought. Soon it would all be over. He would have his vengeance and, if everything went right, he would once again feel the embrace of his beloved Salimah.

In the main room, attendees of the event had already finished their dinner and had gotten up to mingle with one another.

This event was no different than any other. Those in attendance were constantly trying to jockey around the room, seeking out the attention of others in the hopes of parlaying the chance meeting into something else further down the road. Melody hated it, but she also knew that it was part of the game.

For her part, she only had to sit while others flocked to her side to make small talk and have the opportunity to be seen in her presence. She always tried to be kind, but it could be tiresome at times.

Right now was one of those times.

Unfortunately for her, the person making it tiresome was her tablemate, Tippi Fisher. Almost from the moment they had laid their silverware down she had begun holding court, much to the dismay of the others seated at the table.

"One of the things that has been so difficult in this transition is breaking down the 'old boys' attitude that is so pervasive at City Hall," she said. "Of course this has caused a lot of friction with the regular staff, but I have laid down the law and told them it's *my way* or the door."

Some of the women nodded in agreement while others silently glanced around the room looking for an opportunity to break away.

"Strong women, like me, have to constantly prove that they have earned their spots. Not that I don't believe some of the lower echelon people are equally skilled in their roles, like our esteemed police commissioner, but the importance of respecting the proper chain of command cannot be overlooked."

Inside Mary was seething. She looked down at the steak knife that sat on her plate and wondered.

No, too many witnesses, she thought.

Although the ones sitting here at the table might develop a case of *temporary amnesia* and claim that Fisher had fallen on it by accident.

"Excuse me for a moment," Melody said as she stood up, laying the cloth napkin onto the plate in front of her.

Before she left the table she leaned over and whispered "sorry" in Mary's ear.

Melody crossed the room and sat down at the first table with Deb Perez.

In the background, Tippi Fisher continued to drone on, unconcerned whether anyone was actually listening or not.

"Sadly most people don't realize the responsibilities that the position of deputy mayor for operations carries. It is quite a monumental task to oversee the various agencies that provide our emergency services. I have to make sure that they are constantly performing above standards. Some nights I wonder if I will even get a chance to sleep."

Mary reached down, passing up on the steak knife, and instead grabbed the rum and coke in front of her, knocking it back. She looked over toward the waiter, who had been assigned to their table, and smiled as she held up the now empty glass.

Mary turned her attention to Genevieve, who was sitting next to her.

"You okay?" Mary asked.

"No," she said. "I know everyone thinks I was just trying to get out of coming, but I still haven't shaken this bug yet. It's knocking the crap out of me."

"Maybe you just need some fresh air," Mary replied.

She was desperate to get away for a moment, even if it was at the expense of her friend. Genevieve picked up on the hint.

"I need to go check my lipstick," she replied. "Care to join me?"

"I'd love to, dear."

The two women got up and headed toward the main doors. Tippi Fishers audience had now dwindled down to three.

Mary and Genevieve located the bathroom at the far end of the long hallway that ran adjacent to the Grand Ballroom. Once inside the chatter began.

"If she says one more word I'm going to scream," said Gen.

"At least you don't have to listen to her taking digs at your husband. My God this woman got her job via a well-worn pair of kneepads."

"Oh you read about that, too?"

"I would love to know who writes those articles."

City Confidential was a blog that had been referenced in one of the local New York City papers. The writer went by the pen name *Agatha Dixon Ervin* and apparently had an inside track to the salacious goings on at City Hall, as well as other city agencies.

Originally it was believed to be someone from the prior administration who held a grudge. This speculation was further fueled when someone pointed out that the name was actually an anagram for 'I have an ax to grind.' However, the writer seemed to have an intimate knowledge of the players in the McMasters' administration that could only have come from an insider.

The site had appeared within days of the election, hinting about the habits and dalliances of several of the members of the transition team. Everyone assumed that the site would be removed immediately, but over two months later it was still going strong. The Friday afternoon information dump had become the hot topic of discussion at every water cooler in the city on Monday morning.

The latest recipient of the blogger's wrath was none other than Deputy Mayor (Operations) Tippi Fisher. The article was a scathing diatribe which concluded with '*It has been said that Ms. Fisher started her career in politics at the bottom and worked her way up. Unfortunately most of that work was done on her knees, which makes this humble writer question exactly what "Operations" she will be running. At least we can all be thankful that Mayor McMasters didn't select her to run the Board of Education.*'

Whoever had said '*there is no such thing as bad publicity*' had obviously never read City Confidential.

Mary was putting on her lipstick when she looked over at Genevieve in the mirror.

"Hon, are you okay?"

"No," she replied. "I knew I was trying to do too much, too quickly. I have to learn to not be so stubborn."

"Good luck with that."

"Oh don't you go and start sounding like Melody."

"Ha!" Mary exclaimed. "She tells me I sound like you."

"Well, tell her to enjoy Paris for me. I'm going to get out of here. I just want to go home and get into bed."

"Sure you don't want to stay for dessert?"

"No, I think I'll puke if I see any food. Plus I don't want to have to say goodbye to that *she-wolf.*"

"Okay. I'll let Melody know you're under the weather."

The two women walked out and stopped by the coat check where Genevieve claimed her jacket.

"Drive carefully," Mary said.

"Thanks, I will," Gen replied, giving Mary a kiss on the cheek. "Tell Mel that I'll call her when I get home."

Genevieve got on the elevator, as Mary turned to walk back toward the ballroom.

"Mary!"

She turned and saw Janice Craig, the wife of the fire commissioner, approaching her.

"Hi Janice, I didn't know you were coming?"

"I wasn't," the woman replied. "Last minute schedule change and I got freed up. I'm sitting in the back, away from all the nonsense. I need a cigarette break."

"I could use some fresh air myself," Mary replied. I'll take a walk with you."

Inside the ballroom Melody grudgingly returned back to the table that Tippi Fisher now occupied alone. She had waited as long as she could, hoping that Mary or Genevieve would return to the table and she would have someone else to talk with.

"Ms. Anderson," Fisher said. "May I ask you a question?"

"Sure," Melody said with a forced smile.

Fisher motioned toward the vacant seat next to her and Melody sat down. She took the seat just as the waiters started to appear with the dessert trays.

"From what my husband tells me, you are a woman of some renown in the business world."

"I don't know about all of that," Melody replied. "I've tried to do my best."

"Surely you must have had your detractors, those who spoke maliciously about you behind your back. I was wondering how you handled it?"

Melody had been hoping not to get drawn into this issue. She didn't know the woman and would have been content at keeping it that way.

"Honestly, Tippi, I try not to pay any attention to detractors or, for that matter, to those who try to put me on a pedestal. I do the best I can and the only judgment that matters to me is my own."

In a way Melody felt a tinge of sadness. From what little she had seen, it appeared to her that Tippi Fisher was a very insecure person who tried to raise herself up on the backs of others. In her heart, Fisher most likely knew that she didn't merit the position. So she tried to make herself look better at the expense of those working below her. It was a condition that Melody had seen countless times in the business world.

From off to her left, a tray of desserts suddenly appeared and was placed on the table in front of her. She was just about to say thank you, when the hand that previously held the tray came back and suddenly wrapped around her throat.

The move was as vicious as it was sudden. Melody felt her body being tugged backward violently at the same time that she felt the coldness of the gun's metal barrel pressing into her back. She struggled to regain her footing as the room erupted in terrified screams.

From behind her she heard a man's voice shout out.

"*Allahu akbar!*"

CHAPTER EIGHTY-TWO

Southampton, Suffolk County, New York
Wednesday, February 13th, 2013 – 9:15 p.m.

Tatiana stepped out of the shower, grabbing a towel from the rack and began drying off. When she was done, she tossed the towel onto the bed, then walked over to the table and hit the refresh button on the laptop. As she watched the screen, the display updated the vehicles current location. The car was on the Long Island Expressway and had just passed through Medford. Tatiana estimated that she had another half hour before it arrived. From the programs option box she selected the one that would send updates to the cell phone.

She knew that once she left the hotel finding an open Wi-Fi source in this area would prove problematic. At least this way she would get text updates on the vehicles location.

Tatiana got dressed and gathered up her belongings. She checked the laptop one last time, noting the vehicle was just west of Riverhead. She shut down the computer and put it back in its case. She scanned the room for any wayward items and left the room for the last time.

CHAPTER EIGHTY-THREE

1 Police Plaza, Manhattan, New York
Wednesday, February 13th, 2013 – 9:17 p.m.

"Commissioner!"

Rich and James both turned as Luke Jackson burst into the conference room.

"There's been an attack at the Sheraton."

"What?" exclaimed both men simultaneously.

"Reports are just coming in, but from what Operations told me, someone has taken people hostage inside the location."

The two men looked at each other, their faces mirroring each other's thoughts.

James was the first to speak as Rich reached down to grab the phone on the conference table.

"The commissioner's wife and my girlfriend are at an event in that hotel."

A moment later several members of Rich's detail entered the room.

"Anything?"

"Call went straight to voice mail," Rich replied.

James tried calling her cell and after a few rings it also went to voice mail.

Rich picked the phone on the desk back up.

"Operations, Police Officer Snow."

"This is Commissioner Stargold, what do you have on the incident at the Sheraton?"

"Preliminary reports are at least one perp with hostages in the hotel's Grand Ballroom. No reports of any injuries at this time. Patrol is on the scene requesting the duty captain and ESU."

"Show me and the 1st dep as being notified and responding. Notify Chief Ameche about what is going on. Then get the duty chief on the phone and have him respond forthwith."

"Luke, I'm riding with the commissioner, you and Peter follow us up there," Maguire said.

As the men left the conference room Maguire reached into his office and grabbed the navy blue raid jacket that hung on the coat rack.

The trio of Suburban's raced up the FDR drive, their red and blue strobe lights matching the frantic pace of the vehicles themselves as they weaved in an out of the traffic.

Suddenly Rich's phone began to ring.

"It's Mary," he said as he answered it. "Where are you?"

"I'm in the lobby of the hotel with Janice Craig. We were outside when it happened."

"Is Melody with her?" James asked.

"Are you with Melody?"

"No, I don't know where she is. I think she may still be inside. It's a madhouse here Rich, where are you?"

"I'm on my way. Grab a cop, tell him who you are and that I said to stay with you."

"I will, hurry."

The ride uptown took only a few minutes, but to the men in the back it had seemed like a lifetime. When they arrived the street in front of the hotel was closed off. Marked and unmarked police vehicles, including several from the Emergency Service Unit, lined each side of the street.

Rich and James exited the vehicles and were immediately met by a uniformed captain.

"Sir, I'm Captain William Eubanks, C.O. of the 10th Precinct," the man said. "I have the duty tonight."

"Captain, what do we know?"

"So far we have one armed perp with an unknown number of hostages located in the Grand Ballroom on the 2nd floor. I have ESU personnel staged outside the room right now, as well as snipers moving into position on the surrounding buildings. The C.O. of Hostage Negotiation is on his way."

"Is he making any demands?" James asked.

"No sir, no communication at this time."

"Where are the people that were attending the event?"

"We have most of them inside the hotel, one floor down, in the business conference rooms. Your wife is fine. I have her, and the fire commissioner's wife, inside the manager's office with two officers assigned outside the door. Unfortunately some of the others panicked and left the building before uniforms arrived to secure the scene. We have the event coordinator and they are getting us a list of the attendees."

"Rich, I'm going to see if Melody is with the others."

"Okay," Rich replied.

Maguire and Luke Jackson made their way down the staircase and found the room where the attendees were being held.

Two uniformed officers stood outside the room guarding it. One of the officers opened the door as Maguire walked up.

"Community Affairs is inside, sir."

Maguire stepped in and located the Community Affairs Officer who was wearing their traditional light blue jacket.

"Commissioner," the man said. "I'm Officer Pete DeBlasio from Midtown North."

Maguire quickly scanned the room, but there was no sign of her.

"Do we have an attendee list yet?"

"Yes, I have the table seating chart here," the man said and directed Maguire over to a table on the far wall. "We have been marking off who was where."

Maguire examined the list.

"Ah shit," he said and reached for his phone.

"Did you find her?" Rich asked when he answered the call.

"No, but Tippi Fisher is also missing."

"Ah *sonofabitch*, I'd forgotten about her."

"You find Mary yet?"

"I'm on my way inside right now to speak with her. I'll let you know what she says."

Maguire ended the call and went back to the list.

"Excuse me, may I have your attention."

The room grew silent.

"Is there a Sandra Bays here?"

Maguire waited as the people in the room looked around at each other. When there was no response he read the next name off.

"How about a Sheryl Bernard?"

The people sitting in the room looked around at one another again, but there was still no response.

"Okay, how about Kathy Dells?"

"I'm Kathy Dells," a voice in the back of the room called out.

"Can you please come up front, ma'am?"

When the woman got to the front of the room Maguire ushered here out into the hallway.

"Ms. Dells, I'm First Deputy Police Commissioner James Maguire. I'm trying to locate some people who were at your table, Melody Anderson, Genevieve Gordon or Tippi Fisher. Do any of these names ring a bell?"

"Yes Tippi Fisher. God that woman was annoying. She was the reason I wasn't at the table when this happened."

"What about the other two?"

"I don't know who the one woman, Genevieve, was. Most of us walked away from the table after dinner. But I think Melody Anderson was the one that guy grabbed."

"What did you say?" Maguire asked.

"I think she was sitting at the table talking to Tippi. Then all of a sudden this guy grabbed her from behind and shouted something."

"Shouted what?"

"I don't know, it was some foreign language, like *all who akbar*.

"*Allahu Akbar?*"

"Yes, that was it."

"Thank you," Maguire said and walked away reaching for his phone again.

Jackson turned and ushered the woman back into the conference room.

"What did you find out?" Rich asked.

"I think I know where Bashir Al Karim is."

"Please don't tell me it's him."

"Yeah and to make matters worse I think he has Melody and Tippi Fisher with him. I'm coming back to you; I need to talk to Mary."

"We're in the manager's office on the first floor."

"I'll be right there."

CHAPTER EIGHTY-FOUR

Southampton, Suffolk County, New York
Wednesday, February 13th, 2013 – 9:53 p.m.

Tatiana looked at the screen on the cell phone and saw the update for the vehicle. It had just turned south onto Halsey Neck Lane. That gave her a few minutes to get ready.

She pulled out of the parking lot and headed west on Meadow Lane. After a short drive she found a secluded stretch of the road that was between houses. She pulled over to the curb and turned on the Land Rover's hazard lights. Reaching down she engaged the hood's release lever and then exited the vehicle to open it.

It was only a matter of minutes before she saw the headlights of the Mercedes approaching her.

Tatiana stepped out into the roadway and waved her arms.

The vehicle began to slow down as it approached her.

She stepped over to the side of the Land Rover as the Mercedes came to a stop and the driver lowered the passenger side window.

"Are you alright?"

Tatiana felt her heart begin to race. It was the right car, but the wrong woman.

What had gone wrong? She wondered.

She knew she was not going to get a second chance, now that she had been seen. She had to jump on this opportunity and figure how it would all play out later.

"I have a faulty wire on my fuse harness," she said. "My boyfriends a mechanic so of course, rather than just fix it, he just told me how to overcome it. I just need someone to start the engine while I hold it in place."

"Men," Gen said. "Why do they always take the easy way out?"

"If I had the answer to that I'd be rich and could afford to have the car fixed!"

"Let me just pull over," Gen replied.

Tatiana watched as the Mercedes pulled to the curb in front of her and stopped, its flashing hazard lights joining with those of the Land Rover. The woman got out and walked back toward her.

"Thank you so much. Just have a seat and I will let you know when to start it."

Genevieve got behind wheel and waited. Through the gap in the hood she could see the woman moving around inside the engine compartment.

"Okay," the woman called out. "Try it now."

Genevieve turned the key over and the engine roared to life.

The woman slammed the hood shut and walked around to the driver's side just as Genevieve was getting out.

"Thank you so much, I wish I could do something to repay you."

"Oh no problem, glad I could help," Gen said.

"Okay, how about a hug then?"

"Sure," Gen said.

Tatiana wrapped her arms around Genevieve firmly and brought up the syringe, which she had discreetly hidden in her right hand, and pressed it into the woman's left shoulder.

Genevieve yelped and pushed the woman away, but it was already too late. The drug began coursing through her body even as she staggered backward. She made it as far as the back of the vehicle when she felt her body give way under its own weight and collapse to the ground.

Tatiana moved quickly. It had actually gone better than she had anticipated. In trying to make her escape the woman had run to the back of the truck cutting down the amount of work that she had to do.

She swung open the rear door of the vehicle, lifting her up and laying her inside. She then wrapped duct tape around her mouth and zip tied her wrists and ankles.

The interior of the Defender matched the ruggedness of its exterior. This particular one had metal tie down brackets installed. She took a length of rope and secured the woman's body down so that when the drug wore off she wouldn't be bouncing around the interior. After she was satisfied that she wouldn't be going anywhere she covered her with an old cloth tarp. She closed the rear door, walking back to the passenger side and picked up the package that was lying on the seat.

Tatiana walked over to the Mercedes and placed the package onto the driver's seat. She then grabbed the woman's purse and jacket, then shut the door. She would have liked to have had the time to search the vehicle, but time was a luxury she did not have on her side at the moment. As she walked past the back of the car she knelt down and retrieved the tacking device from the bumper.

She got back into the Land Rover, making a U-turn and drove away, the Mercedes fading from sight in the rearview mirror.

CHAPTER EIGHTY-FIVE

Midtown Manhattan, New York
Wednesday, February 13th, 2013 – 9:59 p.m.

Maguire walked into the manager's office where Rich and another man were standing talking to Mary. Maguire noticed that the jacket the man wore had the lettering "NYPD Hostage Negotiation Team" emblazoned on the back.

"James, this is Lieutenant Jack Campbell, he's the C.O. of HNT."

Maguire shook hands with the man.

"Sorry to meet under these circumstances Commissioner," the man said.

"Likewise," Maguire replied.

"I was just explaining to the Lieutenant your suspicions about our perp."

"Mary," James said. "Do you remember seeing Gen inside the room before this happened?"

"Oh my God, I forgot about Gen," Mary said. "She left early."

"Where did she go?"

"She said she wasn't feeling well. I was supposed to tell Melody that she took the car and went home, but then I met Janice and got sidetracked."

Just then an ESU officer opened the door.

"Sir," the man said. "We've deployed the throw phone into the room."

"Mary, stay here," Rich replied. "If you need anything let the officer outside know."

"Please be careful," Mary said. "That goes for both of you."

"Try to reach out to Gen for me and let her know what's going on," James said.

"I will."

She watched as they filed out of the room.

Upstairs in the Grand Ballroom things were decidedly more chaotic.

In one corner of the room a group of women were huddled together. They had missed their opportunity to escape before Bashir Al Karim had gotten his wits about him. He'd selected one of the women to close the heavy drapes that now hung down in front of the windows, blocking any view from the outside. He then forced them into one area, across from the entrance doors, where he could easily keep an eye on them.

In front of him now were the two women who had been at the table when he had put his plan into motion. He believed one of them to be the police commissioners wife, based on the seating chart, but wasn't sure who the other one was. Still if they were sitting here they were important and that was all that mattered.

When the door had opened Al Karim had thought they were going to attack. He had crouched behind the two women, holding the gun to the younger ones head only to watch as a black box came sliding into the room.

"It's a phone," Tippi Fisher explained. "They want to talk to you."

The man stared back between her and the box. Finally he motioned to one of the women in the corner.

"Go get it!"

The woman stood up hesitantly and began walking over to where the box laid. When she reached down to grab it he stopped her.

"Wait," Al Karim shouted, the gun waving in her general direction. His first thought was that they had booby-trapped it. He had seen too many people killed when they had mistakenly picked up something innocent. He would not fall victim like they had.

"Open it up."

The woman opened the box and held it up toward him revealing the phone inside.

"Ok, bring it over here," he instructed her.

When she had placed it on the table he motioned for her to return back to the where the other women sat.

"Pick it up," he said to Fisher.

She reached over and removed the handset from the cradle inside the box. Immediately she heard a voice on the other end.

"Who am I speaking to?"

"This is Tippi Fisher, who is this?"

"My name is Lieutenant Jack Campbell, I'm with the NYPD, is everyone okay?"

"No we are being held hostage by a lunatic; we are far from okay."

Bashir reached down, ripping the phone away from her and put it to his ear.

"My name is Bashir Al Karim and I demand to speak to the police commissioner. I know he is there; I have his wife with me."

Campbell hit the cutoff button on the phone.

"He says he wants to speak to the police commissioner, says he has his wife as a hostage."

"He doesn't know who he has inside," Rich said.

"Let me speak to him," James said.

Campbell looked at Stargold who nodded approval and handed the phone over to Maguire.

"This is Commissioner Stargold," James said. "Who am I speaking with?"

"Bashir Al Karim and if you do not meet my demands I will begin killing women."

"What are your demands?"

"I want an immediate public apology, on live television, from the President of the United States, denouncing the war crimes committed by your military against the peaceful people of Afghanistan. I also demand that he explain to the world how the United States takes care of the people who do their dirty work. You used us to fight the Russians, then, when it was over, you simply left and did nothing for those who had suffered so greatly."

"Is there anything else you want?" James asked.

"Yes, when you have done that, then I will meet you face to face and we can discuss the release of the women."

"You know the President of the United States is never going to issue an apology on national television."

Just then, the sound of a gun shot rang out over the phone, followed a moment later by the sound of women screaming in the Grand Ballroom.

"Then you can tell him that if he does not want to issue an apology he can watch the bodies of these women being removed one at a time on national television."

Bashir reached over and placed the phone back onto the cradle in the box.

CHAPTER EIGHTY-SIX

Midtown Manhattan, New York
Wednesday, February 13th, 2013 – 10:07 p.m.

Melody knelt down beside Tippi Fisher pressing the cloth napkin against the woman's stomach where the bullet had entered.

The lower half of the white satin dress she was wearing was covered in blood and it was expanding at an alarming rate. Melody reached up, removing another one of the napkins and pressed it down on top of the other.

"I'm so sorry," Fisher said.

"Don't be, you have nothing to be sorry about," Melody replied.

"Sure I do, my dear; this is all my fault. If I hadn't put my nose where it didn't belong none of this would have happened."

"Don't think that way. You're the victim here."

"That may be true, but that doesn't excuse my own actions. I'm an abrasive, angry woman with a chip on my shoulder and damn sure can't seem to leave well enough alone."

Melody looked down at the woman's face and watched as she smiled up at her.

"Promise me you won't repeat those words at my funeral."

"You're not going to die," Melody said.

"Yes I am, you're just too kind to admit it," Fisher replied. "But I'm already beginning to feel cold and the only thing I ask is that you not leave my side till after I'm gone."

"You really can't leave well enough alone, can you?"

Fisher laughed, but it brought on a spasm that quickly drove the humor away, replacing it with a sharp pain.

"Tell my husband I was thinking of him when the end came," she said.

"I will," Melody said, reaching down to brush a loose strand of hair from the woman's face.

"It's funny," Fisher said. "We live our lives thinking that tomorrow is a given, as if we have every expectation to it. Then we find ourselves in the surreal circumstances that prove we were wrong. And it is only then that you realize what a horrible, wasted life you have lived."

"What do you mean?" Melody asked, desperately trying to keep the woman talking and focused.

"If I could only have known this morning how this day would end. I would have kissed my husband, instead of criticizing him before he left the house. I would have called my daughter, who's away at college, and told her how genuinely proud I was of her instead of always complaining that she was not working hard enough. I might not even have been a bitch to my staff, and actually thanked them for the job they did, that made me look good every day."

"People know how you feel about them Tippi. They know that just because you may have been critical at some point, doesn't mean that you don't love or respect them."

"Do they? Do they really understand it? Or will they just *want* to believe it?"

"I'd like to believe they will."

"Well, let me give you a word of advice based on the rather unfortunate situation I find myself faced with. Don't let them have to question it. Each day, let them know how you feel so that they never have to guess. So that someone else doesn't have to let them know that you were thinking of them before you died."

"This isn't the end, Tippi."

"I know, my dear," Fisher replied. "I made my peace with Jesus a long time ago, even if I didn't always act like the Christian I am supposed to be. I just hadn't expected to meet Him so soon."

"None of us ever do."

"You have a wonderful man in James. Don't let him go and don't be afraid to do whatever it takes for love, even if that means that you will have to take a risk. Never be afraid to play the queen's gambit."

"Queen's gambit? What's that?"

"You've never played chess, have you, Melody?" Fisher asked with a pained smile. "That's when you are willing to sacrifice the *things* which you feel are the most important, for the *one* who truly is. That is when you know you are really in love."

"I can honestly say that never in a million years would I have guessed that I would be getting lessons on love from you."

"That's okay, my dear, I didn't know that I would be meeting my maker this evening either. Isn't it ironic how life can be at times?"

"Damnit! Stop saying that! You're not going to die, Tippi."

Tippi Fisher looked up and stared into Melody's eyes, a smile forming on her lips.

"Now what are you thinking?" Melody asked.

The woman just stared back at her peacefully.

"Tippi?" Melody replied.

She began shaking the woman, but it was too late. The life had already drained from her body. All that was left was a serene look on her face as if she had been beckoned home from the other side.

"You bastard!" Melody screamed and lunged back at Al Karim.

The two toppled backward as they crashed into the dessert cart that had been abandoned behind the table, ending up on the floor.

The man had not been prepared for the sudden ferocity of the attack, especially from a woman. He struggled to maintain control of the weapon in his right hand while fighting with the other.

Melody, still reeling from watching Fisher die before her eyes, unleashed her fury on the man, pummeling him and taking advantage the surprise attack had given her.

Across the room, the women, seeing what was going on, decided to use what little window of opportunity they had been given and made a dash for the doors. It was only a matter of twenty five feet, but each of those feet was measured in a span of time that no other human could imagine. Seconds dragged by as each anticipated the shot in the back that would end their lives as well.

Hearing the commotion inside the Ballroom, James, Rich and the HNT lieutenant stepped out of the room to see what had happened, just as the doors burst open and the women came running out.

"Down! Down! Down!" Screamed one of the ESU Officers, as those assembled outside the doors leveled off their MP-5 submachine guns at the perceived threat.

Screams filled the hallway as the women encountered this newest threat to their safety and took to the floor.

Maguire bolted toward the door, reaching it before it closed and drawing his gun. Inside he could see a body lying on the ground and a fight going on just beyond it.

He rushed forward, but he wasn't fast enough.

Al Karim had managed to strike Melody in the head with the gun in his hand, dazing her just long enough to gain control back.

He wrapped his left arm around her neck in a choke hold and raised her up off the ground, the small revolver pressed to her head.

"Stop!" He cried out to the man rushing toward him. "I will kill her."

"It's over, Bashir, let her go."

"Over? You must take me for a fool."

Maguire did a quick assessment. Melody appeared to physically be okay, except from some blood trickling down the left side of her face from just above the hairline. Beyond than that he didn't see any other apparent injuries. Al Karim was behind Melody to her immediate right. He was using her as a shield and her height was not helping matters. The man's face was partially obscured and risking a shot, especially in the dim lighting of the Ballroom, was unacceptable. He needed to figure a way to get into a better position.

Behind Maguire, ESU Officers began coming through the door, their weapons aimed at Al Karim.

"Stop! Tell them to get out or I will kill her."

"Then you will die too."

"So be it, *Allahu Akbar*!"

Maguire raised his left hand up, his hand balled into a fist. The ESU Officers immediately stopped their advance.

"Tell me what you want, Bashir."

"You cannot give me what I want."

"Then why are we here?"

"Revenge!"

"For your wife?"

"Don't speak about her!" Bashir screamed out. "You have no right to speak about her, you don't know her."

"Then tell me about her."

"Do you think me such a fool? Do you think you can come in here, talk to me and think this will all simply end?"

"How will it end?" Maguire asked.

"It will end with justice being served."

James looked over to where Tippi Fisher lay motionless on the floor.

"May I?" Maguire asked.

"Don't waste your time. It's too late for her."

"So the whole apology thing was a ruse?"

"I would have given you time to see it happen, but yes, you are correct. It was just about getting you here, Mr. Police Commissioner."

"Is that why you took her hostage?"

"Of course, how else could this end? My wife was taken from me and I never had a chance to say goodbye to her. At least you will get the chance to watch your wife die."

"You do realize that you'll be dead even before her body hits the ground?"

"Of course I do, but I have someone waiting for me and you will have only your memories to live with, memories of not being able to protect her."

Maguire realized that this was spinning out of control too quickly. He desperately needed to get into a better position or slow things down.

"I'm curious about one thing, Bashir."

"What is that?"

"You were with the Mujahideen. You fought against the Russians; they were the ones who killed your wife. Why not take it out on them?"

"Because they were never the real threat, not the way the United States is. The Russians were fools. Clumsy, incompetent fools. But you, you here in the United States, you were not fools. You came in and you talked well, told us what we wanted to hear, how you would support us. But you didn't care about us; didn't worry about what would happen when you were gone. No, you did what you have done everywhere else; you got what you wanted and you left. That's when I realized that the real enemy was not the ignorant invader who had tried to take my country by force, but the intelligent Satan who stood on the side and directed the game for his own amusement."

Maguire could hear the venom in the man's words. It was like watching as the cobra reared back and you knew the strike was only moments away. Whatever needed to be done would have to happen quickly.

"So this is your idea of justice. To take another man's wife and kill her in the memory of your wife?"

"I could kill a thousand of your lying, whore wives and they could never match the memory of my Salimah."

"Do you think Salimah would approve of you doing this?"

Bashir erupted.

"Never use my wife's name again you infidel, son of a filthy whore, bastard."

The man was becoming more disconnected with each passing moment. Maguire had to create an opportunity before the fuse on this psychotic bastard burned down.

Melody watched Maguire as he moved slowly to his left. She knew that he didn't do anything without a reason. There was no wasted movement. She could see that same look she had seen so many months early on the promenade in Vermont. She knew something was coming, but she also knew he was putting himself back in harm's way to save her.

"Allah has willed this path for me and now you will live with the same pain as I have. Say goodbye."

"This isn't about the woman, Bashir," Maguire said. "If it was, you could have killed all of them before we ever arrived here. So why don't we just do this. I'll send the guys behind me outside, I'll put my gun down on the table and you let the woman go. Then it's just you and me, and it can be an honorable fight."

Melody heard the sound of the hammer being pulled back on the revolver pressed to her head.

"Drop your gun on the floor," Bashir said.

He pressed himself tightly against her, shielding himself as much as he could with her body.

She knew that time had run out for her. The man had no intention of letting her or anyone else live. James would drop his gun, because he could not bear to live with the thought that he had not done everything to protect her. But by doing so, the man would have a chance at killing him as well. She stared at James for a moment longer. She couldn't imagine him laying down his life for her, couldn't imagine living without his touch. He truly was the most important thing in her life, and at that moment she knew what she had to do.

Melody dropped her head slightly and then snapped it back violently, feeling her skull connecting with the head of the man directly behind her. The viciousness of the blow had caught him off guard and she felt the arm that had been holding her fall away. Melody lunged forward just as she heard the first shot ring out followed almost instantly by a cacophony of other guns being fired.

Time stood still as her body seemed to hang suspended in midair. Try as she might, she could not will herself to move faster toward the perceived safety of the ground.

The sound of the gunfire was deafening, each shot echoing off the high ceiling of the ballroom. Slowly the ground rose up to meet her and, for a split second, she thought she was safe, that was until she felt the burning sensation in her back as the bullet drove deep inside of her.

A fraction of a second later her body hit the ground with a resounding thud.

Behind her, the body of Bashir Al Karim collapsed to the floor, dispatched to the afterlife by a well-placed round fired from Maguire's .9mm Smith and Wesson.

Even before Al Karim's body hit the floor, Maguire was moving toward him and kicked the gun out of reach. An ESU officer rushed in and immediately flex cuffed the man's hands.

In a game where mistakes were measured in human life, you learned to never take anything, even death, for granted.

Once the threat had been eliminated, Maguire turned his attention toward Melody. He found her being treated by one of the team's tactical medics, while another radioed for EMS to respond forthwith.

Maguire fought every urge in his body to push them out of his way and take her up in his arms, but he knew that they were her best shot at survival. Still, the frantic pace at which they were working over her was not making him feel good.

In the ensuing chaos Rich had rushed into the room, followed by EMT's from the Fire Department's Emergency Medical Service.

"What happened?"

"He was holding her when we came in," Maguire replied. "We had no shot. I think she knew he was going to kill her and she fought back. I fired just as he fired. If I had been a split second faster..."

The words trailed off as he struggled with everything that had happened.

"Don't do this to yourself, James. You and I both know bad things happen to good people and it's not because we weren't fast enough."

They had moved her onto a stretcher now and were beginning to get her ready for transport.

"Go with her," Rich said. "I'll handle things on this end."

"Thanks," Maguire replied and followed the EMT's and ESU cops out of the Ballroom.

As they made their way down the staircase, they passed Mary, who gasped and rushed toward James.

"Oh my God!" she exclaimed. "James, what happened?"

"He shot Mel," James replied. "I've got to go with her. Did you get hold of Gen?"

"No, there was no answer. I'm coming with you."

Once outside, they loaded Melody into the waiting ambulance. Maguire stood at the back, waiting as they stabilized her for the ride to the hospital.

Luke Jackson had already radioed his partner, Peter May, to bring the Suburban up and grab a marked car for an escort.

Mary stopped one of the detectives from Rich's detail.

"I'm going to the hospital with them. Let my husband know, please."

"Yes, ma'am," the detective replied. "We'll take you over in the back-up car."

"I'm going to try calling Gen again. I'll meet you at the hospital."

"Okay, Mary," he replied as he continued to watch.

"James!"

Maguire turned to face her.

"She's going to be fine."

"I know," James said, knowing it was a lie even as he said the words. "Get in the truck; I'll meet you at the hospital."

"Commissioner, we're ready to go," said one of the ESU cops.

Maguire climbed into the back and they closed the doors. The ambulance moved out, as the motorcade of marked and unmarked vehicles led the way to Bellevue Hospital.

James looked down at her and she smiled at him weakly. Her coloring wasn't good and he knew she was losing blood. He reached over and took her hand in his, holding it softly.

"A reverse head-butt? Seriously?"

She shrugged her shoulders, a move which elicited a painful grimace.

"Easy there, angel, the doctors are going to have enough on their plate. No need to give them anything more to fix."

Melody reached up and pulled the oxygen mask from her face.

"Whoa, don't do that," Maguire said, reaching up to replace the mask.

She pushed his hand away and pulled the mask off.

"I love you," Melody said weakly. "I've loved you from the first moment I saw you."

"You don't have to say this now."

"Yes I do. I don't want you to ever wonder how I really feel about you. I never want you to guess."

"I don't," Maguire replied. "I feel the same way about you, Mel. I love you with all my heart and soul."

"I feel so cold," she said.

Suddenly, the monitor, in the rack above her, sounded that all too familiar shrill alarm that signaled Melody's heart had stopped beating.

"Fuck, we're losing her," the EMT cried out.

Up in the cab of the ambulance, the driver reached over, grabbing the radio mic, and transmitted to the hospital that the patient was going into cardiac arrest.

Maguire moved out of the way as the EMT and ESU cops frantically worked to revive her.

He watched as they attached a tab to her upper chest and then one to her side before connecting the defibrillator wires to them.

"Clear!" the EMT shouted before pressing the button on the machine. The manual external defibrillator delivered a jolt of electricity to Melody's heart just as the ambulance arrived at the hospital.

Suddenly the back doors of the ambulance flew open as the medical staff took control. The EMT climbed on top of her and began administering CPR. The stretcher was carefully removed from the back and wheeled toward the emergency entrance.

"Female, Caucasian, late 30's, asystolic with a gunshot wound to the upper back," the ESU cop said to the medical staff gathered around.

"We're going straight to the operating room, folks," one of the doctors called out.

Maguire jumped out of the back and followed them into the hospital. As he walked into the emergency room of Bellevue Hospital it was like *déjà vu* for him, only this time he would have gladly traded places with her. As he watched, she was wheeled quickly down the hallway toward the elevator which would carry her up to the operating room.

As Maguire followed behind, a hospital security officer stepped out in front of him, blocking his way.

The man didn't realize it, but this wasn't going to end well for him.

"Easy, easy," cried Luke Jackson, as he came rushing up from behind holding his shield in his hand. "It's okay this is Deputy Commissioner Maguire, NYPD."

The security officer took a step backward, but held his ground.

"Sir, I understand, but you can't go up there with them," the man replied. "They need the room to work and you're only going to be in the way."

Mary came into the emergency room with her security detail and approached Maguire.

"What's going on?"

"They just took her up into surgery," Maguire explained. "Mary, they lost her on the way here."

Mary turned to the security officer.

"Get us to a private room now," she said. "Have your officers call the head of the surgical department down here immediately."

Something about her tone, coupled with the army of cops that had since filed into the hospital, immediately gave the man pause.

"Yes, ma'am," he replied. "Follow me."

He led them down the narrow hallway to an elevator and took them up to where a private sitting room was located near to the operating room Melody was currently in.

James collapsed into one of the chairs.

Mary walked over to one of the detectives from Rich's detail.

"Get in touch with my husband and let him know what's going on please, and if someone could grab us some coffee that would be fantastic."

"Yes, ma'am," the man replied.

Outside in the hallway plainclothes and uniformed officers kept a vigil outside the door.

Mary sat down next to Maguire and took his hand in hers.

"Melody is going to be fine, James," she said, patting his hand softly with hers. She couldn't be sure whether she was trying to reassure him or herself.

The door opened and a woman stepped inside the room.

"I'm so sorry," she said. "But I need to ask a few questions."

It's okay," Maguire replied and motioned to the seat across from him.

The woman sat down with her clipboard and Maguire began to provide her the information she asked.

"Next of kin?"

The words hung in the air for the briefest of moments before crashing down upon him in all their cold reality. He struggled to come to terms with the question she had asked, but all Maguire could do was stare at the woman.

"Is there a next of kin?"

Finally it was Mary who answered.

"This is her fiancé, James Maguire. Put his name down."

Just then the door opened and a man in a white coat came into the room.

"Mrs. Stargold, I am so sorry, I just got the call," said Dr. Julius Rothman, Chair of the Department of Surgery. He looked down at the woman taking the personal information.

"Do you have your pedigree information for the registration?"

"Yes, but...," the woman began to reply.

"Then that will be all for now," he said. "I'll have you notified when you can come back to complete the rest of it."

The woman got up and walked out of the room without saying a word.

Dr. Rothman took the seat across from Mary and James.

"Is she going to make it, Doc?" James asked.

"I just stopped by the surgical suite before I came in," he said, pausing to take a deep breath.

"Don't sugarcoat it, Doc. I'd rather know the truth upfront and have a chance to deal with it."

The man stared back at Maguire, his lips pursed tightly. This was the second hardest thing about being a doctor and unfortunately it often led to the first hardest thing.

"It's not good, Commissioner," he replied. "She's already lost a lot of blood. They're working on trying to stabilize that now."

James heard Mary gasp and felt her hand grip his tightly.

"I understand," he replied.

"This is going to be one of those situations where we are going to have to deal with one thing at a time. Right now finding the bleeder is the most important. After that we will work on the rest."

"Is there anything we can do?" Mary asked.

"Pray," Rothman said somberly. "Right now the surgical team can use all the help they can get."

CHAPTER EIGHTY-SEVEN

Southampton, Suffolk County, New York
Wednesday, February 13th, 2013 – 11:13 p.m.

Gregor Ritter sat at his desk going over the weekend personnel roster for Peter Bart's security detail.

He looked down at the watch on his left hand and checked the time. He had expected Genevieve to call him on her way home.

Traffic must be really bad tonight, he thought.

He had been worried about her not feeling well lately and had intended on asking her to stay home. But she was not the type of person that enjoyed being cooped, even if it was in a mansion.

Still, something just didn't feel right to him. He pulled up the traffic cameras on the Long Island Expressway on his laptop. There was traffic, but it was moving steady throughout Suffolk County. He reached over to pick up the phone, intent on calling her, when it began to ring. He looked at the screen and saw Maguire's name.

"Good evening, James," he said answering the phone.

"Gregor, Melody's been shot."

"What?" he exclaimed. "How? Where?"

"At the hotel during the charity event," Maguire explained. "It's a long story and I'll tell you more when I see you, but I need to speak to Gen and the calls keeping going to voicemail."

"She's not here," Gregor replied. "I thought she was with Melody."

"She wasn't feeling good. Mary said she left the event early. That was over two hours ago."

"Something isn't right," he said. "She should be home already."

"Try to locate her," James said.

"*Ja*, I'm working on it now."

Gregor got out of the internet browser screen and brought up a separate program. When it came up he clicked on the icon for the Mercedes. A small hourglass popped up and began spinning as the program searched for the GPS coordinates of the vehicle.

As part of the security protocols they had put in place after the attack, each of Melody's vehicles was equipped with their own unique tracking device.

A moment later a map popped up and indicated that the vehicle was stopped a half mile away.

"I think she is broken down," Gregor replied, a wave of relief coming over him. "The vehicle is stopped down the road. I will go and get her, then we will come to the hospital. Where are you?"

"At Bellevue, I'll tell them to be expecting you."

"Okay, be strong my friend, I will be there soon."

Gregor ended the call and got up. He removed the holstered Sig Sauer pistol from the top draw of his desk and clipped it onto his belt. As he went out the door, he grabbed the leather jacket from the coat rack and headed down the stairs.

"Ernst! *Kommen sie hier, schnell*," he cried out, in rapid fire German.

"Sir!" the man replied, leaping to his feet from where he had been sitting on the couch.

Each of the members of the security team had been culled from Europe's finest police special force's teams. Ernst Schmidt had been a member of Austria's federal unit, the Einsatzkommando COBRA. While every member of the security detail had been an elite *tier one* operator before their current employment, Gregor had to admit an affinity for his kinsmen.

"You're in charge," he said. "Inform Mr. Bart that Melody Anderson was shot. She is in Bellevue Hospital with Mr. Maguire. I'm picking up Ms. Gordon and heading to the hospital."

"Yes, Sir!" the man replied.

Gregor headed out the door, sprinting over to where his black H1 was parked. He started the vehicle and headed toward the main gate. He reached over and pressed the remote switch that signaled the main gate to open and retracted the steel bollards that prevented unauthorized persons from driving onto the property.

When he cleared the drive he headed east, racing down Meadow Lane. A moment later he could see hazard lights flashing ahead. He flipped the switch that activated the roof mounted flood lights and began to pull over to the oncoming side of the road.

The H1 came to a stop in front of the Mercedes, the flood lights illuminating the interior of the car parked in front of him, but he could not see Genevieve.

Gregor climbed out of the truck and walked around to the driver's door. She wasn't inside.

He opened the door and peered inside, spotting the manila envelope, addressed to Maguire, on the driver's seat.

"Gen!" he cried out and listened anxiously for the response that would not come.

He rushed back to the truck and lifted the radio microphone, keying the transmit button.

"*Alarm!*" Gregor, called out.

Inside the house, signals began going off and men with automatic weapons began moving to their prearranged posts. Inside the rooftop command center men scanned the compound with infrared cameras. Within seconds the entire house and grounds were locked down.

"Ernst," Gregor said. "I want two patrols out immediately. One is to head directly to Melody Anderson's house looking for Genevieve Gordon. Another is to come to my position approximately 1 kilometer to the east of the main gate."

"Yes, Sir," the man replied over the radio.

"Also alert her security as to what has happened and tell them Ms. Gordon is now missing. Everything is to be secured immediately and the entire grounds searched."

"Right away," Schmidt replied.

Gregor removed the cell from his pocket and called Maguire.

"Yes, Gregor," James said when he answered the phone.

"Gen is missing."

"What?"

"I found the car parked on the side of the road with the hazard lights on," Gregor said.

"Could she have tried to walk home?"

"No, I would have seen her or she would have come to my place. But there is something else, James," Gregor replied.

"What?"

"There is a package addressed to you sitting on the driver's seat. It has to be a message."

Maguire felt a cold chill creep up his back.

"Banning!"

"I thought he was dead?" Gregor said.

"I didn't take the shot," James replied. "I don't know what to believe anymore."

"What do you want me to do?"

"I can't leave Melody," James said. "Secure the car. Have your people scan it just to make sure it's not an explosive. I don't think it is, but with that psychotic bastard I don't want to take any chances. Once the car is swept, I want you to take it back to your place and have your people go over it with a fine tooth comb. That package is his calling card. He's sending us a message."

"I will make sure everything is handled correctly."

"I'll have my people track Gen's cell phone and see if we can't locate her that way. I'll let you know what I find out and call me if anything changes there."

"Okay," Gregor replied.

Maguire ended the call. Rich had joined them now, along with Monsignor O'Connor from the Chaplain's Unit.

"Gen is missing," he said.

"What?" Mary exclaimed.

"Gregor found the Mercedes parked on the side of the road. Gen's gone and someone left a package in the front seat addressed to me."

"I'll call the Chief of Detectives and have him send people out there," Rich said.

"No, that's just a waste of their time. Gregor is going to have his people go over it. If they find something, he'll let us know."

"Okay, do you need them to do anything else?"

"Yes, have them run a trace of her phone. Maybe they can get a ping off it."

"I'll take care of it."

Rich got up and walked to the other side of the room to place the call.

The door opened up and Luke Jackson came in carrying a large coffee carafe and a sleeve of cups.

"Commissioner," he said.

"Yes, Luke?"

"Just wanted to let you know that Mike and Amanda are outside, if there is anything that you need done just let us know."

"Please tell them that I said thank you, Luke. I'll be out in a bit."

"I'll do that, sir."

Rich came back and sat on the couch.

"Okay, our people are going to run the trace on the phone."

"Thanks, Rich."

"She's going to be okay."

"I wish I could say I shared your optimism."

Rich smiled and clapped his hand on Maguire shoulder.

"That's what you have us for, buddy."

"I know," Maguire said. "Thank you."

The door to the room opened up and Dr. Rothman walked back in.

"How are we doing, Doc?"

The man smiled wearily.

"Well, they located where the bleeding was coming from and managed to tie it off," the man said. "But they lost her again on the table. It's really touch and go right now. I think you need to prepare yourself."

Maguire felt as if he had been punched in the gut. He felt everything draining out of him.

"Thank you," James said. "I appreciate the honesty."

He lowered his head into his hand, rubbing his eyes slowly as if to ease the stress he was feeling, but it was just to hide the tears that began welling up in his eyes.

CHAPTER EIGHTY-EIGHT

Northern Maine
Thursday, February 14th, 2013 – 6:53 a.m.

The sun was just peeking out over the mountains in the east. It bathed the landscape in a pinkish hue, which contrasted starkly against the dark blue of the receding night sky.

Tatiana pulled the Land Rover to a stop in front of the cabin and sat there for a moment enjoying the majestic sunrise.

It was something that she had never truly appreciated until she had come here. There was something calming about these mountains, something that chased away the insignificant matters of the day. It forced you to take in the scope and breadth of nature in all its glory.

As much as she was enjoying it, she would have to let the moment go. She'd been up over twenty-four hours already and the night drive had been especially brutal on her. She'd been glad that Banning had the presence of mind to stock up on supplies, including energy drinks.

He really had been a fantastic planner. Not only for the common items, but also for the ones you didn't think you would need. She'd have to learn from that, especially since she would need to restock some of the drugs she'd recently used.

Behind her she heard the muffled movement of the woman under the tarp.

Tatiana let out an audible sigh.

"No rest for the wicked," she said.

She put on her gloves and got out of the vehicle. She opened the cabin door and went inside. It was chilly, even with the portable heater going, but it wouldn't take long for it to get warmed up after she got the fire lit.

Getting the woman into the house was going to be the hard part. She'd been fortunate with Lena in that she had Banning to help her, now she was on her own. She knew it would be problematic for her, so she had saved just enough of the Sumagethonium for just this purpose.

She went to the bedroom, opened the trap door and went down into the bunker. On one shelf was a length of nylon rope which she grabbed and went back upstairs. She laid the rope on the bed and headed back out to the truck.

The pink hue of the rising sun was now replaced with bright golden sunshine. Tatiana opened the back of the Land Rover and untied the tarp.

Genevieve let out a muffled cry and struggled against the restraints.

"Welcome home!" Tatiana said in a cheerful tone before she pressed the needle into Genevieve's thigh. She waited a moment before pulling her free from the truck and laid her on the ground. She positioned herself behind her, lifting her up under the arms, then dragged her through the house and into the bedroom.

When she had positioned her in front of the trap door, she wrapped the rope around her chest. She then lowered her into the bunker without causing too much injury. Tatiana climbed down the stairs and proceeded to drag her to the back room. She laid her next to the bed and attached the cuff around her ankle, before clipping the zip ties.

It was an arduous task on her part and she was physically spent when it was all done. She left the room and locked the door behind her.

She made her way to the living room and began loading wood into the fireplace. Even when exhausted, there was always some work that needed to be done.

After the fire was going she poured herself a drink and sat down on the couch.

She was hungry, but food would have to wait until later. Right now, all she wanted to do was get some sleep.

Tatiana took a sip from the glass, feeling the heat of the liquid as it went down her throat. She sat mesmerized as she watched the flames dancing across the wood logs.

It was an odd feeling not to be alone anymore.

She had almost panicked when she realized that the woman was not Melody Anderson, but instead had just seized the opportunity that had been given to her. Beside which, she'd had her fill of blondes for the time being and this little red head seemed very *spirited*.

On top of that the woman had been driving Anderson's vehicle, so she must have some close connection. This just sent a signal that no one was safe. First Banning had brought the fight to the woman's home and now she had succeeded in kidnapping someone close to her, right off the street. She had to imagine that they would be going crazy trying to figure out why they had not been able to stop it.

Tatiana sipped the drink she cradled in her hand and smiled a victorious smile. She knew that it was all the result of her planning and actions. With the threat of Keith Banning removed, they had all gone back to their ignorant ways.

Now she had one of them tucked safely away and the only clue to her whereabouts pointed a finger back at a dead man.

She wondered how long it would take to figure it out. She was under no illusions that given enough time, and with the resources currently available to him, Maguire would eventually put things together.

It wouldn't be soon, but she knew that it would happen. Tatiana could bask in the glow for a day or so, but then she would have to begin planning for what lay ahead.

She finished the drink and put the glass down on the coffee table. The whiskey had succeeded in making her feel very relaxed and the room was already beginning to feel cozy from the fire. She kicked off the boots she was wearing and laid down on the couch, pulling the afghan that was draped over the back, down on top of her.

Yes, they would be coming eventually, but until then she would just enjoy the peace of the mountains and have some fun with her new house guest.

CHAPTER EIGHTY-NINE

Bellevue Hospital, Manhattan, New York City
Thursday, February 14th, 2013 – 7:23 a.m.

Maguire sat in the small chapel staring up at the ornate wooden sculpture that hung on the wall in front him. He watched as the light from the votive candles flickered off it, casting ever changing shadows against the wall.

Once the hospital had realized that it was *that* Melody Anderson they had pulled out all the stops setting up several rooms to hold the crowd of people that had gathered.

It had been an emotionally draining night for everyone. On top of keeping a vigil, Maguire had to be interviewed regarding the shooting. It would have been tough enough under normal circumstances, but it was made exceedingly worse when Rich had come in and told him she had crashed again.

In the end, the Assistant District Attorney went to great lengths to reassure Maguire that it was a *good* shooting, but James could care less. The woman he loved was dying in a room down the hall and there was nothing *good* that had come out of it. But he played the part, because he knew it needed to be done, and thanked the man. As Maguire left the room, Luke Jackson informed him that another team of doctors had just gone in.

Apparently the bullet had shattered on impact with one of Melody's bones and sent fragments coursing wildly though her chest. What they had originally thought was one bleeder actually turned into two. Maguire wondered if she had not been *that* Melody Anderson would he have already been making the funeral arrangements.

A short time later, he got up to get a cup of coffee when he decided that he needed to take a walk, ending up in the chapel. From behind him he heard the door open gently and a moment later Monsignor O'Connor sat down next to him on the wooden pew.

"There was a time when all these chapels had a Crucifix hanging from the wall. Now they are just empty *quiet* places without direction or someone to pray to," O'Connor said solemnly, his voice still thick with the Irish brogue of his youth.

"I'm not sure if having someone hanging on the wall to pray to would help me right now, padre."

"I imagined you'd be feeling this way right about now, James."

"Where was He?" Maguire asked. "Where was God when she needed Him?"

O'Connor let out a sigh.

It was a question that he had been asked a thousand times before. Often by those trying to make sense out of the senseless acts committed against them or someone they loved. It was a serious question which often indicated a much deeper conflict that lay just under the surface.

"The same place He has always been, James, dealing with the chaos and confusion which we have created for ourselves by exercising our free will."

"That's all well and good, but she didn't do anything wrong. There was no chaos or confusion in her actions. She was at a damn charity event to *help* people and that *sonofabitch* shot her in the name of *his* God!"

He hadn't meant to take his anger out on the priest, but if he was going to be here as God's representative then he had to expect it.

O'Connor turned and looked at Maguire. He could see the hurt and pain on the man's face, could feel the struggle going on inside of him.

He knew Maguire, knew his background. He had first met him when Maguire had been shot. O'Connor had come from the same county in Ireland that Maguire's parents were from. He felt it was his duty and obligation, not only as a priest, but as an Irishman to be there for the lad. He had spent many days sitting in a room upstairs helping him come to terms with everything.

"James," he said. "It's the Church's position that God created man as a rational being. That He endowed us with free will, so that we might seek Him out, of our own choice. Unfortunately, as we both know, man has failed since the Garden of Eden to choose what is good and right. Even to the point of committing evil, all in His name."

"That still doesn't explain why He didn't stop it from happening."

"If God chose to intervene in every moment of crisis, then it negates the whole premise of free choice doesn't it?" O'Connor replied. "I know you're hurting, lad, but I want you to consider something for a moment. Each of us has a life to live. For most of us, we envision that life to be about 80 years, give or take. But we live our lives one moment at a time. We are often amazed when we look back to see how far we have come and what we have achieved. Take yourself for example. From a young man who loved photography in a sleepy town in upstate New York, you went on to be a decorated member of both the Navy and the NYPD. Then you started your own business before coming back and being the number two in the Department. When you were seventeen and living at home could you have ever imagined that? Would you have even believed it could be true?"

"No," Maguire replied.

"Now consider what the next forty years has in store for you. What can you imagine? Will you retire and do nothing? Will you aspire to greater things? Who will be at your side through it all?"

Maguire took it all in and it seemed overwhelming. At the moment he couldn't see past this morning.

"The point I am trying to make, James, is that we all view our lives as a snapshot, like photos in an album. We see our past and present, but the pages of our future are blank. God is omniscient, omnipotent and omnipresent. He is the Alpha and the Omega, the great I Am. He alone knows your life and the life of Melody. He sees our lives not as the individual snapshots we see, but as a movie, from conception to eternity. He sees each of us in that way. He knows everything that we will do and achieve in our lifetimes."

"What will be achieved in her death?"

"James, none of us escapes death. It is the great equalizer of both the rich and the poor, the just and the unjust. We think of life as ending with death, but forget that eternity awaits each and every one of us. It is my earnest belief that God puts each of us here for a specific purpose and period of time. But when that role is fulfilled it is time to return to the Father. Some may scoff at that notion, choosing not to believe in Him, but just because they don't believe in Him doesn't mean that He does not believe in them. Come judgment day I think there will be more than a few who realize the tragedy of their folly."

"How do you explain someone like Bashir Al Karim? He believed he was acting on behalf of God."

"God gets blamed for a great many things, James, but not for what He has done, but rather for what man has done in His name. I have been a priest for nearly fifty years. In that time I have served God to the best of my abilities. I have not always been perfect, but then again, I do tend to an imperfect flock," O'Connor said, giving Maguire a friendly nudge.

"Like when I was laying upstairs and you'd slip me that flask."

"That was strictly for medicinal purposes. Everyone knows Irish whiskey is great for killing all sorts of nasty things you find here in hospitals."

Maguire softly smiled as he thought back on it. None of the nurses could understand how he kept managing to have the smell of whiskey on his breath.

"But I have remained faithful to the vows I undertook, James, and I never engaged in any activity that would diminish my service, even as others did. I know that is something you can understand."

Maguire nodded. Every honest cop knew the sting of being painted with that broad brush when it surfaced that one of their own had crossed the line. There was a well-known saying in the Department that 'one *oh shit* erased a thousand *atta boys.*'

"Understand, James, religion has often been used as a vehicle for man's desire, not God's. In that regard, it has seen abuse by every denomination. But when you inflict pain and hurt in the name of God, it is usually God, and not man, who often bears the blame. Usually this strife is brought about by man's interpretation of scripture. Every denomination and faith has their heretics. Sadly it is they who do the most damage. It led Jesus to say 'Why do you look at the speck that is in your brother's eye, but do not notice the log that is in your own eye?' It has been said that all strife in the world could end tomorrow if everyone picked up the Bible and just did what was written in red. Unfortunately, free will prevents that."

"So ultimately God is responsible for giving us something we couldn't handle."

O'Connor softly laughed.

"Come on, lad, you know that's not true. Just as you know that the criminal is not innocent because he couldn't control himself. In the case of Al Karim he used religion to justify his own actions. God did not put us on this planet for us to wage war with one another. That is Satan's handiwork. The only problem is that we have convinced ourselves that he doesn't exist."

"Why?" asked James. "If we talk about God, why don't we talk about Satan?"

"Because Satan is scary to us," O'Connor replied. "Think about this for a moment. If something bad happens to you, you blame God. Why? Because God is safe. We are taught from an early age that He is a benevolent God who wants only the best for us. Would you act the same way to a stranger? Of course not! You don't know them; they could lash out and hurt you. Now, when something egregious happens, like tonight, do you blame Satan? No, because he is that stranger and he *is* scary. If we acknowledge that Satan is real, and exerting his influence in the world, then we must acknowledge that Hell is also real. Then things start to become a lot more serious. So we pretend Satan doesn't exist, to our own peril and detriment."

"I know it's wrong, but right now I want to hate God."

"He knows," O'Connor said. "You're not the first, and I doubt that you will be the last."

Maguire stared ahead, going over what had happened. Melody had acted on her own volition. He'd seen it. He knew she was going to do something.

"James, when you took your oath, you did so of your own free will. No one forced you to become a sailor or a cop. That was your choice and every day when you went out there you knew the risks. Two thousand years ago God sent His son to earth and He chose to go to the cross to pay the price for man's sins. Before He did, He told His disciples 'Greater love hath no man than this, that a man lay down his life for his friends.' From what you told me of the events of last night it sounds as if your Melody was exercising her choice as well."

O'Connor reached over, putting his hand on Maguire's shoulder and said a silent prayer for both of them.

Suddenly it dawned on Maguire what today was, St. Valentine's Day.

Throughout the world people were celebrating one another's love for each other with symbolic gifts of cards, flowers and chocolate. For a smaller majority, this day would see the placement of a ring on someone's finger and the promise of eternal love. More often than not it wouldn't last. Promises were easy to make in the *good* times, but difficult to keep during the *bad* times.

For Maguire, this day had taken on a whole new meaning.

They should have been waking up in Paris this morning; setting out, hand in hand, to explore the wonders of the city. It was the dream of lovers everywhere.

Instead, he sat here, wondering if it would be his last day with her.

He would have put his gun down. He would have done anything to gain that one extra moment, in the fleeting chance that he could do something more to save her.

Melody knew that too and she knew how it would most likely end. She made the choice to intentionally put herself into harm's way, a completely selfless act, in order to save him.

The words kept repeating in his head.

"Greater love hath no man than this, that a man lay down his life for his friends."

Maguire slowly lowered his head into his hands and wept.

ABOUT THE AUTHOR

Andrew Nelson spent twenty-two years in law enforcement, including twenty years with the New York City Police Department. During his tenure with the NYPD he served as a detective in the elite Intelligence Division, conducting investigations and providing dignitary protection to numerous world leaders. He achieved the rank of sergeant before retiring in 2005. He is also a graduate of the State University of New York. He and his wife have four children and reside in central Illinois with their Irish Wolfhound.

He is the author of both the James Maguire and Alex Taylor mystery series, as well as the NYPD Cold Case novella series. He has also written two non-fiction books which chronicle the insignia of the New York City Police Department's Emergency Service Unit.

For more information please visit us at:

www.andrewgnelson.org

ANDREW G.
NELSON

Made in the USA
Middletown, DE
26 June 2019